Readers Love Gayleen Froese

The Girl Whose Luck Ran Out

"Definitely recommended for those who like to follow mysteries, enjoy engaging characters, and second chance romances."

—Nat Kennedy Reviews

"…the story boasts a soothing, balm-like quality that seeks to heal what has been slivered."

—Delphic Reviews

"I can't wait to read the next book in the series. I believe once more people hear about this book, Gayleen Froese will have a hit on her hands."

—Gina Rae Mitchell Reviews

The Man Who Lost His Pen

"I could read a thousand Ben Ames mysteries and can't wait for another installment!"

—Emily's Hurricane Reviews

By Gayleen Froese

BEN AMES CASE FILES
The Girl Whose Luck Ran Out
The Man Who Lost His Pen

Lightning Strike Blues

Published by DSP Publications
www.dsppublications.com

Lightning Strike Blues

Gayleen Froese

DSP PUBLICATIONS

Published by
DSP Publications

5032 Capital Circle SW, Suite 2, PMB# 279, Tallahassee, FL 32305-7886 USA
www.dsppublications.com

Trade Paperback ISBN: 978-1-64108-526-7
Digital ISBN: 978-1-64108-525-0
Trade Paperback published October 2023
v. 1.0.0

Printed in the United States of America

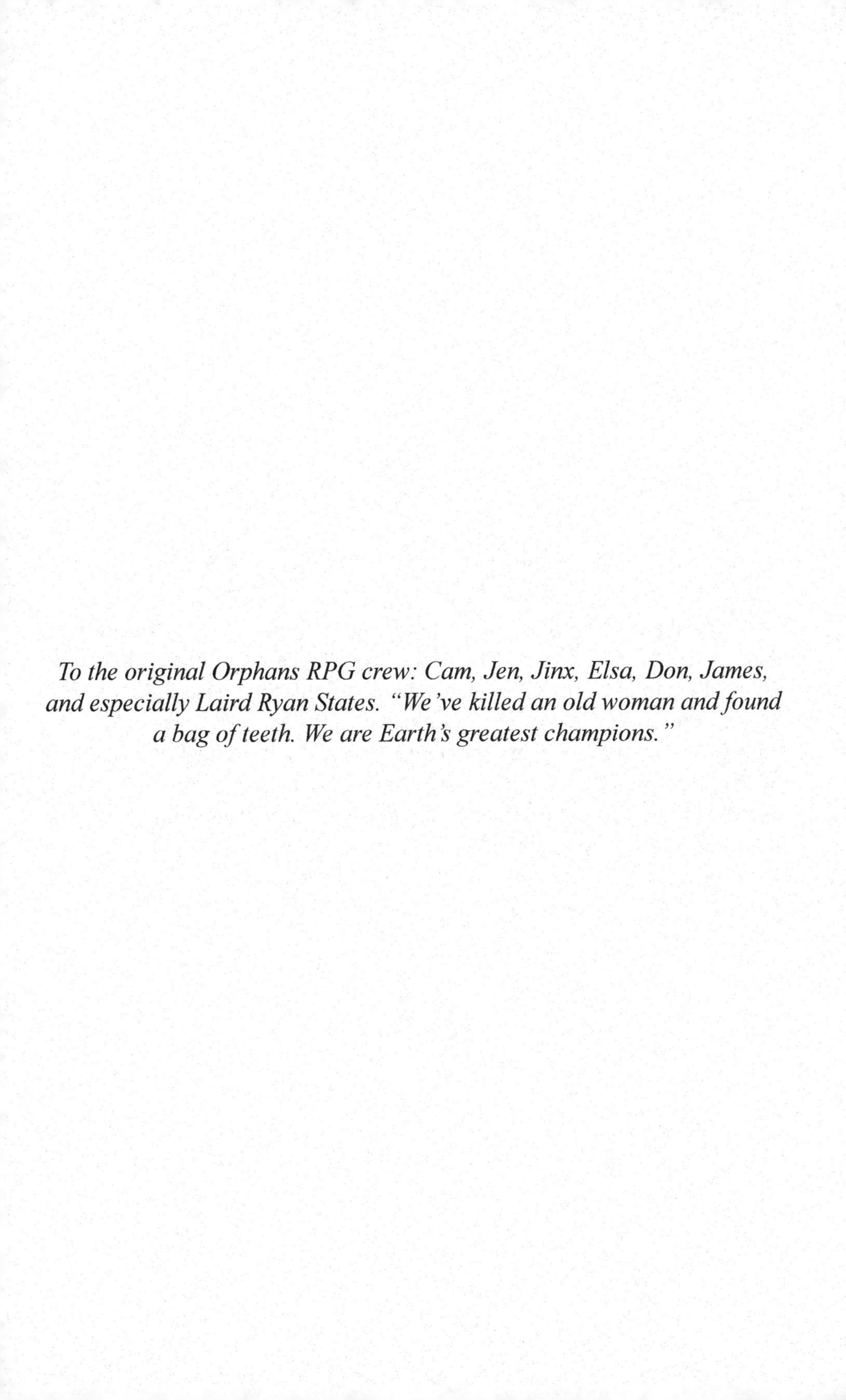

To the original Orphans RPG crew: Cam, Jen, Jinx, Elsa, Don, James, and especially Laird Ryan States. "We've killed an old woman and found a bag of teeth. We are Earth's greatest champions."

Acknowledgements

Thanks to everyone who has joined me in this fictional world over the years, including Peter, Kim, and of course team Orphans. Thanks to my beta readers: Cori, Anne, Deb, and especially Sky. Also thanks to Dr. Steve, who should have been thanked in my last book. I'm on top of things. As always, so many thanks to Gin and Andi and Elizabeth and everyone else at DSP. You're a blast. And to North Battleford.... I know I didn't sell you like the tourist board, but my memories are all sunny days and lakes and my dogs splashing in the river.

Lightning Strike Blues

Gayleen Froese

He's going west. To Edmonton, maybe, if he keeps it up, but for now he has the travel plans of a bottle rocket. That way, as far as the pressure will carry him.

The sky seems bigger than usual, with extra rows of stars. The night is that clear. The casino's spotlight sweeps past, and he wants to get beyond it. Everything will be better the moment he can't see it anymore.

What he knows is this: he is as cold as he has ever been, and as hot. He has been struck everywhere at once. Every nerve is shivering, and every muscle hurts.

And then he's lying on the highway, his bike far behind him, and his clothes have been burned away.

CHAPTER ONE

Gabe

IT WAS a beautiful night in June, but Gabe was not comfortable being outside. Specifically, he was not comfortable standing bareassed on Sandy Klaassen's front porch.

He knocked on the splintering door, casting nervous glances over his shoulder at the street. It was so far from a main drag that it wasn't even fully paved—it merged from crumbling pavement into gravel and dirt about halfway along the row of ill-used duplexes. Still, those duplexes were crammed to the rafters, and the residents came and went without regard to time, so there was no telling when a beater would roll by on its way to the nearest 7-Eleven.

To Gabe's relief, he heard Sandy's footsteps approaching the door. He placed himself to the left side of the porch, assuming Sandy would use the chain, and waited until the door opened the two inches or so that the chain allowed. Then he leaned in so that his face would take up most of Sandy's view.

"Hey," he said. Sandy shoved a dark blond curl out of her face and scowled at him.

"What happened to your key, Gabe? I had to put my book down to be your fucking butler."

"Sorry," Gabe said automatically. A pissed-off Sandy always merited a sorry, in Gabe's opinion, regardless of his culpability. "About that, though, don't open the doo—"

In the silence that followed the door's opening, he said, "It's not my fault you're seeing the goods. I told you not to open the door."

"Oh my God!" Sandy said, one blunt-nailed hand pressed tight across her eyes. "I am not seeing the goods! I see nothing! Get into the bathroom and I'll bring you some clothes."

"Deal," Gabe said, waiting until Sandy had moved aside before heading for the only bathroom. He was relieved beyond words to find it unoccupied—almost as relieved as he'd been not to see either of Sandy's roommates in the living room as he'd scurried by.

He gave the door a good slam to let Sandy know she could uncover her eyes. The sound of her cursing him as she searched for clothes that might fit let him know the message had been received.

"Jesus fuck!" drifted through the air, and Gabe smiled. The bathroom door wasn't the one that had come with the place when it had been built in the sixties. That door had been replaced at some point by the cheapest thing Home Hardware had to offer, and it let bits and pieces of Sandy's rant reach him.

"…naked in the middle of town… your brother is going to… in the horse-raping Christ is wrong with you… will never know…."

"Horse-raping?" Gabe asked the door, as if it might have an answer. He knew better than to expect one from Sandy. Not that it mattered. He had more important things on his mind.

He turned to face himself in the mirror.

Gabe couldn't have said exactly what he'd expected to see. He was together enough to know that he was likely in shock. He didn't have a sense of how badly hurt he might be, but he knew what kind of shape his bike was in and how far he'd slid down the road. So pretty hurt, he figured.

Which was why he stood perfectly still and stared into that mirror for a good long time.

He saw nothing wrong. No bruises. No scrapes. His left hand had a healing cut from when Colin had been chopping up ham to throw in the scrambled eggs that morning and Gabe had put his hand too close to the cutting board. But from a motorcycle accident that he knew, in the dusty sixty-watt light of the bathroom, ought to have killed him, there was nothing to see.

There had to be, though. As he searched himself for a sign that he'd been body surfing a highway for some indication that the friction and fire that had stripped him of clothing had done some damage to the flesh beneath, he came to the uncomfortable conclusion that he must be crazy. Or concussed. He'd hit his head, and he was seeing things. In the sense that he *wasn't* seeing things that absolutely had to be there.

He had an appropriately crazy thought then—that it was good they were all lazy at Sandy's place. Because it had been almost a year since Jerry's birthday, when Sean had knocked out the porch light with a bokken and no one had replaced it. Which meant that Sandy hadn't been able to see how fucked-up Gabe clearly had to be. She would have lost it if she'd seen that. Score one for lazy roommates.

Seconds later, Gabe found himself laughing again, in a spiky way that suggested he might be about to cry. He was laughing because Sandy had knocked on the bathroom door, and the surprise had almost killed him. His heart had stopped for a moment. And then Sandy had shoved a pile of clothes at him and asked what was so goddamned funny. She'd wasted no time in pulling the door shut once the clothes were in Gabe's hands.

"I'm proud of you," Gabe told her, raising his voice a little to be heard through the door. "Someday swearing will be an Olympic event, and you'll represent Canada."

"Fuck yourself," Sandy suggested in response.

The clothes were probably Jerry's, Gabe determined. They were too long but not much oversized in any other way. Jerry was the tallest in the house, and far slimmer than Sean. And Sandy usually dated burly guys. So.

It was nice, really, dealing with a problem that he could solve using logic and basic laws of nature. It was a breath of fresh fucking air, as Sandy might say. Which reminded Gabe that he wasn't exactly cold and hadn't been since this incident had started. He'd noticed the temperature while standing outside. But he hadn't shivered or longed for a cup of coffee. He'd just known that it was cold, the way he knew that it was a clear night or that Sandy's neighbour's ancient pine tree had a tilt to the left.

It had been the excitement, he decided, of the accident. And running from the highway to Sandy's house. And hey, maybe even some of the friction that had worn his clothes away.

And he was probably concussed and crazy.

"I'm coming out," he told Sandy. "With clothes on."

"Waiting with bells on," Sandy answered.

Sandy

OBJECTIVELY, THERE was no reason for anyone with an interest in young men to prefer Gabe with clothes to Gabe without clothes. Sandy wasn't blind, so she knew that. She even knew he was, technically, legal and then some.

But she'd known Gabriel Reece since he was in diapers, and somehow he was always in diapers, as far as she was concerned. Which was surreal on an eighteen-year-old, but there it was. He was always tottering, his baby blue eyes about to darken and black hair coming in thick, grabbing at the supposedly adorable patchwork jeans her parents had seen fit to dress her in and pulling himself up to stand.

He wasn't swimming in Jerry's clothes. They were the right width for him. The impression was that these were his rightful clothes, but someone had taken a few inches out of his legs and arms when he wasn't looking. Before Sandy could ask whether that had happened, Gabe shot her a nasty glare with those disconcerting Reece eyes and said, "Cram it."

Sandy extended an arm toward the living room.

"Who was it," she asked, "that said a 'guest is a jewel on the cushion of hospitality'?"

"Percival C. Crammit," Gabe said. "I'm not sitting on that couch."

Sandy tried to run a hand through her hair, but it got caught in curls about halfway back. She had to relax her fingers and pull her hand up to disentangle it.

"Then don't," she said, trying to make her voice suggest the height to which she had had it with Gabe's shit. "We have other chairs."

Gabe sulked past her to the nubby green armchair Sean favoured, and curled up in it as if he were an orphan girl from a Victorian novel. Sandy's mouth twitched. She told it to stop that. Laughing at Gabe was not a good start to getting information out of him.

Naturally, when Gabe opened his mouth, he said nothing useful.

"You know a cat pissed on that—"

"Oh my God!" Sandy said. "Will this be the millionth time I have told you this? Should we have fucking balloons falling from the ceiling? No cat has ever pissed on that couch. My grandpa had it before me, and he never had a cat."

"So a stray got in one day," Gabe said. "Own up, Sandy. It's not that shameful. A lot of trashy people's couches have been pissed on by cats."

Sandy pressed the heel of her hand to the bridge of her nose and counted, silently, to five one-thousand. Gabe was picking her ass. He was picking her ass because something was upsetting him. This was what Gabe did. Had been since the diaper days.

Funny how knowing that made it no less annoying.

She crossed the room to sit on the couch. It did have a faint cat-piss smell on damp days, along the back on the right side. But the kid would see her eat a live cat, fur and all, before he heard her say so.

"Who," she said as calmly as she could, "actually said it? About a guest being a jewel?"

Gabe gave her a half-hearted smile. "Nero Wolfe," he said. "I lent you that book."

"How'd you wind up naked on my front porch?" Sandy asked as her follow-up.

"Um…." Gabe got a strange look on his face at that. "Do I… do I seem normal to you?"

Sandy checked his eyes. They didn't seem off. She'd seen Gabe chemically altered before, and he wasn't now.

"You always strike me as kind of abnormal," she said. Gabe didn't smile or glare. He just blinked at her in confusion, like he was a curious dog.

"You seem like you," Sandy assured him, since assurance seemed to be what he was after. Gabe nodded, and the confusion cleared.

"Good to know."

"So," Sandy said. "Naked. Porch."

"Oh, thereby hangs a tale," Gabe said.

Sandy nodded.

"Get on with fucking telling it."

"Well," Gabe said, "it started when Colin threw me out of the house."

Gabe

THE GUY'S okay looking. Just okay. But okay is okay, as far as Gabe is concerned, because this guy is about to give Gabe head, and no one has ever done that for Gabe before. North Battleford, Saskatchewan, isn't a place where guys generally offer. And Colin's at the job site until at least nine and probably out with the guys after, and Gabe has the house, so obviously the cosmos wants Gabe to get a blow job at long last.

Gabe's on the living room couch, and he's pretty sure Colin wouldn't like that, but it's not as if Colin is going to know about any of this.

Mr. Okay's a kisser. Gabe could do without that. He barely knows the guy, and it seems weird. The blow job should seem weird too, in fairness. Gabe's probably over the weirdness in that case because he would really like to have a blow job, and his brain will do whatever it has to do to make that work for him. What's more, thinking about any of this crap while a guy who's about to blow him is prospecting for his larynx is not what he should be doing. It is not seizing the day. He should be going with it.

So he slaps his stupid brain into thinking nothing except, Go with it. Go with it. Go with it. *Until his brain is saying it so loudly and persistently that Gabe almost doesn't hear the sound of Colin's truck crunching gravel on the drive.*

And then he does. Nothing could ever be important enough for him not to hear that truck.

Mr. Okay is surprised to be shoved back and lands on the floor ass first, his hands still reaching toward Gabe. It is, objectively, funny. Probably the first time someone has shoved him like that before he could even get down to business. Gabe tells him to put his goddamned clothes on and leads by example. Not that they're completely undressed, but it's obvious what they've been doing, and obvious is not what Gabe's going for. One hundred percent evidence free is more what he has in mind.

"Hey, Gabe, we broke off early," Colin says as he walks in the front door. That's Colin all over, starting the conversation before he even sees Gabe. Drop whatever you're doing, kid. Colin's home. Not that Gabe generally objects.

Now Mr. Okay is showing some hustle. He's got one of his shoes on, and he's already scouting for a back door. Gabe doesn't have the heart or the time to tell him the place doesn't have one.

"You wanna see a movie or something?"

Colin says this over the sound of the fridge door opening and a beer bottle chiming softly. Regular old night at the Reece house. Movies and beer. Gabe is searching for a place to hide Mr. Okay. Behind the couch, maybe? In Colin's room? That one's risky, but Gabe could get Colin out of the house on the way to see a movie and then—

"Jesus Christ!"

That's the sound of the jig being up. Gabe would know it anywhere.

"How old are you?"

Colin has Mr. Okay's shirt in his hands as he asks this, and Mr. Okay is wearing said shirt, so that's awkward. It's a weird question too. Gabe is still trying to figure out why it matters how old the guy is when Colin shoves Mr. Okay toward both the floor and the archway to the kitchen. Kind of an angled shove. It gets the job done, because Mr. Okay lands on the kitchen floor before spinning from lying on his back to being on his hands and knees and then scrambling out the door with no dignity but a pretty good rate of speed.

Gabe, who has always been dazzling with words, looks at Colin and comes up with one for the ages. He says, "So now you know."

He doesn't wait for a riposte. He heads for the kitchen and out the front door, pausing only long enough to put on his shoes and grab the keys to his motorcycle. No jacket or helmet, an omission Colin would not like, but Gabe figures Colin will have to catch his gay ass if he wants to beat Gabe to death.

Which, who knows, he might.

"OH GOD, Gabe…."

Sandy had her eyes screwed tight, her forehead resting on her hand. As if Gabe had given her a migraine by talking.

"I know," Gabe said softly. "He's never gonna talk to me again. I'd better hope he doesn't. If he's close enough to talk to me, he's close enough to kill me, right?"

Sandy raised her head and squinted at him. "You are—could you explain to me again the part where Colin actually threw you out of the house?"

"Well…." Gabe shrugged. "He didn't, like, physically throw me out. But—"

"He didn't vocally throw you out," Sandy said. "He didn't, whatever, figuratively throw you out. There was no throwing of you out."

Gabe leaned his head against the back of the chair and stared at the stippled ceiling. It had little gold and silver flecks in it. Someone, at some time, must have thought that would make it more attractive. Gabe did not understand that person.

"Okay, fine," Gabe said. "I got while the getting was good. Happy?"

"Lord no," Sandy told him. "Why would—look at me, punk."

Gabe rolled his eyes before lowering them to bring Sandy into his field of vision.

"Okay," Sandy said. "Why would you think you'd need to run from your brother?"

"Because," Gabe said, raising a hand and mimicking sign language as he spoke, "he caught me with a guy. Now he knows I'm gay."

"That's obnoxious," Sandy said, stabbing an index finger in Gabe's direction. "You picked that up from Sean, didn't you? That fake-deaf thing? Don't let me catch you doing it again."

"The problem," Gabe said evenly, "remains."

"There is no problem," Sandy said. "Gabe. You idiot. Your brother knows you're gay. I mean, before tonight. He knew."

Gabe put his hands on the arms of the chair and leaned forward, his heart pounding the way it had when Colin had manhandled his date.

"He what? You told him?"

Sandy gave him a look he couldn't read and seemed about to say something when the front door opened and Jerry came in. He appeared beat, his orange-red hair messed up and his face unshaven, which always made Jerry seem as if he'd been eating spaghetti and was slipshod about washing up.

Gabe shot Sandy the best "shut the fuck up" glare he could manage. From the corner of his eye, he could see Jerry looking him up and down.

"You wearing my clothes, Younger?"

Gabe had never found Jerry's habit of calling him Reece the Younger endearing, but it sucked in a special way on this special night.

"I'm trying to pick up your sweet style," Gabe told him, still eying Sandy.

"Good luck," Jerry said. He walked past the living room and veered into the kitchen.

"Long day?" Sandy called after him.

"There was a busted hard drive in Meadow Lake," Jerry called back. "Four hours of driving for a fifteen-minute fix."

"They couldn't get it done local?" Sandy asked. Jerry appeared in the living room entrance with a beer in his hand.

"It's expressly not my job," he said, "to point that out to clients."

"Yeah, really," Sandy said. She turned to Gabe. "I didn't tell him anything. I didn't have to."

"Tell who what?" Jerry inquired, entering the living room and taking the far end of the cat-piss couch.

"Nothing," Gabe said distinctly, glaring at Sandy. She gave him a sweet smile, and Gabe's stomach dropped. Whatever was coming, he was going to hate it.

"Jer," Sandy said, "what would you say Gabe's sexual orientation is?"

"Sandy, shut the *fuck* up!" Gabe said, launching himself out of his chair and then not knowing what to do, because it wasn't as if he could hit her. She could take him.

He stood in front of her, wishing he were dead. Or she were. Or everyone.

"He is gay," Jerry said. Gabe stared at him, speechless. He felt cold again, frozen clear through, the way he had on the highway.

"You sure?" Sandy asked.

"I would say he is less gay," Jerry said, "than Lady Gaga doing an impersonation of Liza Minnelli on a float in the San Francisco Pride parade. But gayer than David Bowie."

"Oh my God," Gabe said. He could barely hear himself. The words felt heavy, almost impossible to push out. "You told everyone."

"Sweetie."

Gabe felt something, a touch to his hand, and glanced down to see Sandy holding it. Pressing it, even. It barely registered.

"Sweetie," she said, "I didn't tell anyone."

Gabe kept staring at Sandy's hand. And his. Seeing the touch made it easier to feel.

"How do they know?" he asked. "I've been really careful."

"We know you," she said softly. "And we don't care, honey. Colin doesn't care. I promise."

Slowly Gabe pulled his hand from Sandy's and backed into his chair. He could believe, maybe, that Sandy hadn't told anyone. She'd promised. She had never broken a promise to him before.

But that was one thing. Colin not caring was something else.

"He threw the guy out," Gabe said, staring now at the way his hands rested in his lap. Was it a gay way of holding his hands? Did he sit gay or something? Or was it all over his face?

"Guy?" Jerry asked.

"Colin caught Gabe with some guy," Sandy said. "Older guy."

"Ah," Jerry said. "Colin gave him the bum's rush?"

"You're a funny man," Sandy said, biting off the words. There was silence for a second or two, and then Gabe heard Jerry taking a pull on his beer. Giving up on his career as a comedian, it seemed.

"Gabe, come on," Sandy said. "If you were Colin's little sister and you'd come home with some skeezy older guy, what do you think Colin would have done?"

"If you were a chick," Jerry said, "Colin would have castrated the guy on your kitchen table. So this actually went better."

"You have to eat on that table," Sandy agreed.

Gabe raised his head and looked from one to the other of them, their earnest expressions, the way they were leaning forward slightly to give their words that extra push in his direction. And to his great surprise, he laughed. Right through to tears, and Sandy laughed with him. Jerry was too damned cool to laugh, but he smirked while he finished his beer, which was effusive for him, and Gabe appreciated it. Because he knew the guy and knew what he was like, and he was okay with that.

"I'll make coffee," Sandy said, getting up and patting Gabe's knee on her way past him to the kitchen. "And then you can tell us how you wound up naked on the porch."

Sandy

IT HAD to be a practical joke. Some terrible fucking joke that Gabe had cooked up, maybe with help from Sean. Definitely with help from Sean, because where else would he get a bike he could do this to?

"Fucking *Sean*!" she blurted, and this, going by the expression on Gabe's face, was about the last thing he'd expected her to say.

He was standing at the side of the highway, stars for a backdrop and wind tossing his hair around, and even in Jerry's too-long clothes, he came off like a goddamned movie star. Or rock star, which he would likely have preferred, considering what a freak he was for music. Sometimes it was stupidly obvious that he didn't belong around there. Sometimes Sandy wanted to slap him for it.

"Was this Sean's idea?" she asked. "Get an old bike and fucking, I don't know, melt it to the highway, and cook up this whole story about Colin finding you with a guy? And haul me and Jerry out here so you can see our faces?"

Gabe had his head tilted a bit to one side. Everything about his expression said that Sandy had lost her mind.

"Your hypothesis," he said carefully, "is that I outed myself to Sean and invented a story that's pretty much my worst nightmare so I could tell you a bullshit story about my bike getting wrecked?"

"That's your worst nightmare?" Jerry asked mildly. "Colin walking in on you?" He was still regarding the bike, or the bike-like pile of melted plastic and metal… metal… stuck to the road. He nudged some of it with the toe of his shoe and shrugged when it failed to move. "It's on there pretty good."

"Careful you don't melt your shoe," Gabe warned. Jerry shook his head.

"Mostly cooled off now."

"What am I supposed to think?" Sandy asked Gabe. "How else could this have happened and you still be… standing here?"

Gabe took a deep breath. A trio of cars passed, not slowing at the sight of three people and scrap metal. People were always in a hurry on that road.

"I think," Gabe said once the cars were gone, "I got hit by lightning."

That got Jerry to stop studying the ex-bike and start looking at Gabe.

"Out of a clear sky," he said.

"Yeah, I know," Gabe said. "But it's the only sky I've got, and I'm thinking lightning came out of it. Something knocked me off my bike and down the highway, burned off all my clothes, and did that to the bike. What else could it have been?"

Jerry gazed at the sky.

"Meteorite?" he offered.

Sandy's stomach lurched. "Come on. Gabe did not get hit by a fucking meteorite. Or lightning. He'd be… he'd…. Jesus, Gabe, you're telling us you skidded how far?"

"About even with the windbreak," he said, pointing out a row of scraggly trees.

"Without leathers or a helmet," Sandy said, staring down the highway. "You didn't even have a jacket?"

"T-shirt and jeans," Gabe said.

Jerry walked around Gabe in a tight circle. "No broken bones. No sprains."

"Nothing," Gabe said. "Not even a scrape."

Jerry whistled. "Somebody up there likes you."

Gabe smiled. "Somebody up there has a love/hate relationship with me," he corrected.

Jerry barked out one of his rare laughs. Sandy thought she might throw up. It wasn't funny. This was so not funny.

"Sandy?" Gabe asked softly. She tried on a smile as another group of cars sped past.

"Whatever happened," she said, "no harm done, I guess. Except to your bike."

"Yeah," Gabe said. "I don't think even Sean's gonna be able to fix it. That's fucked. How am I gonna get up to Cochin next week?"

It took Sandy a moment to remember that Gabe had a summer job lined up at Cochin, teaching people to windsurf on Jackfish Lake. He'd learned like the rest of them, tooling around on Sandy's dad's old board, and he was certified in exactly nothing, but somehow he'd talked his way into the gig. The owners probably thought teenage girls would line up for lessons with the hot guy. The owners were probably right.

"Maybe Sean can lend me a bike," Gabe said.

"We'll figure it out," Sandy said. She put a hand on Gabe's shoulder and steered him toward Jerry's dull red Geo. "You can bunk with us tonight. Tomorrow you can see a doctor and make sure you're really okay."

Gabe stopped, pushing back against her hand. The motion had more force than she expected, and she had to take a step back to keep her balance.

"I don't need a doctor."

"See a doctor," Sandy said, "and I'll make Sean lend you a bike. Don't see a doctor and you're hitching."

Gabe's shoulders dropped as his face fell, giving a general picture of things rushing toward the ground.

"Sandeeeeeeee…."

"You're tall for a six-year-old," Sandy observed. "That's the deal. Stay at our place tonight. Tomorrow morning Jerry will run you by your house so you can talk to Colin before he leaves for work. And then Jerry will drive you to a Mediclinic."

"Wow," Gabe said. "This deal keeps sucking bigger and bigger balls."

"Nobody consulted Jerry," Jerry pointed out.

"Or I could phone Colin right now," Sandy said, ignoring Jerry. "And, I remind you, you will be hitching to Cochin."

"Colin's probably at the bar," Gabe said, as if that won the game for him.

It was bad enough that Gabe and Colin refused to carry cell phones for some bullshit reason, but so much worse that they were obnoxious about it. *You can't pin us Reece boys down.* Sandy stepped closer so that Gabe had to tilt his head back to look her in the eye.

"I will call him at the bar," she said. "I will call all the bars."

She and Gabe stood there for a while, a few more groups of cars' worth. One even honked as though the whole freaking road wasn't enough for his ugly-ass sedan and he resented them taking up the shoulder. They did not, either of them, so much as twitch.

"Have it your way," Gabe said finally.

Sandy smiled and put a hand on his cheek. "Thanks, kiddo."

She stepped back and to his side, then put an arm around his shoulders and led him to Jerry, who was leaning against the side of his car.

"Your chariot," Jerry said, as they approached. "Apparently."

"Until Sean gives him a bike," Sandy assured him. "And I will owe you."

"Story of my life," Jerry muttered, and something in his eyes told Sandy not to ask what he meant by that. Instead the three of them said little as the tiny car full of hard drives and towers and cables bounced from the shoulder to the highway and back into town to take them home.

Chapter Two

Gabe

GABE IS in his bed. He's eight years old, and he feels awful. He doesn't remember a thing since lunch, and it's dark outside now.

Colin crawls in beside him with a book and reads to him about some weird British guys who get lost in outer space. Gabe thinks parts of it are funny, but he doesn't understand a lot of it. He doesn't tell Colin that. He wants Colin to keep reading.

There's wintergreen gum on Colin's breath. The kind that, when it's mints, Colin makes sparks with in the dark bathroom. It's his favourite everything: gum and candy and toothpaste. Gabe remembers smelling it in the dark of the basement, Colin sitting with a hand on Gabe's left arm while their dad puts another needle into the right. Whatever it is, it burns going in, tracing a heavy red line up Gabe's arm. He can feel it moving, the pressure, like someone shoved a wire in there.

He remembers this clearly for a moment, and then the memory fades, like the line on his arm, to Colin's voice and wintergreen air.

Gabe sicks up on his quilt at the smell of it.

Colin doesn't give him shit for the mess. Swaps out the blanket and goes to his own room.

"SORRY ABOUT the yelling last night," Gabe said as he entered the kitchen. Sandy and Jerry were at the table with coffee and bowls of oatmeal and cereal respectively. Gabe wandered by the toaster and pulled a piece of forgotten toast from its clutches. It was still warm, which was reassuring. Otherwise there was no telling how long it might have been there.

"You were dreaming about Colin catching you with a guy?" Jerry asked. Gabe stopped midway between the toaster and the fridge to stare at Jerry without comprehension.

"You said that was your worst nightmare," Jerry explained. "And about three in the morning, you sure sounded like you were having your worst nightmare. So I put two and two together."

"Oh," Gabe said. He pointed the toast at Jerry. "That's funny. You're very funny."

"I'm funnier when I've slept," Jerry said. Sandy swatted him with her coffee spoon.

"Get off him. It's not his fault he had a bad dream."

Gabe used the distraction to get to the fridge for jam and a can of Coke. While he rummaged, Jerry said, "It was more pathetic sobbing than yelling. So you know."

"That's a relief," Gabe said, raising his voice to be heard outside the fridge. "I thought maybe I'd sounded undignified."

"Not for a scared little girl," Jerry said.

"Delightful," Sandy said. "I love sexist fuckwittery with my morning coffee. Gabe, I thought you'd stopped having nightmares."

"Yeah, well," Gabe said, "sometimes I have one for nostalgia's sake."

He spotted a can of store-brand cola and grabbed it. Jam, on the other hand, was nowhere to be found.

"You remember this dream?" Jerry asked. Gabe shut the fridge and opened the cola.

"No."

"He never remembers them," Sandy said. She sounded testy. Also, she was wearing sweatpants and a T-shirt and hadn't even tried to brush her hair, so obviously she'd stumbled straight from her bed to the table. Gabe would have opted not to talk to her, considering those facts, but Jerry had lived with her for a year without losing any important body parts, and this seemed to have made him bold.

"I remember those two years of Colin bitching about getting no sleep," Jerry said. "I'm up on the details."

Gabe dropped the dry toast on the counter. He didn't need it.

"I didn't mean to wake people up," Gabe said. Sandy narrowed her eyes at Jerry before turning to hug the back of her chair and smile at Gabe.

"We know that. You'd have to be a fucking asshole to blame someone for having nightmares."

"What time does Elder work today?" Jerry said.

"Not until ten," Gabe said. "Someone else has to do a thing before the rest of the crew can do whatever it is they're doing."

"It's too bad Colin didn't try to get you a job at the construction site," Jerry commented. "I can picture you now, asking people to pass you the poundy thing so you could hit the sticky-uppy things."

"Shove a poundy thing up your sticky thing," Gabe said. "Colin and I retiled our roof last summer. I've seen you fuck up a Kinder toy."

"Can you both be this charming somewhere else?" Sandy said. "It's not really a question."

"Oh my, is that the time?" Jerry said, standing as he spoke. "Car, young Gabriel."

Gabe raised his drink can at Sandy. "Thanks," he said.

She smiled. "De nada. Say hi to Colin."

The way Gabe's stomach reacted to that told him it was a good thing he'd given up on the toast. In fact, the cola was probably a bad idea. He set the can on the counter.

"Later," he told Sandy and stepped lively to catch up to Jerry, who was already pulling his jacket on at the door. It was going to be too warm for a jacket within the hour, Gabe estimated, but Jerry overdressed for nearly everything.

Once they were squeezed into the Geo, Gabe tugged at his jeans—Jerry's jeans—and said, "I'll switch into my own clothes at my house and give these back to you. Unless you want me to wash them first."

"Ah, wearing my clothes after you've worn my clothes, without washing them," Jerry said, straight-faced and eyes on the road. "Dear *Penthouse Forum*...."

"Dear you," Gabe said. "Fuck you. I'll wash them, and you can pick them up whenever."

"Don't worry about it," Jerry said with a slanted grin. "I can do my own laundry."

He shrugged his right shoulder in a strange, twitchy way.

Gabe frowned. "Something wrong with your arm?"

Jerry stopped smiling. "Boss made me haul some heavy shit," he said. "Not part of my job description. Fucker."

Gabe nodded and stared out the passenger-side window. It wasn't even ten minutes' drive from the duplex to his and Colin's house. Ten minutes tops and he'd be looking Colin in the eye, provided Colin was able and willing to look at him. Well, unless Gabe rolled down the window and leapt from the Geo, but Jerry would probably tell Sandy about that, and then there'd be hell to pay.

Besides, he had to face Colin sometime.

“You’re technically an adult,” Jerry said.

“Your point?”

Jerry shrugged. “It’s your house too, right? It was left to both of you.”

Gabe returned his gaze to the passenger window. “Still not getting your point.”

“You want to nail some guy in your house, that’s your right,” Jerry said. “Colin’s not going to like hearing that, but it might be time he did.”

Gabe had nothing to say to that. He watched the blur of purple outside the window, all the lilac bushes going by. Every year of his life had contained two weeks of mauve hitting him in the eye. He wasn’t sure he’d recognize spring without it.

“Okay, fine,” Jerry said. “You’re right. It’s none of my business.”

They stopped for a train, and Gabe turned his head out of habit to see if he could spot the end. Estimate how long they’d be sitting there. He didn’t know whether he wanted the train to be long or short.

“But someone needs to say it,” Jerry said as train cars rolled by. White letters on dark brown, mostly. Was it grain, heading for the coast? Or did they load that into the tank cars, like silos on their sides?

A few more cars, some tanks, and then Jerry added, “Sandy’s not going to say anything, because she thinks the sun shines out of your brother’s ass.”

It was probably shameful that Gabe didn’t know how grain was shipped or where it went. He was supposedly an adult, and he knew fuck all about so many things.

“Not literally,” Jerry added. “That would be fatal.”

Gabe turned to stare at him.

“Sun shines out of your ass too,” Jerry said, glancing at him. “So you should be glad it’s not a literal thing.”

“Noted,” Gabe said. “You harrowing freak.”

“I’m not the one shooting daylight out my butthole,” Jerry informed him.

“Too fucking true,” Gabe agreed. And whatever might be wrong with Jerry, at least he didn’t look at Gabe cross-eyed when Gabe said things like “harrowing.”

It was a fairly short train, so they were moving again. They'd beat ten minutes, barring some disaster or miracle. Like lightning from the blue.

Gabe brought his knees up to rest along the dash and pushed back against the seat, trying to force the nervous energy out. It didn't even begin to get the job done. He felt oddly numb, like he had the night before. An ache in his muscles but no pain where his kneecaps met hard plastic. Another point in favour of lightning being the reason for his accident. He'd heard it could fuck up your nervous system for years.

"Hey, Jer," he said, "what would it take for you to drive us to, I don't know, Vancouver instead?"

"It would have to be worth both our lives," Jerry said. "I am driving you home and to a Mediclinic, and then I am driving myself to work, and your problems will be your own."

They turned toward Gabe's part of town, a neighbourhood that predated the tidy post-war bungalows and slapped-together late-century apartment units that characterized most of the city. It was the kind of area that would gentrify the second anyone who could spell the word came to North Battleford with more money and optimism than sense. But there was no sign of that yet, and so the gabled houses with thick warped windows and wide verandas merely created a slightly more attractive rundown neighbourhood in a town full of lousy places to live.

Gabe and Colin's pale yellow house was set apart, with an alley on one side and a vacant lot on the other. The alley and their gravel driveway had no obvious demarcations, and in truth, most of their friends saw no difference between the two. They parked on either or both with crooked abandon.

Today, though, Jerry was able to park on the driveway proper, and right up next to the front door besides… because Colin's truck wasn't around.

"Shit," Jerry said. "I guess he went in early."

"Or he went out last night and stayed out," Gabe said.

"Yeah, I guess," Jerry said. He turned off the car. "Either way, you're off the hook."

"For now," Gabe agreed, almost dizzy on the extra oxygen now that he could breathe again. "Lemme run in and change clothes, and then you can drop me at the clinic."

"Make it quick," Jerry said, and Gabe nodded. Colin or not, he didn't feel like spending more time in the house than he had to.

"Back before you know it," he said, his hand already on the car door.

Sandy

"SLOW DOWN, Gabe. I'm not understanding you."

Sandy was holding her phone to her ear with one hand and using the other hand to dig her shoes out from the pile by the door. She had to be at work in ten minutes, so Gabe needed to start making sense in a hurry.

"Colin's gone," Gabe said. His voice sounded harsh over the phone. "What are you not getting?"

"So he's not home," Sandy said.

"No, he's gone," Gabe said. "As in gone, gone. His clothes are gone. His razor's gone. His toothbrush is gone. He is fucking gone, Sandy. He left."

"Okay," Sandy said, "maybe he's taking a little breather or something. Maybe he's giving you some time to cool off. He packed up some clothes—"

"He took all his fucking clothes, Sandy!" Sandy winced and pulled the phone away from her head as Gabe went on. "Oh, Colin knows you're gay, Gabe. Colin doesn't care. Go home and talk to him. Fuck. *Fuck*!"

Sandy shut her eyes. "Is Jerry still there?"

"Yes," Gabe hissed.

Sandy wasn't sure why Jerry's name was drawing that reaction, but she had a feeling there was a reason for it. "Put him on."

"Fine."

She heard Gabe calling Jerry to the phone and Jerry bumping into something and cursing, and then the rustle of the phone being passed from one to the other.

"What can I do for you?"

Sandy sat down in the hallway, next to the shoe pile.

"What's going on over there, Jer?"

"Colin seems to have lit out," Jerry said. He didn't sound alarmed, surprised, or even particularly interested. Jerry and Colin had been best friends since grade school, but hey, easy come easy go, right?

Jerry drove Sandy nuts sometimes.

"Lit out," she repeated.

"Yeah. He packed up his clothes, some personal shit, and his truck's gone. My guess is he got tired of being the drama queen's parental unit and he's taking a mental health break."

"Wow," Sandy said. She glanced at the wall clock in the kitchen. She could continue the conversation on the way to work, but she didn't feel like broadcasting her side of it to the neighbourhood. Might as well resign herself to being late. "Tell me something… is Gabe right there listening to you while you talk this shit?"

"Gabe's a big boy," Jerry said. "Whatever Colin's reason for leaving, it's pretty clear he fucked off of his own volition. There's no reason to get wound up about it. Twenty bucks says he calls by the end of the day."

"Twenty bucks, hey?" Sandy said. "Pretty high-rolling bet. You must be either really uncertain or really broke."

"I can be both," Jerry pointed out. "But I seriously think we'll hear from him."

"We'd better," Sandy said darkly. Not that Gabe was a kid anymore, but running out on the kid was still not cool. "Put Gabe back on, would you?"

"He's all yours," Jerry said. More rustling and then Gabe's voice.

"You can't think this isn't about what happened last night," Gabe said. "Don't even try to tell me that."

"I don't have an opinion right now," Sandy said. "Jerry's right about one thing, though—it sounds like Colin left under his own steam."

"Yeah, that's great," Gabe said. His voice was sharp, the way it got when he was close to tears and determined to hide it. "That reassures the fuck out of me. I drove him out of his house. He can't stand to look at me."

"You're driving me off this phone, drama queen," Sandy warned him. "You don't—"

She stopped because of a loud banging that she realized after a second was the sound of the phone receiver being dropped to a counter or table. In the distance she could hear Gabe asking Jerry what the hell he was doing. If Jerry responded, he was too far away for Sandy to hear him.

After a few seconds, she heard the phone being picked up again.

"Jerry has," Gabe said, "gone into the basement for some fucking reason. He says he wants to check the whole house. I mean, for what?"

"Well," Sandy said, "this is the guy who checks that he locked the door three times whenever he leaves our house, so I wouldn't make a huge deal out of whatever weird shit he does."

"I don't know what to do here, Sandy."

"Go to the Mediclinic," she said. "Go home, maybe take a nap. See whether Colin calls you tonight."

"We have bills and shit," Gabe said. "Not that this is my main concern. But there's a money thing. My summer job will not cut it."

"I know," Sandy said. "I'm sure Colin won't leave you in the lurch. At least give it a day before you panic."

"Yeah, okay," Gabe said. "You should probably be at work."

"No, really?" Sandy said. "I'll call you later, okay?"

"Yeah," Gabe said. "Thanks."

He hung up before she could say anything else. Take care, maybe, or hang in there. Something that tit-useless. She threw her phone into her purse and headed out.

Gabe

IT DIDN'T seem as if the wait would be too much longer. There was an old guy in one of those sweaters that looked like someone ate green and black paint and puked on a loom. A girl in the upper range of plump, probably older than she appeared because her kind of face would always read young, but still not old enough, in Gabe's opinion, to be the mother of the preschooler who was sitting at her feet and coughing on a pile of oversized Legos. Gabe couldn't even imagine being in charge of a kid. He was pretty sure he'd fuck up a goldfish.

He considered reading something, but he preferred not to touch anything. Also he wasn't all that interested in what *Chatelaine* had considered the best one hundred buys under one hundred dollars back in 2018. That meant nothing was distracting him from his intense desire to get up and leave. Doctors gave him the creeps—always had. Which Sandy fucking knew, so it had been real sensitive of her to send him here.

But she'd fuck him over on the bike if he left. He knew that as surely as he knew that she would find out he'd left… somehow.

He'd grabbed an old wristwatch from his bedroom as he'd gotten dressed. He got stares for wearing one, more and more over the years. Everyone else used their phones. But the handful of Bosch promo watches Colin had brought home from a job site had suited them fine, new ones swapped for old as straps and glass broke.

This one told Gabe he'd been in the waiting room for about an hour.

"Gabriel Reece?"

As most nurses did, this nurse called out names as questions. She carefully scanned the four people in the narrow shop-front waiting room. She'd positioned herself before the hallway to the exam rooms like Cerberus with a clipboard, as if she thought the mob might rush the doctor on duty. Her face was as questioning as her voice. *Is there a Gabriel Reece here*? her expression said. *Do I have the name right? Do I have last week's sign-up sheet by mistake? And have you changed your mind about this whole thing, and would you like to run away now?*

Gabe raised a hand and stood to follow the nurse, who had started down the hall as soon as he'd fessed up to being himself.

"Doctor'll be in right away," she told him once he'd dropped into a vinyl-and-steel chair. Same one they had in every doctor's office everywhere. For all Gabe knew, it was impossible to cure anyone of anything unless you had one of those chairs.

"'Kay," Gabe said.

The nurse held a pen to the clipboard. "Why are you here today?" she asked.

"Fantastic question," Gabe said. At the nurse's exhausted look, he relented. "I had a motorcycle accident last night, and I feel fine, but I want to make sure."

"You should maybe have gone to the hospital," the nurse said, seeming like another human for the first time. "If you need X-rays or whatever, we can't do that here."

Gabe tried to make his face say that he was not getting up and going to any damned hospital. Apparently it worked, because the nurse sighed and strapped a blood pressure cuff around Gabe's arm.

"Tell me if it hurts," she said, though it always pinched a little, and Gabe had never known a nurse to care when he said so.

She took her time about the reading, adjusting the strap a few times and even, to Gabe's amusement, shaking the readout dial.

"I'm sorry," she said. "This doesn't appear to be working. I'll make a note for the doctor to do it."

She dropped the clipboard into a Lucite pocket on the exam room's door and left without looking at Gabe again. As if he'd broken the blood pressure thingy and had been too rude to apologize.

Dr. Lam showed up within minutes and politely didn't notice as Gabe scrambled to put back the latex glove box he'd been snickering at. The photo of someone's hand on the side, index finger out and ready for action, was the funniest thing he'd seen in days.

"I understand you had a motorcycle accident," the doctor said, taking the room's other black-and-silver chair.

Gabe almost smiled. If Dr. Lam understood that accident, he was one up on his patient.

"This is going to sound kind of weird," Gabe said, "but I think maybe I got hit by lightning while I was on the highway last night."

"Can you tell me why you think that?" Dr. Lam asked, and Gabe felt as if he'd claimed to have had an alien encounter the night before. Which was also, come to think of it, a possibility. And not much crazier than any other.

Gabe described what he remembered of the accident while Dr. Lam frowned and took the occasional note on the iPad he'd brought in with him.

"Well," the doctor said once Gabe had finished, "whatever happened, it will be good to check you out."

He looked at the chart and frowned again. presumably because he'd realized he'd have to do the grunt work of taking Gabe's blood pressure. And indeed Dr. Lam's next move was to open the exam room door a crack and ask someone Gabe couldn't see to bring him a new spigma something or other.

As they waited, the doctor checked Gabe's eyes and ears. Asked about headache and dizziness. Nodded sagely no matter what Gabe said, which made Gabe want to start speaking Klingon or something, anything to get another expression out of the guy. Even if Gabe only knew three words in Klingon and would be forced to repeat himself.

"Your chart says you're due for a tetanus shot," the doctor said. "We'll start with that."

Gabe nodded, though his heart was racing suddenly. He forced himself to keep still as the doctor prepared the shot and as alcohol was swabbed on his upper arm. He looked away when the needle came out, and—

"—THERE'S NO particular reason to cut them," his father is saying to his friend, the tall one with a face so thin that Gabe can almost see his teeth under his skin. They're in the basement, and Gabe thinks he can see Colin on the next bed, behind the thin guy, and since when were there beds down here? Not even normal beds. The ambulance kind.

"Not unless you want to make a mess and waste blood," his father goes on, expansive on a topic he seems to love. "If you're testing for pain resistance, concentrate on that. If you're collecting blood to work with, there's nothing wrong with using a—"

"SON OF a *bitch*!"

Gabe gaped at Dr. Lam, who had previously not seemed the type to swear, at full volume, in the middle of an exam.

It took a few heartbeats before Gabe was able to understand what he was seeing. Dr. Lam was holding a syringe with a little bit of silver at the end where the needle should have been. He was staring at the exam table where Gabe was sitting. Not staring at Gabe, but beside him. Gabe's eyes followed the doctor's and slowly registered a thin piece of silver. About the size and shape of the rest of that needle.

"I am… I am so sorry," the doctor said, wide-eyed. "I have never seen that happen before. The needle must have been… um… let me get another needle and I'll try again."

Something in Gabe snapped like the damned needle when he heard that. Sandy would be mad, and he wouldn't get the bike, and he might lose his job before it even started, and he did not give a fuck about any of it. He jumped off the table, pushed past the doctor, and ran without concern for who might step in his way or which way the glass doors at the front opened. Full speed, he got outside and kept going—north, through the alleys, to keep people from seeing and staring.

His house wasn't that far away, and Gabe saw no reason why he couldn't run all the way there.

Sandy

"HEY… SANDY…."

Sean probably thought he was whispering as he cut behind the front desk and sidled up to Sandy. Since Sean usually talked like a farm wife calling the hubby in from a cow pasture, maybe a regular inside voice really was whispering to him.

"Sean?" she said brightly, tossing her purse under the desk and shoving back her chair. Sean perched on the counter behind her desk, eyes wide behind thin-rimmed glasses.

"You, uh, can't really be late around here."

Sandy checked the clock on the computer screen, then turned to Sean with raised brows. "Ten minutes, guy."

"Yeah, I know," Sean said. "Boss is kind of a freak about it."

"Thanks again for telling me beforehand about the freak boss at this job," Sandy said, using a genuine whisper in the hopes that Sean would like it enough to develop one of his own.

"Yeah, sorry," Sean said, seemingly unconcerned. He ran a hand over his wiry grey-flecked hair and scanned the shop, probably for the boss in question. "I didn't mean to get you a job or anything. If you don't want me to do that, I can not do that."

He didn't whine his way through that little speech, just put it out there. Sandy patted one of Sean's stocky legs.

"I appreciate the job. Have I been late before?"

"No, no. But if you were late again…."

"Okay, noted," Sandy said. It really wasn't a bad job, service writing for the shop where Sean fixed cars and trucks, mostly, and bikes every chance he got. Yeah, she had to be polite to people, and there was the freak boss, but in general it was reasonably sweet.

"I mean, I don't care," Sean said. "It complicates things for you, though. If you don't have employment. Right?"

Sandy smiled. "It complicates things for most people."

"Well, sure," Sean said. "But… you know what I mean."

Sandy did, and silently thanked him for not bringing it up in the workplace. Even if he was "whispering."

"Uh-huh. Anyway, you can thank the Reece boys for this."

Sean had been starting to stand, presumably with the intention of going back to his own work, but he put his ass back on the counter at those words and eyed Sandy with happy curiosity. The man liked gossip more than anyone who wasn't Andy Cohen, which Sandy found both odd and adorable in someone with grease under his nails.

"Oh?" Sean said.

"Yeah. I guess Colin caught Gabe with a guy last night."

"Heh." Sean adjusted his glasses, transferring grease to the frames. "You know that was gonna happen eventually."

"Tell Gabe that," Sandy said. "Jerry and I already did. Gabe came over to emote about the situation, and he crashed at our place. Where you weren't, by the way."

Sean chuckled and actually blushed a little but said nothing.

"Alrighty," Sandy said. "This reminds me, though—I told Gabe I'd talk you into lending him a bike."

"You're gonna talk me into that?" Sean asked. "How?"

"Favour to me," Sandy said. "He took off on his bike after Colin walked in on him, and he got into an accident. Sort of."

"What sort of 'sort of' accident was it?" Sean asked.

"I don't know," Sandy said. "He didn't hit anything. He was on the Yellowhead, and his bike went over, and he skidded down the road with no leathers. A fucking T-shirt. No helmet either…."

"Shit." Sean's amusement changed to concern. "Is he okay?"

"Miraculously," Sandy said, "he seems to be. Bike's totalled, though. You might want to see it. It's like it's been melted to the pavement."

"That is weird," Sean agreed, enthusiastic again. "You are not wrong. Was he heading west?"

"Just past the bridge," Sandy confirmed. "I seriously don't know what happened."

"Probably what Jerry would call a PEBKAC error," Sean said. "Considering the mood Gabe would have been in."

It was interesting that Jerry had the power to give Sandy a little headache without even being there. He would probably have been gratified to know it.

"PEB…."

"Problem exists between keyboard and chair," Sean said. "It's a way of saying, ehh, the user's an idiot. Because clients don't like being called idiots for some reason. They're funny that way."

"You think Gabe took the turn too fast or something?" Sandy asked.

Sean shrugged. "Sounds like Gabe to me. Okay… now you look skeptical."

"You didn't see the bike," Sandy said. She sounded off, even to herself. She kept picturing the bike, or the remains of it. Jerry kicking the metal lightly and declaring it stuck fast. It was nearly the only thing she could think about.

"So," Sean said, putting a hand on her shoulder and being sickeningly obvious about jollying her along, "you want me to lend a bike to Gabe because he totalled the last one."

Sandy grabbed Sean's hand and returned it to him.

"He has that job in Cochin starting right away," she said, "and he's going to need it because Colin has fucked off."

Sean's eyes popped so wildly at that news that Sandy wondered if they might shove the lenses from his glasses.

"Whoa. What do you mean by 'fucked off'?"

"He was gone when Gabe got home this morning," she told him. "But not gone like he's at work or he's taking a morning stroll. He'd packed up his clothes, and his truck was gone. Fucked right off."

"Like the Dean of Fucking Off at Fucking the Fuck Off University," Sean offered. Sandy stared at him until he shifted uncomfortably and said, "Never mind."

"Jerry bet me twenty bucks Colin will call by tonight."

"So one of you will be asking me to lend you twenty bucks before midnight?" Sean concluded.

"Everyone's a riot today," Sandy said. "Why don't you go do something I can overcharge a customer for?"

"Or I could dig up a bike for Gabe. But he might not like what I find. Just sayin'."

"Honestly," Sandy said, "I think right now you could put that kid on a Vespa and he wouldn't even notice."

Chapter THREE

Gabe

AT FIRST Gabe thought it must be a forest fire. North of the city was pretty much all forest, and a few fires each summer came close enough to make the city smell like a hot-dog roast.

It wasn't until he got to within a block of his house that he realized the smoke was too thick to be coming from a forest miles away. And the air was too damned hot.

Even then he didn't understand that a house was on fire until he cut out of the alley and onto the street, less than a block from his front yard. And he didn't understand that it was his house even as he ran toward it, watching it burn.

It was impossible. That house had been there when he was born and had been built before his parents were born, and it stuck around even after they both left. The very idea that his house could, say, burn to the ground was ridiculous. It didn't do that sort of thing.

Nonetheless it was going up like it had been waiting for this moment all its life. Fire was coming from every window, every air hole it could find, spread evenly across the building, and Gabe had a strange, still moment of wondering if that was normal. Shouldn't it be worse somewhere, or nearly burned out in the place where it had started? Colin would have known. Colin knew about guy shit like that.

That was when it occurred to Gabe that Colin might have come home. His truck wasn't there, but he could have walked or gotten a ride or something. He could have. He could have gone inside before….

Gabe bolted for the front door, which was hanging open, and why, exactly? Did fire open locks?

Never mind—he was going to search for Colin. He'd check the fucking basement if he had to. He'd be thorough, like Jerry.

He had a moment of thinking he'd have to search the house blind. The smoke was crazy thick, almost palpable. He couldn't believe his eyes weren't stinging from it when even the distant forest fire smoke could turn them red. He couldn't believe his chest wasn't aching from the smoke and the heat, that he could stand in the kitchen without wanting to fall to his knees and crawl away.

And then the lights came on.

Not the kitchen lights—they weren't, in Gabe's estimation, ever coming on again. But there was a faint blue glow in front of Gabe, allowing him to see a few inches into the smoke. And a low hum he was sure he hadn't heard upon entering the house.

He was surprised enough that he didn't move right away. He looked from side to side, trying to think where the light was coming from. He heard himself yelling for Colin, which was natural. Colin was good with answers.

He took a step forward, toward the living room, then whirled at noises behind him. Crashing, then coughing. The light landed on a man with close-cropped hair. He was hunched over, reaching a hand toward Gabe. Between coughs, he said something that sounded like "Come on."

It wasn't bad advice, but it didn't work for Gabe. He backed toward the living room, still watching the man approach. The man lunged at him then and grabbed Gabe's arm with both hands.

The instant they touched, the blue light darkened and the hum became a shrill note, like something from a violin. It was louder than the fire. The man was flung backward, hands out in front, and for an instant Gabe pictured Mr. Okay falling to the living room floor, where Gabe had shoved him.

Except Gabe hadn't shoved this time.

The man hit the far wall of the kitchen and slid down until he landed, legs in front of him. Gabe could barely see him and couldn't tell if he was conscious. He had to be stunned at the least. Fucking stunned to chase a stranger into a burning building, but that was beside the point.

Something in Gabe's head did the math for him. Chance that Colin was in the house? Somewhere around one percent, maybe. Tops. Chance that this guy, who seemed to have been trying to save Gabe's life, was right in front of Gabe and in danger of dying? Somewhere around a hundred percent.

As Dr. Lam would have said, son of a bitch.

Gabe moved forward and grabbed the guy's hands to pull him up. The guy didn't help much, but he did try to get his feet under himself, so at least he wasn't going to be dead weight.

"You come the fuck on," Gabe muttered into the smoke as he pulled the guy against his side and half-dragged him to the front yard.

He went nearly to the sidewalk before letting his new travel companion sink to the ground and cough.

"Yeah, do that," Gabe suggested. He reached to pat the guy's back, then thought of the blue flash and the flying body and decided against it. The guy seemed okay anyway. Just a little dazed.

Gabe saw him clearly for the first time. The guy was blond, or blondish—there was enough ash on him that it was hard to tell. His face was defined but not sharp, with good bones and wide blue eyes a few shades lighter than Gabe's own. He seemed young—maybe even as young as Gabe. Certainly no older than early twenties. He was wearing a cotton shirt that might have once been crisp and possibly even white but was now dark grey and textured with debris.

The guy opened his mouth, coughed, shook his head, and tried again. He said, "Colin?"

No one who knew him and Colin would ever confuse them with each other. Not until the day Gabe gained six inches in height and about sixty pounds.

"Uh-uh," Gabe said. The guy frowned, clean lines appearing on his face as the expression put folds in his skin.

"Looking for Colin Reece," he choked out and began coughing again. Gabe put a hand on the guy's shoulder without realizing it.

"Me too," Gabe said. He wanted to say more, or rather to ask a lot of questions, but he was interrupted by the sound of sirens. Evidently someone in his neighbourhood had figured out that a house burning down on a city street was everyone's problem.

"Fuck," Gabe said distinctly, projecting over the noise. "I have to go."

The blond guy frowned again.

"Cops after you?"

"EMTs," Gabe told him. "I have to find my brother. Those fuckers will take me to the hospital, and I'll be stuck in some fucking exam room for a hundred years while they do their goddamned paperwork."

Blondie cocked his head at Gabe, like a bird.

"Waste of time," he agreed and stuck a hand out as if introducing himself. Gabe took it, and Blondie grasped Gabe's hand firmly before bracing himself against Gabe and struggling to his feet. "My car is up the street."

"Whoa," Gabe said, pulling his arm back until Blondie released his hand. "I don't need a hospital, but you might."

"I'm fine," Blondie assured him, then quickly clamped his lips shut over a cough. His cheeks puffed out as he tried to contain it. Gabe sighed.

"Dude...."

"Now or never," Blondie said, pointing his chin at the flashing red lights that had appeared at the far end of Gabe's street. "I need to talk to you."

"Lead on," Gabe said. Because Blondie was an adult and could make his own decisions. Also it wasn't to be overlooked that he was a mysterious stranger who'd shown up at a fire that was burning Gabe's house down—his fucking house down, everything gone—looking for Colin, who was flat-out missing for the first time Gabe could remember in his entire life.

Which meant Gabe needed to talk to this guy too.

Sandy

IT WAS a slow day at the shop, or at least it was once Sandy got done rearranging her daybook and punting everything that could wait to another day. Next week's version of Sandy could handle the people bitching and moaning because their parts weren't in and their repairs weren't done. She could blame it on the supply chain. At the moment Sandy had more important things to worry about.

Not that she was that concerned about Colin. Surely Gabe was exaggerating when he said that Colin had packed up everything—lock, stock, and toothbrush. Jerry had sounded like he thought Colin might have taken off for a while, sure, but not forever. Maybe not even a long time. Hell, he might even turn up before the day was out.

But that didn't mean Sandy couldn't investigate where the jackass had gone.

She scrolled her contacts for Colin's foreman. What was that idiot's name? Carl. Carl had given her his number the week before, when she'd been out for a rare night with Colin's work crew and the foreman had spent ten awkward minutes confirming that she and Colin were not an item before asking if she'd like to go for dinner sometime. She didn't want to because she didn't need more of his thoughts on why the construction industry should be deregulated or how the free market determined the lower value of women's sporting events. But she'd said, "I'm not dating at the moment" instead of "You're obnoxious and I can't stand you," so Carl still thought he was in with a chance.

He caught the call on the third ring with a "Hit me" that seemed too loud even for the level of background noise.

"Hey, Carl," Sandy said, "it's Sandy. From the bar? Do you have a minute?"

"Wha—yes! Of course!"

She heard the background noise lessen, then drop off with the sound of a door closing. Carl must have gone into the trailer. A good thing, since Sandy wasn't able to shout her way through a personal call at her desk.

"That's better. Sandra! It's a pleasure to hear from you."

"It's good to talk to you too," Sandy lied, forcing a smile onto her face. Customers could hear you smile, their freak boss had told her. Always smile on the phone. "I wish it was a personal call, but I'm actually calling about Colin."

"Colin? Is everything all right?"

Sandy glanced at the clock. It was a few minutes past 10:00 a.m., otherwise known as the time Colin was supposed to start that day's shift.

"Is he there?" Sandy asked. "Because I think—"

"No, not yet, but the guys come in a little late sometimes. You know, I'm a fair boss. I just make sure they stay a little late. That's how the system works. Money is exchanged for labour."

Sandy wanted to exchange a punch in the face for the sound of Carl saying *ow*, but that was neither possible nor productive.

"Colin's usually on time, though," she said. "It's one of his things. He likes to be on time."

He was, in fact, an impressively punctual guy. There had been plenty of times when Sandy thought he was going to be late for something, like a meeting with Gabe's social worker or a movie in an actual theatre. He'd tell her he'd be there, running a little behind but it would be okay. And she'd highly doubt it because she'd know he was coming in from too far out of town or had too many errands to run and stops to make. But he always seemed to come skidding in at the last second.

"True, true," Carl said. "I guess it is strange that he's not here yet. But he could have a flat tire or something. I don't know if you know this, but the guy doesn't carry a cell phone."

Nope, definitely no reason Sandy would know that about her oldest friend. She bit her tongue and let Carl continue.

"Yeah, he says it's a government tracking device, and I get it. They're tracking us seven ways to Sunday these days. If you don't have a carbon-fibre wallet, you really ought to get one."

"Right, I'll look into that. But about Colin—I know there's no real way to get hold of him. If he shows up there today, would you be able to have him call me?"

"Sure, no problem. Is there… it sounds like you think he might not be coming in today."

Why hadn't she made notes before picking up the phone, or at least thought things through? She should have known he'd ask something like that.

"The guys thought he might be out of town," Sandy said. "They said something came up. But he didn't tell me or his brother, so I thought I'd call and check."

"I see. Well, I'll miss him at work, no way around that, but he's been a good worker all season. I don't want to cut him from the crew over one no-show. If you hear from him before I do, tell him to give me a call and we'll sort this out."

"Will do," Sandy said.

"Oh, and Sandra?"

Sandy's stomach dropped. She hadn't hung up fast enough. No one to blame but herself.

"Yeah?"

"You give any more thought to dinner?"

She would have liked to say no with more force this time, but she did need him to call if Colin showed up, and she didn't want Colin to get fired because his friend was a bitch.

"You know," she said, "like I said at the bar, I'm taking some time off dating. Could be quite a while. I need to get my head straight after what happened with the last guy."

The silence on Carl's end told her he'd heard about what happened with the last guy.

"Right," he said. "Right, makes sense."

"Thanks again," Sandy told him and disconnected as soon as the words were out. Then she stared at the paper calendar lying across most of her desk. Her scrawled notes were everywhere, along with coffee rings and mustard stains and a couple of squashed mosquitoes. She always loved the start of a new month, when she could tear off the disgusting old sheet and have, for at least half a day, a clean new one.

"You think he'll be good with this?"

Sandy glanced up at Sean's voice and saw him wheeling in a mid-80s Suzuki with tires no wider than her wrist. It was a cute little thing, and Gabe would be cute on it, which would irritate the shit out of him. More importantly, the bike looked like it had been ridden into a mud puddle, abandoned there, towed out with a truck, and hosed off before being thrown into storage for twenty years. But if the thing ran, it might do the job.

"Is it street legal?" she asked.

Sean made a see-saw gesture with his hand. "Ehhh?"

"That's a noise, not an answer."

"Okay, technically the TS125 is street legal. They're dual-purpose. The speed tops out around a hundred, but that's good. Gabe won't be getting speeding tickets on the highway."

"Great news," Sandy said. "Will he be getting other tickets?"

"Busted signal light?" Sean said. "I'm gonna try to fix that. I have some parts I think I can make work."

Sandy put her head in her hands.

"It's not much use giving him a bike if he can't take it anywhere without getting pulled over," she said.

"The cops have better things to do," Sean said. "But I should be able to fix it. I'll give it my thirty-thirty guarantee. Thirty feet or thirty seconds, whichever comes first."

"I don't think he has any better offers," Sandy allowed. "If it's ready by noon, let's bring it by the house."

Gabe

BLONDIE'S CAR was a rental, it turned out. Some anonymous sedan with an interior that had been detailed recently. Someone had probably worked on it for an hour, which made it a shame that two walking ashtrays were now occupying the seats, but sometimes life didn't go the ideal way.

"Direct me," Blondie directed. "Someplace we can talk."

Gabe thought about Sandy's house. Sandy and Sean's shop. The bar, or the other bar, or the Chinese buffet dive, all of them dark and quiet in the middle of the day. But he and the stranger weren't in fit condition even for the dive. This meeting was going to have to happen al fresco.

"Take the alley south," he said for starters. Blondie found the alley entrance without delay and turned early enough that the approaching fire truck didn't have to slow for him. Probably hadn't noticed them. Not as if the fire truck was going to start chasing them or something, but they had radios and might tell the cops if they saw two medium-rare guys booting it from a fire.

A really fucking suspicious fire. Which was something he was not going to think about.

"Where now?"

Blondie's voice was mild, now that he was no longer forcing words out between coughs. He sounded irritatingly calm, but of course he had that luxury since it wasn't his house that had burned down with everything in it. Everything. Everything. Christ. Gabe no longer even owned a change of underwear, a thought that came close to making him need one.

"Where now?"

The guy's voice was still mild, just a bit louder. Gabe blinked and saw the end of the alley approaching.

"Uh—sorry. Right at the next street, and then left at the lights."

Gabe forced his mind to stay on track. Getting somewhere safe and private was the first thing. Finding Colin was the first thing, really, but talking to this guy was step two in that plan, and step one was finding a place to do that.

He directed Blondie onto the bridge and south into Battleford. The sun caught the railings as they drove, and Gabe saw a flash of almost-white, like in the house. That light. The way Blondie had flown against the wall without Gabe lifting a hand.

The thought slipped away so quickly that he couldn't have stopped it if he'd wanted to.

Turn by the gas station, then up the hill and back down along a narrow dirt road to the old steel bridge. It was barricaded against cars but open to lighter things, like bikes and people and pissy seagulls. People came there to fish sometimes. Everyone gave everyone else space.

"Pull in there," he said, pointing to a patch of hard earth a few feet from the barricade. Blondie did so smoothly. He'd driven smoothly the whole way, following Gabe's directions without hesitation. And okay, so it wasn't his house, but he'd been in that house. He'd clearly taken in a lot more smoke than Gabe had. He'd stared into smoke and flames that seemed not merely thick but alive.

That had to bother a guy, didn't it?

Except apparently not.

"So," Blondie said, setting the parking brake, "did you want to talk here?"

"You know, I'd get upwind of myself if I could," Gabe said. "Next best thing, I guess, is to talk outside."

Blondie eyed the environment with clear misgivings. Thick brush leading to the river, with barely-there paths snaking through it. Narrow little pieces of beach below the brush, two of them already occupied by guys with fishing rods.

Gabe left the car and started walking toward the bridge. He didn't check to see if Blondie was following. After a few seconds, he heard a car door shut and then Blondie's footfalls behind him. He followed the ghost of a yellow line on the bleached pavement, walking it like a balance beam. It was a game he'd played as a kid. By the sound of Blondie's steps, he wasn't playing the game. He was just walking.

Midway across the bridge, Gabe stopped and faced his shadow.

"Here's good," he said.

Blondie raised his brows. "Right here?"

Gabe swept an arm at each end of the bridge. There was no way to approach from either shore without being seen. No way, even, to come down the riverbank unnoticed. And nothing but river beneath them.

"Privacy," he said. "Have a seat."

Blondie regarded his pants, which were khakis or something under the grime. He shrugged, all "What am I worried about? Getting my pants dirty?" and Gabe nearly laughed. He wanted to laugh and laugh, suddenly. He was, he decided, in shock. Like the night before.

Blondie sat on the pavement, and Gabe sat across from him, cross-legged, hands on the ground. As a kid he'd always loved the feel of this pavement, heated by the sun and its reflection off the denim-blue water. Now it felt worn and pebbly and cold. Too early in the day, or maybe the season, for its usual warmth.

"So," Gabe said. "You're… you said you were looking for my brother?"

"If your brother is Colin Reece," Blondie said, "yes."

Who was this guy? Not that everyone in town knew Colin, but… yeah, okay, everyone in town knew Colin. Everyone their age anyway.

Blondie wasn't from town, though. He drove a rental car.

"My brother is Colin Reece," Gabe said slowly. He extended a hand. "Gabe Reece."

Blondie shook his hand. "Gabriel?"

Gabe rolled his eyes. "Only when I'm in shit."

Blondie smiled, tiny lines appearing around his eyes to show how he'd look when he was older. Gabe released his hand and said, "Traditionally, this is where you would tell me your name."

"Right," Blondie said. "I'm Eli Samm. I'm a private investigator."

If Sandy's mother had been there, she would have said Gabe was drawing flies by sitting there with his jaw hanging. He closed his mouth and gazed at the river through the rusting beams. It was higher than normal. Heavy snows in the mountains the winter before.

"Seriously?" Gabe said, dragging his eyes back to Eli Samm.

The guy shrugged again, the way he had before deciding to park himself on the ground. "What kind of joke would it be?"

He sounded as if he genuinely didn't know, which told Gabe he ran with very different people from Gabe's friends. Then again, though they might have sent a bogus private investigator to someone as a joke, packing up all of Colin's stuff and burning his house down would likely have been considered going too far.

"Sorry," Gabe said. "I'm just… private investigators are kind of fictional to me."

Eli nodded as if he understood.

"Man," Gabe said. "I can't think of a single fucking reason why someone would pay someone else money to find my brother. He's not hiding. Not usually."

Eli cocked his head again, the way he had on Gabe's lawn.

"I guess I'm asking what you were hired for, exactly," Gabe said. "If you can tell me that."

"I can," Eli said. "I was hired to find Owen Bernier."

"Oh," Gabe said. "That clears it up."

"Does it?" Eli asked, seeming mildly hopeful. Gabe felt like a shit for… well, being a shit.

"No," he said. "I don't know who that is. What does he have to do with my brother?"

"He's missing," Eli said. He took out his phone and showed Gabe a photo of a short, skinny guy with spiky brown hair and his face shoved toward the camera like he was insisting you love it. Gabe did not.

"I don't know him," Gabe said again.

"The last place he was seen was the casino—he works there, but he's been missing from work since two nights ago. He was working a shift and got into an argument with your brother. Colin went into the parking lot, and Owen followed him."

"A fight?" Gabe said, trying not to smile. "Colin and that guy? Did you try scraping the lot with a spatula?"

"I take it your brother has some size on Owen Bernier?"

"Based on that picture? Colin is two of him. But I'm kidding about the spatula thing. Colin doesn't fight purse dogs."

Eli leaned back against the side of the bridge. The sun was hitting his face, throwing harsh shadows to the ground beside him.

"Staff at the casino tell me that Owen was upset about Colin's treatment of one of the other servers. Tracy Howell. Do you know her?"

"Yeah," Gabe said. "She taught swim lessons at the lake one year. I think I was ten. She was maybe sixteen?"

"I'm told she was seeing Colin. You haven't associated with her since then? Maybe seen her around your house?"

Gabe told himself not to roll his eyes. Sandy said it was childish.

"In whose opinion was she seeing Colin? Hers? He flirts a lot, but he doesn't have time to date."

Eli checked his notes on his phone. Gabe doubted he needed to do that. This wasn't a complicated conversation. More likely the guy was buying time while he thought about his approach.

"Staff told me they'd been dating for a few months. Then one night he went cold. Didn't want to sit in her section. Wouldn't speak to her. That's what Owen was upset about."

Gabe frowned. "What's with all this 'staff said' shit? What does Tracy say?"

"I haven't spoken with her. Her co-workers say she's been calling in sick since the night Owen and Colin fought. Ear infection."

"Sounds more like a Colin allergy," Gabe said. "He's at the casino a lot. The place is a fucking hole, but they play eighties rock and the beer is cheap."

"Are you saying Colin has a drinking problem?"

Gabe stared at Eli, trying to figure out if he was for real. The guy didn't seem to be much for jokes, so he probably was.

"Colin," Gabe said distinctly, "is twenty-four. He works in construction. He grew up around here. He. Likes. Beer."

"Normal for his peer group, then," Eli said.

"Yeah," Gabe said. Aggressively normal. Annoyingly normal. Way more normal than his fucked-up little brother.

He kept those addenda to himself.

Eli was watching him as if hoping to find Gabe's mind's construction in his face. He should have learned better than that in grade ten English. Gabe stared back at him and waited for the guy to get tired of it. It wasn't more than a minute or so before Eli sighed.

"I think you can understand why I need to speak with your brother. I'm not accusing him of anything. He's the last person to have been seen with Owen, and I need to find out what he knows."

"Okay," Gabe said. "Normally I'd tell you to check his job site, but I don't think—oh shit! I need to call his foreman and see whether Colin took time off or quit or—shit, shit, shit. I forgot because the phone was in the kitchen and the kitchen was on fire. I need a fucking cell phone. I need some money. I don't have any money. I need to talk to Sandy. I need to—"

"You need to take a deep breath," Eli said, cutting him off. "Breathe in for five seconds. Hold it for five seconds. Breathe out. Do this seven times."

Gabe couldn't think of a response to that, smartass or otherwise. His only option seemed to be doing it. Breathing in… one-one-thousand, two-one-thousand, three-one-thousand. Eli was looking over his shoulder as he did so, out at the water. Enjoying the view, Gabe hoped, since it was one of the nicer ones to be found locally. The sky and water and the grass on the banks were richly coloured and matched in tone, like the scene had been put together by a tasteful, if not very creative, decorator.

When Gabe was done breathing, he said, "I am so fucked if Colin quit."

"You said he works in construction?"

Gabe nodded. "You say 'works in' like he works in finance or something. He does construction. It's a gig. But the money is good."

"And money is a concern for you?"

Once again, Gabe wanted to search the countryside for Eli's UFO.

"Nope. Literally grows on a tree in our yard, and neither of us needs to eat."

Eli glanced at his phone, unbothered. It made sense that he would be so relaxed about sarcasm if he asked dumb questions this often.

"We all need money. I was asking more if there was debt or something else creating pressure."

"We pay our bills," Gabe said.

"Okay. Can you tell me when you last saw your brother?"

"Around nine last night. I went out. I stayed at a friend's house, and I didn't come home until eight this morning."

Eli didn't ask anything about Gabe's sleepover. He was probably assuming Gabe had been with a girlfriend. Or a boyfriend since everyone seemed to magically know that Gabe was gay.

"And you didn't see him this morning? Would he have already left for work?"

"No. He was supposed to have a late start today. Since you won't stop asking questions, here's the situation. Sometime after nine last night, he packed up all of his clothes and every other damned thing he owns, and he was gone by the time I showed up this morning."

Eli didn't say anything to that. He was so still he might have been part of the bridge. He stared at Gabe, steady on. It didn't take long for Gabe's skin to start prickling under the scrutiny.

"What? Why are you staring at me like that?"

"You seem bright," Eli said. "I think you know why."

Gabe looked at the pavement, the yellow line, instead of at Eli. The yellow line didn't have a fucking staring problem.

"He was the last person seen with a guy who's now missing, and he packed up and ran off."

"And?" Eli prompted. Gabe pried up a bit of loose pavement and threw it into the river past Eli's shoulder. Eli didn't flinch.

"And the house burned down," Gabe said. "Man, you don't know Colin, so I won't waste time telling you he's a good guy. He is, but you have no reason to take my word for it. Instead, I'm gonna tell you he's not a complete idiot. If Colin ever did beat some guy into the pavement—which he never fucking would—but if he did, he would not make himself appear this guilty. And he would not burn down our house."

"Gabri—Gabe," Eli said. "I said I wanted to talk to him. It doesn't mean I've decided anything. He's had a busy couple of days, and I'm intrigued."

"Yeah, well," Gabe said. "Right with you there."

He eyed Eli for a while. Staring was a game two could play. And the view was, honestly, pretty good. Not that Gabe had time for that kind of frivolity.

The thing was, this guy was looking for Colin. Whatever he said, he pretty obviously liked Colin as a suspect for whatever had happened to Owen Bernier. And the house thing. Which was crazy, because they barely owned anything besides that house and most of their stuff had been in it. Why would Colin destroy everything they had?

But right, getting back to Eli. Eli thought this kind of thing and was searching for Colin. Which meant that Gabe owed it to Colin to keep an eye on Eli Samm. Make sure Eli was getting the whole story and not jumping to conclusions.

"I think," Gabe said, getting to his feet, "that we should work together on this. No one knows Colin better than I do. And you have a car."

Eli stood and offered Gabe a hand, which Gabe shook. No blue light. He'd forgotten about it, the whole blue-light thing. He'd forgotten that something very fucked-up—maybe worse than Colin, or even the house—seemed to be going on. He'd repressed it, he supposed, because he had enough to deal with right now.

He closed his eyes and tried to repress it again.

"It's good to know I bring something to the table," Eli said. "I also have a hotel room, and I can expense new clothes for you. It's probably best if we clean up before talking to anyone else."

"You're saying I don't look good?" Gabe asked. "That's hurtful. Luckily, new clothes will make it up to me."

"No, they won't," Eli said, giving Gabe the uncomfortable sense that this guy felt sorrier for him even than the circumstances warranted. Which was damned near inconceivable to Gabe. He dropped his gaze, and Eli continued, "Not even if I throw in a toothbrush. But it's better than what you've got right now."

Gabe nodded.

Then they turned at the same time, as if they'd been rehearsing it, and started back to the car.

Sandy

"HOLY FUCKING Jesus!"

Sandy knew where Sean was coming from with that outburst, though she wasn't able to form even the simplest of curse words. She was standing on the sidewalk outside what had been Colin and Gabe's house, staring. Blinking occasionally. Eyes smarting because of the smoke still in the air and tearing up for a couple of reasons.

"Talk about flying off the handle," Sean said. The words didn't get through to Sandy right away, so Sean had finished speaking and even taken a few steps toward the house's remains before she responded.

"What the fuck is that supposed to mean?"

Sean turned to face her. Seeing someone so familiar in front of that charred mess made it, somehow, even more surreal. And it had been pretty surreal in the first place.

"They were fighting. Colin fucks off, apparently…."

"And Gabe burns his own house down?" Sandy said. She knew on some level that she should be quieter. That it might not be the best thing for the whole neighbourhood to hear this conversation. But her volume was climbing anyway. "Hell no! He loves this house."

Then, without knowing she was about to do it, she sat down hard on the sidewalk next to the Suzuki with the maybe fixed signal light.

"Were they in the house?"

Sean looked over his shoulder at the house. "I—"

"They weren't in there, right? Colin was gone and Gabe was at the doctor's. Right?"

"Uh, yeah," Sean said, facing her again.

"He was at the Mediclinic!"

"Uh, yeah," Sean said, facing her again. "I'm sure—"

She was yelling at the poor guy now. She could tell because he was flinching. She didn't sound loud to herself… but then, everything seemed quiet. No birds or cars or lawn mowers. It was like she had cotton in her ears.

"Maybe he's at the hospital or something," Sean said. "He could have gone to the hospital."

Sandy planted her hands on the sidewalk and thought, crazily, that the cement seemed warm. But it wouldn't still be warm, would it? When had the fire happened anyway? She pushed off with her hands until she was able to get her shaking legs to cooperate in her standing initiative. She hoped they would be onboard with walking too.

"We could call the hospital," Sean suggested.

Sandy nodded, reaching for her phone before he was finished. She'd call the hospital. Gabe was at the hospital, probably, with smoke inhalation or something. And he hadn't called her to tell her about the house fire because….

Because….

"Ma'am?"

Sandy was so surprised by the voice behind her that her phone slipped from her hand onto the lawn. It was green and damp and needed mowing. How did lawns do that, stay perky and healthy when the houses behind them burned down?

"Jesus," she said as she turned to find a police officer standing directly behind her. "Jesus."

The cop looked apologetic for scaring Sandy a little bit closer to death. She also seemed no older than Sandy, and Sandy thought for a moment that she could have been that cop. She could have done that job, instead of booking appointments for Sean's freak boss. But she'd heard it was a lot of stress for a paycheque that amounted to a pocketful of loose change.

"Do you know the owners of this property?" the cop asked. "Colin and Gabriel Reece?"

"Jesus," Sandy said. No creative cursing today, it seemed. Just blasphemy, again and again. "Why? Why are you asking me that?"

She felt a hand on her shoulder and nearly slapped it off before realizing that it must be Sean.

"We know them a little," Sean said, and Sandy was terrified for a moment that she was going to laugh. A little. The house she'd spent her first seventeen years in was less than a block away. But you didn't tell the cops anything more than you had to, right? Even at times like these.

"We'd like to speak to them," the cop said, and Sandy nearly sat down again. She had to concentrate, lock her knees, to keep upright.

"They weren't... uh, you didn't...."

"I'm sorry?" the cop said. But it was the good kind: *I'm sorry, I don't understand*. Not a doctor coming out of surgery saying *I'm sorry. We did everything we could.*

So Sandy stayed upright and kept breathing.

"No one was hurt or anything, right?" Sean asked.

"Oh," the cop said. Her eyes widened, and Sandy saw eyeliner, thick and slightly winged at the outside edge. The cop had taken some time to do it. Did she want to look her best while she shoved drunk people into the back of her squad car? "No one seems to have been injured. One of the neighbours thinks he saw two people go in and come out again, but they left before emergency personnel arrived."

"Sounds like Gabe," Sean muttered.

The cop said, "Excuse me?"

"Oh, you said someone was running into a burning building," Sean said. "Gabe's always looking for trou—"

He stopped because Sandy had stuck her index finger into the small of his back as hard as she could.

"Nothing," he finished. "Forget it."

"Well," the cop said, "if you have any idea where they might be...."

Sandy did laugh then. She had never sounded so much like a crazy person, and the worst part was that she had to bite the inside of her cheek to make herself stop. The cop's expression didn't change. Her dark red hair was pulled into a very tight ponytail, though, so it was possible her expression couldn't change.

"We," Sandy said, "uh, we don't know. Where they are. We're really worried because we don't know where they are, you see, and then the house is like this, so we were thinking maybe… that's… where… they…."

It was as far as she could go, but it seemed to be far enough. The cop nodded.

"Okay. Well, I'll give you my card, and you can call if you hear from them," she said. "Also, I'd like to take your names."

Sandy drew her upper lip between her teeth and thought that over. She didn't think she had to say who she was. She wasn't certain, but she thought she could tell the cop to pound sand. And she wanted to, both on principle and because getting involved with any kind of crime was not a great idea. But if she refused to talk, would the cop arrest her? Sandy really couldn't get arrested.

Sean, having seemingly arrived at the same point a few seconds earlier, said, "I'm Sean Boyko," he said. "This is Sandra Klaassen."

Sandy decided to let Sean handle this. He seemed to have his head screwed on straight, whereas hers might be a half-turn off. And it was a delicate situation.

She read the cop's card while Sean talked. Officer Celine Strembosky, North Battleford PD. Sandy didn't know anyone with that last name, so she didn't come from local stock. What on earth would make someone from away decide that coming here to be a cop, of all things, was the way to go?

She'd lost track of what Sean was saying, but he seemed to be doing fine. He didn't mention that the Reeces were fighting or that Colin had fucked off. He gave their address and answered questions politely. Sandy relaxed a little as he spoke. Colin and Gabe hadn't been in the house. They couldn't have been or their… they would have been found. And Gabe wasn't in the hospital or the cop would have known. So Gabe was just… not calling her? About his house burning to the ground? Okay, he didn't have a cell, but people let you borrow a phone when you'd been in a burning house.

That was assuming it had been Gabe that the neighbour had seen going into the house. Gabe and… Colin? Two people went in. Two came out. The neighbour would have recognized Gabe, right? Unless the smoke had been so thick that it had been impossible to make out more than vaguely human shapes.

Sandy's head hurt, and it was only partially from the hazy air.

The next thing she knew, the cop was shaking her hand and reminding her to call when, or if, a Reece got in touch with her. And she was saying, "Yes, of course." And then the cop was leaving, crossing the street and going to a patrol car that Sandy could now see sitting two houses away. Close enough to see who came and went from the Reece property. Far enough away not to be noticed. Jesus. They were watching the house.

"They're watching the house, Sean."

Sean pressed her shoulder, which reminded her that his hand was still resting there. Wasn't his arm getting tired?

"Yep."

"That's bad," she said. From the corner of her eye, she could see Sean nodding.

"Yep."

"Gabe did not burn his fucking house down," she said. Sean removed his hand.

"Okay," he said. "Do you want to see if we can find Gabe? I can get us booked off for the rest of the afternoon if I tell Mike I'll fix his washing machine this weekend."

That was the other thing Sean had not told Sandy about the job. One of the reasons Sean got along with his freak boss, and got to do things like calling in on his lunch break to say he was taking the afternoon off, was that Sean was doing endless shit for the guy off the books and under the table. Which was fine, she supposed, if you were okay with that kind of thing, but she was living in terror of the day Mike decided she should do extra things for him. Girl things, most likely. Washing his laundry or watching his damned kids.

Still, at times Sean's wheeling and dealing came in handy.

"Yeah, okay. We should check the Mediclinic first. Maybe it's a really long wait." She looked at Sean. "He might not know about his house. What if he doesn't know?"

"I guess he might not."

"You tell him," Sandy said. She felt like a shirker, like it was somehow her job to say difficult things to Gabe, but she didn't think she'd be able to get the words out.

"Okay," Sean said. He put the hand that had been on her shoulder against the small of her back and gave her a slight push toward his third-hand Focus wagon. “At least we didn’t get arrested. Even though we didn’t do anything. But I get arrested for not doing anything all the time.”

“Would’ve fucked up my probation,” Sandy said dully, her feet taking her wherever it was she was supposed to go.

“This whole probation thing is a pain in the cock,” Sean observed as they walked. “Was it worth it? To blow up Fitzie’s truck?”

“Fuck Fitzie,” Sandy said automatically. It was what she said every time the topic of her ex-boyfriend came up. “And I didn’t blow up his truck. I just set it on fire.”

“Oh,” Sean said. “My bad.”

“And it was totally worth it.”

Sean nodded. “That’s the important thing.”

CHAPTER FOUR

Gabe

ONE THING that could be said for Eli Samm was that he was a light packer. Left to poke around Eli's motel room as Eli took his turn in the shower, Gabe could find little that hadn't been there before Eli had arrived. There was a backpack on the bed, from which Eli had taken what seemed to be his sole change of clothes. A light coat hung in the closet. Eli either didn't know the prairies well enough, or didn't plan to be in town long enough, to prepare for everything from a heat wave to a blizzard. You could expect either in June. Sometimes in the same week.

It was rude to open drawers, lift the mattress, and search under the bed. Fortunately, Gabe didn't mind being rude. He didn't know for sure who this Eli person was—hadn't even seen a driver's licence, let alone a PI's licence. Did real PIs need licences, or was that a TV thing? Or a US thing… also where was Eli from? Gabe needed more information.

To his disappointment, Eli's wallet and phone seemed to have gone into the bathroom with him. Probably in the pockets of his smoke-soaked pants, and good luck ever getting that smell out. Gabe wrinkled his nose at the smell of his own clothes, which were sitting in the corner of the room wrapped in the bag from the room's garbage can. His new jeans and T-shirt—and underwear—were a good fit, but he'd hated wearing new clothes before they'd been washed ever since he'd read some "stranger than fiction" story in a doctor's office magazine about kids who were poisoned because their discount jeans had been soaked in pesticide during a warehouse accident.

"Fuck that," Colin had said when Gabe related the story to him, and new clothes had gone into their ancient washing machine thereafter.

Gabe found no paperwork in the room, apart from the hotel's express check-out form. No computer. Either Eli had none of these things with him or he was keeping them in the car. The keys to which were… also with Eli in the bathroom, it seemed. As if Eli didn't trust Gabe. Ridiculous.

There had been a shaving kit in the bathroom, and a toothbrush and toothpaste on the bathroom counter. Gabe had taken his new stuff, toothbrush and hairbrush and all that, out of the bathroom with him and tucked it into his new backpack. With everything Eli had bought him, he was set to move onto someone's couch or build a tarp tent under a bridge.

Eli had left a few other personal items around, but they weren't unusual or interesting. No blood-stained knife or bottle of antipsychotics that had been filled three weeks ago and had only one pill missing. Unless those, too, were locked in the car.

Gabe saw the charger for Eli's cell on the nightstand, next to the hotel's phone. Eli had offered to buy him a burner and a charger because, what the hell, he could expense it, but that had felt like too much. Too great an imposition on some rando client who was worried about Owen the missing waiter.

The hotel's phone was old, not even cordless, light beige, and stained with something brown. How did you even stain a phone anyway? The receiver curved downward around the base like a scowl, admonishing Gabe for tossing a hotel room when he ought to be calling his friends.

Sandy had a right to know the house had burned down. Hadn't he and Colin drunkenly told her many times that their casa was her casa? She deserved to know what had happened to her casa. Also, Gabe wanted to bawl like an infant, and he thought Sandy would probably say "There, there" to him rather than tell him to suck it up.

But then she'd say he was going back to the Mediclinic or else, and by the way where was he right now. Oh, a stranger's hotel room? Well, he needed to get out of there immediately. Then he would have had to do all of that rather than hunt for Colin. Or, perilously, he would have to ignore Sandy's direct orders. He preferred to do neither. The house was gone, and she'd find out soon enough without hearing it from him in the middle of her work day.

The thing to do was find out more so he and Sandy would have other things to talk about. Maybe a trip to the casino would be helpful, if Eli was willing to go back there.

The shower stopped. Gabe glanced around the room, checking that everything he'd disturbed was back in place. Close enough, anyway. Eli had expected him to snoop, right? That was why he'd taken the car keys into the bathroom. Unless he'd expected Gabe to take off with the car.

But Gabe didn't really need to be on the run with a stolen car on top of everything else. And besides, though this was completely unimportant, he was sort of curious what Eli looked like with wet hair. He seemed like the kind of guy who'd look good with his hair wet.

Gabe ought to get at least something out of this miserable day.

Sandy

"HOW CAN you be eighteen years old and run away when someone tries to give you a needle? What adult person does that?"

"One who doesn't like needles?" Sean said. Sandy stopped her rapid march down the sidewalk and turned to glare at him.

"Oh, he doesn't like needles? He doesn't wike weedles? I don't like getting a Pap smear, but you don't have to chase me all over town to get me to do it!"

"No, no I don't," Sean said. He sounded as if she'd given him nightmare fuel for a month. "Where do you want to look now?"

Sandy didn't have the first idea. Or she had plenty of first ideas—their house or the library or the middle of that old bridge Gabe liked so much. A restaurant that didn't mind campers who ordered one Coke and sat for hours. The highway, with his thumb out for a lift to Edmonton. None of these possibilities seemed better, or worse, than any other.

"He must have gone home," she said. "When he left the Mediclinic, he would have gone home. It's only a few blocks."

"Sounds right."

"Why the hell didn't he call us?"

"I dunno," Sean said. "Maybe Jerry's heard from him."

It was a long shot, but what the hell. She called and walked up and down the block as she listened to the rings. Five in all before Jerry's voice-mail came on.

"Leave a message," he said. No indication that you'd reached Jerry or apology that he wasn't available. It was surprising he'd bothered to record over the cell company's generic "Hiya, the person you're calling isn't here."

"Yeah, it's me," she said. "Gabe fucked off from the Mediclinic, and the Reeces' house has burned down, so call me when you get this."

Sean was leaning against the outside wall of the clinic, eying her like she needed a tranquillizer dart.

"What?" she demanded. "What now?"

"Nothing. You told him what he needs to know."

"Do you know where he is?" she asked. "Didn't you put that app on your phones that traces where he is? So you could stalk him like the weirdo you are?"

"I didn't know it was weird to meet your friends when you're, like, a block apart," Sean said. He straightened and got out his own phone. "Mine's up, but he turned off location services for his."

Sandy shook her head and waited. Sean sighed.

"It means he can track me, but I can't track him."

He sounded like he'd be reporting that human rights violation to the Hague. Sandy almost felt sorry for Jer, but it served him right for asking Sean to scrounge a phone for him. He ought to have known Sean would do him the questionable favour of setting the thing up first.

"You hungry?" Sean asked. Sandy realized she was. It made sense since they'd spent their lunch break staring at the Reece house ruins and had been at the Mediclinic waiting to see Dr. Lam since then. Sean being Sean, he was probably ready to start gnawing off people's arms.

"Yeah. It's getting stupid hot out here. Do you want to do Dairy Queen?"

"Sure."

Ice cream sounded good to Sandy, for real, but it was also a factor that the Dairy Queen was a block north of the Reece house, and passing that house was the quickest way to get there. Not that she expected to find Gabe there, and not that she planned to hang around, since the cops would still be watching, but it wouldn't hurt to walk by on the way to getting burgers.

If Sean noticed that Sandy had engineered their lunch plans to include a swing by the house, he didn't say so. He didn't even comment when they got a block away and the smoke, not visible but still adding its scent to the air, made him cough. Or when they walked right past the police car. Sandy made a point of not glancing at the car or slowing her pace. She had every right to walk down any public street, including this one.

The front of the house was blocked, now, by the tall blue fencing people put up around construction sites. The back was wide open, but that was understandable. Someone had probably ordered enough fencing to block off a small one-and-a-half-story house without mentioning the vacant lot or the alley to the side or the sprawling backyard.

"Hang on a sec," Sean said and drifted off toward the back of the house. The cops hadn't chosen the best vantage point since there were tall trees on the south side of the alley and they made it impossible to see the back of the house from where their car was parked. Sandy stayed out front, giving them something to watch so they wouldn't wonder what was happening out of sight.

Looking at the house made her feel unsteady, as if the ground were shifting. She knew it too well, the layout, the windows, the furniture. Knowing where everything should be made it clearer how wrong things were now. The fridge and stove stood in place, exposed by the missing walls, but things just as immovable and sturdy, like the stairs, were gone. The basement could be seen through holes in the floor. And little things—scraps of carpet, half the couch—somehow were still intact. Books, for God's sake. Didn't they know they were made of paper? It was ballsy of them to sit in the middle of a fire and not burn.

Then, amid the charred wood and fire retardant and melted plastic, something moved.

Sandy started, then told herself it had to be a cat or a raccoon. Some animal exploring and—

She saw it clearly. For a second, no more.

A tall figure in a dark coat. Far too thin. Bones and teeth visible under the skin. Worse, in spots, through the skin. The summer sun glinted off those spots, making a halo around the face that was staring at her from…

the back of the garage, next to the charred side of her parents' red Corolla

…where Colin's bedroom had been.

There was nowhere it could have gone, stuck in the black wood skeleton of the house and the piles of burned and broken possessions. With holes in the floor and no back door and the rear wall still largely standing. It couldn't go anywhere. But it went.

It was gone before Sandy had a chance to scream.

Gabe

"SERIOUSLY?" GABE said. "Just… all right?"

Eli was in the bathroom doorway, running a brush through his hair.

"Why not? You'll have your own questions, obviously. And they might give you Tracy Howell's address. I wanted to talk to her about what you think is a Colin allergy, but the staff didn't want to give her address to a stranger."

"I have a theory," Gabe said, "that Colin told her the truth and she didn't like it. But she can probably confirm that all Colin did to Owen was tell him to get fucked."

"I hope so," Eli said. "There's also someone who wasn't on shift before that I'd like to talk to. Why did you think I would object to going to the casino?"

"Oh, it's logical to go there, and you're being reasonable," Gabe said. "I'm just used to more arguing. About everything."

Eli nodded as if that made any sense to him, which Gabe didn't think it possibly could.

"Did you call your friends while I was in the shower?"

"I was thinking I'd call them later. When I know more."

Gabe knew the stink-eye when he was getting it, and he was getting it now. Eli did not approve of Gabe leaving everyone hanging. It was weirdly sweet that he'd care about the feelings of people he didn't even know.

"It's better if I know more," Gabe told him. "Trust me."

Eli seemed skeptical but shrugged and gestured at Gabe's backpack, the repository for nearly everything Gabe owned. As in, don't forget to take that with you. As if Gabe could.

"Then let's go."

The car still smelled like a firepit, even though Eli had cracked the windows when they'd left. They both wrinkled their noses as they got in, and Gabe ran his fingertips over the inside of the passenger door, where he'd rested his arm while Eli drove. Black marks came away at his touch.

"They're going to ream you on detailing," Gabe said, "when you give this car back. Did you get the extra insurance? Maybe you'd be better off pushing the car over a cliff."

"It's all right," Eli said as he backed the car out. "The client will cover it."

"Who is your client, anyway?" Gabe asked.

"I prefer not to say," Eli told him. "People change their stories when they know who you're working for."

"Since I don't give a shit about Owen and I don't have a story," Gabe said, "it's okay to tell me."

"Sorry," Eli said, a smile at the corner of his mouth. "I have to keep my air of mystery."

The Mystery Man had obviously learned something on his first visit, because when they arrived, he parked near the door that led directly into the bar. No need to go through the casino itself, squeezing past row upon row of elderly women in pastel sweatshirts who stayed glued to their favourite video lottery terminals like they were stationed in air traffic control.

Not that there were no VLTs in the bar, but the hard-core players tended to stay out on the floor.

"I try not to come to the casino," Gabe said as they entered the bar. Eli raised his brows at Gabe.

"Do you have a gambling problem?" he asked, as courteously as a person could ask something like that. Gabe almost laughed.

"Fuck no," he said. "I have a problem with seeing really depressing shit. But you get dragged here, you know?"

Eli didn't seem as if he knew. He didn't even nod to be agreeable. Gabe sighed.

"You probably come from a place with actual places to go and things to do," he said. "You wouldn't understand."

"Gabe!"

The high-pitched voice from whence that came belonged to a girl Gabe had gone to high school with. Specifically, they'd been in the same guitar class. She was a year older, so that class, an elective that took kids from any grade, had been the only time their paths had crossed. Gabe remembered her fondly as the only one in that class not to make hilarious jokes, like calling him Mini-Menendez or referring to his house as the Parent Death Trap.

"Hey, Cherie," he said. "How's it going?"

"Not bad," she said. She stepped closer, as short and round and rosy as she'd been in high school but with more make-up now. Required by the job, most likely, along with her short black skirt. The thought made Gabe want to throw up.

"Um, Gabe?" she said. Her eyes were even wider than usual now, and she wasn't smiling anymore. "Can I talk to you for a minute? Like, alone?"

"Sure," Gabe said, glancing at Eli. Eli shrugged.

Gabe followed Cherie to the bar, while Eli stood near the door and watched everyone in the room. Slowly, without visible emotion, like a human security camera sweeping the space. It was more than a little creepy if you didn't know he was a detective. Hell, even if you did.

They clambered onto bar stools, a significant clamber for Cherie, and Gabe faced her with a smile.

"So," he said. "You gonna card me?"

She laughed merrily.

"Oh no! You're eighteen, aren't you? I forgot! You were, like, a year behind me."

"Shh," Gabe said, making a show of being furtive. Cherie laughed again.

"Oh my God, Gabe, what are you doing now? University?"

Was he? He had plans, but they seemed ridiculous now, like they were for some other Gabe whose life was neatly on track.

"I guess," Gabe said. "I got into the music program at MacEwan. And I'm working at Cochin this summer."

"Huh—lucky!" Cherie said, punctuating that with a light swat to Gabe's arm. He didn't even feel it. There was a blue flash, soft and almost unnoticeable in the midst of all the lights from the bar's VLTs. Gabe was horrified to realize he'd expected it. Cherie didn't seem to have noticed anything unusual. She kept beaming at Gabe.

"Yeah," Gabe said "Lucky. So… you wanted to talk to me about something?"

"Oh yeah." Her smile disappeared again. "That guy you came in with… do you know him?"

"Not really," Gabe said. "He told me he's a private investigator. He's here about someone who used to—"

"Owen," Cherie said. "He came here asking about Owen. And kind of about Tracy. And your brother."

"What did he ask?" Gabe inquired, glancing over his shoulder to be certain Eli was too far away to hear.

"He never mentioned Colin to start with," Cherie said. "He said he'd been hired because Owen was missing. So we told him about how Colin was… um… pretty mean to Tracy. I'm sorry."

"Mean is in the eye of the beholder," Gabe said. "It's okay. I won't get offended."

"Well, anyway, she was crying, and Owen started yelling at Colin. And Colin said some stuff about how Owen was mad because he was… um, Colin said it a rude way, but he meant that Owen had a crush on Tracy."

"Did he?" Gabe asked automatically, though he immediately realized he didn't care.

"Yeah. Colin was right. He was just rude about it."

"So you told the detective that, and he got interested in Colin."

"Yeah, because Colin said eff you and eff her and eff this, and he went out the side door. He always parks his truck along the side."

"Trust me, I know."

One night, Gabe had made the mistake of parking the truck out front, and Colin had launched into a profane Ted Talk on the risks of parking in the main lot where the casino's patrons would be driving around with a dozen watered-down cocktails in their blood and VLT lights burned into their brains. Always the side lot, Gabriel. Always.

"So I think he was gonna *leave* leave, like get in his truck and go, but Owen ran out there after him."

"That's on Owen, then," Gabe said. "If Colin said they were done."

Cherie gazed at him like she had when the other kids had been mean to him in class. Like she was sorry for him but knew better than to say so. Then she looked at her nails. They were long and zebra-striped and seemed fine to Gabe, though Cherie was running her thumb over the edges like she wished her thumb was a nail file.

"I guess Owen thought Colin wasn't the boss of anything," she said. "Anyways, I think they had a fight, but you'd have to ask Tracy. She went out the side door to the lot, I guess to break it up or something? But she's not here. She's been off sick since then."

"Did she finish her shift and call in the next day? Eli—that's the detective—he made it sound like she went right home."

"Yeah, she totally did. She came in and said she felt awful, and she went home. But she only talked to Jordan, so I don't know exactly what she said."

"Is Jordan around?"

"Yeah, she started a few minutes ago. I'm due to go home in, like, ten. And I picked up another shift tonight, so I gotta go home and sleep."

"Your shifts are insane," Gabe said. "I don't know how any of you have lives."

She laughed merrily. "We don't. Anyway, Jordan's doing roll ups in the back. But maybe don't bring the detective?"

"Why not?"

"Because the stuff with Tracy… it's sort of private? Like, it's your brother's private stuff. And that detective is a total stranger."

She said it the way she might have said he was a total douche, if that had been a thing Cherie would say.

"Colin's a big boy," Gabe said. "Being embarrassed won't kill him. I'll take Eli back there, and if she doesn't want to talk to him, she can say so."

Cherie was kind enough to fake a smile and nod as if she thought Gabe's idea a grand one.

"Okay, sweetie. It was good to see you."

She patted Gabe's knee—not hard enough to draw a flash—and bounced off to find her co-worker. Gabe wondered about the circumstances under which Cherie would walk with anything but a bounce. A funeral, maybe. Of someone she'd really liked. Who'd died in a tragic explosion along with a litter of puppies.

Well, bless people who could be that fucking happy, anyway. Gabe would never understand them.

He crossed the bar, back to the door, and leaned against a VLT, hands in the pockets of his new jeans.

"We need to talk to Jordan," he told Eli. "I don't know this Jordan, but I hear she's doing roll ups in the back. I was also told not to bring you along for this talk, so she may tell you to get bent. We'll see."

"You know the other server, though," Eli said. "You didn't tell me you knew someone here."

Gabe laughed, loud enough that the few daytime patrons of the bar turned their heads.

"I thought you were getting this by now," he said. "Dude. There are thirteen thousand people in this town. I have lived here all my life. That guy by the fire door, in the blue shirt? He taught me eighth grade math. He thinks he's a card counter, which is hilarious, because if he could count cards, they'd stop letting him in. Oh, and the bartender used to work at the 7-Eleven near my house, so he's moving up in the world. He'd get tips here."

"I think your brother left town," Eli said. "You're not going to find him. If everyone knows everyone, the way you say, he'd know he couldn't hide from you here."

For the first time in his life, Gabe was grateful for the presence of a VLT. It was the only thing holding him up as the truth of that sunk in. Colin had his truck. He had not packed for a day. He had taken everything. And he knew there wasn't really any place in North Battleford that he could hide from Gabe if Gabe tried hard enough to find him.

"Okay," Gabe said softly. "You're right. He's probably gone."

Not gone for good, his brain insisted. But gone as in left town. Maybe the province, even. With no set date of return.

"Your best chance of finding him," Eli said, "lies in understanding why he left."

Gabe tried not to show anything on his face, but apparently it wasn't a good enough try, because Eli cocked his head and said, "Oh… you *know* why he left. Don't you?"

Gabe responded to that by pushing off the VLT and heading for the back of the bar. It was easy to spot Jordan at a booth with buckets of cutlery and napkins before her, an Everest of roll ups to one side. She had light brown hair in a loose ponytail and wore the same black skirt as Cherie, though she'd topped hers with a sleeveless white shirt instead of the sequined black tank Cherie had chosen. She seemed healthy and normal, and Gabe regretted the necessity of going anywhere near her. Who knew what might burn down in his wake?

He stopped next to the booth and gave her a smile. "I'm Gabe Reece. Cherie said you were the one I should ask about what happened with Colin the other night."

Jordan looked him up and down. It was a neutral appraisal, from what Gabe could tell.

"So you're Colin's little brother."

"I like to think I'm so much more," Gabe informed her, smiling to let her know he was kidding. Though he wasn't. "This is Eli. You probably heard about him. He was here earlier, asking about Owen Bernier."

Jordan nodded.

"The private dick," she said. It wasn't as obnoxious as it could have been because she said it mostly to herself and not like she'd birthed the Edinburgh Fringe joke of the year. "Have a seat, gentlemen."

They did, Gabe to the inside. Without thinking, Gabe picked up a fork and knife and napkin and started to roll, like he had when Sandy had been a hostess at the steak house and he'd stopped by to cadge the fries from her staff meal.

"You obviously know Colin," Gabe said.

"Kind of," she said. "Mostly from him coming in here. I haven't been in town long. I moved down from Meadow Lake about… God, about six months ago now. Time flies."

Eli was not making himself useful with the cutlery. Instead, he was twirling a sugar packet in thin, precise fingers. Turning it over and over. Gabe half expected him to start walking it over his knuckles like a coin.

"So," Gabe said to Jordan, "this is a little weird. This guy here"—he hooked a thumb at Eli—"shows up from out of town saying he's looking for Colin because some guy named Owen Bernier is missing. I have never heard of this person, and coincidentally, Colin has fucked off to parts unknown, so I can't ask him about it."

"Yeah, weird," Jordan allowed warily. Eli kept twirling the sugar packet. He had a worn gold ring on one finger, and Gabe felt a stab of disappointment before realizing that it wasn't the ring finger. A family heirloom, maybe. Not a wedding ring. And why did it matter anyway? Gabe shook his head and got back to the matter at… well, hand.

"I don't think Colin left because of Owen," Gabe said. "I don't want to get into it, but I really don't think that. But this guy doesn't believe me, so we're going to find out what happened, and then he'll see this thing with Owen was nothing. I assume. Some sniping over Tracy Howell?"

Jordan smiled a little. "Do you know Trace?"

"A little. I haven't talked to her in years."

"She's what my dad would call a cockeyed optimist."

Gabe remembered Tracy standing at the edge of the diving platform, yelling encouragement at Rollie McKay while the poor kid went down for the third time. She'd kept saying, "You can do it!" while the rest of the class had fished him out. Gabe had laughed for years over Rollie, with his old-soul face and Ray Romano voice, saying, "Lady? I *can't*."

"That tracks," Gabe said.

"Even I know better than to take your brother's flirting seriously, but Tracy was convinced they had a connection. I guess they did see each other a few times, movies and whatnot. But it's not like she didn't know about Colin's whole deal."

"Does he love 'em and leave 'em?" Gabe said. "He never talks about this with me. Which is good. He doesn't kiss and tell."

Jordan's smile tightened. "You could say he loves 'em and leaves 'em, except without the part where he loves 'em."

"Sorry," Gabe said. "It's an expression. I guess he doesn't get attached."

Jordan glanced at Eli, then faced Gabe and shook her head. "You don't know?"

"All kinds of things," Gabe said slowly, "I am starting to think. What are you talking about, Jordan?"

She put her forearms on the table and leaned toward Gabe, bent nearly double in her attempt to get as close as she could. Her nails were zebra-striped, a match for Cherie's but not as long. Did the bar make them go matchy-matchy, or did they all go to a salon together after work and bond over the disinfectant tubs? It didn't matter. Gabe shook his head and forced himself to focus on what Jordan was saying.

"…washout. He doesn't seal the deal. He flirts. He takes girls home. And then he goes home. He does nothing."

"Okay," Gabe said, "I don't know what you're getting at, exactly, but a guy can change his mind. So Colin takes someone home and they've got one of those hang-in-there kitten posters and he thinks, okay, I can't do someone this dumb, and he leaves."

From Jordan's distressed expression, he thought for a moment that he'd misjudged her and she owned three of those posters and didn't know there was anything dumb about them. But then Jordan tapped her zebra-striped nails on the table and stared into Gabe's eyes.

"Never, Gabe. Not with any woman in this town. We all got kind of curious after he fizzled out on a couple of us, so we started asking around. Your brother keeps his pants on at all times."

Now Eli perked up, like that was somehow a game-changer. As if he were a paleontologist and had stumbled across a fossil that changed everything. Or, Gabe supposed, a clue.

To what, he had no idea. What did that have to do with this Owen person anyhow, except that Colin probably wouldn't bone him either?

"So to sum up, Tracy had the hots for him, and he had the lukewarms for her," Gabe said.

"He was flirting with her," Jordan said. "And she took him far too seriously. She was pissed off when he wouldn't sleep with her. I think it hurt her feelings. So she got loud about how he was impotent and probably a Ken doll, shit like that, and he laughed her off and ignored her, and that's when she started to cry."

"I'm not feeling too bad for her at this point," Gabe said. "If the genders were reversed…."

"Yeah, I know. Trace was out of line. But Owen felt like Colin had been toying with her, and he hates it when people cry, so he got in there. He and your brother never got along anyway. Colin called him Twinkie and stuff, like he thought Owen was gay. Except I doubt he really thought that because Owen was clearly hung up on Tracy. Still is, obviously. Which Colin got fully into when Owen started beaking at him."

"Did they go to the parking lot to fight?" Eli asked. Jordan tilted her head.

"Yes and no? I think Colin wanted to leave. Owen wanted a fight. The idiot. That's why Tracy followed them outside. So Colin wouldn't one-punch Owen into strawberry jam."

"Does he do that?" Eli asked politely.

Gabe stared at him. "No, he fucking does not! I told you! My brother doesn't fight purse dogs."

Jordan laughed out loud. "Oh my God, is that what you call Owen? That is fucking classic. Nah, I mean, Colin hasn't been in a fight here that I know of. Just, if he did hit Owen, it would be like swatting a mosquito. You don't usually have to hit mosquitoes twice."

"So Colin goes outside," Eli said, "Owen follows, and Tracy follows Owen."

Jordan frowned. "No, that's not…." She grabbed three roll ups and moved two from one end of the table to the other, then slowly added a third. "Like this. Colin leaves with Owen on his heels like a yappy little dog. Tracy sees this, and she goes out after them, but she's not right with them. And she didn't, like, burst on to the scene. She kind of snuck out there and slipped behind the Loraas. I think she wanted to get the lay of things before she decided what to do."

"Then what?" Eli said. Jordan shrugged.

"Then nothing? Colin didn't come back in. His truck was gone too. I noticed that when I took out the garbage later. Owen didn't come back in either. Tracy did, after a couple of minutes. She looked like shit."

"Like she'd been in a fight?" Eli asked.

"No. She was really pale, and she seemed like she was going to pass out. I offered to drive her to the ER, but she said she was getting an infection and needed to go home. So I cut her, and she went."

Eli blinked. "You cut her?"

Gabe and Jordan exchanged a smile. Ah, these funny strangers from out of town who'd never had a real job.

"She ended Tracy's shift. Jordan must be a manager."

"Assistant," Jordan said. "Things were slowing down anyway. But I expected Owen to come back in at that point—like, Tracy never said he'd fucked off—so that wasn't great."

"She didn't tell you what happened in the lot?" Eli asked.

"She seemed like she was gonna boot, so I didn't ask a lot of questions."

"Gotcha," Gabe said. "I don't want to bug Tracy too much if she's not feeling good, but it would help a lot if she could tell us what happened with Colin and Owen. Do you have her address and maybe we could stop by for a few minutes?"

"I don't normally give out staff addresses, but I guess since you know her. I know she's friends with Colin's friend Sandy too."

Tracy and Sandy had come up through school together, and Gabe thought friend was a strong word, but clearly it was better not to say so.

"Yeah. Thanks."

Jordan nodded and went to the bar, presumably to look the address up. Gabe wondered if it would come on a bar napkin, maybe with a little cocktail sword through it.

"It sounds like Tracy saw something upsetting," Eli said.

"It sounds like she was already upset when she went out there," Gabe replied. "But whatever. We'll see what she says."

"Are you okay?" Eli asked suddenly.

"Am I… what?"

"You're hearing a lot of things about your brother," Eli said. "And you've already had a rough day. Very rough."

"I'll live," Gabe said. "And it's always better to know things than not know them."

Whether Eli agreed or didn't, he had no chance to say, because Jordan had returned with the address. It was on an index card, not a napkin. Gabe was a little disappointed about that, and far more disappointed about not getting a cocktail sword.

"Thanks," he said, glancing at the address before pocketing it. Tracy Howell lived on an acreage a few clicks east of town. Close enough that it was probably still on town water. So it would likely be on Google as well. "I really appreciate this."

"Good luck with... well, Colin," Jordan said. She picked up her roll ups and left with them, though she obviously had a few dozen more to go.

"It's like she wasn't enjoying talking to us," Gabe observed.

"In my line of work," Eli told him, "you get used to it. Let's go alienate your friend."

Sandy

"WELL, WELL, well. Look who's here."

Sandy was still shaken by what she'd seen at the Reece house—or, hadn't seen. Almost certainly imagined. But she was on edge, and so her eyes nearly popped out at the sight of Jerry coming toward them. She let go of the handle to the Dairy Queen's door and stepped out back onto the sidewalk.

"What the hell? Aren't you working out of town today?"

"Client cancelled," Jerry said. "I saw on that fucking stalker app of Sean's that he was around here, so I thought I'd come say hi."

"Didn't you say having to see Sean at home and then see him in public was adding insult to injury?" Sandy asked.

"No, I said it was adding public humiliation to injury," Jerry said. Sean added physical injury to that with a light shove to Jerry's arm, putting him off-balance with one foot in the DQ's flower bed.

"Oops," Sean said. "Sidewalk's uneven. I fell."

They went inside and ordered. No line mid-afternoon on a Saturday. No one in the place but staff, in fact. It made sense, since most of the Battlefords' population would be north of town at the lakes on a beautiful near-solstice day.

Jerry saw Sandy ordering a strawberry sundae and fries and insisted she not further embarrass him by dipping her fries in the sundae.

"Floor's pretty uneven in here," she told him, feeling better already about the definitely imaginary thing in the house. "A guy who's not careful could fall into the cake freezer."

They grabbed the large booth at the back, the one they always got shooed out of when there were fewer than eight in their group, and spread out happily. It was the little things, Sandy thought.

"How're things?" Jerry asked around a double cheeseburger. "Aside from the Reece house apparently burning down. What the hell?"

"We don't know what the hell," Sandy told him. "Must've happened not too long after you and Gabe left. The fire department had it out when Sean and I went by at noon."

"Big drama," Jerry said. "I take it no one's seen Elder?"

"Nope," Sandy said as Jerry poured his fries onto his tray. He liked his ketchup evenly spread and claimed the fry basket made it impossible.

"How's Younger taking it?" he asked.

"Christ knows," Sandy told him. "Little fucker ran out of the Mediclinic when the doctor pulled out a needle. Hasn't been seen since. And the cops are watching the house hoping to catch a Reece boy because obviously they think one of them set fire to the place."

"Cool," Jerry said. "Well, he's not at our place. Or he wasn't an hour ago, anyway. I had to go home for a shower because some asshole at the shop spilled a broken toner cartridge on me."

"Oh," Sandy said. "I thought you might have changed clothes, but I couldn't tell for sure, because all your work outfits are so boring that—" She mimed falling asleep on the table.

Jerry flicked the top of her head with a finger. "Hilarious. Anything else I should know?"

"Sandy's hallucinating," Sean said brightly.

Sandy began to protest, then shrugged. "I guess I fucking am. I thought I saw the boogeyman in the Reece house. Like, after the fire."

Jerry laughed, spraying bits of hamburger bun. Sandy glared at him as she picked his food off her fries.

"What, Gabe's boogeyman?" Jerry said. "The one he thought lived in his basement? With the bones sticking out of his skin?"

"That's the one," Sandy confirmed. "Clearly I've lost my fucking mind."

"I'd say."

"Sandy thinks the boys didn't burn their house down," Sean said, as if that were more evidence that she needed to be institutionalized.

"They probably didn't," Jerry said. He paused his eating and sat with his head tilted like a thoughtful and arrogant bird. "The cops have got this one wrong."

"Whoa," Sean said. "You can't say that. I know it seems pretty extreme, but these guys are pretty extreme. Who else would burn that house down? Why did it happen today? I'm not trying to be all disloyal or anything, but I'm thinkin' it was Gabe."

"I'm with Sandy on this," Jerry said. "Sure, he might burn down other things. Who knows. He had bad role models."

This with a flick of his wrist at Sandy, who flipped him off in return.

"But," Jerry went on, "not that house."

"Okay, you say that, but why not?" Sean said. "Didn't their mom die there or something? And wasn't their dad kind of a creep? Apparently? From what I've heard."

"It's worse than you're thinking," Sandy said. "On both counts. Their mother hung herself in the basement. Gabe found her. He was twelve."

"Wow," Sean said. He was so surprised, in fact, that he dropped his burger on top of his brownie sundae. "That is not good. Why did she do it?"

"Her husband was a creep," Jerry said.

Sean frowned. "I thought their father died before their mother. In a car accident or something? Right?"

"Some creeps keep on creeping," Jerry said.

"He did a number on her for years," Sandy clarified. "She was a mess. Always. I never knew her when she wasn't."

Jerry half stood in his seat, something anyone less skinny would have found impossible, and craned his head to look at the staff.

"Yeah, they can't hear us. Okay. Sean, we should probably fill you in a little, given all the shit coming down. Since I didn't meet any Reeces until I was in grade six, I yield the floor to Ms. Klaassen."

"Super," Sandy said. "Should we take this conversation to a place that serves liquor?"

"We can start it here," Jerry said.

"I guess ice cream's just as good," Sandy said. "So… I grew up about a block over from the Reece house. There were a lot of kids in the neighbourhood then. I ran around with all of them. Colin did too, and he had an awesome collection of Matchbox cars, so I was over at his house a lot."

"But I thought his house was creepy," Sean said. Sandy shrugged.

"Yeah… not so much then. His dad was almost never there. Like, really, until Gabe was born, their dad was only home a few weeks out of the year. I was never totally sure what he did—something to do with jewellery. But he was on the road for work. He showed up for Christmas and shit. My mom called their mom the Grass Widow."

"To her face?" Sean asked.

"Why not?" Jerry said. "It's not as if anybody was home in that woman. Ow! What did you hit me for?"

"She was nice," Sandy said. "Yeah, she was always nervous and weird, and she got way worse later, but she was nice when Colin was little. She baked and stuff."

"She didn't bake when I met her," Jerry said. "She might have *been* baked…."

Sandy dipped a fry into the strawberry sauce. It was better when the ice cream had melted a little and she could mix everything. But this would do for now.

"When Gabe was about a year old," she said, "their dad started to be home a lot more. He still travelled, but only… I don't know, a third of the time. My mom said Mrs. Reece must've put her foot down after the second boy was born. You know, about spending time with his kids."

"Your mom never really knew Mrs. Reece, did she?" Jerry said, sounding amused. As if it were funny that Colin and Gabe's mom had stopped making hobo bread and stopped playing the little apartment piano in the living room and stopped talking and then, finally, stopped altogether.

"Is this story cute to you?" Sandy asked. Jerry met her eyes calmly.

"It's fucking absurd," he said. "I always laugh at the fucking absurd. You should try it."

"Maybe," Sandy said, unconvinced. "Anyway, as soon as Gabe was about two, their dad started in with some really weird shit."

Sean nodded. It seemed as if he was bracing himself for something distasteful, but not unexpected.

"I kind of figured he was… one of those abusive guys," he said.

Sandy looked at Jerry, who shrugged. Very helpful. She turned to Sean again.

"Yeeeeeah. He… was. But not like you'd think. Not like hitting them or…."

"Getting priest-like on them," Jerry offered. Sandy stared at him.

"To hell, Jerry. You are going to hell."

"Most likely," Jerry said. The prospect didn't seem to bother him. He turned to Sean. "As far as we know, their dad didn't do any of the usual abusive dad shit. He was way freakier than that."

"Right," Sean said. "Isn't the usual stuff freaky enough?"

"Their dad was really… off," Sandy said. "He was always testing them. Like he'd drop them in the woods and make them find their own way home."

"Like Outward Bound," Sean said.

"Yeah, but they were eleven and five when he started. Or he'd make them stick their hands in ice water, and whoever took their hand out first got punished. Like, no food for twenty-four hours, or they had to walk to the fort and back in the summer with no water. Half the time Colin would throw those things because Gabe was too little for whatever the punishment was. He said that really pissed off his dad."

Sean gaped at that. "What? Was he trying to make his kids tough or something awesome like that?"

"I think that was part of the game," Jerry said. "But there was more going on."

"Definitely," Sandy said. "When we were twelve, Colin told me he'd found little vials of blood hidden in the basement. They were labelled as his and Gabe's."

"That is pretty weird," Sean said. "You are not wrong. What would he… did Colin ever ask him what he was doing?"

Jerry laughed, short and sharp.

"You wouldn't," Sandy said. "He wasn't the kind of guy anyone would ask about anything. Their mom had pretty much stopped talking by the time Gabe was seven or eight. Like, if you asked her a direct question, she might say something, but she never said hello or told you to take your muddy shoes off or—I don't know."

"Initiated anything," Jerry said. "She never initiated. Anyway, the blood thing was weird, and Colin thinks their dad ran tests on them all the time. Sometimes he asked them to do stuff that wasn't bad, but it was weird… put your hand on this piece of metal. Keep it there for ten minutes. Okay, good. Now, Gabe, you do it."

"That's messed up," Sean said. "Didn't anyone report the guy to child services?"

Sandy thought, for a heartbeat, that she saw the boogeyman again. His face in the cake freezer, staring at her. But it was her imagination. Or… something else? A memory? It almost felt like….

She closed her eyes.

"Something wrong?" Sean asked.

"Gimme a sec."

She pressed the heels of her hands to her closed eyes and—

SHE'S EIGHT years old and standing next to her parents in the yard, staring at their burned garage and ruined car. She knows not to say so, with her mom set-jawed and her dad all weepy, but the fire was like TV. She's never seen anything that exciting for real.

And it's not just the fire that's exciting. It's like a party because everyone's there, the whole neighbourhood, and the firemen and now the police. Like it's Canada Day at the park.

Except Colin isn't there. His dad is, but not Colin. Sandy thinks Colin might be in bed, because of the accident. On Monday, after Colin missed school, she went over to see him, and he was all bruised, with a cut on his face, and he said it was because they'd been in an accident. Then his dad had come home and kicked Sandy out. Said the boys needed rest and she was a brat for not leaving them alone.

She'd told her parents at supper that night, and they'd sent her to her room after dessert, which was totally not fair. She hadn't done anything wrong. And then they'd had a fight. She hadn't been able to hear most of it, but she'd heard her mom saying they had to do something and her dad saying it was none of their business. And later she'd thought she heard her mom on the phone.

On Tuesday, Colin wasn't at school, and when Sandy was walking home, she saw a lady in a business suit at the Reece house. She couldn't ask Colin who it was because he wasn't at school on Wednesday either. And then on Thursday he was at school, but he wouldn't talk about it. I don't want to talk about it, Sandra. He never called her Sandra except when he was trying to be serious and grown-up and not two months younger than her.

Now she's looking at the garage, at how different everything is. At the curdled paint on the car. And suddenly a bundle of burned sticks moves, like a giant spider getting up to check its web, and she sees a face.

All teeth and bones with patches of skin falling off everywhere. She's too scared to scream, and she's just been to the bathroom, but she pees a little anyway. It's like a nightmare, one of Gabe's night terrors where he can't say what he was dreaming about.

And then it's over. The sticks are sticks, and Mr. Reece is coming over to her parents. Her mom's nose wrinkles like he smells bad, even though all Sandy can smell is smoke. He smiles at Sandy, all fake like the mean janitor at school. He tells her parents it's too bad about the garage, but they should count their blessings. If your family's healthy, you can't complain.

Her mom sends her inside, and she nearly screams again because Colin is in her room when she gets there. There's a tree outside her window, and they've learned to climb it, every foothold and sturdy branch.

He's standing on her Disney princess rug, and his face is all red like he's been washing and washing it. He smells like her dad's boat when he pours the gas in. Sweet like summer.

"You can't tell your mom things," he said. "Don't tell her things anymore."

She feels so bad that she cries, and he hugs her and tells her it's okay. Everything's okay as long as she doesn't talk about him and Gabe to her parents anymore.

She doesn't hug him for too long, in case he can smell that she peed herself.

"I won't talk about you," she promises, and he gives her a kiss on the top of her head before he leaves.

"I THINK COLIN set my garage on fire one time," she said. "How weird is that? I totally forgot."

"Oh, so he has a history of arson," Sean said.

"So does Sandy," Jerry pointed out, "but that doesn't mean she burned their house down."

"I think his dad made him do it," Sandy said. "It was a threat. Because I told my parents something and they called Child Protective Services. John Reece probably intimidated a lot of people into not doing anything."

"He wouldn't have had to do anything with a lot of people," Jerry said. "He had a way of staring at you like he was seeing your ghost."

"He was scary," Sandy said. She could still almost see her garage, an overlay on the orange chairs and cream tile floors of the restaurant.

"And then he died," Sean said.

"In a car accident," Sandy said. "Near Saskatoon. I don't think anyone really missed him. Money was a thing, but at least the house was paid off and they had insurance. Then I think they went on welfare. It wasn't great, but they used the food bank and stuff. They got by."

"And then she died and there was more insurance, and Colin got a construction job. Gabe did some part-time stuff. I'd say they were better off," Jerry said, "except for the trauma thing. But Gabe got over it."

"It's a point of pride," Sandy said. "All they had was that house and each other, and they made it work. Burning it down would be like burning down everything they've done right for the last six years."

"Okay," Sean said. "I get that. But, ehh, I went into the auxiliary on the way here."

The auxiliary was Gabe's fancy name for the outhouse behind their place, a tilted shack from before that house had gotten indoor plumbing. It was still usable, and given that the Reece house only had one bathroom, there were times when people were desperate enough to use it.

"That thing is still standing?" Jerry said. "Christ. It'll outlast us all."

"Yeah. You know how Colin kept some jerry cans in there to keep the insects away?"

"That's farm bullshit," Jerry said, shaking his head. "It doesn't work. But yeah."

"Well, both the jerry cans are missing," Sean told him. "And they were there last week when I took a leak during the poker game. So maybe the Reece boys didn't set that fire, but someone sure did."

Gabe

"YOU'LL WANT to head east on the highway," Gabe said. "And then I can put this into your—oh, your car has GPS."

"It does," Eli said. "It's a little kludgy."

It was more than a little kludgy, with a lot of unnecessary steps and a touch screen that needed to be slapped like it owed him money, but Gabe made it work.

Eli said nothing until they were nearing the city limits—not, admittedly, a long drive. He broke the silence with, "Why did Colin leave town?"

"I think I told you," Gabe said, "I don't know."

"And you lied," Eli said, the same way he'd have said Gabe had blue eyes. A fact, not up for discussion.

Silence followed. Gabe realized it was noiseless in the car, apart from the sounds of the engine and of both of them breathing. No radio. No Bluetooth connection to his phone. Who drove without music?

"It's not like I *know* know," Gabe said finally.

"I'm still interested to hear it," Eli assured him.

Gabe gazed out the passenger window at the prairie's colours blending while they raced past. Being out here, out of the city, always made Gabe want to drive as fast as he could. Or run. Not to anywhere or from anything. Just run for the joy of it, like horses did.

"Gabe," Eli prompted gently.

"Heard you the first time," Gabe said. "It's kind of personal."

"We were discussing his sex life earlier," Eli pointed out.

"It's personal about me," Gabe said.

Eli smiled. "Well," he said, "that's different."

"Oh, fuck off," Gabe suggested. Eli said nothing. He drove… and waited.

They passed Gabe's bike on the highway. Someone had been out there to clean up the mess, and if it had been a stretch to identify the heap as a bike before, it would have been impossible now. Melted lumps and a few shiny pieces of metal were the only things left.

"You want the next left," Gabe advised. Eli nodded. Perfectly calm, as if he knew Gabe would tell him eventually. Which Gabe wouldn't have except that he could see Eli's point of view. If you didn't know the other reason—the real reason—for Colin's abrupt departure, you might well think it had to do with Owen.

And Gabe preferred that Eli not think that anymore.

"Last night," he said, "Colin came home early from work. Not really early, but he was supposed to work late, and he was earlier than I expected. I was on the living room couch with… uh… a guy. And we were… whatever. We were sort of getting friendly…. Do I have to—"

"I follow your meaning," Eli said.

"Right," Gabe said, relieved. He glanced at Eli, checking for lines on his brow or a shift of his body away from Gabe's. Some sign of disgust. But there was nothing. Just the calmness.

"Colin walked in on us," Gabe said. "I don't think he knew before that. I don't know… maybe he did. But I never told him, and he never said anything to me."

"What happened?" Eli asked. Gabe leaned back in his seat and breathed deep. He almost laughed when he realized he was counting, the way Eli had made him do on the bridge. He stopped deep breathing and started to talk again.

"He got really mad. He threw the guy out. Like, literally. And then I took off, and I wound up at my friend Sandy's house."

Eli glanced at him as if he were about to ask something, but no question followed.

After a few seconds, Gabe said, "I stayed at Sandy's overnight. I went home the next morning before Colin usually left for work because Sandy said I should go home and talk to him. Except I didn't, because Colin had already packed up and left."

More silence. Then Eli pretty much floored Gabe with the words he used to break it.

"I'm sorry."

"Huh?" Gabe said. "Why—did you do something?"

Eli smiled again, though even in profile Gabe could see that his eyes were sad.

"I'm sorry for you," he clarified. "It would be bad enough to lose your home right after your brother left, but thinking he left on your account would make everything even more painful."

"I'm not huge into people feeling sorry for me," Gabe said. Well, except maybe Colin. And Sandy. And only sometimes.

"Today would be a good day to make an exception," Eli advised. "Do we have a turn coming up?"

"Oh… shit… yeah," Gabe said. "In that sense of coming up where we missed it. It's about a quarter of a kilometer back. Sorry."

"Not a problem," Eli told him, slowing the car and turning with the help of a convenient driveway. "You may have been distracted."

The road was oiled dirt, better than gravel in good weather and likely damned near impassable after rain. Good thing it hadn't rained in a billion years.

Eli handled it like a pro. That simple but odd fact made Gabe question, for the first time, his assumption that the guy was city folk. Of course all he really had about the guy was assumptions. He needed to keep that in mind.

As Gabe looked out at the fields, he found himself starting to nod off. He hadn't slept well, and there was only so much adrenalin in him, it seemed, no matter how frantic things still were. The world streamed past his half-closed eyes like water. Sloughs and wheat and canola and a broken-down barn. Horses: chestnut and dun. Colin, standing in the middle of a field.

Gabe jolted and sat up, turning his head to see what they were already leaving behind. He opened his mouth to tell Eli to stop, but his voice wouldn't obey, like he was in one of those nightmares where you couldn't scream or run or use a phone to call for help.

Then something felt wrong with the air pressure, like it was too much for his lungs to fight. After that, everything was impressions—something slamming into the car, the windshield cracking. A violin in ricochet, the bow bouncing down the strings, then thick, loud chords. Taking in too much air as the pressure suddenly released.

The car screeched to a stop. Eli was braced, hands white on the steering wheel and arms locked straight. He was staring, his mouth slightly open, like he'd seen his own ghost.

"Wha-what?" Gabe said. Eli didn't answer. The windshield was cracked in the middle, and the hood of the car had a dent about the size of a hiking backpack. Had they hit a person?

Colin?

Had he really seen Colin?

"There," Eli said, and pointed ahead of them, on the other side of the road. Gabe couldn't tell what it was at first. A light brown pile of fabric and broomsticks. White splotches like spilled paint. Then his eyes focused, and he knew it was a fawn.

"Deer," Gabe said weakly. His heart was punching the inside of his chest, and his jaw was aching.

"It bounced off the car," Eli said, sounding as shaken as Gabe and twice as confused. "Do they do that?"

Gabe had no answer. He'd never hit a deer before. He'd never been in a car where it had happened.

"Are you okay?" Eli asked.

Of course Gabe was okay. The deer was so small and young, and it hadn't even broken through the windshield, just cracked it. Gabe was intact, and the car was mostly intact, and the poor deer was a pile of bones and fur on the road.

"Yeah," Gabe said softly. "Poor deer."

"Poor deer," Eli echoed.

"Can the car still drive?"

Eli started the engine and drove the car, slowly, to the side of the road before putting it into park.

"Seems like it," he said. "I guess it's okay to drive unless we see smoke."

"That's the spirit," Gabe said. "You're starting to sound like a local."

Eli didn't react to the compliment. Instead he drove in silence until he found Tracy's driveway, marked by a bright red mailbox with a perky plastic flag that announced The Howell's in flowing white letters. The height of farmyard elegance.

"You think this is the place?" Gabe asked. Eli ignored that too. Gabe didn't think he was mad. He was focused on driving. Watching for smoke. He wasn't as cavalier as he sounded after all.

When they reached the end of the driveway and stopped in front of the Howells' house, Gabe took a moment to admire the dent in the car. It really did seem like the deer had jumped up and over the front to hit the hood in the middle. That or like an angry god had decided to rain down deer from the sky. Gabe shook his head.

"Dude, I don't care how much insurance you have on this car. When you turn it in, you are screwed."

CHAPTER FIVE

Gabe

"YOU SHOULD get out first."

As he said that, Eli was looking out the car window at a sheepdog of some kind, white and thick-furred and the size of a small pony. The dog was between the car and the ranch-style house, barking loudly enough that it was uncomfortable to listen to, even from inside the car.

"Should I?" Gabe said "Why's that?"

"Because that dog might bite."

He said that as if it were good sense. Which Gabe supposed it would be from Eli's perspective. He wouldn't be the one getting bit.

"You're right," Gabe said. "It might. You should go check."

Eli eyed Gabe as if he wanted to say something. Gabe waited, but it never came out.

"Fine," Gabe said at last. "Sit there and bite your fingernails. I've got this."

He went outside and faced the dog, who was a few feet away and barking up a storm. He took a step forward. The dog took a step back.

"Right," Gabe said. "I'm going into the house. You need anything from inside?"

The dog barked in response. Gabe shrugged and walked past it to the porch, which was fenced by half wagon wheels and lit by a combination of a yellow bulb and a bug zapper. As he climbed the few steps to the door, he heard the driver's door shut. More barking, footsteps across the yard, and then Eli was beside him.

"You ring?" he asked.

"No," Gabe said. "I'm fucking stunned."

"And even-tempered," Eli said.

"Suck it," Gabe said to a surprised Tracy Howell, who had swung open the door.

"Uh…," she said.

Gabe smiled. "I'm sorry," he said "That was rude. You hardly know me."

Tracy continued to stare at him in horror for a few seconds before giving him a shaky smile. She was blonder than Gabe remembered and dressed in the kind of thin black sweats that people wore to yoga classes. The kind you didn't wear white panties beneath.

"Shit," she said. "Gabe Reece? Is that you?"

She sounded sure Gabe couldn't be there, like he'd died years ago. It made him want to pinch himself and make sure he was real.

"Yeah. Jordan gave me your address. I hope that's okay. I need to ask you something about my brother."

"Who's this guy?" she asked, lifting her chin at Eli. As she looked from Gabe to Eli and back, Gabe thought he could see something strange about her eyes. Like she was stoned or zoned out the way his mom used to get. Only not as bad, because Tracy was walking and talking.

"He's a friend of mine," Gabe said quickly, before Eli could ruin it with the truth. "We can talk out here if you want, but I think we're driving your dog a little nuts."

"Oh, sorry," she said. She stood on the tips of her toes to see past them. "Cody! Enough!"

The dog barked once more.

"*Enough*!" Tracy insisted. The dog grumbled and stalked off.

"He's good with sheep," she said, despite no sheep being in evidence on the property. "Come in. Only for a few minutes. I'm not feeling good."

"We shouldn't be long," Eli assured her. She ignored him and waved Gabe into the house.

The house had an open plan, with a living room directly before them and a combined kitchen and dining room to their right. Large windows at the back of the house looked out over a garden with a row of trees behind it.

"This is your place?" Gabe asked.

"No, my parents'," Tracy said. "I want to get an apartment."

"If they cook and do your laundry," Gabe advised, "don't be hasty."

Tracy seemed confused for a heartbeat, then nodded. "Oh, right. You're on your own, aren't you?"

"Me and Colin," Gabe said.

Tracy's face changed when he said Colin's name. A flinch, like someone had thrown dust at her eyes.

"You and Colin."

Tracy eyed Eli again. When she turned her head, Gabe could see that one of her ears was the colour of a cherry popsicle. The skin around it was flushed too, so maybe the redness came from a heating pad or something, rather than the infection. Still, it seemed Tracy wasn't malingering. Gabe and Colin believed that sick leave shouldn't be wasted on a day when you felt like shit, but to each their own.

"Did he send you here?"

Gabe almost laughed.

"Hell no," he said. "He'd have to talk to me first."

Tracy's mouth turned down at the corners.

"He's not talking to me either," she said.

"Don't feel bad," Gabe said. "He's not talking to anybody. He fucked off out of town last night and didn't tell anyone."

"Oh!" Tracy wavered like she was about to fall. Eli caught her arm to steady her.

"Are you okay?" he asked "Maybe you should sit down."

"No, no, I'm good." She gave him a broad, loopy smile. "I'm so good. Do you think he's going to come back, or…?"

"Dunno," Gabe said.

Tracy's smile shrank to half its previous size. "Oh. Well, he's gone for now."

"Okay," Gabe said, "I get that my brother hurt your feelings, and I'm genuinely sorry if he led you on or something, but can you not throw a gone-away party with me standing right here?"

Tracy's smile shrank further. It was the Aral Sea of smiles. "You apologize. He doesn't, but you do. Everyone says you're the nice Reece."

The nice Reece? What the hell was that supposed to mean?

"I guess," Gabe said, "Colin was too busy raising me all by his damned self to go to fucking charm school."

Tracy flinched again. Eli put a hand on her shoulder.

"This is a little personal for Gabe," he said. "If you'd like, he can wait in the car."

Oh, like he'd acted up at the Safeway over some toy his mom wouldn't buy him. Gabe shot Eli a glare and got a glare right back. Gabe dropped his gaze and studied the tile floor. It didn't feel like tile. It was that new lino, maybe. Tracy didn't have a lot of lights on, so it was hard to tell.

"No," Tracy said. Gabe looked up in time to see Tracy turning her head toward him. "It's okay. This is his brother we're talking about."

Gabe knew what was on her face now. It was impossible for him to miss, considering how much of it he had seen after his mother's death.

Goddamned pity.

"S'okay," he muttered.

"Can you tell us what happened with him and Owen?" Eli said. He was using that soothing tone again, the one he'd used in the car when he'd asked Gabe why Colin had left. "We know they argued in the bar and that Owen followed Colin outside, but we don't know what happened there."

"I… can you walk with me? I need more hot water."

They followed her into the kitchen, and she turned the hot water tap on, letting it run to warm up. Gabe saw a bottle of pills next to the sink. Ativan. He knew that one. He'd been on it after his mom died. It was supposed to make him feel better or something, but all it did was make him not feel much of anything. Which at the time, he had considered okay.

Tracy was staring into the water, occasionally touching her finger to the stream to test the warmth.

"I followed them out," she said. "I went behind the dumpster so they wouldn't see. They would've told me to go back inside."

Gabe believed that. He'd been sent back inside, or outside, or upstairs, about a zillion times in his life.

"Did they see you?" Eli asked.

Tracy shook her head. She grabbed a hot water bottle from the counter, poured out the old water, and refilled it.

"Wrap a towel around that," Gabe warned. "You'll burn yourself. You might have already."

"Oh… right." Tracy pulled a tea towel from the rack and tucked the bottle into it. "I hate ear infections so much. I always get them when I'm stressed."

"What did you see?" Eli said.

"So Colin was in the lot, and someone had parked an SUV behind his truck. I think it was a Yukon. And… um. You should look at my phone."

Eli and Gabe exchanged glances.

"You filmed it?" Eli said.

"Yeah. I thought if they were fighting, it might make them stop."

She grabbed an iPhone from the counter and pulled it toward her to unlock it.

"There. Just… you can hit play."

Eli took the phone and held it up so Gabe could see it too.

The video showed the back of a Loraas-brand dumpster in its signature red, then tilted as Tracy got herself into place. For a moment, the screen was filled by a few tough strands of false chamomile and the cracked pavement it grew from. Then it moved again and locked in on two people in a parking lot. Colin and a guy who had to be Owen.

Owen was standing still, not yapping at Colin like Gabe had expected. Not even talking. Because Colin was busy.

Colin had discovered that someone's shitty parking job had left a Yukon pinning in his truck, and he was doing something about it. Not kicking in a taillight or leaving a note. Not slicing the tires, which would have been an overreaction, but Colin was clearly in a mood, so Gabe wouldn't have 100 percent put it past him.

None of that was happening.

What was happening was Colin was crouched behind the SUV, picking it up with both hands.

It was, to start, the kind of thing you'd see on the news sometimes. Mother has surge of adrenalin, lifts car by rear bumper and saves trapped child. Except this was a Yukon, not a car, and Colin didn't stop at lifting the bumper. Seconds later, he'd slipped under the vehicle and was getting to his feet, lifting it over his head. Which was impossible, but Gabe didn't dwell on that because the next thing Colin did was lean back, bowing his spine, still holding on to the SUV. It wasn't propped on his hands. He was gripping it.

Then he whipped forward and pitched the vehicle over the strip mall beside the casino into the lot on the other side.

It could have been an empty beer can, arcing toward a doused firepit while Sandy told Colin to pick that up and put it in the recycling, damn it. It had taken more effort than that, sure, but it flew nearly as well. Glass broke and metal crunched off-screen when it landed.

The camera shook and caught the navy sky for a second. It dropped to the back of the dumpster and stayed there, orange-red filling the screen. Gabe could hear Tracy breathing heavily, a shrill panicked note at the back of her throat. Trying not to scream or cry, he thought. Trying to hide.

Farther off, he heard an "Oh Jesus, oh Jesus," and a "Please, please don't," and then a scuffle and a thud. Gabe knew that last sound. He'd gone hunting with Sean and Colin and Jerry once and helped them throw a kill into the back of the truck. Not a deer. A Charolais calf Jerry had got by accident… or because he liked veal and knew a guy who was into home butchering if you were willing to split the meat.

That calf hadn't been dead when they got to it. Jerry had shot it again because it would have kicked and fought and scratched up the bed of Colin's truck, and the only other option was leaving it there.

Purse dogs who didn't know when to stop barking, though… they weren't half-dead calves. Give them a good thump on the head and they'd keep still, wouldn't they? It didn't have to mean they were—

Eli made a soft sound, a little "Huh." Like something finally made sense to him. The video ended and started to play again. They all watched it once again, twice, before Gabe touched the screen to stop it.

It was equally impossible every time. And equally believable to Gabe, bone-deep. Though he'd never seen it before and barely believed his eyes, it seemed being able to overhand an SUV was on his internal list of things a guy might be able to do.

Like walking away from a motorcycle crash or zapping someone across the room.

"Did Colin see you?" Eli asked. "Did he know you were there?"

"I'd be dead if he had," Tracy said. "Wouldn't I? He didn't notice me."

"And then you went home sick," Eli said. "And you haven't been back since."

"What if he's there and I *look* at him and he knows I know?" Tracy said softly. "He'd see my face and he'd know. I've been here the whole time thinking I might be crazy, but what if I'm not crazy? He'll kill me."

"You're not crazy," Eli told her. Which implied, what, that Colin would kill her?

"Colin wouldn't hurt you," Gabe said.

Tracy started to cry. Not loud. Just tears falling, one after another, rain on a windowpane. She'd put the hot water bottle back on the counter, and her ear was glowing under the pot lights.

Gabe knew he should hug her or pat her shoulder or hand her a towel or something… but he couldn't move. He couldn't let go of the counter behind him. His legs were gone for all he knew. He couldn't feel them, or any part of his body, really. Only the counter under his hands. She probably didn't want to be touched by a Reece anyway.

"I'm sorry," Tracy sniffed, grabbing the towel from around the hot water bottle and swiping it across her face. "I thought I had a grip. I've been… I keep watching it."

"Of course," Eli said gently.

The three of them jumped at a sound from the kitchen. Gabe turned around, heart pounding, before realizing that it was the buzzer on the oven. Tracy took a deep, shaky breath and went to turn it off.

"Sorry," she said. "That's for my antibiotics. You have to take these ones four times a day. I left them in the bathroom."

She went past them, out of the kitchen and down a hallway, and took the first door on the left into what was probably the washroom. Left alone in the kitchen, Gabe and Eli looked at each other.

"You're… pretty calm about this," Gabe said. "You don't even seem surprised."

"It's complicated," Eli said.

Gabe was about to ask, complicated compared to goddamned what, but that was when they heard the shot.

Sandy

"OH MY God, I am not answering that," Sean said. They were sitting around the kitchen table over the bottle of Kraken they'd agreed to open well before cocktail hour in honour of the day.

"It could be Gabe," Sandy pointed out. "Or Colin. They might not have their keys."

"They have keys," Sean said, at the same time as Jerry said, "Tough."

He was slouched so far down that his chin was resting on his chest.

"Fine," Sandy said. "I will do everything around here. As per fucking usual."

Jerry played the world's smallest violin as Sandy pushed her chair back and shambled down the hall to the door. The damned thing had no peephole and no side window. She'd complained to their landlord about it many times. He'd seemed to find it funnier each time.

Pulling the door open as far as the chain would allow gave her a vertical slice of two cops. Or she assumed they were both cops anyway. One was the uniformed redhead who had spoken with Sandy and Sean on the Reeces' lawn. Officer Strovinsky? Strembosky? That was it. The other was a stranger in a suit. Everything about him, from his suit to his hair to his skin, was grey. He seemed annoyed to be breathing.

This was exactly the kind of situation for which Sandy would have liked a peephole. With a peephole, you could see who was there, quietly back away from the door, and move or hide or flush anything you felt you should before going back and opening that door. This way, with the chain, it took more chutzpah than she had to pretend she wasn't at home.

She shut the door, hissed, "*Cops*!" over her shoulder at Sean and Jerry, unhooked the chain, and opened the door again as Sean and Jerry scattered to other parts of the house.

"Ms. Klaassen?" the redhead asked. "May we come in?"

It was Gabe's fault that Sandy didn't know what to say. The day of her sentencing, he'd smirkingly met her outside the courtroom, waving a flyer for a "You and the Law" course at the community centre. "Given your delicate legal position," he'd said. Because he'd been a dick about it, she'd crumpled up the flyer and jammed it into his Big Gulp. Fat lot of good that was doing her now.

"Uh… sure," Sandy said, stepping back from the door and letting them past her into the hall. "Is this about the Reece boys?"

"Ms. Klaassen, this is Detective Palmer," the redhead informed her.

"North Battleford has a detective? What's there to detect?" Sandy asked, realizing only as she spoke that the detective might consider that rude.

To her relief, he simply directed heavy-lidded eyes at her and said, "You might be surprised."

"What can I do for you?" she asked. It crossed her mind that she should probably invite them to sit down, or offer coffee or tea. But that would only encourage them to stay.

"Ms. Klaassen," Detective Palmer said, "do you know an Owen Bernier?"

That didn't sound a thing like, "When did you last see the Reece brothers?" or "Do you know any arsonists, other than yourself?" What the hell?

"What? No. Why?"

Palmer gestured at his partner, who took out her phone and showed Sandy a photo of a guy with hedgehog hair and a narrow face. He was sitting on a restaurant patio in what appeared to be Saskatoon, nestled between a pair of assembly-line twentysomething girls. They were mostly legs and eyelashes, any distinguishing features masked by contouring and concealer. Owen and his friends were holding wine coolers in one hand and flashing vees at the camera with the other, identical glittery nail polish on everyone.

"Oh shit, that guy," Sandy said. "He works at the casino. I don't think I've said ten words to him."

"Owen Bernier," the detective said, "left work during his shift two nights ago. He went into the parking lot with Colin Reece and hasn't been at work since. No one has been able to contact him."

"Okay?" Sandy said. "Shouldn't you be asking Colin about this?"

"We haven't been able to find Colin Reece," Palmer said as if Sandy hadn't spoken. "Have you seen him recently?"

"Like I said earlier," Sandy said with a nod to the redhead, "I don't know where either of the Reece boys is right now. And they don't have cell phones, so good luck tracking them down."

"When did you last see Colin?" the detective asked. Sandy was starting to think he had a script he'd memorized, or there was a teleprompter behind her head that she couldn't see. No matter what she said, she got what seemed to be his preordained next answer.

"I saw him last Saturday," she said. "At the Taphouse. We were there from about nine until… one, I guess."

"And have you communicated with him in any way since then?" Palmer inquired.

"No."

Not even a phone call, and how weird was that? When had they started going a week or more without talking? Well, except when Colin had been on jobs out of town, the fly-in stuff where he was gone for ten days or whatever. But otherwise they usually talked all the damned time.

Palmer nodded slowly. His face said this was only the latest in a terribly long line of disappointments, and he expected the future to hold more of the same.

He said, "Please excuse this question, which may seem unnecessary to you. Where do you think Colin Reece would be right now?"

"I have no idea," Sandy said, hoping that the truth of it was in her voice and on her face. "I would have thought, with his house burned down, he would have come here. I guess he knows people from work and everything, but Colin's an old friend, and he even has a key to this place. I don't know where he is or why I haven't heard from him."

Palmer sighed. It seemed to be a sigh of disappointment, not irritation. "Fine. What about Gabriel Reece?"

"Same thing, except I saw him this morning. He starts a job at that windsurfing rental place in Cochin on Monday. If you haven't found him by then, you could check there."

"All right," Palmer said. Strembosky glanced at him and at the door, and Sandy thought she was probably dying to leave. How embarrassing would it be to get dragged along merely to identify someone—yep, that's the chick I met on the Reeces' lawn—and then have to stand there like a big dummy?

Sadly for his partner, Palmer didn't seem quite ready to leave.

"I understand," he said, "that a Sean Boyko and Jerome McClelland reside here as well?"

"Yeah," Sandy said. "Please call him Jerome. And let me watch."

Palmer gave her a perfunctory smile. It might have been the only kind he had.

"I'll need to speak with both of them. Individually."

Of course. Sandy answered the insincere smile with one of her own. "Wait here. I'll get them."

Gabe

SOUND WAS tricky. It was always difficult to tell exactly where something loud and ringing, like a gunshot, had come from. But as far as Gabe knew, there was only one other person in the house, and he knew where she was. He headed for the door Tracy had gone through, Eli close behind him. Neither of them arrived at their destination, though, because someone stepped out of that door and blocked their way.

He was tall and thin, so thin that Gabe could see his bones…

see his teeth under his skin

…wearing through his skin, the skin red and tattered and white bone right there, exposed. Yet the guy was standing, head cocked, smiling at Gabe from behind his dark…

sunglasses that he always wore, always, even in the basement with almost all the lights out

…sunglasses, instead of falling over the way a corpse should if you stood it up in a hallway and then let it go. He was smiling and holding a gun, a handgun, which Gabe didn't see a lot of. Mostly rifles and shotguns around here. Mostly aimed at deer and beer cans on fences and not at Gabe's heart.

"Hello, Gabriel."

standing over Gabe, curious, taking his blood, running electricity through him like

lightning

out of nowhere

And Gabe stopped thinking about anything at all.

"You look like shit, Jack."

Gabe hadn't known Eli's voice could sound so harsh. It shook him, like a slap to the face, and he was breathing again.

Eli stepped forward to stand beside him. Stupid. Stupid. Behind Gabe, he'd been safe from the gun.

"Eli," the man said. Was his name Jack? Or had Eli said it like you'd call someone Buddy or Mac, a name for any guy?

No. It was his name. Because Jack knew Eli too, didn't he? Knew Eli's name. The way he'd known Gabe's. Hissed it, with air escaping all over the place. Around the bones, through all those little holes.

"You haven't killed him yet," Jack said. Was he talking about Gabe? He was talking to Eli, and there was no one else around.

"Get out of here," Eli said.

"I will," Jack told him. "But you do me a favour. Wait for the police."

His gun moved to point at Eli's heart. Without thinking, Gabe stepped between them. He barely realized it when Jack fired because the sound was immediately swallowed by a thousand violins hitting the same note at once. It filled every space in the house and in Gabe, his mouth and lungs. The blue light was so bright it was impossible to see anything else, like they were fifty feet down in the clearest, emptiest ocean.

And then it was dark and silent, and Jack was gone.

Gabe moved one foot up and down, feeling the solid floor beneath him. He was still standing. Shot in the heart and still standing.

Shot with a blank. Or the gun misfired.

God, it was quiet. The dog wasn't barking. No one was moving. Jack was gone. Just gone.

It startled him when Eli said, "Are you going to say he missed?"

Gabe turned his head. Eli was still beside him. He didn't seem to be shot. Tired and confused and upset, but definitely not shot.

"You okay?" Gabe asked.

"I'm not the one he shot," Eli said. "Are you going to tell me he missed, Gabe?"

Gabe turned completely, and Eli turned to face him.

"I'm not dead," Gabe said, unable to get any force behind it. Eli stared down at his own hands, then raised the right one and gently laid it onto Gabe's chest. Over his heart. And Gabe hadn't felt much in hours, not since the night before. He'd been numb, he realized, to rough edges and hard chairs and so many tiny hurts.

But he felt that.

"He shot you right here," Eli told him, *I'm sorry* running through every word. As if Gabe really were dead. "He shot you, and nothing happened."

Their eyes met, and Gabe wanted to put his hand over Eli's. He wanted to step backward until there was a solid wall behind him and haul Eli up against him. Sex and death. He kept his hands still. Eli's hand dropped to his side.

"That's impossible," Gabe said.

"You saw the video," Eli said. "And when he shot you, you saw the flash. You heard that. You saw that light in your house, Gabe. In the fire. Are you going to tell me he missed?"

Gabe swallowed hard. "No."

Eli nodded. "Okay."

Gabe's vision blurred. It wasn't until he saw, hazily, sorrow on Eli's face that he realized he'd started to cry. For the first time in all of this mess. He blinked hard. Not now. Not now, not now.

"Can you tell me what's going on with you?" Eli asked, so kindly that Gabe almost started to cry again.

"No to that too," Gabe said. Eli put a hand on Gabe's arm and pressed it, not hard enough to draw a flash.

He said, "Then I'll tell you."

Sandy

IT WAS hard to remember everything she might need to hide, and that was of the things she knew about to begin with. Sandy was well aware that Sean and Jerry both thought whatever she didn't know couldn't hurt her. Or more likely that whatever she didn't know couldn't hurt them or get them yelled at or evicted. The lease, the trump card of all trump cards, was in her name.

There was Jerry's hillbilly heroin, which he kept in its prescription bottle in the medicine cabinet like it was his by right. Unless Rochelle Simons was secretly his legal name, Sandy was pretty sure it didn't belong with him. Sean had some knives that weren't allowed, though she wasn't an expert on which. The parachute knives, she thought. Those were a definite no.

The various pick-me-ups and lay-me-downs they all kept in tins and bottles around the house, they could be anywhere. Sandy had some Xanax from her mom, the last of a prescription her mom hadn't wanted to finish. Everyone's pot was fine, except what hadn't come from a dispensary. Like Sean's, since Sean thought his dealer gave him better deals.

"We're a bunch of delinquents," Sandy said under her breath.

The attic was the place to stick everything. She could use the stepladder and get up high enough to shove things onto the attic floor, a few inches past the ceiling trap door. That door was barely big enough for someone Gabe's size, and wouldn't Palmer be searching for Colin if he decided to go through the place? He'd take one look at that door and move on.

To make sure the plan would work, she got the ladder, popped the door, and slipped her hand onto the floor. It felt like usual, like sawdust and maybe some raccoon shit. And… something solid.

The hell?

She tapped the side of whatever it was and heard a hollow noise, like a bongo. It felt smooth, like varnished wood. She got hold of the thing and tugged at it, shifting it this way and that until it was positioned the right way to slide through the door. Finally, Gabe's guitar fell into her hands.

SANDY IS in the Reeces' kitchen, making grilled cheese for one. Waiting for Colin to get home while Gabe hides in his room. Wondering whether there'd be any point making a second sandwich and whether she could make it fit under Gabe's door.

She hears Colin's truck in the drive and the front door opening, Colin hanging his jacket in the hall.

"Can I offer you pizza instead?"

Sandy plates the sandwich and shuts off the stove before turning to see that, yes, Colin has indeed brought home an extra-large pizza from Family, which was fine but no goddamned Venice House, and that was a hill she'd die on.

"I'll always take pizza. But I don't know if that's enough to get the sulk monster out of his lair. He got suspended at school today. And he broke his violin."

But Colin already knows, somehow. He knows that some kid asked Gabe whether his dead mom haunted his house on Halloween and that Gabe broke his violin over the kid's face. That Gabe caught suspension and the other kid got nothing, supposedly because Gabe was violent and the other kid used words.

But really, she and Colin agree, it's that the Reece boys will always be something ugly to this town. Like crows on a telephone line, a bad omen you hope will go away.

Colin drops the pizza box onto the kitchen table and heads upstairs to get Gabe. Sandy watches him go because, though he's too much like family to date, she can still enjoy the view.

Unlike his brother, Colin seems like he belongs. He's broad-shouldered and muscular, made for tight white T-shirts and Levi's. His black hair is curly, not wavy, and his face says that he knows who he is and likes it. He's not a show-stopper like Gabe, but he's got charm, and in some ways that's better.

Sandy puts out beers for her and Colin and a Coke for Gabe. Plates. Napkins. She's barely done when Gabe slouches into the kitchen and takes a seat. He doesn't pull up to the table or take any of the pizza, but he's there.

Gabe doesn't say that he's been suspended, but it's not that he's trying to hide it. Sandy knows better. Gabe told her, and he knows she's told Colin, which is all the confession he needs. His priest will take it up with God.

Nothing is said for a while. Colin and Sandy take seats and eat pizza and drink beer. Gabe nurses his Coke, hugging the can to his chest between sips.

"I have," Colin says at last, "two things I need you to know."

"Shoot," Gabe says without enthusiasm.

"You and I are never going to run this piece-of-shit town."

Gabe laughs and seems startled by the sound of it. "I didn't need to be told that. We'll get run out *of this town, maybe."*

"Nah. Not until we're ready to go. Look. People don't like it that our parents are dead. They think it's—"

"Like carelessness," Gabe says darkly.

Colin regards Gabe for a long moment before continuing. "Something like that. People see us and they think about dead parents and orphans, and who the fuck wants to think about that shit? You get why they don't want us around."

"It's not your fault," Sandy adds, putting a hand on Gabe's arm. It's awkward because he's still clutching his Coke the way a monkey clutches a baby, but she manages. "It doesn't mean there's anything wrong with you."

"Oh!" Colin laughs and gently slaps Gabe's other arm. "No. Man, there is a lot wrong with us. Don't kid yourself."

For the first time, Gabe seems… hopeful? It must be something else he's feeling, but that's what's on his face.

"Yeah?" Gabe says.

"We're what the minivan drivers of the world would call traumatized. Those people are pussies, but that's what they'd say."

"Okay."

"Do you want a beer for this?"

"No." Gabe's eyes are locked on Colin's, pitilessly. "I'm good."

"All that stuff you remember our dad doing—all the needles and the tests—that all happened. You weren't imagining it. Are you sure you don't want a beer for this?"

"Still good," Gabe says. Sandy, on the other hand, thinks her stomach might be rolling around on the floor between the table's uneven legs and down the tilted linoleum to the mudroom door. She and Colin have sworn not to talk about any of this with Gabe. But she can tell there's no stopping it now.

"Our dad was a fucking lunatic," Colin says breezily, as if recounting a story about a bad day at work. "I don't know what he thought he was doing or what he was giving us, and probably it was nothing. You know? It was some bullshit he got off the internet. Like homeopathy. It did nothing. So I thought it was better to tell you that you'd imagined it. Even though I knew you didn't believe me."

"We could have told a teacher or something," Gabe says. "If you'd come with me and backed me up. We could have made him quit."

"No one wanted to mess with our dad," Colin says. "You know that. Even if they believed us, they would have pretended they didn't. And God knows what Dad would have done."

Gabe was holding the Coke too tight now, starting to bend the metal. "You could have tried."

"I could have got us put in foster care, maybe. Best case scenario. No way would anyone have left us with Mom. The only reason they left us with her when Dad died was that no one came around to investigate. Did she even say two words a day? Do you remember her going anywhere she wasn't pushed?"

Gabe opens his mouth, and Sandy knows what he's about to say like she knows what's going to happen when she reaches the top of a roller coaster. "There's one place," he's going to say. "She went one place without being pushed." She kicks him before he says it. He looks at her sharply, so grown-up sometimes with his expressions and his knowing eyes. He's angry. But he shuts his mouth and keeps it shut.

"If you think we'd have been better off in foster care," Colin says, "you need to shake your fucking head. Things were okay when it was us and Mom, and they're okay now, so it worked out."

The way he says it sounds almost like taking credit. Like everything went to plan. That's stupid because John Reece's car accident was an accident. But sometimes Colin raises the hair on her neck, no matter how long they've been the best of friends.

"Sometimes," Colin says to Gabe, "when Dad was on business trips, I searched the basement. You ever do that?"

Gabe doesn't move.

Colin smiles. "Guess you didn't find anything either. I thought maybe I'd find out what was in that shit. I don't know, Gabe. Maybe it was nothing too bad and that whole thing is over, or maybe we're gonna grow second heads someday. I decided, after Mom died, all we can do is move on."

Colin gets up to get himself another beer and sets one in front of Sandy as well. The idea of pouring something down her raw throat is horrifying to her, but she accepts the beer with a closed-lipped smile.

"You'll go away to school in a few years," Colin continues.

"I don't have—" Gabe starts, and Colin sets his beer down decisively.

"What? The grades? You're on the honour roll. The inclination? I've seen you on websites. You think I don't notice shit, but I do. MacEwan? In Edmonton? You can afford it."

Gabe raises his brows. "Really."

Sandy knows what he means. This kitchen echoes Gabe's "really" in a dozen ways. The scuffed and pitted floor. The oven that has to be set fifty degrees too high to get to the right temperature. The toaster that only works on one side. If there's money, Sandy hasn't seen it.

"I've been putting money aside," Colin says, like it wasn't merely possible but easy. "You'll go, and I swear I will be cheering you on. But if you ever feel like you're too weird for the human race, come back to this house and I will remind you that you are not ever alone. I know this is a fucked-up home to come to and a fucked-up place to belong, but don't ever think you don't have one. Okay?"

Gabe sets down his Coke and puts his hand on Colin's arm. Colin turns his arm and they clasp each others' wrists, like Romans in the movies.

It seems a long time before Colin takes his arm back and says, "There's also that second thing I need you to know."

"All of that was only one thing?" Gabe says. "Jesus. I aged while you were going on."

Colin swats Gabe with a paper napkin before going to the mudroom and returning with a guitar case in his hands. He hands it to Gabe across the table.

"Guitar?" Gabe asks. Not in the sense of is it a guitar? More why are you giving me one?

"Yeah," Colin said. "The second thing is that violin is for pussies. Learn to play a real instrument, for God's sake."

Gabe laughs. His eyes are bright. "You are such a redneck," he tells his brother. "You're like a sack of rattlesnakes, shotgun shells, and dicks."

He opens the case as he speaks and marvels at the steel-string inside, which even Sandy can tell is a nice one. Expensive.

"Thanks, man," Gabe says softly.

Colin puts a hand on his shoulder.

"First time I hear the fucking Mountain Goats coming out of your room, you and that guitar will both be on the street."

THIS GUITAR, it should have burned with everything else in the Reece house. Everything except those few pieces of furniture and those stubborn books. It should have been gone, not here in her hands, feeling warm as if it had just come from a fire. The attic. It got impossibly warm on long summer days.

Sandy set it on the floor. An impulse took her back up the stepladder. She felt around some more, stood on her tiptoes on the top of the ladder like everyone said not to do. Finally her fingers brushed it. She reached, reached, caught it. Brought out one more thing, the thing Sandy had scraped together the cash to buy Gabe after his suspension.

A second-hand violin.

Gabe

ELI WAS in the washroom, checking on Tracy. Gabe didn't see any point to following Eli in there. There was nothing in that washroom that Gabe needed to see.

"Did he shoot her?" Gabe called from the foyer.

"Yes," Eli called back.

"Is she dead?"

"Yes."

Jesus. Jesus. Gabe saw her hot water bottle lying on the counter, a memento from minutes earlier when her ear infection had been the biggest problem she had.

"Is that guy really gone?" he asked.

"Yes."

How had he gotten out of the house? How had he gotten into the house?

"The dog didn't bark," Gabe said.

Eli came out of the washroom, wiping his hands on a towel that was turning pink, even red in spots.

"What's that?"

"Cody didn't bark at Jack. It's like that Sherlock Holmes story. The dog didn't bark."

"Jack teleports," Eli answered.

Oh, well. Of course. He teleported. Gabe should have known.

"We should go," Eli said. He dropped the towel in the sink and put Tracy's phone into the back pocket of his pants.

"Are you sure she's dead?" Gabe asked, "Maybe we should call an ambulance. In case—"

"Gabe. She's dead. I'm sorry."

"Don't say you're sorry to me," Gabe said. His stomach was twisting in on itself. "Say it to her. Tell her we're both sorry we came here."

Eli took a deep breath.

"He would have found her eventually. I'm also not thrilled that we made it easy for him."

"He wanted to shoot you."

"I know. Thank you, by the way. I didn't say thank you."

Gabe felt himself blushing. He looked away, at the dog bowl by the door. Poor Cody.

"If it makes you feel better," Eli added, "I doubt Jack wanted to shoot you."

"Did you?" Gabe said, suddenly remembering. "Do you want to shoot me? What did he say about you not killing me yet?"

"I'll tell you in the car. Jack wasn't kidding about calling the cops. We have to go."

"Not so fucking fast," Gabe said. "You can't tell me that some shambling zombie murderer expected you to shoot me and then tell me to get my ass in the car."

"Okay," Eli said, stepping around Gabe to the front door. "I get that. But I haven't killed you yet. I think I'd rather not. And I wouldn't shoot you, because we both know that would be a waste of my time." When Gabe didn't move, Eli held the door open and waved a hand at the great outdoors. "Get your ass in the car."

"You think you'd rather not?"

"Gabe…," Eli said, sounding so much like Colin when he was nearing the end of his patience that Gabe's stomach made another vicious turn.

"Fine," Gabe said. He moved fast, past Eli and the door, down the steps, past the barking sheepdog, and to the car door, which beeped and unlocked as he reached it.

"Enough, Cody," Eli said as he passed the dog on his way to the driver's side. Cody ignored him. A bad idea, Gabe thought. For all Cody knew, Eli might shoot him.

"Is that dog going to get fed?" Gabe asked once Eli was in the car. "Should we put out some food?"

"She lives… lived with her parents," Eli reminded him. "I assume they'll be home soon."

"Oh," Gabe said softly. "Right."

So her parents would find her, shot to death in their bathroom, maybe with a bottle of antibiotics in her hand.

"Did you leave prints?" Gabe asked as they left the private driveway and turned onto the dirt road. South. Away from the highway. "Hey—where are you going?"

"We're going somewhere we can talk," Eli said. "No, I did not leave prints. Did you?"

"Uh… maybe," he said. "On the counter in the kitchen."

Eli thought for a moment, eyes narrowed. Then his face smoothed.

"No. Not the way you were gripping it. You're fine."

Neither said anything for a few minutes. The fields rolled by without any sign of deer or farmers or Colin. The sky was as bright as midday, though Gabe's watch told him it was late afternoon.

Seemingly at random, Eli picked a dirt road, thinner and bumpier than the one they'd been on, and took it for a kilometer or so before pulling over and turning off the car.

"He teleports?" Gabe asked. Eli, eyes fixed on the steering wheel, smiled.

"Something like that. I've never nailed down exactly what it is." He eyed Gabe. "I've misled you."

"No shit," Gabe said, as pleasantly as he could manage.

Eli smiled again, for a second. "I am an investigator, kind of. But I'm with an organization that finds people with unusual abilities."

Gabe felt himself starting to smile. Not that he was happy, but it was so ridiculous that smiling seemed the only logical response.

"Like being bulletproof. Or picking up SUVs."

"Yes," Eli said.

"So you're a recruiter?" Gabe asked. "For Xavier University? You're looking for people to join the Super Friends? Wow… I can't even believe I'm saying this shit. Are you hearing this?"

"I am," Eli confirmed. "But Gabe… I'm going to be honest. I'm not a recruiter. There's a reason Jack thought I was going to kill you."

This was the kind of thing Sandy meant when she told Gabe not to be so trusting of strangers. Well, not exactly this. But the thing where they secretly intended to kill you, and you didn't realize it because they were smart and kind of funny sometimes and you liked them more than you should for no reason at all.

"Should I make a run for it?" Gabe asked. Eli smiled again.

"You can if you want to. I know this won't sound better, but if I had intended to kill you…."

"I'd be dead already?"

"Yeah."

"I know Jack," Gabe said. A new subject. Anything to talk about other than Eli killing him. As if that would put off his demise. "He used to come to the house when I was a kid. He was a friend of my father's. I didn't know his name."

"He would have known your father," Eli said. "Your father knew mine."

He stopped there and breathed in and out, slow and deep. Like this topic was hard for him.

"Hold it for five seconds," Gabe said, and Eli laughed. It was the first straight-up laugh Gabe had gotten out of the guy. He felt oddly proud.

"All right," Eli said. "My father was a kind of scientist… and a kind of… I hate the word magician, but it's not proper science. It's not. He figured out a process that would give people abilities, like you and your brother have. He thought he could make people who could do good things, like cleaning up oil spills or planting a thousand trees an hour. So he brought in partners who were willing to try the process on their kids."

Eli seemed both embarrassed and miserable to be saying that. Gabe sympathized. Embarrassed and miserable was how his own father had usually made him feel. With some terror thrown in.

"How did he know my father?"

"I don't know," Eli said. "There's a lot I don't know. I don't know who everyone was or where to find them. I don't know how my dad found them in the first place. If there were criteria… there must have been, but I don't know what they were."

"You're not a very good PI," Gabe said, "if you don't know all those things and it was your own dad running the operation."

Eli looked exasperated. "I'm not a PI. Of course I'm not. Are you being this way on purpose?"

"Yes."

"Great. So… my dad eventually felt like this had gone wrong. There were always things that went wrong. Like Jack. He was an early subject. My dad kept him on the payroll because…."

"What else was Jack going to do?"

"Exactly. Jack wasn't always this crazy, either. I don't remember him from before. He was already like that by the time I was born. But my dad did this to him when he was an adult. He volunteered. I read my dad's journals, and there's a different Jack in there. He was all about human potential."

"That's not necessarily great," Gabe said. "Like, you could have said the same thing about Hitler."

"I don't think Jack identifies with humans anymore. Your brother and whoever else is out there, that would be his family now. He's trying to protect them from what he thinks of as animals. Killing Tracy to keep Colin's secret? It would have been like shooting a bear that was charging his kids. And killing me is practically self-defence because he knows I'm coming for him."

"I don't think proactive self-defence is a thing," Gabe pointed out. "Except maybe in Florida."

"All things are possible in Florida," Eli said. "Anyway… my dad. He figured out he needed to start the work with kids so that their bodies would adjust instead of falling apart like Jack's did. I don't know how many other failures he had before he dialled it in. Those should be in his records, but they aren't."

"So there could be way more people like Jack out there?"

Eli shook his head. "I really don't know. But you and your brother were lucky. You got the system that worked. See, the process is a lot of work when the kids are small, and then you wait for them to pass puberty and there's a thing you can do… like a trigger. You set the powers off."

Like lightning, Gabe thought. Was it like lightning? Maybe what he'd thought, that he was somehow invulnerable and then lightning had hit him… maybe it made more sense to assume the lightning had been something else, and that was the moment this had begun.

"What are you thinking?" Eli asked. He sounded nervous, like he'd asked Gabe out and Gabe hadn't replied. Or some other scenario from Gabe's dream world of things that would never happen.

"About triggers and stuff, I guess," Gabe said. "I wasn't… I don't think I was like this until last night."

"You should never have been like this," Eli said. "One of my dad's rules was that there could only be one kid per family. I used to think it was in case something went wrong—so the people wouldn't lose all their children. But now I think… it was about power."

"What do you mean?"

"He didn't want too much power in one family," Eli said. "He was scared of what that might become."

A raven was calling from a nearby tree. Gabe wondered whether it had bothered to fly into the tree or had walked straight up it in that determined try-and-stop-me way ravens had. He wouldn't put anything past them.

"You said he thought it wasn't working out," Gabe said. "But wasn't it? Colin and I can… do things, I guess. And we don't look like Jack."

"It wasn't the powers," Eli said. "It was the people. The kids who got them. They didn't turn out to be the kind of people who'd plant trees or rescue manatees. They turned out…."

"Messed up?" Gabe offered. He could hear Colin over pizza years ago. *There is so much wrong with us.*

Eli shook his head. "My dad died a few years ago, and before he died, he told me I had to stop them. Because there was something badly off with all of them."

"Something wrong," Gabe said.

"Yeah. My dad used words like sociopath. Psychopath. But what I remember most is that he said the children had grown up to be cruel."

Sandy

IT WASN'T super smart to crawl out a window with a violin in one hand and two cops in the living room. Sandy knew that, but there she was anyway, lowering herself out the bathroom window onto the portico above the back door.

From the portico, on her stomach, legs dangling, it was a short drop to the ground. They'd all practised it the previous fall when Sean had decided they needed to up their fire safety game. He'd also brought home a fire extinguisher labelled Property of the University of Saskatchewan, and upon reflection, that was one more thing Sandy hoped the cops wouldn't see.

She kept low through the back yard, though no ground-floor rooms had windows on the back wall. Through the fence with the rusty gate, a squeak that got louder the quieter she was trying to be, and into the alley. Sandy didn't know how people skulked around in those new neighbourhoods where the yards were back-to-back. Maybe they went rooftop-to-rooftop, like Spider-Man.

"Colin?" It was more of a cough than a word. "Colin Anthony Reece. Are you around here? Have you been in my house?"

The neighbours' ash trees rustled in the wind, and Sandy stared at them like she thought Colin might leap to the ground from behind the leaves. They hadn't climbed trees together in years, not since they were fifteen and Colin had broken a branch on the tree behind her room. Too heavy for it, all that football muscle weighing him down. The next year he'd been old enough to work, and the football team had been discarded like it had never meant a thing.

"Goddamn it, Colin, why was this violin in my attic?"

She saw something move. A shadow along a fence line. Way too big to be a cat. It was heading for the park that connected to the west end of the alley. The hairs rose on the back of her neck, and she felt cold, despite the warmth of a sun that wouldn't even think about going down for six hours or more. Her voice was unsteady and too high as she said, "Colin?"

A mosquito landed on her arm, and she slapped it with her free hand. A second landed on the back of the hand she'd used to slap the first. So they were going to be like that, were they? She was tempted to start swinging on them with the violin, but she didn't think it would end well.

The only remedy was to get moving. She stayed low and went fast.

The west side of the park was usually jumping on warm days, all the families who couldn't escape to the lakes bringing their kids to the spray pool and the ancient playground. It still had the long metal rocking horse that Sandy had ridden as a kid, pressing her bare legs to the scalding sides and refusing to give it up to the big kids from the subsidized housing to the north.

The east side was different. Someone had planted pine and spruce a long time ago, and the trees made a tiny forest now, cool but mosquito-ridden and too full of needles—from trees and from meth heads—to be popular with parents and kids. The forest went up to the edge of the alley, and Sandy crossed into it quickly, holding the violin against her leg so it couldn't be seen from the road.

It was dim enough in the trees that her eyes needed a second to adjust. She saw shapes at first. Green and brown and grey. Drizzles of light between the branches. A shadow moved as her vision cleared, and Colin was standing in front of her.

"Jesus!"

"No, just me."

Colin was in his usual T-shirt and jeans, a wry little smile on his charming face. Sandy wanted to punch him square in the middle of it.

"What in the everloving fuck have you been up to, Colin Reece? And where the hell have you been?"

"Good to see you," Colin said. "Nice day. Bit of a warm one. You wanna try greeting me again?"

They stared at each other. To the west, kids were shrieking as they ran under cold water. They pumped that water straight from the river, and it was like ice every month but July.

"Your brother thinks you left because he's gay. You have ten seconds to tell me that isn't true."

That knocked the smartass smirk off Colin's face.

"What? You know that's not…. I know he's gay. We've talked about it. I don't care. Did he tell you he brought home some fucking creeper, though? That guy has forty in the rear-view. I guarantee it."

Sandy sighed. "Yeah, Gabe told me. He didn't say exactly that. But you know Gabe. He thinks this is all about him."

"His kind love their drama."

It took most of Sandy's willpower not to throw the violin at him.

"Do not make jokes like that around him right now. He doesn't think any of this is funny."

"I know," Colin said. "That's his problem right there."

"It is? And not his house burning down?"

Colin opened his mouth to say something—that it was a bummer, or he must have left the stove on, or that he didn't even know it had burned down. Sandy didn't have the patience. She held the violin in front of her like it was warding off a vampire. Colin closed his mouth.

"Yeah," Sandy said. "That's right. You want to explain what this was doing in my attic?"

"No."

Though Sandy hadn't been swimming, she had an urge to knock water out of her ears. She could not have heard him right.

"No?"

"No, and put the violin back where you found it. Don't say anything to Gabe about it until…. I'll let you know."

She let her arm, and the violin, fall back to her side.

"That's not good enough. Where have you been? Did you… was it you with the house? Your own house?"

"Well, it wasn't Gabe," Colin said. "Look, I only came to talk because it seemed like you were going to make some kind of a scene."

Sandy's eyes widened so far that it hurt.

"Am I… hysterical now? Am I overreacting? Like a damned woman or one of the gays?"

Colin sighed. If he did that one more time, he was having a violin for dinner, and Sandy would have to buy Gabe another one.

"I'm having a rare one, Sandy. You don't even know. And—" He held up a hand. "—you're not going to know. I want you and Gabe and the two stooges to stay out of this."

"Your whole house. Why the fuck would you do that?"

"Something from our past is catching up with us," Colin said. "Our dad's past. I'm dealing with it. I know the house thing seems a little drastic, but I have reasons."

"You have reasons. Do you even have insurance?"

"No. But it'll work out. Just… put the violin back, do not tell anyone you saw me, and go on with your life like normal. Let me deal with this situation. Please."

The kids in the playground, laughing and screaming, sounded like a Greek chorus to Colin's nonsense. Sandy rubbed her forehead.

"I don't normally have cops in my living room, you shitheel. They think you did something to that little punk with the spiky hair, from the casino. Owen something-or-other. Did you set him on fire too?"

"Tell the cops you haven't seen me," Colin said. "Say you don't know anything. This isn't that hard."

"I don't even know where your brother is," Sandy said. "He's gone off half-fucked, and he's not checking in. God knows what he's doing right now."

"He's an adult," Colin said, which marked the first time Sandy had heard Colin say such a thing. "He'll be fine."

Sandy raised her arms to the heavens, like Colin was an asshole orchestra she was trying to conduct.

"It was his. House. Too."

"Reeces land on their feet," Colin said, which was rich from a guy who'd buried half his family before he was out of his teens. "I have to go."

He stepped back into the shadows. She went after him, but he'd always been fast, and he knew his way around in the trees. He was gone.

CHAPTER SIX

Gabe

ELI GOT out of the car after that and found a new place to sit. They were next to a cow pasture, and a wooden fence lined the road, old-fashioned, with wide posts and logs between them. As good a bench as any in town.

"Colin punched a cow once," Gabe said out of nowhere. A memory of the last time he'd been in a cow field. Eli raised his eyebrows.

"He picks fights with livestock?"

He sounded as if this were kind of what he'd expected, but also a new one on him.

Gabe smiled. "No. It's not.... Colin's not like you think."

THEY'RE IN Colin's truck, some late July evening in the summer between grade eight and nine for Gabe—the jump from elementary school to high school. Colin's not in school anymore; he's nineteen and has a job. A real grown-up job that pays for things around the house since he's Gabe's guardian now. And Gabe thinks, Four more years. *He feels like a shit about being in school while Colin works, and he swears he's going to get a real job, not more of the under-the-table shit he scrounges up now, as soon as he gets out of high school. Even though Colin says he's going to university and that's that.*

Colin's taking a short cut to a bush party, bringing Gabe along because, okay, the kid'll be at a bush party, and that's not ideal, but at least Colin will be able to keep an eye on him. At least that's how Colin described it to Sandy on the phone.

They're bouncing across a field, taking it reasonably slow over the dips and bumps, when something scrapes the bottom of the truck and Colin decides to check it out right then and there. As if there's anything he can do at the moment even if he did fuck up the muffler or something. But the truck's his baby, so Gabe says nothing. He's not in a rush, anyway, to get to some party where Colin will be pulled in a dozen directions, each of them away from him, and he'll be the kid brother, watching. Not even allowed to have more than a couple of beers.

Gabe turns the radio to a pop station from Saskatoon. Nothing against classic rock, but he's already had enough for the night, and there'll surely be more at the party. And Colin might be too distracted to notice that Gabe has changed the station. For a while, anyway.

A cow wanders over to see what's going on, approaching on the driver's side. Gabe likes her for that, for being more curious than scared. He waves at her, and she steps closer.

"Incoming," he alerts Colin, who is kneeling beside the truck, trying to see beneath it.

He turns, then stands and smiles. "Nice cow," he offers and, since the cow is right beside him now, scratches between her eyes.

Colin gets back in the truck and starts to say that it must have been nothing, that scraping sound, when he notices the radio and glares at Gabe. Even Gabe has to admit the current song is annoying, a cotton-candy dance thing that he, as a gay boy, is supposed to like.

"Whose truck is it, Gabe?" Colin inquires. Gabe knows the right answer is, hey, man, it's your truck, and lemme change that station right back, but he can't say that because there's something approaching Colin's open door, and Gabe can't believe it. So he says nothing, and Colin is leaning over the radio, trying to change the station, when the cow tries to climb into Colin's side of the truck.

Colin shoves at the cow, and his arm brushes the radio, turning it up full blast, so now he's wrestling with a Holstein while Whigfield sings "Saturday Night" all the way to the back forty, and Gabe knows he should be helping—or at least turning the radio off—but he's laughing so hard he can do neither of those things.

The cow makes it nearly halfway into the cab before Colin gets in a good shot, an uppercut to the bottom of her snout, and she sniffs and backs away with what Gabe could swear are hurt feelings. Colin pulls the door shut, and they hightail it after that, muffler be damned. Colin shuts off the radio with a slap of his palm to the controls and thanks Gabe very much for all his help, and Gabe keeps laughing.

"Colin Reece," he sputters out as soon as he can talk. "Irresistible to women."

Colin tries to glare at him again, but he laughs instead. They laugh almost all the way to the party. Colin says, "Is it weird that I feel bad about the cow?" Then he says, "Tell no one about this, Gabe. I swear I will kill you."

So of course Gabe tells everyone in sight.

"HE'S NOT some monster," Gabe said. "He's not cruel. You don't know him. He felt bad for the cow."

"I don't know him," Eli said. "You may be right."

"But you came here to kill him," Gabe said softly. "Us."

"Gabe, I have never met one of these… subjects… who wasn't a mad dog. I don't know your brother. As for you…."

Gabe's stomach dropped, and cold sweat popped out on his back and hands. Even if he was bulletproof.

"I don't understand you," Eli finished.

Gabe coughed out a laugh. "Nobody does," he said. "I'm a freak. Freakier than I even thought, apparently."

Eli shook his head. "I mean, you're not like them. You worry about someone burning herself with a hot water bottle, or whether a dog is going to get fed. It upsets you that Tracy Howell died. That is not normal for someone… like you."

"Did it upset you?" Gabe asked. "Does it? That she died?"

"Of course," Eli said, and Gabe believed him. It wasn't on his face, that he was sad and sorry, but it was in his wide blue eyes.

"And are you like me?"

Eli didn't say anything.

"I said—"

"You're right next to me," Eli said. "Do you really think I didn't hear you?"

"Okay," Gabe shrugged. "So you're just rude."

Eli sighed. "Give me that pocketknife you got at the dollar store."

"It's a multi-tool," Gabe said. "The knives are probably for shit, but I don't like not having anything."

"Not having a weapon?" Eli asked.

"Not having a fucking screwdriver," Gabe told him. "Almost everything I own is constantly breaking down. I mean… it was. That's one problem I don't have anymore."

"You can get new things now," Eli said. "With the insurance."

"I love how you think we've got insurance on our home. Okay, here. Are you going to take the car apart at superspeed? Don't do that unless you know how to put it back together."

Eli took the tool and went through the three knife blades, feeling the edge on each. As Gabe had suspected, they might have been able to cut through cottage cheese. Still, Eli took the tool in one fist, with a blade pointed down at the back of his other hand, and took a breath.

Gabe was so convinced that no one would do what it seemed like Eli was going to do that he didn't reach out to stop Eli until it was too late and he had already slammed the blade about an inch into his hand.

Gabe yelped like it was his own hand, and Eli actually stopped to look at him, puzzled, before pulling the knife back—

"Don't do that!" Gabe said. "Leave it in there!"

Too late. It came out with a squishing noise, and Eli set it on the fence between them.

"Jesus Christ," Gabe said. "What the fuck—"

"Wait."

Before Gabe could ask what he was supposed to be waiting for, he saw it. The bleeding stopped first. A bruise appeared, then faded. Blood clotted, knit the wound together. Made a scar. The scar took the longest to go, and Gabe thought he could still see it after a few minutes had passed, but he could have been imagining that. It would definitely be gone within the hour.

"Holy shit."

"Uh-huh."

The cows were watching them now. They'd heard the yelling. Maybe smelled the blood. Gabe had no idea how well cows could smell.

"What would have happened if Jack had shot you?" Gabe asked.

"I don't know. I've never been shot before."

"Wild. You ever tempted to try it?"

Eli gave him a twist of a smile. "It does hurt, you know. I've tried a few things so that I know what to expect, but I'm in no hurry to get shot."

"I guess not. Well, anyway. You don't seem like a sociopath."

"I hope I'm not one," Eli said. "I don't want to be. But maybe I'm kidding myself."

"If I'm different, why can't you be?"

"You might be different," Eli said. "Or you might be very good at hiding your… ah… dark side. Better than anyone I have ever seen. What is so funny?"

Gabe left one hand on the fence for balance and put the other to his mouth to try to keep the giggles from spilling out.

"I'm sorry," he said, once he had some shred of control again. "I thought I was in the closet until last night. Apparently my closet has glass walls. I am the worst. I thought I was bad at keeping a secret, but I am the actual worst."

"You're not great," Eli said. "You're either very bad at hiding what you're feeling or you're one of the best actors on the planet."

"And that's why you haven't killed me," Gabe said.

Eli stared down at the fence. At his hands on the fence. Did he use his hands, kill people bare-handed somehow?

"Yes."

"How do you do it?" Gabe blurted out. "You say these people have all kinds of… I don't even know what powers…."

"It's random," Eli said. "Even my father didn't know what I would get."

"Okay, so they have, like, flying and throwing heavy shit and healing fast and whatever. How are you killing them?"

Eli looked at him reluctantly, his expression almost shy. "I can't tell you that."

Gabe's shoulders dropped. "In case I'm a really great actor."

"Or in case powers corrupt." Eli said. "You're new to this. You said you only got this way last night."

"Yeah. I sort of got hit by lightning."

"Lightning?"

"After my fight with Colin, I got on my motorcycle and left town. I was on the highway and… what I thought was that lightning must have hit me. It melted my bike to the road. I thought I was the luckiest guy in the world not to be dead."

Eli hesitated, then put a hand on Gabe's leg. Gabe told himself not to stare at the hand. Or at Eli. Or in general. Don't stare. Or blush. Or say something stupid.

Breathe and count to five.

"That must have been terrifying," Eli said gently. "Did it hurt?"

"For a few seconds. Then no." Gabe shrugged. "You know how it is."

For the second time that day, Eli laughed. "Welcome," he said, "to an awful club."

"But not your other club," Gabe said. "The one where you go around killing the evil superpeople. Do the rest of them do what you do? Do they have powers too? I'm seeing a lot of potential problems. Have you thought about this stuff or—"

"I'm not going to talk about them," Eli said. "I only tell my own secrets."

"But how do you recruit people? Are they the families of the people you're… hunting? Is that the right word? Did your dad start this club before he died?"

Eli mimed zipping his mouth shut, locking it, and throwing the key away.

"Be that way," Gabe said.

He slapped his hand against the fence, as hard as he could. He saw a faint light and heard the same violin-string hum he'd heard in the house, for a moment. And felt nothing but light pressure. What would happen if he tried to cut himself, or if he jumped off a building or got hit by a car?

He slapped it a few more times, playing with the light and sound. It got stronger the harder he hit things. Could he learn to control it?

Could he rescue people from a burning house? And what could Colin do, if he could lift something that heavy?

What could they do if they worked together?

"This situation is fucked-up," he said. "I get that, but… this thing I've got, whatever it is, could be kind of cool. I mean, don't you like healing up fast?"

"It's not free, Gabe," Eli said. "None of these… talents… are worth it. You'll find out."

"I don't know if you're thinking about this right," Gabe said. "I could help people. Colin and I could help people. You could too. Think about it."

"I help people," Eli said, "by doing what I do."

"You kill people," Gabe said softly. Eli met his eyes.

"There haven't been very many. But I understand that it's not normal to kill people. I understand that what I do would have to seem monstrous to you, given your circumstances. You don't know what kinds of things they do. And I don't want to be the one who tells you."

"Do you kill them because of things they've done? Or things you think they might do?"

"Things they've done," Eli said. "That's how I—it's how the organization finds them, usually. We're on message boards, looking for unexplained events. And we have some ads out there."

"Is that how you found Colin? Is there some Reddit board out there for mysterious flying SUVs?"

"No. It was a tip. Anonymous. We have a tip line. The caller said to go to North Battleford, Saskatchewan, and ask at the Red Tail Casino about Owen Bernier. At first I thought this was about Owen. Even when I started searching for Colin, it was so I could ask him where Owen might have gone. But then I met you, and there was that thing in the house where you shoved me. I couldn't see in the smoke, so I wasn't sure, but it felt like I got shoved by a wall, not by someone's hands. So then I figured this was about your brother. Or maybe you."

"Why wouldn't this tipster tell you to go get Colin if they already knew so much?"

"I don't know."

Gabe regarded the face less than a metre from his own and couldn't see a monster there. Though here the guy was, admitting to multiple homicides. Cold-blooded. And Gabe hadn't known any of the people Eli had killed, so how did he know what kind of people they'd been? Maybe they'd been like him, innocent—well, relatively innocent—and confused.

Except Eli hadn't killed him yet.

"I'm going to be an exception," he said.

"Good," Eli said firmly.

"So will my brother," Gabe added.

"I hope so," Eli said, and Gabe believed that he meant it. He simply wasn't very hopeful, was all.

"We'll find him," Gabe said, trying to ignore the twist in his stomach that said maybe he shouldn't lead Eli to Colin. Just in case he.... Just in case. "And you'll see."

"We'll find him," Eli agreed, "and I'll see."

Sandy

IT WAS harder getting back into her house than it had been going out. The back door was out of the question since the only hall leading away from it went straight to the living room. Sandy tucked the violin down her shirt, found the ladder with a busted rung that Colin had scavenged from a job site, and got herself onto the portico. From there, it was a struggle to get into the window, worse because she didn't want to make noise or crush the violin.

The whole production took so long that she'd barely gotten in and put the guitar and violin back in place when she heard Jerry calling from downstairs that the coast was clear.

"Down in a sec," she said.

Ceiling panel shut. Step ladder away. No sign that she'd been up there. Or outside, except for dirt from the portico that she brushed away.

"How'd it go?" she asked as she gave her hair a quick shake for pine needles and went down the stairs.

"They're looking for some guy called Owen Bernier," Jerry said. "They seem to think Colin killed him and threw his body into a swamp."

"That's an exaggeration," Sean said. "They're not sure the guy was dead before Colin threw him in the swamp."

"Have they actually found a body in a swamp, or are you being comical?"

"We're being comical," Sean said. "But, ehhh, the cops are talking like something bad happened to this guy. You gonna sit down and stay a while?"

Sean and Jerry were in the living room, sharing the cat-piss couch. That was more company than Sandy wanted on a good day, or on a cold day, and this was neither. She took the chair by the window.

"They asked me about that Owen guy too," she said. "Do you know him at all? If I've said ten words to him, four of them were 'get me a beer.'"

"Yeah, us too," Jerry said. "We've been at the casino with Colin more than you have, so we saw him more often, but there was no law saying we had to talk to him."

"So we didn't," Sean finished.

"If Colin gives a shit whether that guy lives or dies," Jerry said, "I haven't heard about it."

"Cool," Sandy said. "Is that how you put it to the cops?"

"No," Jerry said, at the same time as Sean said, "More or less."

"Awesome," Sandy said. "I hope you weren't so fun to talk to that they decide to do it more often."

"We were politely useless," Jerry assured her. "I suggested they talk to Colin's construction buddies."

"Better the cops than us," Sandy said. "I don't get how you can stand to go out with that crowd."

Jerry shrugged. "They buy rounds. The drunker I get, the less they annoy me."

"They're not that bad," Sean said.

Jerry met Sandy's eyes. "Sean thinks they're not that bad."

"Sean thinks Charles Manson wasn't that bad," Sandy said.

"Sean thinks Thanos was misunderstood," Jerry returned.

"Sean thinks Godzilla means well, but he's a little clumsy."

"Okay." Sean got up. "Sean thinks Sean needs a beer."

It didn't feel great, not telling them she'd seen Colin. She could have said something anytime: As Sean went to the kitchen. As he got beers for them all. As he and Jerry argued about what had happened to their pedestal fan and was it downstairs maybe and, if so, who was going to get it. Any of those moments she could have stopped everything and said, hey, funny story, I saw Colin in the park. And each of those moments passed without her saying a word.

What she'd do when Gabe finally turned up, she had absolutely no idea.

Gabe

GABE LIKED to think that, if he'd had time, he could have come up with a less embarrassing way of getting from his seat to the floor of the car. Less ungainly. It had been a spur of the moment thing, though, inspired by the sight of a cop car unsubtly tucked into an alley across from Sandy's house.

"Keep driving," he'd hissed, and Eli had done so without asking questions. He'd gone two blocks up, turned, and parked on a side street. Now Gabe was slowly extricating himself, dusting off his clothes as he slithered back up to the passenger seat.

"Sorry about that," Gabe said. "There were cops."

"I saw them," Eli said. "You think they're waiting for you?"

"Me or Colin," Gabe said. "Or both. Probably about the house."

"That seems likely," Eli said. "But it's possible the police are there for your friends. I don't know what your friends are like."

Gabe grinned. "They're behaving themselves right now. Sandy's on probation. She blew up her boyfriend's truck. Ex-boyfriend."

"You spent the whole drive here trying to convince me that we should tell Sandy everything and ask her what to do. Because she's sensible."

Gabe laughed. "I know how it sounds, man. She was crazy about that one thing. She's really good most of the time."

"If you say so," Eli said, with a straight face and without inflection. Regardless, Gabe swatted his arm.

"Shut up. Oh fuck. It's not just the house, is it? I went to talk to someone, and now she's dead. Jack called the police… they'll have found her… they'll talk to her co-workers, and the co-workers will talk about us…."

"I was planning to stay away from my hotel room," Eli admitted. "It didn't occur to me that the police might stake out your friend's house."

Gabe looked out the passenger window. It would be hours yet before they'd have anything like the cover of darkness. Even sitting here, blocks away from the cops, he felt uncomfortably obvious. This neighbourhood was low on garages, or even driveways, so people tended to view the curbs in front of their homes as their personal parking spaces. Even by parking on the street, they were going to attract stares.

"We could phone in a tip," Eli said, "saying you're somewhere else."

"They'd probably send a different cop to check that out," Gabe said. "It's whoever's close—hey!"

"Hey?" Eli said.

Gabe twisted in his seat to face Eli. "There are, like, five cops in this town. Okay, more than that, but there aren't a lot of them. If something happens close to here, that car watching her place will have to respond to it. Like, say, if someone tried to break into the school."

"Broke a few windows, you mean," Eli said. "From a distance? With rocks?"

"It would set off the alarm system," Gabe said.

"I like it," Eli said.

Gabe told himself not to beam with pride. That sort of thing was embarrassing.

"It's low-risk anyway," Gabe said, as casually as he could manage. "If it doesn't work, we can try something else."

"Agreed," Eli said. He turned the car off, and they left. It seemed they didn't have to discuss the details of the plan, that they'd be going to the school on foot and walking—quickly—to Sandy's house from there. It was understood.

"You're easy to get along with," Gabe said as they headed down a back alley. They were both scanning the ground for rocks small enough to carry and throw but large enough to break windows.

"You are the first person ever to have said that to me," Eli said. He sounded amused and... pleased? "Gabe... about your new abilities."

"Uh-huh?" Gabe stooped to grab a rock about the size of his fist. It was dull pink and dark grey, mottled. Polished and flat, it would have resembled the countertops he'd helped Colin install in rich people's homes two summers before.

"I know you want to tell your friends," Eli said. "And who you tell is your decision. But there are risks for them and for you."

Gabe grinned, turning his head to hide his face from Eli. "So I can't take out billboards?" he said, trying to sound disappointed. "No Facebook ads?"

"Give this at least a minute or two of serious thought," Eli advised.

"Okay, okay," Gabe said, tossing the pink rock up and catching it as he walked. "I get it. I don't want to wind up shot down by the army or locked in a secret government lab."

Eli was crouching beside a small ring of rocks that someone had placed around a steel garbage can. They'd written their address on the can in black marker, which wouldn't keep the neighbourhood ruffians from taking the can and using it as a beer tub.

"Anyone you tell, you need them to be able to keep a secret," Eli said as he eyed the rocks, head cocked. Hunting, it seemed, for the perfect one. Because you couldn't throw any old rock through a school window.

"Sandy gets the concept," Gabe said, more sharply than he had intended.

"Good," Eli said, plucking a rock and straightening. "But please don't tell her about me. You can tell her about my organization and my father. I guess you have to do that because she'll want to know why I'm in town. But don't tell her there's anything weird about me personally. I don't share that with strangers."

"You told me," Gabe pointed out, slowing a bit to let Eli catch up. "You don't know me."

"We're in the same stupid boat," Eli said. "You won't tell her?"

"I won't tell her," Gabe promised. "Also, it might be a moot point because she might shoot me on sight. I can think of about four reasons why she wouldn't be real happy with me right now."

"Good thing that's not a serious threat to you."

Gabe smiled. "Hey, as long as we're discussing things not to tell people. No matter how pissed at me Sandy is… if you tell her you're here to kill me and Colin, she will feed your nuts to squirrels. I don't think you want that, even if they do grow back."

"I'm not certain they would," Eli said, one corner of his mouth slightly raised.

"Then you shouldn't risk it," Gabe told him. "Tell her you're here to… assess the situation or something."

"You're advising me on how to hide the fact that I've threatened to kill you," Eli said. "So that your friend won't be angry with me."

It was ridiculous, Gabe knew. Even the magpies on the rusted-out car beside him seemed to be laughing at him.

"It was conditional," Gabe said weakly, then laughed and clapped a hand on Eli's shoulder. "Man, I really don't think you're gonna kill me. I'm sorry. I believe you're badass and everything. I just don't believe you'll do it. You know, in this case."

Eli eyed him. He wasn't laughing. He seemed troubled, his eyes somehow intensely focused on Gabe's and yet distant.

"I would really rather not," he said. He sounded as troubled as he looked and then some. Gabe moved closer, so their arms brushed as they walked.

"I promise I won't make you," he said.

Eli sighed. "Maybe you won't," he said.

Gabe put a hand on his back and left it there. He might have flushed a little when Eli didn't object.

"I won't," he said. "Come on. Let's get your mind off your troubles and vandalize a school."

Sandy

"…MIGHT HAVE hitchhiked to Saskatoon," Jerry was saying. Sandy was out of her chair and on her knees in front of the fan, which Sean had found in the basement and tried to plug in without a wipe-down. He'd rolled his eyes at her, as if she were ridiculous for not wanting a year's worth of basement dust shot into her face.

"I told you," she said as she ran a damp paper towel around the blades, "Gabe isn't going to run off. He wants to find his brother."

"And that's what I mean," Jerry said. "What if Gabe gets it in his head that he should be searching for Colin in Saskatoon? Or Edmonton? Or—"

Sandy couldn't remember Jerry ever stopping mid-sentence, not for anything. She turned to see what had brought that on as Sean said, "Speak of the devil."

He pointed out the window. Sandy got up and looked out front to see Gabriel Reece coming up the walk, seeming tired but unburned. A slim blond was behind Gabe, gazing at the front door with apprehension. So Gabe had not only spent the day failing to check in, but he'd dragged a stray to her house.

"No one say anything," she said to Sean and Jerry with a warning jab of her finger. She didn't know what she thought they'd say, but she was sure it would be stupid, and she didn't need something stupid scaring Gabe away.

She opened the front door and greeted Gabe with a "Hey."

"Hey," Gabe answered. He'd stopped at the bottom of the stoop like a dog who'd been told to stay. Waiting for permission to come to the door.

Sandy wanted to tear him a set of new ones for not calling, for leaving the Mediclinic without his tetanus shot, for getting on his bike the night before without a helmet or leathers, and for bringing some random person to her house. Gabe had made bad choices, and the responsible thing to do was to turn him into Swiss cheese so he wouldn't forget it.

She was at least as surprised as Gabe when, instead, she opened her arms and said, "C'mere."

Gabe's relief was obvious as he went in for the hug. Sandy could feel him keeping his eyes shut tight as he pressed his face against her shoulder. Still trying not to cry.

He smelled of some new soap and shampoo, and the clothes were new too. Never washed, by the feel of them. The tags he usually removed were still in the neck of his shirt. Why had he needed to change his clothes?

Sandy let go and put her hands on his shoulders while she looked him up and down.

"You seem intact," she said. "I was thinking you might be dead."

"I know," Gabe said. "I didn't call."

She sighed and dropped her hands.

"You're lucky the cops weren't out front when you got here. They must be on their dinner break."

"I heard some punks threw rocks through a school window a couple of blocks away," Gabe said. "Really shocking behaviour. They probably got called away for that."

Ah. Sandy hoped there weren't security cameras around that school. But if there were it would be the least of their problems anyway.

"Have you been home?" she asked.

Gabe's shoulders dropped, and there was something about his face, like he'd put on a couple of years since that morning.

"Yeah. I saw it. I don't… there's no insurance. I have about fifty bucks in the bank and a toothbrush and this backpack that Eli here was nice enough to get me. I am deeply screwed."

And a guitar and a violin, but Sandy wasn't going to say so, was she? Apparently she wasn't.

"You've got a bike," Sean said. "It's out front. And, ehh, you're gonna have pizza as soon as I go pick some up."

"That's a good idea," Sandy said. Gabe cast a glance at Jerry and back at her. She wasn't positive about his intent, but she took a guess that Gabe had been hoping to find her home alone. He'd always preferred unburdening himself one on one. "Hey, Jer, why don't you go with him? Maybe get some more beer while you're at it."

"I don't have Sean's supervisor on my business card," Jerry bitched, but he got up anyway and followed Sean out the door. They both had to edge past Gabe and the blond guy as they went, and each of them gave the blond guy a look. Somewhere between curious and hostile, with Sean leaning more toward curious and Jerry the other way. The blond guy gazed right back without aggression or fear.

Once Sean and Jerry were gone, Sandy ushered Gabe and his friend fully into the house and shut and locked the door behind them. Then she turned to the blond—Eli, Gabe had said—and offered him a hand.

"I'm Sandy Klaasen," she said. "Who the fuck are you?"

He smiled at that, so either he wasn't too uptight or he'd been warned about her.

"Eli Samm," he said.

"Well, Eli Samm, why don't you and Gabe have a seat in the living room, and I'll get you some ice water. You can have beer once you've hydrated."

Gabe gave Eli a look that Sandy knew well. I told you so. Exactly *what* he'd told Eli was a mystery.

She heard them finding seats while she got water from the fridge and tossed in the last few ice cubes. Then because she was an adult, she filled both that tray and the one that one of her infant roommates had put back empty and set them neatly in the rack. The goddamned simplest of adult chores, and her people couldn't even do that. It didn't give her optimism about the shit they were facing now.

She delivered water to Gabe in the window-side chair and Eli on the cat-piss couch. He was sitting all the way to one side, perched at the front of the cushion. Had Gabe warned him about that too? She turned the fan on as she crossed to take the remaining seat.

"What a day," she said, raising her ice water in a toast. Gabe raised his glass. Eli didn't. He was studying them like they were a card in that Eye Witness game her parents kept at the cabin. Like he was expecting a quiz about the details of the scene.

Since he was staring, Sandy stared back. The guy had an intelligent expression and a pleasant face under wavy light blond hair. His clothes were blandly nice, a white cotton shirt and olive chinos. Nothing to object to or take exception to. Nothing to pin a role on. He could have been an undercover cop or a bike courier or the second runner-up from *Canadian Idol*. He seemed to be twenty, twenty-one at most. It was a shame Colin wasn't there to see him since he felt so passionately about Gabe making friends his own age.

"Did you want to tell me where you found this guy?" Sandy asked Gabe.

"You're not going to like it."

Why did Gabe think it was helpful to front-load things like that?

"Go on," Sandy said.

"It was in the house. The house was on fire when I got back from the Mediclinic, and I went inside in case Colin was in there."

"You went into a burning building," Sandy said. Her tone must have tipped Gabe off to her opinion on that because he set his glass down and raised his hands.

"I know," he said. "I know. But obviously I'm fine."

She slammed a hand down on the arm of her chair.

"No thanks to you, Gabriel! First you get on that bike without a helmet and now this? Is it a death wish I'm seeing? Did you come by to borrow one of Sean's guns or some razor blades?"

"I thought Colin could be inside," Gabe repeated, as if that were all the answer anyone should need. And this was Gabe, so it was.

"I was coming up to the house, and I saw him go inside," Eli said, "so I went in to pull him out."

Sandy blinked in astonishment. It made her aching eyes feel better, so she did it a few more times.

"You went into the house after him."

"It was a bad fire," Eli said.

"That was a very brave thing to do for a stranger," Sandy said.

Gabe and Eli exchanged glances.

"Luckily," Eli said, "we're both okay."

Sandy sucked an ice cube into her mouth and cracked it. Gabe jumped a little at the sound.

"What were you doing at the house?" Sandy asked Eli. "Pouring out the last of a jerry can? Flicking a match?"

"Hey!" Gabe said, as if she had accused Smokey the Bear of lighting the place up. "It wasn't him!"

"You've played board games that lasted longer than you've known this guy," Sandy said. "Give your head a shake."

"She's right," Eli said. "I didn't do it, but technically I could have."

Sandy pointed a finger at him. "Nobody asked you."

"You kind of did," Eli said mildly. "You asked what I was doing at the house. I was looking for Colin Reece."

Sandy turned to Gabe.

"What?" Gabe said. "He was looking for Colin. I was looking for Colin. He had a car. I figured we could both go looking for Colin."

"Sweet blistering Christ. You met a stranger at the scene of a crime—a stranger who, for some reason, was trying to find your brother—and you got into a car with him because you thought it would be… convenient? Do I have that right?"

"Efficient is a better word," Gabe said.

Sandy grabbed the nearest loose item—one of Jerry's go mugs—and whipped it at him. Gabe ducked, and it hit the window.

"Good thing that was plastic," Eli said.

"We're not out of fucking go cups," Sandy warned him. "Are you a serial killer? Are you a very lazy serial killer who puts things off all day?"

"No."

She stared at Gabe. "You're lucky, aren't you? Because he could have been a fucking serial killer."

Gabe was spinning his water glass without looking at it, which seemed to Sandy like a good way to accidentally push it off the arm of the chair.

"Do you want to hear this?" he said. "I'll tell you who he is and what he's doing here if you stop throwing things and listen."

"I threw one thing."
"A cup and a tantrum," Gabe said.
"I have more cups," Sandy said again.
"Great," Gabe said. "Hold on to them until I'm done."

CHAPTER SEVEN

Gabe

HE TOLD her the lies first. What Eli had told him on the bridge, about being a private investigator. About Owen. About their trip to the casino. And about the clothes and everything Eli had bought for him, because he wanted Sandy to get a full picture of the day.

Apart from the few times she'd seemed like she was going to run from the house screaming, Sandy took it better—and more quietly—than Gabe had expected. Eli didn't say much either. A clarification here and there. Sandy had more or less called him an arsonist and a serial killer within ten minutes of meeting him, so Gabe could understand why he'd want to keep his head down.

"She told you Colin doesn't seal the deal," Sandy said, after Gabe repeated what Jordan had told him. "How the fuck would she know?"

"Tough to prove a negative," Gabe agreed. At Sandy's puzzled look, he added, "They only know Colin wasn't sleeping with *them*."

"Well, fucking exactly. I didn't know he was dicking Tracy around. That's too bad. She's all right. A little boring."

In a way, she'd become as boring as it was possible to be. Gabe felt himself about to laugh and pressed his lips together.

"Did I say something funny?" Sandy asked.

"No," Gabe said. "Actually it's very not funny. We went to see her and it was… bad."

"Do you want me to tell her?" Eli asked.

That sounded great, but it also sounded like passing the buck, and Gabe preferred not to do that. Not with something like this.

"No," he said. "I will."

He didn't know how else to do it, so he told her how it was. He left out thinking he'd seen Colin, and the deer hitting the car. From when they'd pulled in at the farm, though, Gabe told it straight. Sandy listened with some impatience to the business about the nice Reece and the hot water bottle. She stopped shifting in her seat and casting glances at the front door—where were Sean and Jerry, anyhow?—when Gabe started to describe the video.

When he finished, he wondered if he should describe it again, the way he and Eli had watched it three times over. Sandy wasn't giving anything away. She was staring at him, unmoving, her lips thin and straight.

Then, without warning, she leapt to her feet and went to Gabe, who automatically rose to meet her.

"You are *fucking* with me!"

"I'm not," Gabe said. "Do you think I would joke about something like thi—"

"You come in here with some bullshit story after the fucking day I've—"

If Sandy was going to yell over him, two could play that game.

"The fucking day *you've* had? Everything I own is—"

"—and dragging your brother into this—"

"—and throwing a fucking Yukon to the… to the fucking *Yukon*—"

"—Sean and Jerry in on this practical joke? You all think it's hilarious to fuck with me? I suppose Colin is in on it too—"

"—the old burning-my-house-down gag? It's a classic. You've been punked. You think I think this is funny? I got *shot* tonight! And Tracy *died*!"

Sandy froze in the sudden silence. She took a few backward steps to her chair and sat. Gabe did the same.

"She what?" she said, her voice barely above a whisper.

"I'll get to that," Gabe said. He could feel tears in his eyes, damn it. Not spilling yet, but ready to start at any moment. "I have to show you something first."

"What do you mean, you got shot?"

"I'm fine," Gabe said. "Get me a knife, okay? A good one."

He waited while Sandy got a knife—and a beer for herself, and no beer for him or for Eli. Eli was still keeping quiet at the end of the cat-piss couch. Gabe tried to see the scar on his hand and couldn't, but it was dim in the room with trees in the yard and the sun making its way to the side of the house. Or the scar could have been gone.

He took the knife from Sandy, by the handle like she'd taught him the first time they'd made ants on a log. He set it on the floor beside him.

"You remember how my dad used to do all kinds of weird stuff with Colin and me? Like he was doing experiments or something?"

"Yeah, I think I remember your house being the source of nearly all my childhood nightmares," Sandy said. "I vaguely recall that."

"Mine too," Gabe said. "So, uh, Eli here, his father did those experiments too. Actually he kind of invented them. There are other people who can do stuff like Colin can do."

He paused and waited, in case she wanted to start yelling again. Instead she took a pull on her beer. Ten seconds. Twenty. Gabe decided it was safe to go on.

"Eli's dad died a couple years ago, and before he died, he asked Eli to find everyone who'd been experimented on and see how they were doing. So Eli has a group that does that. That's why he came to the Battlefords. He'd heard about Colin. Kind of. He has to go looking for people because I guess his dad didn't keep records of where they were."

Sandy glared at Eli. Eli remained calm.

"You a YouTuber?" she asked him. "Videographer?"

Was that her theory now? That Eli was an intern for *Impractical Jokers*? Eli didn't rise to it. He said, "No."

Sandy waved a hand at him dismissively and turned back to Gabe.

"Okay. What do you need the knife for?"

"I'll show you," he said. "And then I'll tell you about Tracy. But you'll want to put down that beer."

Sandy

"THAT IS amazing," Sandy said. She was sitting on the coffee table in front of the couch and stabbing at Gabe's chest with the largest knife in the house. The largest kitchen knife, anyhow. Lord knew what Sean had stashed under his bed.

"You can stop now," Gabe said. Sandy continued staring at his chest, almost hypnotized by the flashes of light and the bursts of music. It might have been possible to play him like an instrument by hitting him in different places with different amounts of force. Like he was a better looking Muppaphone.

"I'm not sure I can," she admitted. "It's fascinating. Are you sure it doesn't hurt?"

"The knife's not going in," Gabe pointed out. It wasn't. It had taken Sandy a while to really grasp that Gabe wasn't being hurt, that he had a… force field or something. She'd worked her way up from flinching as Gabe unsuccessfully cut at himself to taking the knife and making a tentative swipe at his arm to, finally, lunging for his chest with all her strength.

"Unbelievable."

She thought about pulling the curtains. What if someone saw the flashing blue light? And then she'd twitted herself for that stupid thought. No one was going to see a flashing blue light and think it was the force field on an eighteen-year-old smartass. No one except the boogeyman.

Gabe had told her the whole story, about the boogeyman shooting Tracy for knowing too much. Trying to shoot Eli for the same reason, more or less. As Eli had put it, he was hunting for people with powers, and a lot of them didn't want to be found. So the boogeyman was hunting him. Maybe Gabe now too. And how delighted would he be if he realized Gabe had told the secret to her?

It was all terrible, from Tracy dying for no reason to someone shooting Gabe from a metre away. But somehow the thing that sat in her like a block of ice was knowing she hadn't been imagining things when she thought she'd seen a monster in her parents' garage.

The saving grace in it all was seeing Gabe and getting the whole picture. That if monsters were real, it meant that something like magic had to be real too.

"You could be… I don't know," Sandy said. "A fucking Avenger. And not a second-stringer like Ant-Man."

"I was thinking about that," Gabe said. "There's a lot of good someone could do if they could… I mean, I could walk into burning buildings and pull people out."

"I told you that was a bad idea."

Gabe was, apparently, surprised enough to hear from Eli that he stopped speaking and stared at Eli instead. Sandy set the knife down on the floor and did the same.

"You're not the first to have thought you could do some good," Eli said. "But you're drawing from a poisoned well."

"Power corrupts, blah, blah," Gabe said.

"You know what I think."

Obviously they'd talked about this, and maybe Eli had a point she wasn't seeing, but Sandy wasn't getting it. What was the harm in Gabe rescuing some people from burning buildings, if that was a thing he could do?

"I'm not clear on what you're doing here," she told Eli. "Did you come here to try to talk Gabe out of using his… powers, I guess? Sounds lame when you say it out loud."

Gabe gazed at Eli with open curiosity, as if he were dying to know what Eli might say next.

"I want to make sure these abilities are not being used by anyone," Eli said carefully. "I hope to talk Gabe out of using his."

"I kind of can't help it," Gabe pointed out. "I'm going to stub my toe sometimes. Probably more, now, since it won't hurt."

"Try to avoid situations where you'd have to deflect a bullet," Eli said. "Unless you're doing stupid things, it shouldn't be a problem."

"He does all the stupid things," Sandy said.

Eli smiled. "I've noticed."

Sandy found herself sharing a look with the guy, as if they'd both known Gabe for about a billion years and had been frustrated with him for at least that long.

Her phone made its little blipping noise to tell her she had a text, and she glanced at it. Sean, telling her they'd be late with the pizza. He wanted to stop by the Reece house first, sneak behind the fence and see if he and Jerry could save a few things.

kk, she sent back.

"…but come on," Gabe was saying. "You expect me to never get bumped or pushed or prodded?" Even as he said the last word, he coloured. "Never mind prodded."

"You think that could be an issue?" Sandy asked, eyes widening.

Seemingly desperate to change the subject, Gabe blurted out, "Did Dr. Lam tell you the needle broke when he tried to give me my tetanus shot? How am I going to get the flu shot this year? What if I ever needed surgery?"

"He told me the needle broke and you ran for the hills," Sandy said. "The receptionist had to dive for cover."

"You were a spectacle?" Eli said in a "let me get this straight" tone. Gabe treated him to a baleful glare.

"Oh, fuck me ragged for being scared," he said. "You want a spectacle? See what happens after Dr. Lam breaks off a few more needles. Now all he thinks is that he got a defective one."

"Fair enough," Eli sighed. "I forget that normal people will make up reasons for what they saw, no matter how weird it was."

"Normal people," Sandy said. "Like people who aren't in that group of yours."

"Yes."

"What is this group, exactly?" Sandy said. "Where are you based? Who funds you?"

"I really can't discuss that," Eli said. "I'm sorry."

Sandy leaned forward, hands on her knees. "I think you really can discuss it," she said. "Start now."

Eli showed no sign of concern.

"I meant that I won't discuss that," he said.

It was nearly as amazing as Gabe's… power, or whatever it was. Sandy wasn't used to people remaining unruffled when she tried to intimidate them. Maybe she hadn't done it hard enough.

"You're not Teflon Boy, here," she told him. "I bet you can get hurt."

"Don't threaten him," Gabe said, putting a hand on Sandy's arm, above the elbow. "Please."

Sandy stared at him.

"Why on earth not? Everything is going to hell. Colin is missing, you're a fucking one-man band with a light show, and this stranger swans into town claiming to know things and refusing to tell us half of them. You don't want to beat the information out of his smug face?"

"No," Gabe said, meeting her eyes. "I don't."

She couldn't think of a coherent response. All she could do was shake her head and mumble that sometimes she didn't think she would ever understand him. Which, for some baffling reason, made Gabe laugh his stupid ass off. It didn't matter, Sandy reminded herself. It didn't matter why Gabe was being an idiot. It only mattered that he was.

"Gabe," she said, reaching desperately for patience, "this guy sitting beside you? He is some stranger who blew into town… when?"

"This morning," Eli said.

"Blew into town this morning," Sandy said, "around the same time as your life got on a luge to hell, and he told you a pile of fucked-up shit about you and Colin and your dad. You need to ask yourself who the fuck he is and why you are trusting him. No offence, Eli."

"No," Eli said. "What you say is reasonable."

"Oh, stow it," Sandy said, feeling a billion times more patronized than she could stand. "I'm not interested in how reasonable you think I am."

Gabe met her eyes and, infuriatingly, shrugged. "I believe him."

"Did he tell you how he heard about Colin?"

"Anonymous tip," Gabe said. "They've got a tip line."

Sandy pinched the bridge of her nose, trying to chase away a headache that wanted to start right there.

"So who left the tip, Gabriel? Did you listen to the message? He must still have it. It's got to be someone we know, right? Since we know everyone in this one-dog town?"

Gabe was regarding her with deep respect. Sandy thought about taking a photo to save the moment.

"Eli?" Gabe said.

"The voice was disguised."

"For fuck's fuck," Sandy said. "Can you at least tell us what the message said?"

"That we would find something of interest," Eli said, "if we investigated the death of Owen Bernier in North Battleford, Saskatchewan."

"Death?" Gabe and Sandy said at once.

"The cops asked us about Owen too," Sandy said, realizing suddenly that she'd never said so to Gabe. "They came here for Colin, and I thought it was about the house, but it wasn't. It was about Owen. They never said he was dead."

Gabe turned to Eli. "You know he's dead? You've known this whole time? You told me he was missing."

"That's what the tip said," Eli said. "As soon as I started talking to people, I realized no one had found his body, so I said missing instead. He might be. The tip could be wrong."

"And Tracy," Sandy said. "She thought Colin killed Owen."

"Yes," Eli said. "She as much as said so."

"That's horseshit," she said. "It's sour grapes. Colin flirts, but he's not serious, and it pisses a lot of women off. So he's got this reputation for being cold, you know? An asshole. It's the same as how if a woman is good-looking and she doesn't put out, a lot of guys will say she's a bitch. Colin's not an asshole, and he's definitely not a murderer."

"Gabe is very attractive," Eli said. "And equally unattainable. But Tracy called him the 'nice Reece,' and the server at the casino seemed fond of him. Why does he have a better reputation than Colin does?"

"Gabe doesn't lead people on," Sandy said automatically, then wanted to go back in time and slap herself. "I didn't mean it like that. Colin's just—hey! Wait a minute—how did you know Gabe was unattainable?"

Gabe had vivid colour along his cheekbones and at least three emotions fighting it out on his face.

"I told him why I left the house last night," he said, then stink-eyed Eli. "Can you keep a better lid on the gay thing?"

"Of course," Eli said. "But you could also not be ashamed of it."

Sandy could see how Gabe had forgotten so easily that the man was a stranger, and a creepy one at that. He was likeable, but in a self-possessed, take-me-or-leave-me kind of way. A here's-my-unvarnished-opinion way. Like he wasn't out to hurt your feelings, but also he wouldn't bullshit you, and if he paid you a compliment, you'd done something to earn it.

It was a nearly ideal personality for a con man. Or a serial killer.

"It's not your choice," Gabe said, biting off the words.

Eli inclined his head toward Gabe. "That's true. I apologize. Again. For whatever that's worth."

Eli smiled, and Gabe smiled back. Oh hell.

Gabe liked the guy—*liked* him, liked him. Sweet Jesus. Sandy wanted to cry, or bang Gabe's head against the wall. Or cry while banging Gabe's head against the wall. Gabe thought this was a good time and place and fucking subject for a puppy-dog crush?

"You are an idiot," she hissed at him. He stared at her with confusion for a second, as an idiot would. Then his eyes widened. He stood, his knees bumping against hers, and grabbed Sandy's water glass as a pretext for going to the kitchen. He followed that by going upstairs to the washroom. She hoped, anyway. Gabe also knew how to let himself out the window.

"Did I miss something?" Eli asked. Sandy chewed on the inside of her cheek, keeping herself from saying anything too quickly.

"No," she said after a few moments' thought. "He's being Gabe."

"I'm not being secretive for fun," Eli said. Off Sandy's incredulous gawp, he added, "I'd like to tell you everything, but I don't really know you either. I've already said more than I should have. But I want to trust Gabe like he wants to trust me."

Sandy looked at the knife she'd dropped on the floor. Gabe hadn't grabbed that when he'd decided to clear away her mug. She should put it somewhere before someone who wasn't an Avenger stepped on it and hurt themselves.

"This is all crazy," she said. "You know that, right? I'm going with it, but I could be having a nightmare."

Eli smiled. "That sounds like a healthy way to think about things. Until you adjust."

"Okay," Sandy said, silently hoping that she would be able to wake up rather than adjust. "Assuming this is real… let's also assume there are freaks out there playing 'what does this button do' with people's genes. And they generate a guy who can fly. And you find out about it because someone calls your tip line. Because you're Superman Stoppers. Do you pay out like Crime Stoppers?"

"We don't generally get tips," Eli said. "Mostly we keep an eye on discussion boards. And the news."

"You watch the news," Sandy said. "For flying people."

"We know what we're looking for," Eli told her. "Go on."

He seemed so ordinary, sitting there and answering her questions.

"What do you do when you find these people?" she asked. "Like Gabe. Will you open a file called Gabe Reece and make some notes and move on?"

Eli glanced at the stairs when she said that. Checking that Gabe wasn't hanging around eavesdropping. Eli seemed sad and a little guilty, and the expression made Sandy's head hurt worse.

"What," she said distinctly, "do you do?"

"That depends," Eli said. "You seem to have some influence over Gabe."

Sandy narrowed her eyes. "What. Do. You. Do?"

Eli leaned forward and stared at her with enough intensity to make her uncomfortable. His voice was low and rough as he said, "Keep him out of trouble. His brother too, if you can. But that's a trickier proposition, isn't it?"

Sandy saw the knife from the corner of her eye, and it crossed her mind that maybe no one knew Eli was here. Not *exactly* here, in her house. Or what he'd found out. And what were the odds that he was as knife-proof as Gabe?

She didn't know what she would have done if her phone hadn't rung.

Gabe

GABE WAS halfway down the stairs when he heard Sandy's phone ring, and he quickened his pace so he wouldn't miss the conversation. Half of it anyway.

It turned out he wasn't missing anything because Sandy was sitting in the living room staring at her phone as if it had grown fangs. Even Eli seemed shaken.

"Get a grip, guys," Gabe said. He picked up Sandy's phone and brought it into the kitchen with him. He'd forgotten that he meant to get himself a beer.

"Hello?"

"Gabe?"

It was a relief to hear Sean's voice, not the voice of a cop or a disguised tipster or the little girl from *The Exorcist*.

"Yeah," Gabe told him. "I've got Sandy's phone."

"I'm at your house, and there's something you—"

The last sound was more of a grunt than a word. And then the phone clicked off.

Gabe dropped the phone onto the kitchen table.

"Hey!" Sandy protested. "Good money was paid for tha—"

"Something happened to Sean," Gabe said. "He said he was calling from my place and that something strange was going on, and then it sounded like he got hit or something, and the call was cut off."

Sandy and Eli were on their feet before Gabe had finished talking.

"Sean and Jerry went to your place to try to save some things," she said. "Sean texted me a few minutes ago."

Eli went to the front window and stood with his back to the wall, peering through the gap between the curtain and the glass.

"The cops are back," he said.

"Shit," Gabe said. "Sandy? Can you pull them away?"

"I could drive to the Sev," she said. "Or the bar. If I left in an ass-busting rush, I bet the cops would follow me. They'd think I was meeting you or Colin."

"We have a car two blocks from here," Eli told her. "Once the cops are gone, we can go to it."

"Okay. Shit. Gabe, when are you gonna get a fucking cell?"

"So you can bitch at me every time I turn it off for five minutes?" Gabe said. He grabbed Sandy's purse from the pile of shoes beside the door and tossed it to her. "Get going."

Eli was moving, going around Gabe to the hall table. He grabbed a pen and a flyer for a new pizza place.

"This is my cell number," he said, writing quickly. "Don't let the police find it on you."

He handed it to Sandy, and she smiled at him with seeming sincerity before folding the flyer and tucking it into the front pocket of her jeans.

"You boys should get away from the door."

They went to the kitchen. Gabe was certain his heart was pounding loudly enough that the cops could hear it from across the street. Eli put a hand on his shoulder, and Gabe shut his eyes, tried to pay attention to nothing but that.

The door opened. Closed. Locked. He could hear Sandy's car starting. It had a grinding sound to it that Gabe was almost certain wasn't right, but Sean kept insisting that it was fine, which either meant that it was fine or that he didn't think he could fix it and didn't want to tell Sandy she was going to need a new car. Because Sean was soft-hearted that way—and kind of a doofus sometimes.

And in some serious trouble because of Gabe.

"I fucking wish you could shoot me," Gabe muttered, opening his eyes and turning to Eli.

"That's not productive."

Eli went to the front window again, checked, and declared it clear.

"Let's go."

They took the alley to the car. Running, which in that neighbourhood would have made them seem like thieves.

"You drive," Eli said once they got there. He threw the keys to Gabe. "It'll be faster. Just—"

"Don't get pulled over," Gabe finished for him. He crossed to the driver's side, and they were off, circling wide to avoid the 7-Eleven where

Sandy had led the cops. As they waited at a red light, Gabe's leg bouncing with impatience, he said, "There's this thing called call display now. For your tip line."

Eli glared at him. "I checked the number out. It was a cell phone, registered to a state in Germany."

Gabe stared at him, forgetting his hurry for a moment. "Fucking Germany?"

"Yes," Eli said. "I called it. Someone answered the phone, but they said nothing. After thirty seconds, they hung up."

"And you didn't think…?" From the corner of his eye, Gabe saw the light change. He pulled forward, leaving some rubber for the road to remember him by. "You didn't think, hey, why the fuck would someone be calling about North Battleford, Saskatchewan, from fucking Germany?"

Eli was looking out the passenger side window. Anywhere but at Gabe.

"I didn't care," he said. "I was going to come here and kill whatever I found. What difference did it make how or why I got the information?" He looked at Gabe then. "Does that answer your question?"

Gabe kept his eyes on the road. "Yep."

At the next red light, Eli said, "It makes a difference now."

Gabe nodded. "I concur."

If the drive to his house from Sandy's had seemed like the blink of an eye that morning, it seemed interminable now. Gabe bit his lip, trying to redirect the energy that was telling him to go faster. He couldn't risk speeding, at least not more than was normal for this town.

"Whatever happened has already happened," Eli said. "It happened while you were on the phone. We're not going to stop it."

Gabe glanced at him. "Did you mean that to be soothing?" he asked.

"I'm saying it's not in your hands," Eli said gently. "No matter how fast you drive."

Gabe ducked around a Safari van, rusted green with tinted windows. How could any of those things still be on the road?

"Eli," he said as he pulled back into the right-hand lane, "no offence, but please don't try to reassure me anymore."

Eli's response was to put a hand on Gabe's arm. It was almost certainly another attempt at reassurance, but it was sort of working, so Gabe decided to let it go.

"See any cops?" Gabe asked as he turned onto his street. Eli was scanning the sides of the road carefully, leaning forward to see better.

"No. But they should be here."

Gabe huffed out a laugh. "Remember what I said about the Battlefords having, like, five cops? They would have had to choose between my house and Sandy's house."

"Even though they're after you and your brother for arson and murder," Eli said, shaking his head. "That must be frustrating for them."

"Two murders," Gabe corrected, then swallowed hard. He'd nearly thrown up with the words. When he'd woken up that morning, his only problem had been that Colin probably hated him.

As he neared the house, he saw a single figure standing on the lawn and sighed with relief. Sean was okay.

Then he got closer, and it wasn't Sean. It was Jerry, behind an opened fence panel. His shoulders were hunched, making him seem closer to Sean's height, and he was staring at something in his hand.

Gabe pulled up alongside the fence, next to Jerry. Jerry didn't look up.

"Jer?" he said as he and Eli left the car. Jer turned his head, his back still hunched. Everything was grainy in the late sun. Overexposed.

"Hey," Jerry breathed. Gabe could see now what Jerry was holding. An iPhone. Sean's, maybe, though Jerry had a matching one of his own.

"What happened here?" Gabe asked. He took a single step toward Jerry and then stopped, instinctively treating him like a deer that had wandered into someone's yard.

"I came to see if there was… anything left."

"Sandy told me," he said. "Thank you."

Jerry nodded and looked over his shoulder at where the house had been. Eli came around the side of the car and stopped at Gabe's side, shoulder to shoulder with him.

"Is that Sean's phone?" Gabe asked.

Jerry stared at his hand and blinked as if he were realizing for the first time what he was holding. "Yeah."

Gabe took another step closer. Eli moved with him.

"What happened to Sean?" Gabe asked.

Jerry shook his head. "I don't know."

Gabe took a deep breath. The air still reeked of smoke and chemicals. Things that had melted in the fire and things that had been used to put the fire out.

"He called Sandy."

Jerry nodded. "Yeah. I guess he did. I saw him talking to someone."

Okay, so Jerry had seen Sean on the phone. Gabe bit his lip again, trying to keep from speeding.

"I answered," Gabe said. "He tried to tell me something, but he got cut off."

"Oh," Jerry said. His eyes were wide, and it was strange to see them that way. Jerry usually kept his eyes half closed, as if there was nothing interesting enough to merit opening them all the way. "Oh, yeah."

"What happened, Jer?" Gabe repeated, taking one more step forward.

"I don't know," Jerry said. "Maybe aliens?"

Gabe stopped and blinked a few times. Aliens? Really? Like he needed aliens today after everything else? He felt a hand on his arm. Slight pressure suggesting that he stay quiet for a bit.

"What did you see?" Eli asked, his voice low and even. Jerry looked at him. The turn of Jerry's head was quick, birdlike.

"Nothing. Sean was here, talking on his phone. Then there was a blur and some noise like… wind. And then Sean was gone. Just… gone."

Now Eli took a deep breath. "If someone moved very, very quickly," Eli said, "would that have been like what you saw? A person moving fast?"

Going by the way Jerry was staring at Eli, Gabe might almost have thought that Eli had read Jerry's mind.

"Could've been," Jerry said. "Nobody can move that fast. But it was like that."

Suddenly he seemed embarrassed. Embarrassed and a little disoriented. It reminded Gabe of Colin when he was sleepwalking and Gabe said his name to wake him.

"Sorry," Jerry said. "That's… it's fucking stupid."

Gabe closed the distance to him and pulled him into a hug.

"Fucking stupid," he assured Jerry, "is the order of the day."

Sandy

THE COPS were gone. Sandy had watched them through the plate-glass windows of the 7-Eleven as they'd pulled up, realized she was simply getting coffee and a chocolate bar, and pulled away. Not coming in for their own coffee, it seemed.

She'd taken the long way to the Sev, in the interest of giving Gabe and Eli more time to get to Gabe's house. And she'd made a few detours for good measure. She'd dropped a pair of sunglasses into a friend's mailbox, as if she'd borrowed them and was giving them back. Checked the hours on a coffee shop she'd already known was closed. Dropped an empty envelope from her glovebox into a mailbox. It had almost been fun, knowing the cops would be getting excited every time she stopped and knowing there was nothing they could legally do to her no matter how bad she wound them up.

If she hadn't been so goddamned worried about Sean and Gabe and Colin and even Jerry, she might have had a good time.

She made her purchase, then went to the back of the store, where a recessed ATM created a semi-private space, and set her food on top of the machine. Then she took out the pizza flyer and gave Eli a call.

"Yes?"

It was funny, how familiar Eli's voice seemed already.

"It's Sandy," she said, in case her voice hadn't made an equal impression on him. "I've lost my tail. I mean, I didn't lose them, but they left."

"Then meet us," he said.

"Okay," she said. She wanted to ask about Sean, but she'd find out soon enough. "At the house?"

"No," Eli said. "We aren't staying. The neighbours have probably been told to call the police if they see anyone here. Name another place."

She thought a moment. North Battleford was too damned small. At any moment they might run across a cop who was on the lookout for them.

"My parents' cabin," she said finally. "Gabe knows where it is."

"We'll see you there," Eli said. Then, a bit awkwardly, he added, "Take care."

"Take care of my boys," she responded and hung up.

Her car had about a third of a tank left, and a nasty habit of bottoming out after it hit the one-quarter-tank mark. She'd bitched to Sean about it many times, and he'd shrugged and told her to keep it at least half full. Because she should anyway. Like everyone did all the shit they were supposed to do with their cars.

Eli would have said if Sean wasn't okay, right?

No. Probably not. Probably wouldn't have wanted to upset her.

Good thing she wasn't upset.

She filled the car with Sev gas and picked up some groceries, in case there was nothing at the cabin. Her folks usually stocked it over the Victoria Day weekend each year, but they were in the States for a few months, so she wasn't sure that had happened.

Anyway their absence was coming in handy now. She headed north, taking side streets wherever she could. Eventually she'd have to get on the main road toward Cochin, and there might well be Mounties on it, but all she could do about that was hope for the best.

Gabe

GABE DROVE again. Not that they were in a rush this time, but they'd agreed it would be simpler than him giving Eli directions. Especially once they got into the cabin country, with all the long driveways and the rutted roads that were little more than paths.

Jerry was in the back seat, so quiet that Gabe could hardly believe it was him. He still had Sean's cell phone in his hands, holding it the way someone might hold the leash from which his dog had escaped. Eli, in the passenger seat, was checking his own cell phone. Flipping through the call list from what Gabe could see in his occasional glances. Thinking about the origin, perhaps, of the mysterious tip-off call.

"My dad dumped me and Colin out here once," Gabe said, pointing with his chin at the forest to the left of the car. "I was six and Colin was twelve. Dad said the first one to get back to the house wouldn't have to do chores for a month."

"To the house?" Eli said. "Your house? From here?"

"Yeah," Gabe said. "We hitched after we found the road."

"You went home together?"

"Colin wasn't going to leave me out here," Gabe said. "He's not that kind of guy."

HE'S FIVE years old, and pine needles are pressing into the palms of his hands. He's sitting on the forest floor with his hands on the ground. His head is tilted back to regard Colin, standing over him. Colin is bigger and stronger than Gabe will ever be. Colin always laughs and says Gabe will grow up, Gabe will catch up, but Gabe doesn't think so.

"Get up," Colin says. He sounds angry. He doesn't try to help.

Gabe hates making Colin angry, but he can't get up. They've been walking for hours.

"I'm not carrying you," Colin tells him.

Their dad said whoever got out of the woods first could get off chores for a month. It's supposed to be a race. Colin shouldn't be here.

"You win," Gabe said. "You can win."

Colin looks really mad now, but he holds out his hand.

"I told you," Colin said. "Fuck our dad and fuck the chores. We'll get out of here together. Come on."

Colin swears a lot.

"I'm tired," Gabe says. He knows he sounds whiny. He's embarrassed, but he can't make his voice sound grown-up like he wants.

"No one cares," Colin says. "Gabe, no one is coming to get us. You can't sit around waiting for someone to help you. The only way out is to suck it up and do whatever you have to do. Or you'll die."

Colin doesn't say how he'll die. It could be a bear. How would it feel to be eaten by a bear?

Gabe lifts his hands and stares at the pine needles. Slowly he brushes them off. He traces his fingertips along the indentations in each palm. Then he reaches up and takes Colin's hand. Colin pulls him up, hard enough that his arm hurts. Gabe doesn't say anything. No one cares.

Colin puts an arm around his shoulders and pulls him in so he's leaning against Colin's side.

"You remember that animal show," Colin says, "about the birds and the chicks and how the weak ones die?"

Gabe nods.

"You can't be weak," Colin tells him. "Be the weird fucking goofball you are. You don't have to be like me. But toughen up, because I can't do it for you."

Gabe thinks about that.

"The sun sets in the west," he said. He read it in Chickadee. *He reads it at the library every month.*

"So that way's east?" Colin said. "We'll get to the road if we go that way long enough."

"You're supposed to leave me," Gabe said. "Dad'll be pissed."

"You're supposed to hit me over the head with a rock and crawl inside me for warmth. Like in Star Wars.*"*

Gabe hates that scene, always looks away when it's on. Colin squeezes his shoulders.

"He'll be pissed at both of us," Colin says, and Gabe wants to say, "Why go home, then?" The road goes both ways, right? It goes north, all the way to Meadow Lake and maybe all the way to the Arctic. They can live with a pack of wolves.

But Colin never wants to leave, and Gabe has stopped asking.

"It's getting dark," he says instead, and Colin nods.

"So let's go."

"I DON'T UNDERSTAND why Colin never wanted to leave home," Eli said. Gabe shrugged, and Eli added, "You didn't. Leave, I mean. You probably wanted to."

Eli glanced worriedly at the back seat. Gabe could have told him not to be concerned. He'd been checking Jerry with the rear-view mirror and had seen no sign that Jerry was listening to anything outside his own head.

"There's no reason to test the subjects," Eli said. "You give them the shots and do some procedures, and then you wait. What your dad was doing… it was pointless. It was just abuse. I know people stay for abuse, for all kinds of reasons, but I don't understand."

"Colin stayed partly because I was there," Gabe said, and it was amazing how guilty that still made him feel. As if it had been his idea to tie Colin down. "And there was our mom. She wasn't real participatory, but she was still our mom. We weren't gonna leave her with him."

"And, I assume," Eli said, "you loved your father."

"Colin did," Gabe said. He was close behind a camper now. He dropped back for a better read on the oncoming traffic. Not being in a hurry was fine, but there was no way he was driving behind a fifth-wheeler all the way to the cabin.

"You didn't?" Eli asked.

Gabe shrugged. "Maybe? I felt strange when he died. But Colin was like a dad for me. So I didn't need my real dad that much."

"I'm sorry," Eli said.

Gabe stared at him for long enough that he nearly ran right up the ass of the Triple E trundling along before him. "Shit!"

"Sorry about that too," Eli added.

"Why do you keep saying you're sorry to me?" Gabe asked. "About my dad, I mean. I can't be the saddest case you've ever heard of. At least I had Colin."

"I'm sorry you have to deal with any of this," Eli said. "It would have been nice if you could have just… gone to school. Or whatever you were planning to do. Maybe you still can, but you've got a hell of a mess to clean up first, and that's not fair."

Gabe set his jaw and cut into an opening in traffic that seemed long enough. Eli's rental car didn't move the way Gabe's bike did, but it got the job done.

"Fucking RVers," he said as he slipped back into his lane. "Gas hogs. And all these people are, like, a million years old, so what do they care what they do to the planet?"

Eli pulled a cable from his pocket and plugged his phone into the car's cigarette lighter to charge. Gabe didn't think he'd be able to remember to do that if he had a phone to charge. It would be dead all the time, and Sandy would be perpetually annoyed that she couldn't get hold of him.

The lake appeared through the trees on their left. It was brilliant with the sunset, or the lying low of the sun anyway. Pink and orange sky, and diamonds glinting off the water everywhere. The lake was silky smooth, and Gabe could imagine how soft the water would feel. It always seemed like his true bed, his right and proper home. He'd heard someone say on some science podcast that life was only able to leave the oceans by taking it along—packing a tiny salty ocean into every cell.

"It's nice country up here," Eli said inadequately. "Once you get out of town."

"Yeah," Gabe said. "I'm becoming a big fan of getting out of town. I guess, depending on how this situation goes, I might have to."

"We'll see," Eli said. Gabe found that infuriating from most people. That phrase—we'll see—which always seemed to mean "Shut up. I don't want to talk about this, Gabe. It's not important."

But Eli said it more like "I'll see what I can manage." And there was something reassuring about that. In that phrase, the way it came from Eli's mouth, he got the reassuring thing right.

Sandy

THE BOYS were waiting on the front porch when she pulled into the cabin's driveway, between the two tall pines and over the roots of whatever had once stood beside them. Well, not the boys. That would have been Gabe and Jerry and Sean and Colin, not half that group plus some weird blond guy from out of town. But two of her boys were there anyway, sitting at the tilted picnic table under the yellow bug light one of them had apparently thought to plug in.

She saw the porch differently for a moment. The gang around it, her parents in bed, and fucking Fitzie off at some goddamned podunk rodeo to see his asshole buddy rope calves. Jerry smoking—he still had, last August—and the campfire making them all gag every time the wind blew toward the cabin, because….

"GODDAMN IT, Sean, the next time you claim to be a fucking woodsman, I will beat you with a tree limb."

Colin says it with conviction, but Sean laughs anyway. Even though his eyes are redder than any of theirs.

"Sixty percent of the time," he says, "it works every time."

"Scuh-rew you," Jerry coughs out. "Scuh-huh-huh-rew you."

Sean swore to them that the moss he'd gathered from tree limbs behind the cabin would drive mosquitoes away. Throw some on the fire and the bugs disappeared. Like magic. Guaranteed. He was puffed up with pride over his woodsy know-how, so Sandy can't blame the guys for threatening him now that they're all choking on thick, foul smoke while slapping as many mosquitoes as before.

"Did Cyrus tell you about the moss?" Gabe asks sweetly. Sandy hides a smile behind her hand. Cy is one of Sean's co-workers, and he's Cree, so Sean figures the guy must have a direct line to Mother Nature. Which means, of course, that Cy has been trotting out worse and worse bullshit for months,

wondering what it will take for Sean to catch on. He has the wonder and joy of Christmas morning in his eyes every time Sean swallows another one.

Sworn to silence, Sandy says nothing.

"I hate to tell you this," Gabe continues, "because it's pretty funny and I've been enjoying it, but Cyrus fucks with you. Like, constantly."

Sean turns to Colin. Colin smiles sadly and puts a hand on Sean's shoulder.

"Sorry, man."

"Cy's hilarious," Gabe says.

"Hell of a poker face," Colin puts in.

"And you may be," Jerry finishes, "the actual last person in town to know that."

"Cy never told me about the moss," Sean protests, cheeks burning. "I read it. Somewhere."

"Think of it this way," Colin says, pausing to cough. "He got all of us this time."

"How about you shut up and deal?" Sean asks, and Colin takes his advice, dealing out the next hand of Wizard. They open another round of beers to go with it and pass a dwindling bag of Oreos. Sandy twirls her finger into a burn mark on the table, left the summer before when someone knocked over a mosquito coil and didn't notice. She is, for the moment, perfectly okay.

"WHERE'S SEAN?" she asked as she climbed the broad steps to the porch.

"We can talk about that inside," Eli said, and Sandy nearly threw up her coffee and chocolate bar right there. She'd still half thought someone would say he was in the outhouse, or that he'd gone down to the lake. But something had happened, it seemed. Something they'd have to talk about inside. Something that wrong.

"Okay," she said, moving swiftly to the door and flipping through her keys to the one with the orange plastic ring around the end. Her father always did that, put plastic on keys. After all, who could tell them apart any other way? Bless that far-sighted man. Sandy wished he were here now to tell her what the fuck she should do.

The screen door was loose on its hinges, and the inside door needed a good shove. Stepping inside, Sandy wrinkled her nose as the pent-up air hit her face, then put her back to the door to make room for the others to pass.

"Jesus!" Gabe said as he stepped onto the doormat and automatically wiped his shoes. "This place smells—"

"—like it's been shut since December?" Sandy asked.

"I was gonna stop at 'smells,'" Gabe said, grinning. Sandy swatted him across the head.

"It's not my parents' actual job to clean the place just so you can be an ungrateful bitch all summer."

"Hey," Gabe said, raising his hands. "What do we do now?"

"Open windows," Sandy said, putting a hand on his back and giving him a shove. She flicked on the living room light and was pleased to see the bulb hadn't burned out.

"Sorry about the smell," she said to Eli as she ushered Jerry and Eli past her into the living room. "It gets musty."

"It's not important," Eli said.

Sandy smiled and handed him a broom from beside the door. "Then it's no big deal if you have to sweep out the cobwebs, right?"

To her surprise, Eli gave her a warm smile in return.

"It's no big deal," he agreed and went to do as directed.

Sandy turned to Jerry. "Jer? How're you doing?"

He looked terrible, distracted and pale with worry. None of that made her stomach feel better. She put a hand on his shoulder, and he gazed at her without, she thought, really seeing her.

"What?"

Maybe a chore would help. Something simple. She pointed to the white plastic bucket under the washstand in the kitchen.

"You remember where the pump is, right?"

Jerry nodded but didn't move.

Sandy got the bucket and placed it in his hand. "Go fill this, okay?"

She thought for a moment that he might keep on standing there, bucket in hand, until his legs gave out. But then he moved, turning slowly and going back out the door. She watched him until he reached the road, making sure he went toward the lake. The pump was only a few hundred metres down. He'd been to the pump a thousand times. He'd be okay.

"No running water?" Eli asked. Sandy stepped inside and pulled the screen door shut behind her.

"This is a cabin," she said. "Not a fucking cot-tage."

From one of the bedrooms, she heard Gabe snicker.

"My mistake," Eli said mildly. He was sweeping carefully, getting every last strand of cobweb and every dried pine needle. Sandy wanted to tell him again that this wasn't a cottage, that a half-ass job was probably a quarter-ass too much. What the hell, though. The place needed a good cleaning.

She'd sic him on the outhouse next.

"So," Sandy said as she opened the kitchen window and drew a JCloth along the sash, "who wants to tell me what the fuck happened to Sean?"

Gabe

GABE TOLD her what the fuck had happened to Sean, in as much as he understood it. He could have let Eli talk—would have preferred to really—but he knew it was important for Sandy to hear this from a friend. Even if Gabe wasn't certain what "this" was.

"So let me get this straight," Sandy said. She had paused in the middle of the living room with her arms full of grey wool blankets. They smelled even worse than the cabin as a whole, and Gabe hoped she meant to shake them out on the porch before making the beds. If she didn't, he'd do it. "Sean and Jerry were at your house sifting for unburned objects. Sean called to tell us something, and then…."

"A blur," Gabe repeated. "A noise like wind. And Sean disappeared. That's how Jerry described it."

Sandy nodded sharply, then marched outside. Through the dusty front window, Gabe could see her hanging the blankets on the clotheslines strung around the outside of the porch. Good. Half an hour outside would make a world of difference. He hoped anyway.

"So he didn't actually say that he saw anyone in particular swoop in like fucking Superman," Sandy said upon her return. "Though you're both looking at me like you think it was Colin."

"No," Eli said from the second bedroom, where he had taken himself and his broom. "He didn't even say it was a person. I asked if it was something like a person moving quickly, and he said it could have been. Which was strange. Most people would reject a suggestion that bizarre."

"Jerry's not in a reacting mood," Gabe reminded Eli.

"True," Eli allowed. "Anyway, there's no need to mention anything about powers to Jerry."

"I don't know," Gabe said. "Not that I love having share sessions with Jerry, but the guy's in this with the rest of us. And he saw whatever happened to Sean, so what's the point in being coy with him?"

Sandy sat on a short bookshelf along the cabin's east wall. On either side of her legs, Gabe could see the same jumble of half-missing board games and torn paperbacks that he'd picked through as a child when rain had driven them all from the water. Time stood still at the lake.

"Coy," Sandy said. "Thanks, Jane Austen."

"You need to learn this," Eli said, fixing Gabe with a gaze that was annoyed at best. "Only tell people what they need to know. I don't want to sound melodramatic, but it's better for him if he knows nothing."

"Phew," Gabe said. "Close one on the melodrama. You barely avoided it."

"Could you be some completely different way?" Eli said. A snort from the bookshelves drew Gabe's eyes to Sandy.

"I know, but he's right," she told Eli. "Jerry and Colin have been friends since they were kids. Jer has as much right as anyone to know what's going on."

"Not that we know what's going on," Gabe put in.

"Well, as much as we do know," Sandy said.

"There's an exponential increase in danger with each person you tell," Eli said, as if he were quoting a well-known mathematical fact.

"I would think you'd be happy," Sandy said, "to have more minds on this problem. Oh, wait, I forgot—you have a whole organization. What fucking golden nuggets of advice do they have for us?"

"I'm the one on the ground," Eli said. He seemed uncomfortable, as he generally did when they asked about the group. "It's my job to investigate. Until I do that, my organization has nothing to work with."

He'd said it with such conviction that Gabe forgot, for a moment, that the purpose of Eli's investigation had been to find the superpowered person and destroy them. Not exactly a case worthy of Hercule Poirot.

"Jerry's gonna be back any second," Gabe said. "We're going to be talking about this in front of him, so—"

"So we stop talking about it," Eli said, as if the matter were already decided.

"Don't be ridiculous," Sandy ordered at the same moment that Gabe said, "Come off it, man."

Gabe looked at Sandy in the ensuing silence and found her staring at him. He shrugged and returned his attention to Eli.

"We have to talk about this," Gabe said. "We're missing two people and have no plan for how we're going to find them. We don't know that Sean is with Colin. He could be in real trouble. This is not the kind of shit you can sleep on and hope it'll all be better in the morning."

"No," Eli agreed, drawing the word out. "That's true. But there are—"

He didn't say what there were because steps on the porch make them all look out the window. Jerry was back, carrying the bucket with both hands on the thin steel handle. He dropped the bucket on the porch, sloshing about a cup of water to either side as he did so, and grabbed one of the blankets from the line. Then, without so much as glancing at any of them, he marched into the house with his blanket and went straight for the big bedroom in the back. The one with the double bed that Sandy's parents always claimed.

"Jer?" Gabe said.

Jerry's response was to slam the bedroom door behind him. Sandy raised her eyebrows, then went to the porch for the bucket. Eli carried the broom to its place by the door and left it there.

"Problem solved," Gabe said. "Right?"

"I guess," Eli said. Sandy opened the door and handed the bucket to Eli.

"Put this under the washstand in the kitchen, would ya?"

Eli nodded and did so. Either he was determined to be helpful, or he'd figured out that shutting up and obeying orders was one of the quicker routes to Sandy's heart.

Gabe took a seat on the couch and watched as Sandy tossed logs and kindling into the firepit a few metres from the porch. She never built twee little pyramids when she was making a fire. She threw everything together, squirted a bottle of lighter fluid on the mess, and tossed in a match or ten. In retrospect, they shouldn't have been so surprised when she'd lit up her boyfriend's truck.

"Good lord," Eli said. He'd arrived back in the living room in time for the woof and flash of the fire starting. "What did she start that with? Gasoline?"

"She would in a pinch," Gabe said. "But there was some lighter fluid under the porch. Which seems like a shitty place to keep it, actually."

Gabe watched the fire, the new flame reaching eagerly for the almost-dark sky. It seemed like a different thing from the fire that had consumed his home. That one had been rough and menacing. This one was like a lithe cat after a string.

"So," Gabe said to Eli. "Shall we…?"

"Sit around the fire with a pyromaniac?" Eli said. "Sounds great."

CHAPTER EIGHT

Sandy

GABE AND Eli had brought the blankets inside rather than leave them out to catch smoke. That was 100 percent more foresight than Sandy had at the moment, and had she been feeling jaunty, she would have saluted them for it. Clever boys. Both of them.

Whatever reservations she might have about Eli—that he'd come out of nowhere, for example, with a fishy story on the day everything went to shit. Oh, or that he was clearly hiding something. But whatever reservations she might have, she had to admit he seemed bright. Maybe as bright as Gabe, who, despite being ten kinds of idiot, was the smartest person Sandy had ever met.

"There's pop and chips in my car," she informed the clever boys when they joined her around the campfire and sat on rickety lawn chairs with missing slats. There were better chairs locked in the shed. These were the spares her parents left outside on the assumption that no one would steal orange and green cross-woven chairs from the late 1970s. So far that assumption had been correct.

Sandy had briefly considered going to the shed for the good chairs before remembering that she didn't give a shit.

"Not hungry," Gabe said wearily. He wiggled his chair around a bit to grind it into the sand surrounding the firepit. It was the only way, on the uneven ground, to keep the chairs from rocking.

"Well, the food's there if you want it," Sandy said. "I got some other things too. I'll leave it in the kitchen before I go."

"Go?" Gabe asked, tilting his head. His face was all angles in the firelight.

"I have a job," Sandy reminded him. "I'm on the weekend schedule. Even if—" She swallowed past the lump and pushed on. "—even if Sean's not there tomorrow, I have to be. And I'll have to tell them… I don't fucking know. That he went out and never came home, I guess."

"Keep it as simple as possible," Eli advised. "And stick to that."

Of course this guy would have advice on how to lie.

Sandy rubbed a flake of ash from the tip of her nose and nodded. "Jerry's on weekends right now too, but I'll call him in sick. You can let him sleep in."

"So we'll wake him around suppertime," Gabe said, and Sandy smiled a little in spite of everything. Jerry loved his sleep.

"If he's not up by noon," she said, "give him a kick in the ass. Tell him it's from me."

Gabe smiled and held his hands out to the fire. Then his smile died, and he pulled his hands back. Was it that he couldn't feel the warmth, being the way he was now? Sandy wanted to ask, but it seemed rude somehow.

"I guess… should I report Sean missing to the police?" Sandy asked instead.

"You should report him missing," Eli said. "Wait until morning. Then say you're concerned because… oh, you could say it's because this isn't like him."

Gabe was kneading the arms of his chair, and one of his knees was bouncing. Too much energy. Gabe got that way when he'd been sitting for too much of the day.

"Do you want to go for a walk or something?" she asked.

Gabe seemed startled by the question. "No. Why?"

"You seem antsy," Sandy said, pointing to his leg.

Gabe watched the bouncing for a few seconds, then grinned at her. "I didn't even know I was doing that. Uh… I'm gonna go to the lake for a bit. If that's okay."

"Sure. Let me grab my windbreaker," Sandy said.

Gabe shook his head. "No—I need some time. A few minutes, anyway."

Eli was eying Gabe speculatively, saying nothing. Sandy wanted to swat him. He was Mr. Practical. He ought to be saying no.

"Don't be an idiot," she said when it became clear Eli wasn't going to. "Oh gee, two people are missing, so let's split up? You moron."

"Sandy," Gabe said, "as heartwarming as your concern is, what do you think is going to happen to me? If someone grabs me hard enough, they go flying. I can't get shot. I can't get stabbed. I think I can manage a few minutes at the lake by myself."

Before she could respond, Gabe sat up straight in his chair, alarm on his face. “Unless you’re worried about me leaving you guys alone here. Are you?”

Sandy hadn’t even considered that. Should she be afraid to be alone? It was a disgusting idea.

“No,” she said firmly.

Eli was smiling at Gabe, all smug reassurance. “No need.”

Oh, for the love of fuck. Did he have superpowers too? It should have occurred to her before now. Why wouldn’t he, if his own father had invented the supersoldier serum, or whatever the fuck it was?

Hell, maybe everyone she knew had powers and they’d all been keeping it from her. Laughing about it behind her back. Levitating and spitting fire or whatever when she went to the washroom at sleepovers. Quick, everyone, stop violating the laws of nature. Sandy’s coming back.

“If you’re sure,” Gabe said, to Eli and not to her. She wanted to smack both of them then, and it occurred to her that she could have saved herself the bother of starting a fire. She could have just slapped Gabe over and over until the sky glowed blue.

Ah, but it was never a bother to start a fire.

“Enjoy your nature walk,” she told Gabe. “Don’t stay out too late.”

Gabe

THE ROAD to the lake sloped steeply down from the subdivision where Sandy’s folks had their cabin. When they’d been kids, Colin and Sandy and Jerry had dared each other to ride their bikes the whole way, not pedalling or braking. Gabe had followed them, feet off the pedals so he couldn’t chicken out and use his coaster brakes. His plastic training wheels had bounced wildly on the washboard road.

It was much slower to walk the road, but it still took no more than a couple of minutes. He kept to the side of the road where the trees draped shadows over him.

Beyond the cabins and next to a woodlot, he passed the sturdy green-handled pump and smiled at the familiar sight. Jerry had gotten that shit job for once. Gabe hated wiggling the pump’s handle, trying to make it vomit ground water into the wash bucket. He’d never understood why they couldn't draw water from the lake instead. The place, he joked to Sandy every year, was too damned civilized.

It wasn't, though, in the sense that it was still possible to be there and be alone. Gabe followed the road to a gap in the trees and went through it to see the lake, dark beaches empty. Quiet and perfect, only the lake and him, with small waves pushing sand back and forth as if they were redecorating and couldn't decide where it should go.

He walked straight to the lake the way he'd walk up to Colin or Sandy, with confidence that he was going somewhere he belonged. The water spilled onto his runners and wet them, but he didn't feel it soaking through. Not the cold or the damp. He glanced over his shoulder, checking again that no one was anywhere near. There were campsites further up the beach and set back into the trees, but they were far enough away that their sound and light barely reached him. The concession was closed and dark, the playground still.

As quickly as he could manage, Gabe got out of his clothes and into the water.

It felt, to his relief, soft and soothing. He was rocked by the slight push and pull of the waves. He'd been afraid he wouldn't feel any of it, but instead he seemed only to be missing the cold and the… wetness. When he raised his hand from the water, droplets raced away and left it dry.

He was lucky, he realized, that he could still eat. Surgery would be a problem, as he'd noted before. He was fucked if he got diabetes or something. But he could still eat. What if this… field, or whatever it was, had blocked his mouth? It seemed designed to protect him, but what if it had noticed a hint of pesticide on his food and slammed the gates shut? What if his lungs had refused to breathe imperfect air? The thought made his stomach twist for about the hundredth time that day.

He breathed deeply and gratefully as he lay on his back and gazed at the stars. They were brighter here than in the small city he'd left behind. Out of place in the dim twilight.

Gabe sculled with his hands to keep himself from drifting back to shore. It was easier than it should have been to move his hands. Less friction, he guessed.

What if Colin hadn't known about his powers—hadn't even had his powers—until… when? The same time Gabe got his? And he'd freaked out, maybe. He'd thought he might hurt someone. So he'd left town.

Maybe he'd grabbed Sean so he could explain everything. Maybe Colin and Sean were talking, and Sean would come home and tell them all what was going on.

What if Colin really had been in the field earlier? He could be watching Gabe now, like a guardian angel. People had said that to Gabe after his mother died. She's your guardian angel now. He'd wanted to pull out his Swiss Army knife and ask them which of their relatives they'd like for an angel.

"Colin?" he asked. He heard nothing but the water passing by his ears.

"It's like I'm fucking praying to you," Gabe said. "That is messed up, man. If you're around, can you please come here and have a real conversation with me? Please?"

He was surprised by dampness on his face and realized he was crying for the second or third time that day. Colin never seemed to cry. Gabe didn't remember ever having seen it. Sometimes Gabe felt like it was another chore they'd designated. Colin mowed the lawn, and Gabe cried for both of them.

"Okay," he said. "I'm not praying, but I'm begging. And I'm pissed. Do you know what kind of a mess you left me with? I need to talk to you. You owe me that. Come on."

Either Colin didn't agree or he wasn't listening, because he didn't appear. Gabe considered asking for a sign of some kind, but that was far too much like praying, and he was not going there. Colin could throw SUVs until the cows came home, but it would never make him a god.

Fuck it all. Gabe rolled over, then swam for the diving platform, an AstroTurfed block of wood that had been chained in place at the far edge of the swimming area. He climbed onto it, still amazed not to be wet or cold. It was a good night for diving—in the sense that the waves had washed most of the gull shit away. Not that diving, exactly, was what Gabe had in mind. Forgetting the form he'd been taught one summer by a friendly pair of sisters, he instead threw himself at the water face first, arms spread wide.

It didn't hurt, of course. The flash was blue and flat, the sound of strings choppy and fast. He was an instrument. He wondered if he could learn to play the force field like a theremin. He could perform concerts. Except Eli the killjoy would probably consider that indiscreet.

Was it weird that Gabe's main reason for wanting to jump off a building was to hear the music that came off him when he landed?

He treaded water, his back to the shore and angled so that he couldn't see either of the cabin subdivisions. No lights at the far end of the lake. Just him and trees and the water. Trillions of cells coming home.

As was his custom, when no one was around to call him out on his dorkiness, he sang to the lake. "Carrickfergus" on this occasion. A good song for open water.

His voice seemed to widen, become richer as it glided over the waves. He could probably be heard on the far side. Water was funny that way. Well, if someone over there didn't like it, they'd have to come find him to make him stop.

"Neither have I wings to fly," he added under his breath, once the last line of the song had stopped ringing in the bowl of the lake. "Why don't I fly instead? Why did we get what we got?"

Without waiting for an answer, he dove under and swam to shore. His lungs ached. The thing to do was go to the surface for air. Unless… what if he'd brought the air down with him? He must have brought some, at least, if he was staying dry. He pursed his lips, like he was drinking through a straw, and pulled lightly. A breath of air came in. He wasn't sure how much air he had. It couldn't be too much, with the water displacing around him almost normally. He'd be pushing water like a rowboat if his field had formed a diving bell before he'd gone down.

But he could choose to do that. He was suddenly as sure of it as he was that he could throw a ball in the air and catch it. He couldn't have explained the physics, but he knew how it would feel, and he trusted that his body would get it done.

He popped his head up once the water was too shallow for swimming and froze in place. He was still horizontal in the water, and his hands gripped the rolling sand of the lakebed to keep himself in place. He'd seen something, someone, in the trees along the road. Watching. He could feel the eyes on him. There for a heartbeat and now gone.

Some stranger, probably, taking one of the goat paths that led through the trees. There were trails everywhere at this lake, secret passageways between the public places.

He shook the sand from his clothes before pulling them on. The beach had dark gold sand, large grains that got punishingly hot under the sun. You didn't want to take even a few steps with bare feet. You had to leave flip-flops close to the water and hope the sneaky little wavelets wouldn't carry them away when your back was turned.

It was the simplest thing, a tiny human inconvenience. Gabe wouldn't have to feel it again. The thought made him feel hollow and infinite, whatever part of him was… him… floating away to a nowhere that had no heat or cold or coarse gold sand.

He shook his head and put on his shoes. He pressed his feet hard to the sand as he walked, though it made the grains slip from under him and make his stride ungainly. He was better on the gravel of the road, crunching stones into the dirt with every step.

It was as he was passing the pump again that a voice came from the woods.

"Remember when Jasper chased that skunk?"

Gabe felt untethered again, shocked loose from the Earth. He closed his eyes and made fists, driving his nails into his palms. Letting himself feel it. Then he opened his hands and his eyes and turned to look at his brother.

Colin was standing between the pump and the woodlot, a few metres back from the road and the few yellow lights that marked the turn from the main park road into the subdivision. If he hadn't spoken, Gabe would have walked right past him.

"It was right around here," Colin added. Gabe couldn't get his head around Colin's words at first. Then he remembered. Sandy's cousin's dog, chasing a skunk, getting sprayed while everyone was in hot pursuit and well within the spray zone. They'd spent the afternoon in the coin showers, getting peroxide-and-baking-soda scrub downs.

"Fucking Jasper," Gabe said. "Where's Sean? Is he with you?"

"I'm gone a day and everyone's manners go straight to shit. Hello to you too."

Gabe took a step toward Colin. It surprised him a little when Colin didn't flee.

"Seriously, where's Sean? If you didn't grab him, somebody else did, and—"

"I'm on top of the Sean thing," Colin said. "Don't worry about it."

Gabe cocked his head. "Don't worry about it?"

"Gabe. What does 'I'm on top of it' mean?"

"It means stop asking you."

"It means I'm taking care of it."

"No offence," Gabe said, stepping closer, "but you might not have everything one hundred percent locked down. Like, our house is gone. For starters."

"I'm aware," Colin said. "Come here."

Gabe had regarded that invitation with suspicion since shortly after learning to walk. It could mean come here for the Revello I got you at the corner store. Or it could mean come here because Jerry found the biggest spider ever and we were thinking we'd put it down the back of your shirt.

"You gonna throw me over a building?" Gabe asked, as amiably as he could. Colin looked at the sky. Praying for patience or figuring out a trajectory?

"Come here and we can have that conversation you wanted without waking up campers."

So Colin had heard him from the lake. Not impossible with the way sound carried over water, but Gabe hadn't spoken loudly. Superhearing seemed to be part of whatever gift package Colin had received.

"Why don't I whisper from here?" Gabe whispered.

"Funny. Yes, I can hear you. I can hear a lot of things."

Like what? Like everything Eli had said after Tracy had been shot? Like Jack threatening them in the hallway? Like someone burning down their home?

As Gabe stood thinking about those things, Colin approached, a careful step at a time, until he was standing in front of Gabe.

"We'll be okay," he said. "I have money. I know we lost things in that house, but we'll be okay."

He put his arms around Gabe. Gabe felt something buzz under his skin, like his field was getting ready to go off. *It's Colin*, he told it silently. *Chill out*.

Colin hugged him tight, and Gabe's field behaved itself. Gabe smelled Colin's shampoo and their laundry detergent. Faintly under it all there was smoke. He'd been by the house. Changed clothes, like Gabe had, but the smoke stayed in your hair.

For a moment, Colin relaxed against him like he was sinking into a sofa at the end of a twelve-hour day.

"Are you okay?" Gabe asked. Colin made a sound that wasn't a laugh or a sob. Something between.

"I'll live," Colin said. He dropped a kiss to the top of Gabe's head, then pulled back and put his hands on Gabe's shoulders. "I didn't leave because I caught you with a guy. You know that, right?"

"You seemed pissed at the time," Gabe pointed out.

Colin smiled. "You can hook up with any guy you want, as long as he's younger than the internet."

"I can't exactly have my pick," Gabe said. Colin rolled his eyes.

"Get out of the Battlefords and that's exactly what you'll have. Wait, did I say any guy? How about anyone who isn't planning to kill us both. You can stop mooning over the assassin."

"Wow, where to start," Gabe said. "First, I don't even know if he's into guys. I haven't asked. I've been weirdly busy all day. Second, he's not planning to kill us. If you were eavesdropping on us, and it seems you were, you know this already. He's not going to kill us because we're not bad people. Come talk to him and we can sort this out right now."

Colin dropped his hands from Gabe's shoulders. "I will never understand how someone can grow up the way you did and still be so fucking naive. He's going to kill both of us because that's what he does. The reason he hasn't killed you yet is that he wants you to lead him to me."

"I'd have to find you first," Gabe said. "After we have this talk, you're gonna… what? Superspeed your way out of here? Teleport? Turn invisible? Fly to the moon?"

"Probably fly," Colin said. "I fly. Looks like you got a force field of some kind. Flying's better, but a field is pretty good."

Like Gabe had pulled a good prize out of one of those machines at the supermarket where you put in a loony and got some shitty toy inside a plastic ball.

"Maybe we can play catch sometime," Gabe said. "You throw SUVs at me, and I'll bounce them back to you."

Colin looked at the sky again. Was he expecting someone?

"I'm sorry you saw that. I'm sorry you found out about any of this. You weren't supposed to."

"Because bad things happen to people who find out?" Gabe asked.

"Sometimes they do, Gabe. Jack goes after people. You know that."

"Yeah," Gabe said. "He does. But he wasn't there when that Owen guy saw you—"

"That Owen guy is fine. I rang his bell a little, gave him a ride to the edge of town, and suggested he keep his mouth shut and not come back. I guess he took my advice."

"The police need to know he's okay," Gabe said. "They're asking about you."

"The police are welcome to try to find me. This shit will sort itself out."

"Do you even care that your friend died? Or girlfriend, whatever she was? She's dead because she saw you lose your temper. That is incredibly fucked-up."

"I feel bad about it, but there are bigger stakes. I can't hang around here all night. I have shit I have to do."

"Like finding Sean?"

"I told you I am on top of that, Gabe. Everything Eli Samm told you was basically true. He might even be right that no one with powers is a nice person. But we exist, and we're not going to let him wipe us out."

"We," Gabe said.

"Jack introduced me to some people, and we're looking out for each other. I also do things for those people sometimes. I made a deal that you and Sandy and the idiots could be left out of all this. Now I don't know what to do because someone set off your powers and the deal is fucked, but I'm not going to let Andrus Samm's prissy little private-school kid take me out. We all still agree on that."

"You know what? If you want me to stop hanging around with Eli, I can do that. I can go with you now. You can introduce me to your friends."

"They are not my friends. You're safe with Eli as long as he thinks you can bring him to me. What you need to do is find out how he kills us. Is it a technique? A device? A charm, an incantation? No one has lived to talk about it. Get him to tell you. He has the hots for you, so that'll help."

"He…."

"Don't tell anyone you saw me. Especially not your little buddy. Not even Sandy."

"Wait, you never—"

He never told Gabe what happened to the house or how long he'd had his powers or what they even were. Never even let Gabe finish that sentence. Just up, up, and away, straight from the ground into the sky, without so much as bending his knees to jump.

So that was a no to meeting the others, then.

Gabe headed back to the cabin to hang out with the assassin instead.

Sandy

SHE WAS rattled, obviously. It was the only excuse for her not realizing until Gabe had left that Gabe would be leaving her alone with Eli.

Now she and Eli were sitting across the fire from each other, squinting against the smoke that a light wind was tossing around. Sandy knew she ought to have a billion things to ask the guy, but she couldn't seem to think of any of them. Should she go inside, knock on the bedroom door, and insist that Jerry come out and make this less weird? The state Jerry was in, she doubted it would help.

It didn't matter, as it turned out, because Eli broke the silence.

"I've noticed," he said, "that people are careful what they say around Gabe."

What in the hell did he mean by that? They all swore like sailors in front of Gabe, and they didn't hesitate to talk about… whatever. Sex or drugs or anything that came to mind. Gabe was an adult now, technically, but they'd never worried too much about what he overheard.

"I have no fucking idea how to respond to that," Sandy said.

Eli smiled. "Specifically about Colin."

"Okay," Sandy said, "again I'm not following you."

"Does Gabe have a clear picture of his brother? Or is there some hero worship?"

Sandy grabbed a coat-hanger wiener stick from its place against a nearby tree and gave the fire a few good pokes. Sparks scattered, and she was captivated. It struck her then that it would have been terrifying and miserable to see the Reece home burn down… but beautiful too. A tiny part of her was sorry to have missed it.

"Colin and I sort of raised Gabe," she said, pushing logs around as she spoke. "I feel dumb saying that because it's not like we bought his school supplies or anything, but we were six years older, and his parents basically sucked. He figured that out really early—even before he started school. So yeah, he turned to us."

"That's understandable," Eli said. He had his hands out to the fire, the way Gabe had held his hands before. Except Eli seemed to be getting some benefit from the fire's heat, because he kept his hands there.

"Are you trying to say that people don't talk smack about Colin around Gabe? And are you asking why?"

"Yes," Eli said.

Sandy shrugged. "They're family," she said. "You don't talk smack about someone's brother unless you know they hate their brother or something. Even if they do hate their brother, you can still get it in the teeth for talking smack."

"But you're Gabe's de facto family, so you'd be free to say whatever you liked."

Sandy gave the fire a hearty poke and stared into it as she replied. "You think I'm going to shit-talk my oldest friend because his brother's not here? Is that what you're looping and winding your way around? Whatever you want to ask me, spit it the fuck out."

She was proud of herself for not adding the words "you douche."

"Fine," Eli said briskly, rubbing his hands together, then placing them on his knees. "I want to know what Colin Reece is really like."

Sandy shoved the stick until it stuck and left it there. "He gets speeding tickets, and he's lousy about doing the dishes. What the fuck do you want me to say?" She looked at Eli, whose face was serene. Being snapped at by someone with a red-hot poker seemed to bother him not at all. "He's not perfect, and he's not a murderer. Christ. What am I supposed to tell you about Colin that Gabe doesn't damned well know? They're brothers. They're fucking acquainted."

Eli drew in a deep breath through his nose, likely getting a snootful of smoke. "Like I said, I don't know if Gabe sees Colin's flaws."

Sandy's jaw tightened. "Colin does not have serious flaws. Not like you mean."

Eli cocked his head. "What do I mean?"

A rattling sound from the cabin made them both jump a little. Sandy recovered first and laughed.

"Squirrels, man. They throw pine cones at the roof. Usually they do it in the morning, but I guess the solstice fucks them up."

Eli nodded. "Solstice," he said thoughtfully. He was staring at the sky as if it were an eye chart he couldn't quite read. After a minute, he gave up on it. "Sorry. What do you think I mean?"

"Well…." Sandy's shoulders hurt. Tension, she thought, and moved them back and forth. It didn't help. "Okay, murder. You're asking if he's a guy who could kill someone."

"And is he?"

Eli might, from his tone, have been asking whether Colin was a gearhead or a Sagittarius. Something of no real importance.

"Of course not!" Sandy said.

"Almost anyone might kill under the right circumstances," Eli said.

"Sure, okay, self-defence or something," she said. "But he's a normal guy."

"No," Eli said. "He's not. Were you surprised when Gabe told you Colin had packed up and left?"

"It wasn't like him," Sandy said.

Eli raised his brows. "He doesn't do that?"

"Like fucking off to the city or something? No. Excuse me." Sandy went to her car and got her jacket. She shouldn't have needed it with the fire, but the night had turned colder than she'd expected. On the way she got an eyeful of the rental car for the first time.

"Fuck almighty! What happened to your car?"

"Got hit by a deer," Eli said.

Sandy eyed him. "I think you mean you hit a deer."

"Do I? It came out of nowhere while we were on the way to Tracy Howell's house."

Sandy turned to him. Her hands had gone to her hips like she was her mom about to scold Jerry and Colin for trampling the begonias.

"You think Colin dropped a deer on your car."

"I think someone might have. Gabe says deer can jump right into a car sometimes, so maybe it was that."

"That's insane."

Sandy proceeded to her car and got her jacket, leaving Eli to decide whether she'd meant that dropping a deer from the sky was insane or whether his suggestion that Colin had done it was insane. She wasn't sure herself.

"Does Colin take construction work out of town?" Eli asked when she returned.

“Sometimes,” Sandy said. “So what? This is a small place. You go where the work is. Why don’t you go interrogate Jerry about his runs to Meadow Lake or wherever the fuck? If you think there’s something criminal about leaving the city limits.”

Eli pursed his lips. Sandy was starting to wonder what it would take to ruffle the guy. Maybe a burning log to the head.

“Why do you think he left this morning?”

A loon called from the lake, and Sandy heard herself laugh. It was a shriller sound than she usually produced.

“He’s looney?” she said. Eli didn’t smile. Sandy shook her head. “I. Don’t. Fucking. Know. I have no idea. Gabe thinks it’s because he came out, but trust me, Colin knew. He didn’t care. It must have been something else.”

“I agree,” Eli said. “Gabe is a bad liar. So I believe you that Colin knew he was gay and didn’t leave on account of that.”

“So basically I don’t know why he left,” Sandy said. “*Je ne sais pas—*”

“Does Colin do a lot of strange things?” Eli asked.

“No,” Sandy said, hugging her jacket closer. “He’s a normal guy. I’m telling you. Little bit thoughtless, kind of a dick sometimes, always ready to help his friends, loves his brother to pieces. He’s the normal one.”

“And Gabe is the nice one,” Eli said, seemingly to himself. “How did their parents die?”

Sandy was about to recite the old story about the car accident—that John Reece must have nodded off while driving—but what did it matter? It wouldn’t have been possible to take away the insurance money now.

“Both parents committed suicide,” she said. “Their father had a deliberate car accident when Gabe was ten and Colin was sixteen. He used Colin as a witness. He let Colin out of the car and then drove into the oncoming lane. Colin pretended he’d been in the passenger seat and told everyone it was an accident.”

Eli leaned back in his chair, then changed his mind when the chair nearly tipped over. Sandy almost smiled.

“Didn’t anyone think it was strange that Colin was unharmed?”

“Yes,” Sandy said. “But his father wasn’t wearing a seatbelt. Colin said he had been wearing one, and that’s why he lived. He was sixteen, and his dad had just died. Nobody wanted to get shitty with him about it, you know?”

"I do," Eli said. "And their mother?"

"Suicide," Sandy said. "Two years later. She hanged herself."

"So," Eli said, "Colin helped his father commit suicide. His mother killed herself two years later. That has to change a person, doesn't it? Don't you think it's weird that he acts like a normal guy?"

"Am I a fucking shrink?" Sandy said. She shoved her chair back from the fire and stood. "Are you? Colin and Gabe keep it together, okay? Gabe's neurotic, and Colin gets in bar fights and is a jerk to women. That's what's wrong with them. Stop talking like Colin's got to be some kind of fucking… psychopath. And what about Gabe, by the way? He grew up in that house too."

"You may want to sit down," Eli said gently. "And be quieter. There are lights in the cabin across the road."

Sandy would have preferred to shove Eli's chair over and walk on top of him to get to her car, but she needed an answer to her question, and that wouldn't get her one. And he did have a point about the noise.

"Fine," she said, taking her seat again. "What's the difference?"

"I don't know that there is one," Eli said. "I haven't met Colin. I have met other people who were part of this experiment. They are typically not very nice."

"Colin and Gabe are good people," Sandy said. "They're not always polite people, but that's different."

She grabbed the poker again, then drew her hand back with a yelp. Metal conducted heat. She was pretty sure she'd heard that somewhere.

"You should put ice on that," Eli said. "Or cold water."

"Fuck it," Sandy said. "I have known Gabe since he was born. I have known Colin since he was very young. They are not whatever you think they are."

"The abilities might make a difference," Eli said. "I've never met any of these people before they received their… upgrades. It might change them."

"Well, Gabe got zapped last night, right?" Sandy said, ignoring the bile in her throat. "So?"

"So," Eli said, "he's not what I expected."

He gazed at the fire and said nothing more.

"What do you mean?" Sandy prodded.

"He wiped his shoes," Eli said, and yet again that day, Sandy thought she might be losing her mind.

"What did you say?"

"He wiped his shoes," Eli said. "Before going into your cabin. You say he's not polite, but I think he is. For the right reasons. He worries about other people, animals, even property. Maybe he's still changing, since he was… zapped… so recently. I don't know. I'm cautiously optimistic about Gabe. As long as he stays out of trouble."

Sandy could only stare for a few moments. Stare and blink a little in the haze.

"You've been doing a lot of thinking about my friend," she said.

Eli smiled. "I've spent all day with him. There's a lot to think about."

"But your opinion is that Colin's a lost cause? Based on… nothing?"

"He's had his powers for a long time," Eli said. "At least eight years."

The loon called again, as if it could understand the crazy shit Eli was talking. Sandy wished she could invite it to join the conversation.

"Eight years," Sandy repeated.

"Vehicle accident," Eli said. "Not a scratch. That doesn't ring any bells with you?"

Sandy wanted to say he was being fucking ridiculous. She even opened her mouth, but the words refused to leave.

"Uh," she said.

"Hell of a coincidence," Eli said. "Don't you think?"

"Uh," Sandy said again.

"I think Colin was in that car. Otherwise witnesses to the accident would have seen him by the roadside. They would have seen him getting into the car after the crash."

They would have. Sandy knew that. She'd always known that, she guessed. She just hadn't wanted to think about it.

"Okay," she said softly. "Fine. But that doesn't mean Colin's a bad person."

Unless he'd grabbed the wheel like she'd heard someone whisper in the grocery store a few weeks after it happened. Unless it hadn't been an accident. Even so, though, the way their father had treated them… even if Colin had yanked the wheel, did that make Colin a bad guy?

"I could take that position," Eli said. "I could assume that Colin's what you think he is, even though I know the odds are against it. But do you really think it's in Gabe's interests for me to do that? I don't think Gabe needs one more person telling him there's nothing wrong with his brother. I think he's better off getting an alternate opinion. In case I'm right."

"You're wrong," Sandy said firmly.

"Hope so," Eli said. "It would be nice."

Sandy stood. "The Reeces are exceptions to everything," she told him. "I'm going back to town. You have my cell number."

"I do," Eli said. "Drive carefully."

Did he mean don't get hit by pseudo-lightning and given weird, superhuman powers? Or did he mean, don't get picked up by the police?

Maybe all he'd meant was drive carefully.

"Will do," Sandy said.

CHAPTER NINE

Gabe

GABE PASSED Sandy's car on the road and gave her a wave, which she returned. He wanted to flag her down and tell her he'd seen Colin and that Colin seemed okay, basically, but he was acting weird and talking about making a deal with some pretty awful people, including the boogeyman, and did she have any thoughts on what they should do next? But Colin had been clear about not telling her, specifically. As much as Colin was being an asshole and pissing him off, what if he had a good reason for asking Gabe to keep his mouth shut?

Hell, what if he had good reasons for all of it?

Why the fuck wouldn't he come back to the cabin and sort things the fuck out so they could all deal with this fucked-up situation together?

The fire was out when Gabe got back to the cabin. He could see Eli puttering around, putting the kettle on the stove and checking his face in the small shaving mirror that someone had hung above the washbowl, despite all shaving taking place, mirrorless, in the woods.

Gabe went inside, and he and Eli exchanged nods. Nothing to say, it seemed. Or too tired to say it.

If Gabe said something about Colin, like saying Beetlejuice three times or Bloody Mary into a mirror, the guy would probably show up. The eavesdropper. The flying Superman spy. He'd have to work something out.

Unless his way of working things out was to ring Eli's bell and leave him at the edge of town.

Or unless Colin was right about Eli, and the second he got Colin in a room with him, he'd wipe Colin and Gabe off the earth and be back in Saskatoon in time to get a morning flight to anywhere.

Well, Calgary and then anywhere. But the principle held.

Eli checked his phone, then wandered into the living room. Knelt in front of the bookshelf. Gabe could have told him what was there because it had never changed. *Reader's Digest*s and *Pet Sematary* and the *Berenstains'*

B Book and *The World According to Garp*. Which of those would an assassin like best? Eli didn't seem impressed by any of the options.

Gabe grabbed the scratched aluminum kettle from the gas stove moments before it started to whistle. Jerry was pretty out of it, but Gabe didn't want to take the chance that the kettle would startle him. Jer didn't seem like he needed any more scares.

"I regret to tell you," Gabe told Eli, "that there's only one decent bed in this place, and you're going to become much closer to Jerry if you try to sleep in it."

He filled a pair of enamel mugs into which he'd placed tea bags of unknown age and type. They'd been in a mason jar in the cupboard, next to an ancient campfire percolator and, bizarrely, a melon baller.

Eli returned to the kitchen, took a mug and teaspoon, and poked at the tea bag floating in the water.

"You don't recommend the bunk beds?"

The cabin's other bedrooms were fitted with heavy wooden bunk beds of varying lengths and unvarying cruelty to the backs of their occupants. Gabe had loved them as a kid—loved the security of having Colin and sometimes Jerry in the room with him—but they'd lost their allure as he'd grown.

"If you like walking around like the bell ringer at a French cathedral," Gabe said, "they're terrific."

"I'd heal up," Eli reminded him. "But it doesn't sound relaxing."

"The alternative," Gabe said, "is the couches in the living room. I'll be taking one of them. I'm told I don't snore, so you might be okay on the other one. Unless you're worried about sleeping in the same room as a nancy boy."

"It wouldn't be the first time," Eli said. "Which couch do you prefer?"

Gabe looked into the living room. One couch, long and low with burnt-orange frieze upholstery, was against the front wall, directly below the window. Orange-and-rust polyester curtains hung above it. They had a pattern of huge oval holes, ensuring that the curtains would block neither daylight nor anyone's view.

The other couch, along the left-hand wall, was a stained and legless heap with a hunting scene repeated across its length—men and pheasants and feathered retrievers. Neither would get a five-star rating for comfort.

"The orange one," he said. "It's the one I usually get."

They set their tea bags in a dish by the sink and carried their mugs into the living room, then set about placing sheets and blankets and pillows on couches that weren't meant to be beds. Gabe had never been able to decide whether it was better to tuck the sheet around the couch cushions or to drape it over them. Everything seemed to be a tangled mess by morning no matter what he did.

Eli was tucking his sheet in with almost military crispness. A neatnik, apparently. Or maybe, given the chaos of his life, he took order where he could find it.

"I hate," Gabe admitted as they worked, "the idea of Sandy driving back into town by herself."

"I've only known Sandy for a few hours," Eli said, "but I think she could handle driving through a herd of zombies with fire raining from the sky and a smart bomb following her car."

Gabe considered that. "Herd?"

"Yes, or pack," Eli said, as if he were a court-recognized expert on the matter. "My point is that Sandy can take care of herself."

"So you say," Gabe said. "Of course, for all I know, you've murdered her and buried her in a ditch."

He said it as lightly as he could, but Eli seemed to have heard the stress in his voice anyway. He went to Gabe and put a hand on Gabe's shoulder.

"I was with you when Sean went missing."

"I know," Gabe said. "I know that. I was kidding, man."

"She'll be fine," Eli said. "Probably safer than being here with us."

"I don't know about that," Gabe said. He lowered his voice on the distant chance that Jerry might be listening. "I'm a superhero or something, right? And so are you."

Eli shook his head and tightened his grip on Gabe's shoulder. "Road to hell, Gabe."

Gabe dropped his blanket on the couch and sat down next to it, taking himself out from Eli's grasp.

"If I can't follow my good intentions," he said, "I really don't know how to decide anything. My instincts are all I have. And, okay, my father's moral education, but I don't think following that is going to improve my behaviour. Do you?"

Eli finished making his bed, unhurried, before turning to Gabe again.

"It's the powers," he said. "They're the problem. Don't make anything of them and you'll be okay."

Sandy

A BUDDY IN the RCMP had told Sandy once that people who went exactly the limit on the highway seemed suspicious to them. The theory was if you weren't speeding a little, you had to have something illegal in your car. So she was going about ten over the limit now and making good time.

She remembered taking this highway on a frosty November night. Nearly out of gas and not wanting to be in suspense about whether she'd make it to town, she'd pushed the car up to 160 while the boys yelled at her from the other three seats. Wusses. She'd had everything under control. They'd coasted into a gas station as the engine had sputtered out.

Little had she known that Colin could have picked the car up and thrown it to the Petro-Can.

And that, for some reason, was it. She was crying, from zero to sobbing in seconds, and barely made it to the side of the road before she was entirely unfit to drive.

She didn't even know what she was crying about exactly. Sean or the house or having been lied to for what was probably such a long goddamned time.

She kept it up until her face was red and ugly and her forehead ached. As her sobbing wound down, she heard the Hip on the radio, singing about the hundredth meridian. Something from the good old days before, as Gabe liked to say, they'd crawled up their assholes. The fields were as the song said, huge and haunted. She felt as if someone was watching her, maybe from the trees across the highway.

People didn't know when they were being watched, no matter what the internet said. Jerry had waved some studies under Sean's nose a few months ago when Sean had insisted people had some sixth sense about being stared at. She knew it was bullshit, thinking she could sense eyeballs aimed her way.

And yet.

It was a hangover from her spooky day. She pulled onto the highway again and got up to speed, wiping her nose with a crumpled napkin from the cup holder. She'd feel better after she'd slept. Oh sure, everything would still be fucked-up, and Sean would probably still be missing, and she'd have to get questioned by the fucking police, and it was going to be one of the worst days of her life. But she'd have slept. And she'd go to Timmy's for breakfast and have the biggest fucking maple cream doughnut they had, or maybe two of them.

She'd have sleep and sugar and coffee, and she'd get through it.

Gabe

EVEN WITH the lights out, Gabe could clearly see Eli's face from across the room. The bunk bed rooms had heavy vinyl pull-down shades, the old kind that snapped back up when you tugged it too far down. Old and ugly, but they kept the light out. This room was going to be bright far too early for Gabe's liking.

At least he could tell that Eli wasn't asleep either.

He could hear Jerry snoring through the bedroom door. Gabe had thought Sandy was being a little hysterical back in May when she'd given Jerry a twenty-minute lecture on his need for a CPAP, but it was possible she'd had a point. At least the noise meant it was safe to have a conversation.

"You know something weird?" Gabe asked.

Eli looked amused. "Yes," he said.

Gabe laughed. "Okay, here's one more thing—I swam in the lake, but I didn't get wet."

"Well," Eli said, drawing it out as if he were explaining shoelaces to a slow child, "you seem to have some kind of force field, Gabe."

"Really?" Gabe said. "This is the first I've heard of it. The reason it was strange, asshole, is that I got wet when I took a shower at the hotel. Remember?"

Eli pursed his lips. "You're right. That's strange."

"Thank you. You asshole."

Eli smiled. "It's funny someone so oversensitive would develop a force field. Isn't it?"

"Do you think that?" Gabe said. "Do you think we get what we want? Or need?"

"I don't know," Eli said. "And I don't know why the shower got through and the lake didn't. Maybe you subconsciously allowed the shower through, or it got through because it was at a better temperature. Or it's possible your field has been growing stronger throughout the day."

"I jumped flat onto the water from the diving platform, and there wasn't any more light or sound than I'd expected. I don't think it's getting any stronger."

Eli sat up. "You did what?"

"Jumped flat," Gabe said, drawing out the words as Eli had done earlier, "onto the water—"

"In public," Eli finished. "I keep telling you—"

"There was no one around," Gabe said, surprising himself with the speed and conviction of his lie. Eli seemed to buy it. Instead of eyeing Gabe and demanding the truth, he lay back and stared at the ceiling.

"You know, I'm not harping on this to be… an asshole. You're in serious trouble."

"Right," Gabe said. "Because the CIA is lurking by the mini-golf course, waiting for me to do something freaky."

"Because," Eli said, "whoever called me with that tip was trying to get you killed."

Now it was Gabe's turn to sit up. "Excuse me?"

Eli turned his head to Gabe. "Think it through. I normally kill people like you. Someone fired up your ability on the same night that they told me there was something unusual going on in North Battleford."

"They also told you to investigate Owen Bernier," Gabe pointed out. "It sounds to me like someone was setting Colin up."

"Colin left town," Eli said. He sat up. "I was called into town and Colin left. It's obvious that once I started hunting for Colin, I'd find you. You're new with your powers, so you were going to be sloppy with them. I think the idea was that I would kill you."

Gabe cocked his head, trying to shift a funny idea that was sticking in there. "Wait—am I still alive because you're pissy about being manipulated?"

"You're still alive because I think there's hope for you."

"Anyway," Gabe said, "you're talking like Colin set me up."

"Am I?" Eli's face and voice were carefully neutral. Gabe wondered how neutral he'd sound while being dragged behind the car.

"He left town," Gabe said. "He would have been your target if he'd been here. You wouldn't even have noticed me."

"I'd have noticed you," Eli said, and Gabe was warmed until he went on. "I'm good at my job. And yes, I think your brother set you up. It might not have been him. Jack, or someone else, might have told him to leave town without telling him why. But the simplest explanation for all of this is that Colin was worried about this business with Owen drawing unwanted attention, and so he triggered you, tipped me off, and left."

He doesn't know Colin, Gabe told himself. *He says these things because he doesn't know.*

"Colin did not do that," Gabe said.

"Maybe not," Eli said.

"You'll see," Gabe said one more time. No telling when Colin would fucking relax and let Gabe straighten all this out, but it would happen eventually. "Hey… I've been wanting to say, this thing your dad asked you to do? It sucks. Like, for you. It sucks for you. I bet this isn't what you wanted to do with your life."

"I think your father might have been worse than mine," Eli said dryly. "But thank you. There aren't many people I can talk to about him."

Gabe frowned. "Not in this organization you belong to?"

Eli stared at the worn blanket covering him. He seemed suddenly uncomfortable.

"The organization is about doing what needs to be done," he said. "It's not for counselling."

Gabe smiled a little. "That's okay. I'm sure you could go to any old shrink and tell them your story and you wouldn't get locked up at all."

Eli laughed and shook his head. "Good night, Gabe."

"Good night, Dread Pirate Roberts," Gabe said.

"Excuse me?"

Eli sounded confused rather than irritated.

Gabe smiled. "Because you'll most likely kill me in the morning?"

"Oh." Gabe was about to explain further when Eli said, "Oh, right. That. Good night—I'll most likely kill you in the morning."

Was Colin outside the window, watching and listening? Wanting Gabe to ask how Eli would do it. What the secret was. So he could get around it and take Eli out first.

Gabe rolled over to face the back of the couch. He couldn't be seen from outside that way. And he couldn't see Eli. He could pretend to be alone, on the water, staring across the lake and making up his own mind.

What if he led Eli to Colin and Eli turned on them both? What if he didn't find out Eli's secret and then Eli used it to kill his brother? Gabe was lying here making jokes like that was never going to happen. But what if it did?

Or what if Eli was right about Colin's new friends—

They are not my friends

—and they would both need Eli's help to get Colin free of whatever deals he'd made with them?

What if someone else was a bigger threat to all of them?

There was no way to know what was right. All Gabe had was his instinct that Eli was, in spite of everything, a decent guy. Someone you could reason with. And he might be the most important person Gabe or Colin could have on their side.

It wasn't exactly the old saying about how it was better to have someone inside your tent pissing out than outside pissing in, but it was something like that. It was, in Gabe's estimation, usually better to make friends.

"I'm on top of this, Colin," Gabe breathed into the scratchy fabric of the couch.

Just in case.

CHAPTER TEN

Sandy

IT WAS the sugar rush from the second doughnut that pushed the rest of the sleep from Sandy's brain. Until she'd eaten it, she'd completely forgotten that she needed to call Jerry in sick. She pulled out her cell as she walked out the side door of Tim Hortons and headed for her workplace across the lot.

"Dynamic Solutions. We put the Dy in Namic."

Oh Christ. Lloyd was answering the phones.

"What kind of way is that to answer the phone?" she demanded. "What if I'd been your boss?"

Lloyd chuckled. "You couldn't be my boss," he said. "I've never had a boss with legs that good."

Lloyd was one of Jerry's compatriots in the service-and-repair trenches. He looked the way Jesus would if he were myopic and fond of *Battlestar Galactica* T-shirts, and he had no business being anywhere near the reception desk.

"Where's Cora?" Sandy asked.

"In the can," Lloyd said cheerfully.

Sandy pinched the bridge of her nose. "No, Lloyd. She's not in the can."

"No, she is. I saw her go in there with a copy of *InStyle*, so she's probably gonna be a while."

"But you don't tell people that," Sandy said, swerving around two gulls that were fighting over a discarded coffee cup. "You say she's fucking indisposed or away from her desk. Only you don't say fucking—oh, the hell with it. Lloyd, can you tell your boss that Jerry's sick today? He won't be in."

"What?" Lloyd said, his voice rising with indignation. "That guy is never around."

"It's not like Jerry asks to get sent to fucking Meadow Lake all the time," Sandy said, her protective instincts firing up.

"But—"

"Tell your boss, okay?" Sandy said. "I've gotta go."

She hung up before Lloyd could bitch about the office coffee machine or tell her anything further about Cora's bathroom habits. He was an okay guy and everything, but she could only take so much Lloyd on a good day. And this wasn't one.

She walked into the shop expecting chaos. She'd half expected it not to even be there, to have been burned to the ground or picked up and pitched into the forest. The only thing she hadn't been prepared for was what she found. Business as usual.

Everyone was where they were supposed to be. Well, except Sean, who was supposed to start half an hour before she did and was, obviously, not around. But everyone else was acting as if this was just another day, which was crazy. It was the first day after everything got fucked sideways. How could people not know that?

"Hey, Sandy," one of the mechanics called from the coffee stand. "Where's your roommate? We've got customers coming out our asses."

"Stop eating them," the shuttle driver advised on his way out the door. The mechanic, Bruce, laughed and saluted with a raised coffee cup.

"Yeah, about that," Sandy said, meeting Bruce by the coffee. "Sean never came home last night."

"I hear he didn't come home night before last either," Bruce said, waggling his eyebrows and smoking an invisible cigar. "He's gotta be coming somewhere."

"Funny, Groucho," Sandy said, and Bruce brightened. He was older, maybe fifty, and he liked it when the kids got his references. "He was… somewhere… two nights ago, but not last night. I'm kind of concerned, actually."

"Aw, kiddo, don't worry about it," Bruce said. "It's young love. He probably forgot to call you."

"Yeah, probably. I'll call his cell."

"Right," Bruce said. "I've got to get back to it. Have a gooder."

It wasn't likely that Sandy would have a gooder, but the thought was nice. She went to her desk and stared at the phone. Occasionally it rang, and she let voice-mail pick up. Voice-mail was at least as capable as she was at the moment. It couldn't book appointments or answer questions, but she didn't feel like doing those things. She didn't feel like doing anything, except maybe changing her name and moving to Brazil.

Finally she decided she had to get it over with. Not the moving to Brazil—she'd keep that in her back pocket. What she had to get past was calling the goddamned police. She picked an open line and pulled a card from her purse.

"Detective Palmer?" she said in response to the hello.

"This is he," the voice said.

"You don't say police or anything when you answer," Sandy said. She wasn't even sure why she said it.

"You have to hold back sometimes. Speaking of which, who are you?"

"This is Sandy Klaassen," she said. "You were at my house yesterday evening."

"I remember," Detective Palmer said. "Was there something you wanted to tell me?"

It sounded like an invitation to confess. Yes, Detective. I held him while Colin folded him.

"I called to tell you," she said, "that one of my roommates didn't come home last night."

"Curiouser and curiouser," Palmer said. He didn't sound curious. He sounded as if he wished people would stop committing crimes while he was trying to nap. "Ms. Klaassen, are you at work?"

"Yes," she said. She imagined she could hear his nod over the phone.

"And where do you work?"

She gave him the name of the garage and the address.

"Stay there," he said. "I will come by as soon as I can, and I will buy you a cup of coffee."

"Yes, sir," Sandy said. She'd already had all the coffee she wanted for the morning, but at least he wasn't offering to shine a bright light in her eyes. "I get a coffee break at ten fifteen."

Sandy hung up and watched the phone answer itself for a few more minutes before forcing herself to stand up and start walking toward the boss's office. Because it seemed she might have another unscheduled absence coming, and also his favourite employee wasn't going to be in that day, and she had to break the news to him. Which was freakin' delightful since odds were he would not take either of those things very goddamned well.

Gabe

BIRDS, DAYLIGHT, or squirrels bouncing pinecones off the roof. Those were the three things most likely to wake Gabe when he was at the lake. He took it as a sign of how badly he'd needed sleep that none of the three had gotten through to him.

What had gotten through was the aroma of coffee from the kitchen, smelling wonderful—much better than in the city. Gabe could normally take coffee or leave it, but it was different in the woods. Whether you were in a shabbily comfortable cabin or a lean-to you'd made out of rope and a tarp, you could believe you had your shit together if you'd made coffee in the wilderness.

Gabe slowly became aware of himself. He was on his stomach, his blanket on the floor where he'd apparently kicked it during the night. He was wearing a pair of navy blue sleep pants he'd scavenged from the main bedroom before Jerry had taken it over. His clothes and toothbrush and nearly every other damned thing he owned in the world were tucked into the backpack beside the couch.

This was his life now. He was a guy whose stuff fit into a backpack. He was hanging around with a cute, if peculiar, blond who'd come to town to bump him off. He was missing one of his best friends. And the cops probably thought he'd committed murder.

"Didn't you say things would seem better in the morning?" Gabe crabbed at Eli.

"I would never have said that," Eli said, unruffled. "There doesn't seem to be a toaster, so I'm toasting bagels in the oven. I assumed you'd want at least two."

"Fucking right," Gabe said. He located his left arm and brought it up to his face to check his watch. "Jesus! It's almost noon! Why didn't you kick my ass?"

"We didn't have anything specific planned," Eli said. "I thought it would be good for you to sleep."

"I should've been doing something," Gabe muttered. He rolled over, planted his feet on the floor, and grabbed the handle of the backpack. "Back in a sec."

He changed in the cramped second bedroom, elbows bumping against the bunk beds. A child's butterfly kite was nailed to one wood-panelled wall like a preserved specimen. Its name, Flutterburt Butterwink, was written across one wing. Old Flutterburt. It had been there as long as Gabe could remember, probably tacked up by Sandy's mom when she was a girl and her parents had owned the cabin.

A quick rub of his face told Gabe he likely didn't need a shave today. His hair, thank God, was long enough to put in a tie again. Finally. He'd cut it the previous winter after losing a bet to Jerry.

Which reminded him.

"Where's Jerry?" he asked Eli, stepping out of the room with his backpack in one hand and his toothbrush and toothpaste in the other.

"Still asleep, I guess," Eli said. His hands were busy putting jam on a bagel, so he raised his chin toward the closed bedroom door. "You and Sandy said he liked to sleep in."

"Like Rip Van Winkle," Gabe confirmed. He pulled a mug from one of the kitchen cupboards. It was green on the outside, white and coffee-stained on the inside, and might have predated the butterfly kite.

Gabe grabbed a ladle from beside the water bucket, half filled the mug, and took it out back to brush his teeth.

As he spat onto the spongy ground, he saw that Jerry had opened his bedroom window during the night. The screen was still missing from the summer before. If this had been an ordinary trip to the lake, Gabe would have done something with that. Caught a few frogs and tossed them onto Jerry's bed, maybe. Frogs were always good for a laugh.

This wasn't a prank kind of trip, though.

When Gabe got back inside, he realized that Eli probably hadn't boiled water for the washstand, the way Sandy's mom always did. She boiled water and mixed it half and half with the cold water from the bucket so everyone would have warm water to wash with. Because the woman was a saint of some kind, and Gabe had never seen it.

"If you found that jam in the fridge," Gabe said as he washed his hands, "you might not want to eat it. It's probably been there since fall, and the power's been off. I realize I should have said something earlier."

Eli, who was holding a plate with nothing but crumbs on it, smiled. "Sandy brought the bagels last night, and the coffee was here, but I got the jam from the store by the lake."

"Well played," Gabe said. "You mentioned you'd toasted a couple of those for me?"

"Help yourself," Eli said, stepping away from the oven. Gabe poured himself a cup of coffee and retrieved the waiting bagels. He'd read somewhere that real, fresh bagels from a proper bagel place should never be toasted. These were bagels from a convenience store and a few days old at best, so he figured that rule was out the window.

"You changed clothes," Gabe said, regarding the tan shirt that had replaced Eli's white shirt from the day before. "You must have put your shit in the car at the hotel. I didn't notice you doing that."

Eli blinked in confusion, then smiled back. "My shit is still at the hotel. I always keep stuff in the car. You never know when life will get complicated."

Gabe leaned back against the counter and sighed. "I used to know. You wanna know how often my life was so complicated that I needed to stash clothes and a toothbrush in multiple locations? Never."

Eli said nothing, but his eyes said, "Get used to it." Gabe decided he might as well eat. No telling when he'd have another chance.

Sandy

"SANDRA MARIE Klaassen," Detective Palmer said. "Born and raised in North Battleford. Employed by Janowski's Auto Repair. Currently on probation for arson involving the wilful destruction of a half-ton truck belonging to one Patrick Fitzgerald."

"That's me," Sandy admitted, drumming the nail of her index finger slowly against the heavily varnished table. Palmer had opted for a restaurant that was always quiet in the mid-mornings, a Greek place pretending to be Italian. Pizza with feta, baked spaghetti… and souvlaki because the menu writer had given up on the scam.

"In my defence," she added, "it was a fucking GMC."

"Yes," Palmer said dryly, "well, the arresting officer and the judge seemed more impressed by the care you took not to endanger anyone or anything aside from the vehicle. That appears to be the reason you are on probation and not in jail. The sentence, Ms. Klaassen, could have been a more serious one."

Sandy leaned against the crushed velour covering the high backs of the booth. The material was dark, with a busy pattern that could, and likely did, hide dozens of tomato sauce stains.

"If you're here to intimidate me," she said, "it won't work. I haven't broken my probation, so you can't get me in trouble for that. And I honestly don't know where Colin Reece is. I wish I did."

Palmer nodded. "Maybe you don't. There's a good chance, however, that you know where Gabriel Reece is."

"Nope," Sandy said, grateful for the dim lighting that masked her face. Each booth had its own plastic Tiffany lamp hanging above it, and each lamp held what appeared to be a forty-watt bulb. The place had no windows and no lights apart from those faux-Tiffanies. It was a hazardous place for a waitress—one of Sandy's friends had tripped at least twice a shift while working there—but it was a fine place to be interrogated.

"It has not escaped the attention of my colleagues," Palmer said, "that you are on probation for an arson charge and that the Reece home was destroyed by fire."

"Wow," Sandy said. "Throwing a Molotov cocktail into some asshole's truck box is now considered equivalent to burning down somebody's house?"

Palmer laced his fingers and set his hands on the table. "Most people, Ms. Klaassen, have never made Molotov cocktails."

"Guess I'm not most people," Sandy said.

"I was curious about you," Palmer said, "so I spoke with an old friend of mine. Marcia Hagen."

"Mrs. Hagen?" Sandy asked, not quite believing it. Hagen had taught English at her high school.

"She had you, your housemate Jerry, and both of the Reece boys as students at various times," Palmer said.

"And?"

"I asked her what she made of you."

"A *C* student," Sandy said without malice. English had never been her thing. The essay questions were always something like, "Why did Willy Loman commit suicide?" and she hadn't been able to come up with much beyond, "Because he was a douche." Which Gabe had later told her wasn't wrong, exactly. Just incomplete.

HE PAUSES on the edge of explaining it to her. He's bouncing her rolled-up exam off his knee as they sit together on the bleachers behind the high school, waiting for Colin's practice to be over. She can see him thinking how to phrase it, how to put the knowledge across. So fucking earnest, even though she knows he doesn't like Death of a Salesman *any better than she does. Maybe less, because it seems to offend him somehow, instead of boring the shit out of him the way it does her. But he read it because, though he's only nine, he reads everything Colin is taking in school. And he wants to talk about it.*

He wants to make a gift of whatever he knows.

And then he stops, the way they've all taught him to stop, and thinks about the kind of gift he's about to give. Like socks to a five-year-old boy, unwanted and worse. Annoying in the distance by which they miss the mark.

No one wants the information. No one cares. It's stupid old socks.

Gabe smiles instead, as if he's making fun of some other guy now, that earnest kid in the front row with his hand up. What a loser, his smile proclaims. And he says, "You should have said Willy Loman was a total *douche."*

"ACTUALLY," SANDY added, "I doubt she remembers me. She's taught a lot of kids."

"She remembers you and the Reece boys," Palmer informed her. "And Mr. McClelland."

"Okay," Sandy said. "I don't see why she'd remember any of us. Except maybe Gabe."

"She remembers both boys," Palmer said. "And you. She says you are, overall, a decent young lady."

Sandy coughed then as the Pepsi she'd chosen instead of coffee went down the wrong pipe. She held a napkin to her mouth and waved off Palmer's hand as he reached to pat her back.

"Sorry," she said. "That makes it sound like I wear white gloves to church."

Palmer, to her surprise, smiled a little. "I asked her if you could tell right from wrong, and she felt that you generally could, excepting certain… excesses of the heart. I find Mrs. Hagen to be an exceptional judge of character."

"Um… all right," Sandy said, not sure what Palmer expected her to say.

"Between her assessment of you and the disturbing news that another of your friends has gone missing, I thought it might be worthwhile to present you with some information."

"What huh?" Sandy asked, the sounds well out of her mouth before she gave any thought to them. "I… I mean, I thought you guys didn't like to tell people stuff. Especially not, you know. Suspects."

Palmer patted his tie as if trying to calm it. He must have thought it had shifted, though Sandy couldn't imagine why. It wasn't as if he moved at all, most of the time.

"Oh, do you mean the arson?" he asked. "Of the Reece home? Is that what you believe you're suspected of doing?"

"See," Sandy said, straightening in her seat, "that's the kind of thing I mean. You're telling me it was arson? For sure? Like, you did some CSI thing?"

"I don't believe there was ever much question about it," Palmer said. "But yes, we know it was deliberately set. Not with a Molotov cocktail."

No, of course not. With two jerry cans of gas, maybe, formerly residents of the old outhouse.

"No," Sandy said. "That would never work."

Palmer gave her his half smile again.

"I feel as if I shouldn't tell you. I can say that there was an accelerant involved and that the perpetrator did not seem concerned about the crime being found out."

Like somebody knew he was going to have fucked off by the time the cops got involved.

"We've found Mr. Reece's truck," Palmer said.

Sandy gawked at him. She didn't figure it was the coolest she'd ever looked. "You've what?"

The server stopped by at that moment to warm Palmer's coffee. She noticed Sandy's empty glass and asked if Sandy would like another. These pseudo-Italian places didn't have free pop refills the way civilized places did. They brought narrow plastic glasses of nearly flat pop and charged you handsomely for each one. But fuck it, the cop was paying. Sandy nodded, and the server went away.

"The truck was located behind a windbreak a few miles east of the city," Palmer said smoothly, as if they hadn't been interrupted. "There's no sign of an accident. We believe it was abandoned there deliberately."

The hell? Colin loved that truck. Of course, she'd thought he loved his house too. But the truck was his only form of transportation, as far as she knew. So how had he been getting around?

"Do you think he hitched after that?" she asked.

"We're interested in your opinion," Palmer told her.

Sandy laughed. "You don't want it. If you'd asked me a week ago whether Colin would skip town like this, I would've said never. No way would he take off on Gabe like that."

"Did he take off on Gabe?" Palmer inquired. "Are you certain?"

Sandy accepted a new glass of Pepsi from the server and drained half of it before she answered.

"You think Gabe knows where Colin is?" she said. "You think he's lying? I've seen Gabe trying to lie since he was three years old. He was shitty at it then, and he's nearly as bad now."

"That is his reputation," Palmer conceded. "He also has a reputation for hotheadedness."

Sandy shrugged. "He got picked on some at school," she said. "For the smart thing, mostly. He's smart. So Colin taught him how to hit people. And yeah, he's dramatic sometimes, but he's eighteen, and he's—"

She stopped, nipping her tongue in rebuke.

She expected Palmer to start in on her. But he nodded instead, and she thought that he'd probably heard from others what she'd opted not to say. That Gabe was gay, after all. Didn't he have a certain birthright when it came to drama? He'd probably have been a little high-strung even without his fucked-up childhood for an excuse.

Or maybe not. She didn't know a lot of gay guys. Actually, for guys she *knew* knew instead of knew from serving her in restaurants in Saskatoon or whatever… there was Gabe. For the first time, it struck her how fucking lonely that had to be.

"Do you believe he might have burned down his house in response to his brother leaving?"

Sandy shook her head. "No. Especially after Colin took off, Gabe would need it. Not only for a place to live. So he could leave a light on for his brother, you know? A place to come home to?"

Palmer was nodding as if what she'd said made sense to him. She felt a little better. Maybe it would be possible to get through to this guy. Maybe this was her chance to do that.

"About Colin leaving," she added, "Gabe's not mad—he's hurt. He thinks he did something wrong or upset Colin. That's how Gabe's brain works about Colin."

"All right," Palmer said. He unfolded his hands and picked up his coffee cup. "Now, do you know a Tracy Howell?"

Oh shit. So the boogeyman really had called the cops. And the cops had been to the ranch house, and they'd been to the casino, and that, when you got right down to it, was what Palmer was doing here.

"We came up together," Sandy told him. "We're not really friends."

She did not ask whether he'd asked Mrs. Hagen about Tracy too.

"Gabe visited the casino yesterday in the company of someone named Eli Samm, who identified himself as a private investigator. Do you know him?"

Sandy shook her head. “Should I?”

“Ms. Howell was found dead in her parents’ home last night,” Palmer said, as if she’d said nothing. “She had been shot in the chest. The wound was not self-inflicted. It’s possible Gabe or Mr. Samm might have seen something, or that she might have told them something that could help us.” Palmer said it in that same chatting tone he’d been using all along, except he wasn’t chatting. He suspected Gabe. Of course he did. He’d have to.

The impression she’d had that she could talk to him and he was really listening, all fair and impartial and shit, he’d used that casual tone to give her that impression. And she’d fallen for it. She’d told him all kinds of things.

She wanted to throw up.

“I realize this is upsetting news,” Palmer said. Sandy fought the urge to punch him in his lined and weary face, all fake with compassion.

“I’m sorry,” she said. “I really don’t know where Gabe is.”

Palmer placed his hands flat on the table.

“Ms. Klaassen, I am telling you these things, which I would not ordinarily tell a member of the public, because I want you to understand the seriousness of the situation. There has been arson, and there have been two murders.”

“I get that, but Gabe didn’t kill anyone,” Sandy said. “And neither did Colin. So you—” She stopped, a chill running through her. “Did you say two murders?”

“We found blood and hair inside a freezer we took from the basement of the Reece home,” Palmer said. “Apparently someone failed to realize that arson would not destroy evidence inside a freezer. Again, I would not be telling you this if I didn’t think you needed to understand.”

“Blood?” Sandy said. “So one of the Reece boys cut himself deboning chicken, and then he put the chicken in the freezer.”

“This was a large amount of blood,” Palmer said. “It was spread throughout the freezer. We believe it will turn out to be Owen Bernier’s. We’ve sent it for testing, along with samples from his apartment.”

“It could have been from all kinds of things,” Sandy said. “The boys are carnivores.”

“We don’t believe that to be the source of the blood.”

“Sir… are you dicking me around?”

“I beg your pardon?” Palmer said.

“You expect me to believe,” Sandy said, “that my friends killed some guy and kept him in their freezer? My honour roll friend who cries at Dodo videos? And my friend who's been supporting his kid brother since he was a teenager? Those friends? Are you fucking serious?"

"As I've said," Palmer replied, "I consider this very serious. You need to understand that what you're doing right now is not the same as protecting your friends from a B&E charge or something of that nature. At least one of your associates is a dangerous person, and you are not safe. You need to tell me what you know."

Was it possible that Colin had… he wouldn't have done it on purpose, never, but he was strong, wasn't he? Could he have hit that Owen guy too hard without realizing it? An accident, that's all. A terrible accident. One you could never explain because how did you explain being so strong?

God, how did he manage to go through life without breaking things all the time?

She couldn't say any of that. It was a life-and-death secret, about the powers. Eli annoyed her in a few special ways, but she knew he was right about that.

She placed her own hands in the middle of the table. "I hear you," she said in the tone she used with irritated customers. "Obviously something fucky is going on, and Gabe and Colin need to come home and maybe get lawyers and straighten this out. If I hear from them, I'll tell them that, okay?"

"Ms. Klaassen—" Palmer started.

"No," Sandy said. "That's all I have for you. Oh, except, what did Mrs. Hagen say? I bet you asked her if Gabe and Colin were likely to kill some waitress, right? So what'd she say?"

Palmer tilted his head. "She said she didn't think Gabriel would do any such thing."

Sandy stared at him in silence for a few moments. Then, still staring, she felt for her purse, grabbed it, and slipped from the booth.

"Be careful, Sandra," Palmer said as she walked away.

Gabe

"THIS IS ridiculous," Gabe said, sitting at the living room table with his second bagel and eyeing the closed bedroom door.

"I agree," Eli said.

"Jerry should be up by now," Gabe said.

"I agree," Eli said.

"So," Gabe concluded, "you should go wake him up."

Eli glanced at the door.

"You think I should wake your friend."

"You think I should do it because he's my friend? I think you should do it because you don't have a friendship with him to damage."

"The bedroom door's locked," Eli pointed out.

Gabe raised his eyebrows. "You think I'm gonna crawl in the window? The ground under that window is a cup of water away from being a bog. How about you pick the lock, if your PI licence is so real."

"You knock first," Eli told him. "Picking a lock without knocking first is considered rude."

Gabe smirked. "PI school teach you that?"

"Experience did."

Gabe nodded, then made a show of slowly tucking into his food. Can't knock on Jerry's door. See? Busy eating. Eli rolled his eyes, then went to the bedroom door and knocked three times.

"Jerry? It's almost noon."

No response. Eli knocked again.

"Jerry."

Gabe frowned, dropped his bagel onto his plate, and set the plate on the counter.

"Jer?" He crossed the room and rapped on the door. "Jer, stop fucking around."

"Hmm," Eli said. He leaned in to study the lock. Moments later he was rummaging through his backpack.

"Do you have actual lockpicks?" Gabe asked. "That is so cool."

"Normally I use a pick gun," Eli said as he dug to the bottom of the pack. "But I've had trouble taking them on planes."

He slipped past Gabe to the door and knelt in front of it, scowling at the lock. "Get out of the light," he said. After a second he added, "Please."

"Since you asked nicely," Gabe said as he moved, but his heart wasn't really in badgering Eli. He was starting to worry about why Jerry wasn't answering the door. Sure, the guy liked his sleep, but he'd gone to bed reasonably early the night before. A good long time before Gabe had in fact. Also, how the hell had he slept through two guys knocking on the door and calling his name? Or through the smell of coffee, for that matter?

Once Eli cracked the lock and pushed the door open, Gabe saw the answer to his question. Jerry hadn't slept through anything. Jerry wasn't there.

"He slept on top of the bed," Eli said, entering the room and looking around. He was being careful, Gabe noticed, not to touch anything. That was crazy, since they had every right to be in the cabin and weren't at a crime scene or anything, but it was probably a habit for the guy.

The nubby white cotton cover that Sandy called "Mom's fucking matelassé," which had been relegated to the cabin after ten-year-old Sandy had spilled grape juice on it, was in place but rumpled. Jerry might not even have slept. He might have lain awake in the sagging centre of the old mattress faking a snore and waiting for everyone else to fall asleep before taking off through the open window.

Eli was at the window, gazing below. "It's very spongy ground," he said, as if Gabe hadn't just told him that. "He wouldn't leave footprints."

"Uh-huh," Gabe agreed, standing on his toes to peer over Eli's shoulder. "When do you think he left?"

"He stopped snoring around midnight," Eli said, still staring at the ground as if it had disappointed him. "Could have been anytime after that. Why do you think he'd leave?"

"I dunno?" Gabe offered.

"I thought this was your good friend."

"Sure, I guess," Gabe said. "He's more Colin's friend, you know? I tag along. But Jerry's always been a law unto Jerry. Maybe he left because he was freaking out and wanted some alone time, or maybe he left because he realized there's no Cap'n Crunch at the store and it's what he's eating for breakfast this month."

"I need real possibilities," Eli said, "not jokes."

"I'm not joking," Gabe told him. "Jerry would fuck off over Cap'n Crunch. The guy's weird, okay? I'd have trouble crawling into his head under normal circumstances, and these aren't them."

Eli shut his eyes and hung his head. It occurred to Gabe that he hadn't asked Eli how he'd slept or if he needed anything. He wasn't used to being a sort of host.

"You, uh, sleep okay?" Gabe asked.

Eli smiled, his eyes still shut. "Fine."

He hadn't. Even Gabe could tell that.

"Jer must have hitched out of here," Gabe said. "I mean, provided he left under his own steam."

"If someone had taken him, there would have been noise," Eli said. "Jack could have popped in and out and grabbed him, I guess, but I still think there would have been a few seconds of noise. There wasn't any disturbance at all."

"Except in Jerry's head," Gabe agreed. He ran his hand flat over the bedspread, sliding his fingers down the cotton bumps as if they were Braille. He'd heard somewhere that blind people who played guitar had trouble with Braille sometimes. Calluses on the fingers.

"He was pretty upset," Eli said, "for a man who didn't really see anything."

"Well, he saw his friend disappear," Gabe said. "That's got to be upsetting."

Eli stood up straight, away from the wall. "You saw that video of your brother throwing that vehicle. You were shaken, but you kept going. I think Jerry might have seen more than he was willing to share."

Gabe lay back on the bed. It smelled faintly of Jerry's aftershave and strongly of old, stale air.

"Maybe that's why he took off," he said. "Maybe he wanted to talk to Sandy alone."

Eli returned to the window. "How easy would it have been for him to hitchhike back to town?"

"Depends," Gabe said, studying the stains across the ceiling tiles. "In the middle of the night, he would have had to walk back to the highway. Even then it might have taken a while. If Jer waited until morning, he could have gone down to the store and hitched with a delivery truck. There are a few people in the cabins who commute into town for work too. So that would have been simple."

"And would Jerry have known this?" Eli asked.

"Yeah." Gabe sat up. "He knows this place as well as I do. We've all been coming here for years."

"Then he probably left in the morning," Eli concluded. "Unless your brother came to get him. Colin could have driven up here and parked on the main road. Though he probably finds driving painfully slow if he's got superspeed."

Gabe stared at the floor between his feet. Braided rug on a piece of roll-end lino. It was no wonder he loved this place, really. It was full of old, stained, discarded stuff that didn't quite measure up in town.

"You think that's what happened to Sean?" Gabe said. "Colin whisked him away?"

Colin hadn't said that Sean was with him, or even that Sean was okay. Only that he was working on it.

Eli shut the window before facing him. "I think that could have happened to Sean. I also think one of the other players in this game could have made off with him."

"Too bad you haven't killed everyone yet," Gabe said.

"I don't know why you think that's funny," Eli told him.

Gabe shrugged. "Me either." He went into the kitchen and put a kettle on for dishwater.

"See if there's dish soap in that cupboard, will you?" he asked Eli.

"I can do the dishes."

"I won't turn that down. Oh, hey, can I borrow your phone for a sec?"

"To what end?" Eli asked. He sounded neutral, curious as to what Gabe intended.

"Thought I'd call Jerry. Even if he's avoiding us, there's no reason not to answer his phone, right? He can always tell me to fuck myself."

Eli paused in the middle of clearing ash-tree seeds from the dishwashing tub.

"I wonder if Alexander Graham Bell ever imagined people would one day use phones to tell other people to fuck themselves."

"My physics teacher said Bell considered phones a nuisance," Gabe said. "Which they are. Colin and I are on the same page about that."

"Good thing you can get by without one," Eli said dryly. "Go ahead. It's in my pack. Outer pocket."

"Thanks," Gabe said. "If the dish soap isn't in that cupboard, then it's in another one. Or it's nowhere. Except probably at the store."

"Thank you for breaking that down for me," Eli said. Gabe flicked the back of Eli's head with one finger before crossing the room to his pack.

Gabe found the phone quickly and decided not to poke around in the pack, tempted though he was to find out what Eli might be carrying in there. The guy was lending Gabe a phone, and he was also doing the dishes, so Gabe owed him a little consideration.

Sandy

JERRY WAS the person to talk to. Sandy was almost sure of it.

As much as Colin loved Gabe, and as close as the two of them were, there were things he would never have said or done in front of Gabe. When it came to his brother, Colin liked to come across like Captain America's better, stronger, nicer counterpart from a world in which everything was a little bit more awesome.

And there was shit Colin didn't tell Sandy either, because… well, she wasn't sure. Because she was like a sister, or because she was a girl, or because she'd disapprove and bawl him out. She'd known for a long time that Colin kept things from her. She hadn't thought it was anything important.

Live and learn.

Anyway, Jerry was the source if anyone was. Maybe he knew about the… powers, whatever… and maybe he didn't, but he would definitely know more about what Colin got up to than Sandy would. Far more than Gabe would. He might even know where Colin had gone.

Sandy was about to call Jerry's cell when a thought came into her mind. She didn't care for it and told it to keep walking, but it stayed. It turned and turned, tromping down a crop circle in her brain. Demanding to know if it was possible that Lloyd might not have been bitching out of turn.

Because here was the thing—when she'd called Jerry in sick that morning, Lloyd had complained that Jerry was never around. And she'd thought Lloyd was being unfair, because Jer wasn't skipping work. He was in Meadow Lake and Turtleford and every other godforsaken place, attaching dingles to dongles or whatever the hell.

Except wouldn't Lloyd have known about the out-of-town work? They had a schedule or something, Sandy was pretty sure.

So maybe….

So maybe, the thought insisted, something was off. And maybe she should talk to Lloyd again.

God help her.

"Dynamic Solutions."

Ah. Good. Cora was back at her post. No one was answering the phone with "Dynamic Mortuary. You stab 'em, we slab 'em. Dynamically." If Sandy had held Cora's job, she would have unplugged the landline and taken it to the bathroom with her. Whatever it took to keep the guys from ever, ever, picking up a call.

"Cora, it's Sandy," she said. "Can I talk to Lloyd?"

"Sandy, hi!" Cora said, sounding pleased as always to be speaking to a fellow adult.

Cora was somewhere between forty and sixty and as big around as a young redwood. Sandy could almost see her upon hearing the sound of her voice. Keen blue eyes behind rhinestone glasses. White-blond hair pinned high on her head and a slash of rose-pink lipstick missing half her lips. She had been known to send employees home with instructions to take a shower and, for God's sake, change their underwear.

"Lloyd's on a call right now. Is there something I can help you with?"

Cora could help, without question. There was nothing about the comings and goings of the service techs that she didn't know. But Cora would also know that Jerry's sick days were none of her business, whereas Lloyd didn't ever seem to care what questions were asked of him or why—he enjoyed having the answers.

"Well," Sandy said, "uh, you know Jerry's out sick today."

"Mm-hmm," Cora said, her voice a little too sweet. And that, right there, was almost enough. The unspoken *Here it comes and what is it this time*?

"He asked me to check how many sick days he had left," Sandy said, "when I called in for him this morning. But I forgot. I thought I'd ask Lloyd instead of you because he's the one I was talking to this morning."

"Oh, honey," Cora said. "I'm sure he's forgotten all about that by now."

Either he had, or he'd remember it until Mt. Everest eroded to nothing. Always one or the other with Lloyd.

"Anyway," Cora went on, "I'm really not supposed to release that information to anyone but Jerry."

"Yeah, I know," Sandy said. "It's just, you know how guys get when they're sick. He is the whiniest bitch right now."

"Oh, I know," Cora said. "You don't have to tell me. You'd think they got different viruses from us."

"Right?" Sandy said. "So he's going to be a bitch tonight when he wakes up with a half degree of fever, and then on top of that, I have to tell him I didn't find out his sick days."

"A half degree of fever," Cora repeated. "Oh, that's a good one. That's about it, all right. Well, I suppose in a sense you're like his wife…."

Acid invaded Sandy's throat at those words, but she swallowed it and said nothing.

"So," Cora said, "I don't mind telling you. He doesn't have any sick leave left at all. He used the last of it earlier this week. Today's going to have to come off his vacation time."

Earlier that week? Another surge of acid. Sandy would have liked to blame it on multiple Pepsis, but she knew better than that.

"Wow," she said with a little cough to smooth out her voice. "He's not gonna be happy to hear that."

"He should learn not to call in sick over every little thing," Cora said. "Or maybe if he spent less time going out with his friends and *getting* sick. I don't mean you, dear."

"No, I hear you," Sandy said. "Hangover is a preventable illness. Thanks, Cora."

"Anytime, dear. You tell Jerry he'd better hurry up and get better. Fast."

"Will do," Sandy said. "Take care."

Gabe

GABE THOUGHT at first he'd screwed up. The sound of a phone ringing inside the cabin made him think that somehow he'd managed to call himself. It wasn't until Eli turned from the dishes, frowning, that Gabe realized the ringing was coming from the bedroom.

"He left his phone?" Eli asked. Gabe followed the ringing to find Jerry's phone lying on the floor beside the bed. From where it was lying, Gabe thought it might have been bumped off the nightstand. He picked it up and took it to the kitchen.

"Must have forgot it," Gabe said.

"Really?" Eli said. "Assuming he did leave of his own accord, he was planning to hitch a ride or walk along the highway. Do you think he would have forgotten his phone?"

"I think he did," Gabe said pointedly, waving a hand at the phone. Then he cocked his head and took a closer look. "Unless…."

"Unless?" Eli said, turning back to the dishes.

Gabe leaned against the counter beside him. "Sean and Jerry have iPhones. Same model. Same case and everything. Jerry got a deal through work and convinced his boss to let Sean have it too."

"He had Sean's phone last night," Eli said. "You think he left with Sean's phone."

Gabe nodded and opened Jerry's phone. It was lucky he'd shoulder-surfed Jerry's lock code earlier that year, for a prank that had never happened.

"Guess I'll call Sean," he said. After a long pause, the phone connected, and he heard one ring, followed by a voice explaining that the cellular customer was not available.

"Tell me something I don't know," Gabe muttered. Off Eli's questioning glance, he added, "No answer. Anyway, I might as well call Sandy."

He called Sandy's cell, figuring he could tell her that Jerry was probably headed into town, but he was put through to her voice-mail.

"It's Gabe," he told it. "I've got Jerry's phone, and he's got Sean's. Call me."

"You could have left a more detailed message," Eli pointed out.

Gabe took a plate from the drying rack and applied a tea towel to it. "A more detailed message would have wound her up, and then I would have a call back saying what do you *mean* Jerry's not there, and *when* did he leave, and *how* do you know he's got Sean's phone, and *why* am I hearing about all this *now*? Seriously, it's better if I can get her on the phone and give out the information in controlled doses."

"That's assuming you're still alive when she calls back," Eli said.

"I'm gonna make a wacky outside bet," Gabe said as he put the plates back into the cupboard, "that I'll be breathing in half an hour. You know, unless you kill me."

"Can you let that go unless or until I actually try to kill you?" Eli said.

"I'll try," Gabe said. He picked up Jerry's phone again and started to flip through apps.

"What are you doing?" Eli asked.

"Jerry and Colin are bestest buds," Gabe said. "There might be some kind of clue in here about where Colin went. Like the number for an Airbnb in Boca Raton. It's not as if we have a ton of other fantastic leads, right?"

"We only have a ton of fantastic problems," Eli agreed.

"We have the kind of problems you see on a milk carton," Gabe said. "Oh, hey, this is a very weird number."

"What is it?"

"It starts with zero one one," Gabe said.

"That's for international dialling," Eli said. "Overseas."

"Ah," Gabe said. "I don't have anyone overseas to call. Unless you count one nine hundred numbers in Thailand."

What's the next part of the number?" Eli asked, ignoring Gabe's hilarity.

"Four nine three oh—" Gabe said. Eli held up a hand to stop him.

"The first two numbers are a country code," he said. "Did you say four nine?"

"Uh...." Gabe checked the phone. "Yeah."

"That's Germany," Eli told him. "The three zero would be a type of area code. In this case, it's for Berlin."

Gabe let his hand with the phone fall and stared at Eli. "Why is Berlin ringing a bell?"

"Could you please hand me my phone?"

Gabe grabbed Eli's phone from the counter and handed it over. Eli began searching for something, pressing buttons and scrolling. Gabe waited, glancing down occasionally at the phone in his own hand. Why would Jerry have been calling Germany? Who could he possibly know in Berlin? A fellow geek, maybe—an internet friend of some kind. Or a supplier. Jerry bought parts sometimes. But he wouldn't use his personal phone for that, would he?

"Read me the rest of your number, please," Eli said. Gabe did so. Eli looked as if he was getting a worse and worse headache with every digit.

"That's it," Eli said. "Whoever called to tip me off about Owen Bernier called from that number."

CHAPTER ELEVEN

Sandy

SANDY WAS halfway to the break room door when her phone rang again. She glanced at it, thinking it would be Gabe. She nearly dropped the phone when she saw Sean's name on the display.

"Jesus fuck, Sean, where are you?" she demanded.

"Ow," a voice that wasn't Sean's responded. "Can you tone it down to, say, jet-engine volume?"

Sandy held the phone away from her ear to check the display again. It still said Sean.

"Jer?" she asked.

"Yeah," he said. "I guess I grabbed Sean's phone by mistake. Sorry about that."

No big deal, Jerry's tone said. Which was funny because Sean had grabbed Jerry's phone by mistake once the previous winter, and Jerry had lost his shit about it. Far out of proportion to the crime.

"Give me a fucking heart attack," she muttered.

"I said fucking sorry about that. I need to talk to you."

"How convenient that we both have phones," Sandy observed.

"It's marvellous," Jerry said. "But I'd rather talk in person. Without the kid around."

Sandy sat on the arm of the break room couch and stared at the bulletin board. A poster encouraging people to contribute to the Secret Santa drive was hanging on from the previous December, now splattered with something dark brown that she could only hope was coffee. Should she take it down? Ah, what the hell. It was early for next year.

"I was thinking the same thing," Sandy told him. "I don't think I can get out of here before closing, but I can meet you after. Want to get dinner somewhere?"

"I'd rather not be seen in public," Jerry said.

"Aren't you still at the cabin?" Sandy asked.

"No. I hitched into town. I've had enough of Gabe's new buddy."

Sandy flicked a piece of lettuce off the couch to the floor. Someone would sweep it up eventually. She could use it as a gauge to see how the cleaning crew was doing.

"I think the guy's probably okay," Sandy said. "But I guess we don't really know."

"Damned fucking right we don't know," Jerry said. "Fuck that guy. Tell you what—I'll meet you on the island, at the trailhead."

There was an island in the river with nature trails on it, and had someone asked Sandy previously whether she'd ever hear Jerry suggest going there, she would have laughed. But it probably wasn't a bad idea as long as she went there straight from work. A lot of people used the park, but the crowd thinned around dinnertime, when kids were starting evening sports and suppers were being served.

"I'll come after work," she offered. "Except I'll stop at Subway or something. You want anything?"

"A bus ticket to the moon," Jerry said. "I hate this town."

"You get that ticket," she said, "get one for me too. I'll see you later."

Sandy glanced at the phone's screen again and saw that she had a message in voice-mail. From Jerry, it said, but playing the message revealed that it was Gabe, helpfully explaining that he had Jerry's phone and Jerry had Sean's. And asking her to call him. He didn't sound panicked, so she assumed nothing was on fire. He probably wanted to know if she'd heard from Jerry, since she was willing to bet Jerry hadn't said goodbye or even left a note. Not with the mood he was in.

Anyway she could talk to Gabe later. If her boss noticed her taking any more break time today, she was going to be looking for a job at Subway instead of just a sandwich.

Gabe

"SO WHOEVER called you," Gabe said slowly, "and said, 'Hey, you might find scary superpeople in North Battleford,' called from that number in Berlin."

Eli nodded. "Right."

"And Jerry has placed—" Gabe checked Jerry's phone. "—at least three calls to that number since yesterday morning. His call log only goes back a week, though. He could have called it a lot more."

Eli was sitting on the back of the couch with his feet on the seat, which would have gotten him banished to the porch if Sandy had been around. Never mind that he'd taken off his shoes.

"Either way," Eli said.

"And you said… you think whoever called you with that tip was trying to set me up."

"Yes," Eli said. "If that number is on his phone, Jerry has been talking to whomever set you up. Were they long calls?"

Gabe scrolled, then held the phone out to Eli. "Under thirty seconds," he said.

Eli took the phone and scrolled in turn. "The first call was after you discovered Colin had left," he said. "The last was shortly after Sean's disappearance."

"And one between when I went to the Mediclinic," Gabe said, "and when my house burned down. It's like… like he's reporting in. Telling someone what's going on around here."

"Or asking for instructions," Eli said. "From your brother?"

"You think Colin is in Germany giving Jerry instructions for, like, arson."

"He could be. I'm sure he gets around. But you're right, there could be other people using that number. I know there's a little club of them working together. Jack's involved, of course. The bad news is that obviously your brother is too."

Eli was right, though Gabe couldn't tell him so. Neither could he say that, yes, Eli had the facts down, but things weren't what they seemed. Gabe wanted to explain, tell Eli that Colin was working with them because they'd promised to leave the other people in Colin's life alone. And they were scared of Eli, too, so they were banding together because of him, and maybe some of them wouldn't be in that club at all if they weren't afraid of being killed.

Since Gabe officially knew none of that, or any of the other things Colin had told him, he went a different way.

"Where does Jerry come into this?" he asked. "I can buy that maybe the people with powers all talk to each other. But Jerry's only power is driving to Green Lake to turn a computer off and on again. What does somebody like Colin need from a crabby IT guy?"

"Interesting question," Eli said.

Gabe stopped pacing and stared at him. "No. It isn't. The answer is, he does not need Jerry for anything."

"It's too bad Jerry isn't answering his phone," Eli said. "We could ask him to settle this."

"So helpful," Gabe said. "Aw, fuck. I gotta call Sandy and tell her this."

"Tell her to stay away from Jerry."

Gabe reached for Jerry's phone, making a "gimme" motion with his hand. Eli gave him the phone, and Gabe took a step away before saying, "We've known Jerry since elementary school. He's an asshole, but he's not a monster. If he's involved in this at all, he doesn't know he is. Colin could have asked him to leave a message at that Berlin number. Or Colin could have borrowed the phone. I truly hate standing up for Jerry, but there's no reason to think he's actually involved."

"I wouldn't say no reason," Eli said. "Tell Sandy to stay away from him."

Gabe chose Sandy's work number this time, the one he wasn't supposed to call, ever, because it was for customers and he wasn't one, are you, Gabriel? Are you a customer?

"Janowski's Auto Repair."

Sandy sounded like her mom when she answered her work phone. Gabe had never had the nerve to tell her so.

"Don't hang up," Gabe said. Eli raised his brows, and Gabe turned his back to Eli. He didn't need distraction.

"Gabe, for fuck's sake!"

Now that was Sandy as Gabe knew and loved her.

"If you kept talking fancy to me, the people at your end would never know I wasn't a customer," Gabe pointed out.

"They would," Sandy told him, "because I don't threaten to break my foot off in the asses of customers. What do you want?"

"We've found something out," Gabe said. "Jerry is connected with whomever tipped Eli off about Owen Bernier. Eli has the number of the person who called him with the tip, and we found that same number on Jerry's phone. Also, it's for a phone in Berlin."

Sandy didn't say anything for so long that Gabe thought maybe she'd hung up.

"Well," she said finally, startling him. "That's pretty weird."

"Isn't it?" Gabe agreed. "We need to talk to Jerry."

"Definitely," Sandy said. "Whatever's going on, he and Colin must be in it together. He's been calling in sick to work a lot lately—I found that out when I called him in sick this morning."

Gabe sat on the arm of the couch Eli had slept on. "Like this week when he said he was in Meadow Lake? He wasn't?"

Sandy laughed. It was short and sounded as if it had hurt her throat on the way out.

"Maybe he was," she said. "But he wasn't fixing computers there. I'm gonna talk to him."

"Okay," Gabe said. "But you'll have to find him first. He left here sometime—"

"I know," Sandy said. "I don't know when he left, but he called me to say he was in town. I'm meeting him after work."

"Oh." Gabe leaned back. He felt a tiny bit more relaxed. "Good. That takes care of that. Where should we meet you?"

"How does nowhere strike you?"

"I'm afraid I'll have to counteroffer," Gabe said, "with somewhere."

Gabe heard Eli move on the other couch. Getting up to get in his face, most likely.

"He doesn't want to talk in front of the new guy, and he really doesn't want to talk in front of you. He probably promised Colin not to tell you some shit. Whatever it is, I'll get it out of him, and then we can all deal with it."

Sandy was pretty good at managing Jerry. It might not be the worst idea to let her do it.

"Yeah, okay," Gabe said. "He'll probably be easier to deal with if you settle him down fir—*hey*!"

Sandy

"HEY!"

It was the last thing Sandy heard from Gabe before the sound of a scuffle, complete with Gabe cursing and bursts of violin as Gabe's field went off.

"Gabe?" she called into the phone, as if that would make a difference. What the hell was going on there? Where was Eli?

"Give me that!" Gabe said, sounding distant.

"In a minute," Eli said, closer. It sounded like Eli anyway.

"Eli?" Sandy asked. "What the fuck?"

One of the mechanics glanced up from the coffee stand a few feet away. Right. She needed to keep her voice down.

"Gabe won't tell you to stay away from Jerry," Eli said. "I think Jerry might be danger—*oof*!"

Another scuffle, this one shorter, and Gabe's voice was back.

"Sorry. Someone thinks he can take the fucking phone away from me without asking."

"Hey, Gabe?" she said.

"Yeah?"

"Can I talk to Eli?"

"Very fucking funny," Gabe said. Sandy took a moment to breathe. She was pleased to see that the mechanic wasn't staring at her anymore.

"Gabe, I really do want to talk to Eli. Please?"

"He's gonna talk a bunch of shit about Jerry," Gabe said.

Sandy wished she were in the cabin, standing next to him so she could slap him upside the head. "Gabriel. Put Eli on the phone."

Gabe sighed theatrically, but the sound of footsteps and the phone changing hands told her he had decided to comply.

"Jerry could be dangerous," Eli said a moment later. "Is he with you right now?"

"No," Sandy said. "I'm meeting him later."

"Don't," Eli said. "Tell me what the arrangements are. Gabe and I can meet him."

It was funny, almost. It would have been under different circumstances. Here was some guy she'd known for two days—not even—saying she was supposed to trust him further than she trusted one of her oldest friends. Not to mention the part where this was all supposed to be too dangerous for her, but dragging the kid along was fine.

"No deal," Sandy said.

From the way Eli was breathing, she could almost see him summoning patience.

"Sandy, I really think—"

"Do you know something about Jerry that I don't?" she asked. "Is there something Gabe hasn't told me?"

"No," Eli said. He hesitated, as if he were about to say more. She waited, to give him a chance, but he seemed to decide against it.

"Then, no offence, but I've known this guy a lot longer than you have, and nothing I've heard today has convinced me that he's a psycho killer. He's definitely a lying asshole, and I'm sure he knows things he should have told us already, but that's kind of Jerry's style. Okay? I can deal with this."

"One person is dead," Eli said. "Another is missing and probably dead."

Sandy thought about the freezer, and the blood. She said nothing.

"And your friend Sean is missing," Eli added. "Whatever you've caught Jerry lying about before, it was probably not this serious."

Sandy eyed the row of business cards in front of her, Sean's among them. He was supposed to carry them to give out to potential customers. He never did, though. He always wound up writing his number on napkins or bar coasters or the backs of receipts. At least once a month, someone called saying they'd found this number on a napkin without a name or anything, and what the hell was it, anyway? Jerry had laughed when she'd told him that, particularly when she'd told him that all of the callers were women.

"These are my people," Sandy told Eli. "I will deal with them."

"Can we be there while you do?" Eli said, "I won't say anything."

"Then Jerry will tell me fuck all," Sandy said. "And by the way, if you think something is that dangerous, leave Gabe out of it."

"Gabe is bulletproof," Eli said. Now Sandy wanted to slap Eli upside the head. Maybe the thing to do would be to knock Eli's and Gabe's heads together.

"Because he has that field?" she hissed, turning slightly away from her desk and toward the wall. "Does it need to be recharged somehow? For all you know, he can only take one bullet a week, and then he needs to build it up again. Maybe I drained it stabbing him yesterday. We don't really know anything about it."

There was a pause before Eli said, "You make a good point."

"Fucking right I do," Sandy said. "I will give Jerry your regards."

Whatever Eli said to that was lost on her, as she had already hung up.

Gabe

THEY HADN'T wasted any time getting on the road, backpacks thrown into the car and the cabin door left unlocked because Sandy hadn't thought to leave the key.

Gabe let Eli drive and got settled into the passenger seat, his feet up on the dash. As they left the park, he was leaning against the passenger door and staring out the window to the tops of trees. There were some damned tall jack pines in the area. They had to be older than anyone he knew.

They'd been on the main road for a few minutes when Gabe said, "What good point did she make?"

Eli glanced at him, brow wrinkled almost comically. "What?"

"You told Sandy she'd made a good point. What was it?"

"Oh." Eli breathed deep. "She said we don't know much about your field. It might get drained if you use it too much. I was thinking, too, it could get weaker or stronger under certain conditions. And we don't know about its limits. You probably shouldn't jump out of any planes."

"Wasn't planning on it," Gabe said. "Although actually I think terminal velocity would be my friend. Right? Like, it probably wouldn't be any worse than jumping off a tall building."

"Don't do that either."

"Roger that," Gabe said. "Oh fuck—that reminds me. Speaking of rogering…."

"We weren't," Eli said quickly. Gabe laughed.

"Sorry, man. I don't mean to make you uncomfortable, but I'm not gonna talk about this with Sandy."

"I'm sure you could," Eli said. "She doesn't seem like a bashful flower."

"She's not," Gabe said. "I am. Seriously, man, with this field and everything… how am I supposed to get laid?"

Eli's mouth curved up on one side. "Looking the way you do," he said, his eyes firmly trained on the road, "if you walk into a gay bar and can't get laid, you must be doing something so wrong that I doubt anyone could help you."

"You know that's not what I mean," Gabe said. He pulled on the lever between his seat and the door and was pleased to find that the seat reclined. He shoved it back with his shoulder until he could curl up on his side, facing Eli. "How do I know my field won't go off when I'm having sex with someone?"

"You could settle for holding hands and gazing at the stars," Eli suggested. Gabe swatted Eli's shoulder, causing a quick flash without sound.

"It's fine for you to joke about this," Gabe said, "but it's pretty fucking serious to me."

Eli shook his head. "I can't believe this is your primary concern, under the circumstances."

Gabe grinned. "I'm eighteen."

"Don't I know it," Eli sighed. "I'm not trying to be an asshole. I was eighteen two years ago. I don't know how, but I'm sure you'll work something out. Considering how important this is to you."

Gabe watched Eli's face. It told him nothing. There was still a trace of a blush there, though, from when Gabe had mentioned sex in the first place.

Gabe placed a hand on his own leg and ran his fingertips over the seam in his jeans, the slight roughness calming him. He could feel that, though he couldn't feel fire or wind. Maybe he had more control over this than it seemed.

"Maybe I can let things through if I want," he said. "That'd be good—in case I need, I don't know, a face lift or something. To keep looking this great."

Eli laughed. He always seemed surprised before laughing.

"Maybe you've got the ultimate sunscreen and moisturizer," he said. "Actually you might want to take vitamin D pills, if that's the case. Since you won't be getting enough sun."

"Right now this field seems to go on and off by itself. It makes its own decisions. But I'm getting better with it, I think. I didn't get a hole in my shirt when Jack shot me, even though I lost all my clothes in the bike accident. I might eventually learn to control it."

"You might," Eli said. "Or you could not use it."

"I'll figure it out," Gabe said. "I hope it doesn't flicker out on me when I'm jumping off a skyscraper."

"A problem easily avoided," Eli said, "by not doing that. Don't put yourself in situations where you have to rely on this field."

"Otherwise you'll have to kill me," Gabe concluded.

Eli raised his brows at Gabe. "Otherwise I might *not* have to kill you," he said.

Gabe snorted a laugh. "Okay. Point taken."

"I doubt it," Eli said.

"I wonder why Colin's not getting laid. Do you think he has a field or something?"

"Dunno. He might be worried about his strength. Maybe he can't stay in control of it when he's worked up."

"Gross," Gabe said. "That's awful."

"It's not great."

There was another thing. A stupid thing, really. Gabe wouldn't have even brought it up if Colin hadn't said what he'd said. About Eli being maybe kind of sort of attracted. To Gabe.

"So, when we were fighting over the phone," Gabe said, "back in the cabin? And you were on top of me at one point? You seemed kind of… into it. I mean, I noticed. Is what I'm saying."

Eli's jaw tightened. Gabe told himself not to smile.

"I know that doesn't necessarily mean anything," he went on. "Obviously I know that. Like, so well. But you've made a few comments about my appearance, and I kind of get the sense tha—"

"Yes," Eli said sharply. "All right? I said you were attractive. I meant it."

"Obviously I'm not here to judge you about that," Gabe said. "Or anything else, really."

Eli said nothing.

"If I were, though," Gabe added, "here to judge you? Overall, I'm impressed."

Eli shoved the palm of his hand against the steering wheel. It was a short, rough strike that had probably been hard enough to bruise. For a minute or two anyway.

"You are a lot of trouble," he said. "And this isn't the time to parse all the kinds of trouble you are. We are going to talk about something else now."

"Just because I'm *in* trouble doesn't mean that I *am*—" Gabe started.

"Shut up or walk!" Eli said.

Gabe stared at him. "I'll shut up."

"Good."

The woods blurred into prairie. Gabe watched birds circling the bright little sloughs. They were acting as if everything was the same as it had been a week ago.

"Knowing what you know about Jerry," Eli said. "What you found out today. Can you think of anything suspicious Jerry might have done over the past few weeks? Is there anything you see in a different light?"

Gabe wasn't even sure what he knew about Jerry. He knew Jerry was up to something. That Jerry knew more than he was saying about this whole situation. And that he'd been skipping out on work, which was something Eli didn't even know.

"Sandy says Jerry's been missing work," he said. "She found out when she called him in sick today."

"Not surprising," Eli said. "You still think Jerry's not involved?"

"It could still be all the sketchy shit they do. Low-key criminal bullshit. It doesn't have to be the superpower thing."

"Criminal bullshit. But you insist that your brother is a good man."

Gabe banged his head lightly against the seat, trying to shake the right words into place.

"They're sketchy!" he said. "We're poor, and we're on our own. Colin had to take care of me somehow. Everything costs money. The whole world is a fucking crime scene if you want to know the truth, because we're all getting ripped off by, like, the same fifty people, and those people put the rest of us in jail for selling loosies. Fucking billionaires are your really bad guys. My people are honourable where it counts."

GABE KNOWS he should turn around. He's not supposed to be here on so many levels. It's a bar, and he's fifteen, and it's mid-afternoon on a school day. He should turn and run and be grateful that his brother didn't see him.

The thing is, though, he doesn't know what his brother is doing here. Not Jerry either, actually. They're both supposed to be at work, and Colin's on a job out of town for two days, so what the hell? There's no way they should be in a pine booth at the back of O'Leary's, holding a pair of beers that are about to join a legion of dead soldiers.

Gabe edges closer, wanting to hear what they're saying. Their faces are serious, and they're leaning forward a little, as if concerned about being overheard in this nearly empty bar.

The light's dim and yellow, and it's hard to be sure, but he thinks he sees red on Jerry's shirt and the side of his face. Rusty red, like dried blood. Ketchup, maybe? Gabe takes another step, fixated on the stains, and that's when Colin sits up straight and looks at him, quick and sharp as a hawk.

"What in the Christ are you doing here?"

It's quiet enough that the bartender doesn't seem to hear it, but plenty loud to Gabe's ears. He goes to the booth and stands in front of it. No sense in running. He's been spotted, so the damage is done.

"Cutting class?" Gabe offers. Colin's raised brows tell him this isn't a good time for wisecracks.

"Put that together myself, Gabriel."

Gabe nods. The best hope he's got is the truth. So he tells it.

"They've got a blues band here tonight, and the guitar player does this thing I'm having trouble with. I thought if I showed up around soundcheck, maybe I could get him to teach me."

Colin's expression changes a little. Not so anyone would notice if they didn't know his face, but he's not as angry now. Still serious, but.... Gabe studies him, the lines of his tanned face and the vivid blue eyes under long black lashes. It's relief, Gabe decides. He's seeing relief.

Jerry, on the other hand, is like a kid who's seen the class nerd get a swirlie.

"Lemme get this straight," he says. "You cut class and snuck into a bar so you could get a guitar lesson?"

Gabe shrugs, like he doesn't care about whatever is so fucking funny. "So?"

Jerry finishes his beer and taps the bottle against Colin's. Gabe can see Jerry's fingernails under the hanging light, dirt and that same rusty red beneath them. Colin eyes Jerry with bland curiosity.

"Colin," Jerry says, "you want my advice? You need to stop worrying about raising a delinquent and start worrying about raising a fucking dork."

Colin nods thoughtfully. He seems angry again, but it's another of his subtle buried expressions. Like a drawing of an angry face that was made a dozen sheets of notepad ago.

Still, Jerry can see it. Gabe can tell by the way Jerry sits up, pressing his back against the booth and pulling his beer to his side of the table.

"Nobody wants your advice, Jerry," Colin says. "Leave now."

Jerry scoots out of the booth so quickly that Gabe has to jump aside to avoid being run over.

"Pleasure as always," Jerry tells Colin. Colin doesn't move. Jerry snorts and leaves, Trooper playing him out over the bar's tinny speakers. Good old "General Hand Grenade."

Colin gestures at Jerry's empty seat, and Gabe takes it. This is where he gets the shit he's about to catch. Gabe knows that. But he's almost too curious to care.

"I don't want you cutting class," Colin says, as if Gabe might have thought otherwise.

"I know," Gabe says. "But I really wanted to talk to this guy, and he's only in town for one day, and I've got a ninety-five in soc anyway."

The corner of Colin's mouth rises as if someone has tugged on it with a string. "You might be a dork," he says.

Gabe grins, pressure lifting from his chest. "I'm a guitarist," he says. "I am automatically cool."

"Of course," Colin says. "My mistake."

"What are you doing here?" Gabe asks, unable to hold the question in any longer. "You're supposed to be up at Turtle."

Colin nods. "Yes, I am."

Gabe frowns. "What was that red stuff on Jerry? It kind of looked like—"

"Gabe," Colin says, "I lied to you about the job at Turtle. And Jerry has blood on him, and I will tell you it's from a deer, okay? Because I don't want you getting crazy shit in your crazy head. It's deer blood, and we're not in any trouble. But that's all I'm going to tell you."

"You're kidding, right?"

"No," Colin says.

Gabe wants to reach for Jerry's beer, see if maybe there's some left, but he doesn't really want to drink from Jerry's bottle. Besides, anything that might remind Colin that his kid brother is in a bar is probably a bad move.

"You lied to me."

"Right."

"You can't do that," Gabe protests. "You told me you would never lie to me."

"I said that before Mom died," Colin says. All the anger is gone from his face now. "Gabe... you're crowding me. The truth is, I don't want to talk to you about everything I do. I don't want you to know about everything I do. I need some privacy."

"So you've been lying to me for, like, two years?" Gabe asks. "Telling me you were out of town and then doing fuck knows what with Jerry?"

"I'm not going to discuss that with you," Colin tells him, and Gabe would prefer that Colin break one of the empties and cut him with it, because he's pretty sure it would hurt less than Colin using that end-of-discussion tone on him.

"I thought you said we were in this together," Gabe reminds him. "After Mom died, you said that."

Colin nods, and his expression softens again. "We are. In general. But there's a zone where I'm your guardian, and we're not in that together. It's my responsibility."

Gabe leans back and rolls his eyes. "Come on. That's legal bullshit we had to do so I could stay at home."

"No." Colin sets his beer down so hard that people from across the bar glance at them. Gabe tenses, though he knows he won't be hit. It's just the force of Colin's anger and frustration, slamming into him across a table that seems far too narrow right now. "Being your guardian is the most important thing I do. I am serious about it, and it means you can't be my buddy the way Jerry is. Not for a while."

"Why the hell not?" Gabe demands.

"Because," Colin says, "you can't ground your buddy."

"So don't ground me," Gabe says.

"Don't cut class," Colin shoots back. "Gabe, when you're eighteen and you've got your high school diploma, I will be proud and happy to be your friend. I mean, if you don't still think I'm a dick for grounding you. But until then we're not friends."

"Damn right we're not," Gabe says. He knows he's being petulant, even as he's being it, but his chest hurts and his eyes hurt and he can't help it. "If you're fucking deer hunting with Jerry and telling me you're at work."

Colin smiles tightly. "I am twenty-one years old, Gabriel. I get up to some shit that is not age-appropriate for you. When you're eighteen and we're friends again... that'll be different. For now, there are parts of my life that I'm keeping you out of."

"Uh-huh," Gabe says. He starts picking at the label on one of the bottles. It gives him something to do, something to look at that isn't Colin's face. "So when you and Jerry don't come back sometime and all I know is you were supposedly at work—"

"That—" Colin says. "Gabe, look at me."

Gabe does so. He doesn't want to, but he has trouble not doing what Colin says when Colin sounds hurt.

"Gabe. That will not happen. I promise. I am not going to get arrested or disappear. I'm not going to bail on you."

Gabe could point out that Colin could get hit by a truck or fall off a girder or have a blood vessel in his head pop, like this guy on a TV show Gabe saw. He doesn't, though, because he can tell that Colin means this.

"Okay," he says instead.

"Okay," Colin answers. He reaches across the table to squeeze Gabe's forearm. "Good talk. Now get out of here."

Gabe puts his hand on Colin's for a second, then slips out of the booth. He's halfway to the door when Colin stops him.

"Hey—one more thing."

Gabe turns to face him. "Yeah?"

"You're grounded for two weeks. You don't go anywhere except school unless you're with me."

"But—"

"Whine and get three weeks. Another thing. If I find out you've been cutting class again—and I will find out—you will get far worse. Now get the fuck back to school."

Gabe is surprised to find himself smiling. "So you know," he says, "I think you're a dick for grounding me."

Colin returns the smile. "I love you too."

Gabe starts to leave again, but he's only taken one step when Colin says his name. Gabe spins around.

"What, dude? I'm getting whiplash here."

"Talk to your guitar guy," Colin says. "Then go back to school."

"DEER BLOOD," Eli said.

"It could have been," Gabe said. "Or calf or lamb. They poached. Stop trying to make this into something. The point is that Colin and Jerry being kind of dirtbaggy doesn't mean they're bad guys."

"Again, Gabe, I remind you that you're not stupid."

"Oh, I'm being dumb? We're just south of lake country, and there are deer all over the fucking place, but Jerry probably had blood on him because he was murdering sorority girls?"

Gabe was prevented from making further arguments by Jerry's phone ringing, the sound hitting him like a bell being slammed against the inside of his chest.

"Why does everyone put up with these things?" Gabe said as he unlocked the phone. "Yeah? Hello?"

"I forgot to tell you something."

It wasn't until he heard Sandy's voice that Gabe realized it could have been anyone calling. It could have been Berlin. And he'd answered it all casual, like an idiot.

"You what?"

"Am I interrupting something?"

Sandy sounded irritatingly amused by the notion of what she might be interrupting. Gabe wanted to tell her to stick it, since he'd been shot down only a few minutes earlier and damned if it wasn't still stinging, but he wasn't going to talk about that with the shooter beside him.

"One of the worst days of my life," he said. "That's about it. What did you forget?"

"That cop came to see me—did I tell you that? The detective guy?"

"You did not mention that," Gabe said. "What did he want?"

"He wanted to good-cop me," Sandy said. "But, Gabe, he told me something—the cops have your freezer."

The funny thing was the sky was blue and the trees were green and pretty normal looking, and they were driving behind a boring little Hyundai, and in general the world did not seem like crazy bizarro land. So obviously Sandy had not said that the cops had his freezer. Because that would have been nuts.

"Come again?" Gabe asked.

"The cops have your freezer," Sandy said distinctly. "It didn't burn up in the fire."

"No, I guess it wouldn't," Gabe agreed. Apparently Sandy was determined to have a nutty conversation, so why not play along? "Do the cops need someplace to store their Pizza Pops?"

Eli shot him a look. Gabe stared out the passenger window. He heard Sandy sigh.

"This is fucking serious, Gabriel."

Gabe shut his eyes and laid his forehead against the glass.

"Why did they take our freezer?" he asked.

"Because, apparently, there's blood all over the inside of it."

Gabe's eyes opened. "The fuck?" he inquired.

"They think it's that Owen's blood, but they're having it tested to see."

He had a mad impulse to say that it had probably been a deer.

"Colin probably cut himself or some shit," Gabe said. He couldn't see Eli, but he didn't have to. He knew there were eyes boring into him, all "I told you so." Like this proved anything.

"The cops don't think it's like that," Sandy told him.

"They have their minds made up," Gabe said. "Everything seems like proof to them because they already think he did it. It's bullshit."

"Bullshit like that lands people in jail," Sandy pointed out. Gabe said nothing. He was too busy trying to keep his breakfast down. She added, "Maybe we should talk to a lawyer."

"Sandy, if you don't wanna talk to Jer alone…."

"Oh, fuck off," Sandy said. "You've been listening to your new buddy, haven't you? As if I can't have a conversation with Jerry McClelland. That will be the motherfucking day."

"Yeah," Gabe said. "Okay. Sorry."

"I'll call you after I'm done with him, okay?"

"I look forward to it," Gabe said.

"Oh, and they found Colin's truck. The cops. It was a few miles east of the city, but they probably towed it or something. It's probably not still there."

"Jesus! Take your sweet time telling me, Sandra!"

Eli made a soft questioning sound. Gabe ignored it.

"I almost forgot," Sandy said. "It's not a big deal, Gabe. We know Colin cut out, right? So he ditched his truck a few miles east of town. The cops said there was no accident or anything. He ditched the truck."

"Fuck. Is it in the fucking impound?"

"I don't know," Sandy said. "Leave it for now."

"They charge you to get stuff out of impound," Gabe pointed out. "Like, a lot."

"I know," Sandy said. She sounded tired. "Leave it for now. We'll figure something out later."

"Okay," Gabe said.

"Okay," Sandy replied.

After a few beats of silence, he decided Sandy must have hung up. He did the same and put the phone into his pack again.

"So the police found Colin's truck," Eli said. "And they found blood in your freezer."

"You put that together," Gabe said with bright wonder, "from sitting right there while I talked about it? You really are a detective."

"Sarcasm will not make this better," Eli informed him.

Gabe wanted to say that sarcasm always made things better, but he knew it for a lie.

"Have they identified the blood?" Eli asked.

Gabe shook his head. "They're testing it. Sandy said it takes a while."

"It does if they're DNA testing," Eli said. "Typing it and distinguishing human from animal is much faster."

"I guess they're DNA testing," Gabe said. "They probably already did the other stuff."

"Probably. When we get to town, I think we should check the remains of your house. I doubt Jerry would have been digging through it for mementos. He was probably looking for something important."

"Okay," Gabe said. "We can dig through the ruins. There might be cops watching the place, though."

"So think up something to do about that," Eli said.

It couldn't have been more obvious that he was giving Gabe a chore to get Gabe's mind off… well, everything. But Gabe couldn't really object. The truth was, he was grateful for it.

"Two-person cow suit?" Gabe offered. "Like in *Top Secret*?"

"Keep thinking," Eli said crisply. He did not quite manage to hide his smile.

Sandy

BOYS AND their penises. That was, Sandy decided, the heart of all the problems she was dealing with. Gabe, presented with a good-looking blond guy, was—after one day—trusting that guy over Jerry. Sure, Jerry had been a friend to both Gabe and Colin for nearly a decade. Sure, that one time that Gabe had gotten food poisoning and Colin had been away at a job site, Jerry had taken Gabe to the hospital, filled out all the paperwork, and stayed with Gabe until the hospital kicked Jerry out for not being a relative. And yeah, Jerry had filched an old laptop from his job and added bits and pieces from other junkers until Gabe had something he could use for high school. But Jerry wasn't a mysterious blond from out of town, so apparently none of that mattered.

And then there was Colin, fucking around with bar girls and breaking their hearts and pissing off their co-workers because God forbid the guy should get a nice steady girlfriend and stop being the asshole of the county.

By the time Sandy reached the front of the line, she was toying with the idea of castrating the lot of them.

"Hey, you."

Sandy shook herself out of her thoughts and smiled in relief at seeing Abby's wide grin on the other side of the Subway counter. Abby was a sensible human being. She and Sandy had bonded during a few high school detentions.

"I was scared the crazy chick would be on," Sandy said.

Abby laughed. "Oh. My. God. She threw a sub at a customer last week. I was so unsurprised—when they told me, I swear to God, all I said was, was it a hot or cold sub? Like, a meatball would have been the worst."

"I can't believe they haven't fired her," Sandy said. She glanced over her shoulder to check for waiting customers and was pleased to see that she'd been the last person in line. She and Abby would, with luck, have a few minutes to chat.

"She's got to have, like, video of the district manager doing a goat," Abby agreed. Then her heart-shaped face fell.

"Is it true that the Reeces' house burned down? And that the cops are looking for them? And about Tracy from the casino being dead or whatever? Are the cops really looking for Colin about that?"

"Where did you—" Sandy started but stopped as she realized she didn't care. And she wasn't surprised, really, that the word was out. A murder, a disappearance, and a house fire.... It didn't get much more exciting than that in her town.

"Yeah," she said. "The cops have some stupid idea about this shit. I don't know. The boys did nothing."

"Well, Gabe," Abby said. "I mean, as if Gabe. Or, uh, Colin. They're the Reeces, you know? Like they're big criminals?"

"They're not," Sandy confirmed. "They're petty criminals."

"Yeah," Abby said. "Oh, hey, I feel like a total shit, but... do you think they're hiring at the casino? Because it would beat the hell out of this job."

Abby probably could get on at the casino, with her big brown eyes and thick blond hair and curves that might run wild one day but were all in place for now. She could have been working at the casino already, Sandy guessed, if she'd applied.

Like the dead girl or the missing guy.

"This place is chiller," Sandy said "Um... six-inch ham on brown."

"Not toasted, right?" Abby said. "And the white cheese."

"I should have ordered it as my usual," Sandy said.

Abby nodded. "I try to remember customers' orders," she said. "It keeps me awake. Oh, hey, you should've seen Gabe the last time he was in here. He got Liz—you know, the crazy chick?"

"The sub thrower," Sandy said.

"She asked Gabe if he wanted white or yellow cheese, and he was all, those are not kinds of cheese. Those are colours. He kept asking her what the cheese really was, and she was, you know, it's *orange*, and no, that is a *colour*, not a kind of cheese, and back and forth like that for, like, at least five minutes. It was just Gabe and Jerry in here, so it was okay. I mean, the nutritional stuff is in that brochure by the register, and Gabe could have looked it up, but you know Gabe. And he hates Liz, I think. Like, more than the other customers do."

"Not more than I do," Sandy said. "I'm pretty sure."

"Or the guy who got the sub thrown at him," Abby said. "Anyway. You want chips or anything?"

"Yeah, chips and a drink," Sandy said. "This is supper."

"I've got a couple of broken cookies," Abby said. "If you want. Like, for free. We're not supposed to give them out, but what else are we gonna do with them?"

"Sold," Sandy said. "Thank you. And can I have whatever Jerry usually gets, for Jerry? I'm meeting him at Finlayson after this."

As she grabbed a cup and went to the fountain, it crossed her mind that she should tell Abby not to apply at the casino. It seemed dangerous. But then as she tested a few jets to find one that seemed like it was mixed right, she decided that wasn't accurate. The casino probably wasn't dangerous in general.

"Take care," she said instead as she headed for the door.

"You too," Abby said. "Seriously."

Seriously. Sandy gave her a wave and left.

Gabe

"I DON'T MEAN to rush you on the plan," Eli said, "but we're about five minutes out of town."

"Can you shoot?" Gabe asked.

Eli glanced at him. "I didn't bring my gun."

"But you can shoot," Gabe said.

"Yes."

"A handgun, or can you—we're going to need more range than that."

"I can shoot," Eli repeated.

Gabe shrugged. "Turn left at the lights."

Gabe directed him carefully through side streets and alleys to the back of a three-floor walk-up.

"I need something out of the back of that truck," Gabe said, pointing out a venerable green pickup with a tiny propeller welded to the trailer hitch and an I Took the Red Pill decal along the cab's back window.

"The owner seems classy," Eli observed.

Gabe snorted. "You have no idea. But his life is about to suck, so it's okay. Pull in next to the dumpster."

"This a friend of yours?" Eli asked as Gabe opened the passenger door.

"Not hardly," Gabe said. "He's my brother's foreman, and he's a total fedora. Keeps hitting on Sandy. It's creepy. Hey, actually, Lockpick Man, can you get the lock on that box?"

He indicated a wooden box in the back of the truck. A padlock was keeping it shut, holding together a hasp set that was half pulled out of the box's weathered boards.

"I was gonna pull it open," Gabe said. "But it might be easier…."

"Your way's easier," Eli said. "Whatever you're doing, do it quickly."

Gabe clambered into the truck box, careful to keep his head down, and grabbed the tire iron from the middle of a spare tire that lay under a canvas tarp. Eli turned out to have been right—two quick tugs and the splintered wood spit the hasp out. Gabe rubbed the iron off on his jeans, dropped it, and quickly pulled a rifle and ammo from the box. Seconds later he was back in the car and Eli was heading down the alley to the street.

"Colin told him he needed a better lockbox," Gabe explained quickly. "The guy would not listen."

"I agree with Colin about something," Eli said. "Directions?"

"First left after the stop sign," Gabe said. "We're going a ways uphill."

Gabe didn't feel the need to say much when they'd reached their destination, a dirt road at the top of a rise. There was cover from caragana, and a good view of Gabe's former home through the branches of the shrubs. A patrol car sat in a nearby alley.

"Are you a good shot?" Gabe asked. "Really good?"

Eli turned from peering through the caragana to stare at Gabe. His face was unreadable. "You want me to shoot a police officer?"

"What?" Gabe's stomach lurched. "God, no! I want you to shoot her car. Maybe get the lights on top or something. So she'll come up here to investigate."

Eli seemed both relieved and incredulous, which Gabe considered impressive. They weren't expressions often found together.

"She'll call it in," Eli said distinctly, as if Gabe had proven himself irretrievably slow. "On the radio. Cars will come. We'll be trapped up here."

Gabe laughed. "It's the Battlefords. First she'll be confused about what happened because she is not used to being shot at. Then she'll get out, see the damage, figure some shit out, and decide the shot came from this location. By this time, we're gone. She calls it in, but she's the closest of the fuckin' two cars they've got on this side of the river, so she has to come up here to investigate. Now we are long gone. And maybe she sees us at the house—maybe—but she's up here searching for a shooter, so she's got bigger issues."

"We can't just vandalize another school?" Eli asked.

"We can if you love it that much," Gabe said. "But I think the cops might remember that we did that to them yesterday."

"You want me to shoot a police vehicle with a rifle," Eli said.

"Only if you're a good shot," Gabe stressed, meeting Eli's eyes. "I don't want there to be any chance that you'll hurt someone."

"And… leave the rifle here?"

"If you would be so kind," Gabe said pleasantly. "Carl's probably got an alibi, and his gun was clearly stolen, but he'll get charged for keeping it in that stupid box, and the cops will be right up his ass. Let me have a small ray of light in this shitty day."

"And you don't believe the cop will recognize this as a distraction."

"Maybe," Gabe conceded. "But she'll have to come up here anyway. Besides, cops in this town…. I don't know exactly what they make, but those servers we met at the casino yesterday? They make more. City cops around here get no money, and I bet they get shit for training. I'm not saying she's dumb. She's just not prepared to deal with this."

"Okay," Eli said. "If you're certain."

Gabe blinked. "Seriously? You'll do it?"

"It's far from the craziest thing I've done," Eli said calmly. He went to the car and took a thin pair of gloves from his pack, then pulled out the rifle and loaded it. Gabe got into the driver's seat and put the key into the ignition. He didn't have to wait long before a single shot came from the left of the car. Seconds later, Eli was in the passenger seat.

"Go," he said. Unnecessarily, since Gabe was already rolling.

Sandy

SANDY HAD half expected Jerry to be hiding in the bushes or something. Maybe wearing shades and a wool hat and holding a newspaper in front of his face. But he seemed to think he'd go unnoticed on the island, because he was leaning against the trailhead sign with his face hanging out when Sandy arrived.

"Fancy meeting you here," Jerry said.

"Hell of a coincidence," Sandy answered. She looked around the gravel parking lot and only saw one other vehicle, a Jeep that had been left topless by its owners. Sandy would never have enough faith in her fellow human beings to leave an open convertible in an unsupervised place. Not a motorcycle either. But possibly she overestimated the number of people around who both could and would hotwire things.

"I got you a cold-cut combo," Sandy said, holding up the plastic bag.

"I told you not to get me anything."

"Then throw it in the river."

"You here by yourself?" Jerry asked. There was a strain to his voice, and she saw now that his casual stance, leaning on the sign, was misleading. His limbs and face were tense.

"Am I dropping off ransom money?" she asked. She tried to make it light, a joke, but her own tension was in the words. Jerry raised his brows and, at the same time, stood up straight.

"I don't want to see Reece the Younger right now."

"Is that why you ran out on him this morning?" Sandy asked.

Jerry huffed air out through his nose. "Christ, Sandy. He's eighteen. It's not like I abandoned a child. You need to cut the cord."

Sandy took a few careful steps back until she was next to a picnic table a few feet from the edge of the parking lot. She sat on the table part, eyes still on Jerry.

"I never said you abandoned a child," she said calmly. She opened the plastic bag and began freeing the sandwich from its wrap. "Maybe I fucking baby him, okay? I'll own that. But he could be eighty years old and you leaving without saying goodbye would still be rude."

"Yeah," Jerry said. "Well."

Sandy felt stupid for suggesting that Jerry would care about being rude. As if to drive that point home, Jerry took a seat across from her and grabbed his sub without a thank-you.

"You're avoiding Gabe why?" Sandy inquired before taking a bite of her sub.

"I'm not avoiding him," Jerry said. Sandy rolled her eyes, and he shook his head. "Not exactly. I want to tell you some shit, and Colin wouldn't appreciate me saying it in front of the kid."

"Colin can get fucked," Sandy commented as she brushed bread crumbs from her face.

Jerry snorted. "Yes and no," he said. In response to Sandy's curious glance, he added, "Never mind. I'm not gonna say he's not being a dick. He is being a dick."

Sandy sat up. Her hands, and sandwich, fell forgotten to her lap.

"Jerry McClelland, what do you know?"

"Shh," Jerry said. He'd stood and taken a step backward as she spoke, into the trail. "Just… finish your food, and we can talk about it on the trail."

Sandy felt a little guilty getting pushy with Jer, since she still hadn't told anyone—not even Gabe—that she'd seen Colin the day before. But there was a difference between seeing the guy for five minutes and knowing where he'd gone or what he was up to.

"Do you know where he is?" Sandy hissed, leaning forward.

"Shut the fuck up," Jerry hissed back. "I-I'm sorry, okay? We need privacy."

Sandy surveyed the abandoned parking lot and waved an arm at the trees surrounding them. "You're worried the chipmunks are gonna talk?"

Jerry shut his eyes. His brow was pinched. "Can I have one damned thing my way, Sandy? One time only?"

In Sandy's experience, Jerry had all kinds of things his way. But it was true enough that he went along for simplicity's sake a lot of the time.

"Okay," she told him, picking up her sub again. "This one time."

Gabe

GABE WASN'T pulling his weight. He knew that. While Eli was combing through ash and melted plastic and bent metal for any hint of a clue, Gabe was standing where the freezer had been. The stairs to the basement were gone, and he'd had to lower himself into the pit, but there was enough debris that it wasn't difficult. He was even optimistic about his ability to climb back out.

He hadn't been down there since the night before last, when he'd been on the way to get chicken from the freezer and Colin had—

Hey, Gabe, wait. Let's get pizza.

—stopped him. Because he'd wanted pizza instead of chicken or hadn't wanted to cook. Because he'd gotten a lot of overtime recently and was feeling flush.

Not because there'd been a dead guy in the freezer and Colin had known it.

It was ridiculous, and yet Gabe couldn't stop staring at the square on the ground as if confronted with the entrance to a lost pharaoh's tomb. Nothing beneath the freezer had burned, and there was still a scrap of wrapper there from a box of ice cream sandwiches. Gabe knelt to pick it up for no reason except the impossibility of its survival. Well done, little scrap of paper. You chose your hiding place well.

Then he saw something else. Not paper. Plastic. Glossy and curved, striped in white and black. Gabe picked it up, trying to understand where it had come from. A button off something? A piece of decoration? He turned it over, saw the shape of the curve, and realized what he was holding.

A fake fingernail. Zebra-striped.

He dropped to the rubble, his knees sinking into ash.

He could see the women from the casino, how he'd pictured them before, gathered at the nail salon. Now Owen was in the image too. Laughing and asking to have his nails done to match.

Gabe tried to imagine something else. Tracy, at their house for dinner some night when Gabe wasn't around. Going downstairs to bring up something for Colin. Vanilla ice cream to go with a pan of fresh brownies. Colin never had women over, but what if he had?

And she'd lost a nail and not noticed? Not looked for it? Left it on the floor, waiting to be kicked under the freezer by the next person who walked by?

Gabe didn't believe any of it, but he kept trying.

He shut his eyes, and all he could see was Colin, gazing at the sky all "heaven help me" because Gabe was being crazy with his talk about disappearing Owens and suspicious cops.

Gabe opened his eyes. Flipped the nail over and over. Under his breath, he said, "Who's crazy now?"

He whirled at footsteps behind him. Eli. Gabe put the nail into his pocket, the little watch-fob pocket they still put at the front of jeans. Now it was a murder pocket. Tuck your crimes away, like a condom or a loonie you'd got back in change.

"Gabe?"

The Reece boys covered for each other. They'd never have made it this far any other way.

Because he was a loyal brother.

Because things were a little fucked-up for them.

Because Colin did what he had to do.

Hadn't he kept a secret of the things Colin had told him at the lake?

He felt something brush his arm. Eli had crouched beside him.

"I was wrong," Eli said. "I can't find anything here that's going to help us find Sandy. And we've got to. We have to figure something out."

Gabe turned his head to Eli.

Then, silently, he took Eli's left hand and turned it palm up. Eli kept his hand that way and waited. Gabe took out the nail and placed it in the centre of Eli's palm. Eli regarded it silently, and Gabe thought he'd have to explain. He'd have to get the words out. But then he saw Eli putting it together, from their visit to the casino to the blood in the freezer and the freezer-sized clean mark on the floor in front of Gabe.

"Oh no," Eli said. "Oh, Gabe. I'm so sor—"

He finished the word, most likely, but Gabe couldn't hear it over the gunfire.

Gabe turned to see where it was coming from. Eli put a hand on his back and shoved him to the ground. Gabe's field flashed.

"Fuck!" he said, turning his head to see Eli on the ground beside him. Instinct drove him forward, to a place he'd used in countless hide-and-go-seek games. Under the charred remains of the mud room, he could see a trap door, still mostly intact, and he went for it.

There had once been, Gabe and Colin supposed, a root cellar under the house. It had been filled in, probably at the time the full basement had been dug, but there was still a funny half flight of stairs leading from that trapdoor into an earth-floored crawl space about four feet tall and the length of the house along one side. Few people knew it was there.

Gabe dove into the crawl space, Eli right behind him. Gabe shuffled forward, away from the stairs, to give Eli room.

Both Gabe's body and heart stopped when he ran into something hard.

Not hard like a brick wall or a tree trunk. Soft, actually, to the touch. But hard to move—too heavy to dislodge when brushed. Gabe gave it a good shove, and a drone of low strings sounded as Gabe's blue light flashed and Gabe saw….

He dropped gracelessly to the packed earth.

It had only been a flash of light. A second. He'd imagined what he thought he'd seen. It wasn't real. It wasn't true.

Behind him, he heard Eli rummaging for something. He had his pack with him. Of course he did. Fucking boy scout.

"Don't," Gabe muttered. Eli put a hand on his shoulder and squeezed gently. Careful not to set off the light.

"Close your eyes," Eli said. Gabe did and heard the snick of a lighter. He heard Eli draw in breath, then move around him to get closer to Se— To whatever he was looking at.

Gabe felt stupid and useless, sitting there with his eyes shut, pretending none of this was happening. As if somebody would make this better if he ignored it long enough.

He opened his eyes and saw Sean lying face up on the ground, a bullet hole in his forehead. His eyes were open, and he was dead, of course, because you didn't get shot like that and live.

Eli was looking Sean over. Gabe didn't see the point, but he wasn't a detective. There were probably things to see. His vision blurred, and he realized he was crying without sound. Just tears, steady and strangely cold on his face.

But someone took Sean, he thought. Why would they take him and shoot him and bring him back? Jerry had said someone had….

Jerry had said.

Jerry said a lot of things.

Gabe was perfectly still, barely breathing. Thinking. From the corner of his eye, he saw Eli watching his face. He didn't care or not care. He barely noticed. Thinking.

He hadn't heard a shot when he'd spoken to Sean on the phone.

He hadn't heard Jerry's voice.

But Jerry could have hit him in the stomach or maybe the throat. Taken the phone away. Cut off the call.

And then….

Jerry knew the crawl space. He and Sean had tried to grow shrooms down there one summer. Gabe could almost hear them in the darkness. Bickering. Trading insults. Deciding they never liked shrooms anyway, and they were going to get drunk instead.

Walking to Jerry's car with Sean's hand on Jerry's shoulder.

Gabe slapped a hand over his mouth to keep himself from being sick.

Then everything settled. His stomach and his shaking hands and legs calmed. There was only one thing that mattered.

Gabe started to crawl up the steps. Eli's grip on the back of his shirt stopped him. Gabe turned on him.

"Sandy's with him," he hissed.

"You can't go out there," Eli hissed back. "You'll get shot."

"So what?" he said. Eli glared at him in the dim yellow light.

"If someone sees your field go off—" he started.

"Fuck it," Gabe said and, with regret, raised a foot and kicked Eli in the chest. Not too hard, but hard enough to send Eli sprawling back onto….

Onto Sean.

Gabe ran both away and to, then. To Sandy, wherever she was, but also away from Sean being dead and lying there screaming that at him. That he was right there and dead and therefore not okay somewhere else and also not ever coming back.

He heard Eli curse and follow him.

He was nearly at the car before he realized there was no more shooting. No more shooting from above. No cops coming up the street. Silence.

It had to be the calm before the storm.

Sandy

"IS THIS far enough?" Sandy asked. She and Jerry had been walking for a few minutes, and she could no longer see the parking lot through the trees. Jerry, walking ahead of her, shoved his hands into his jeans pockets and shrugged. It was a small, tight movement, and she thought his shoulders probably hurt. He had problems with them, and with his wrists, from work.

Not that the guy, apparently, went to work all that often.

"Yeah," Jerry said, neither slowing nor turning around. Sandy considered grabbing his arm to stop him, but he seemed as if he might lash out on instinct.

"Okay, so… about Colin being a dick?"

Jerry did slow a little then.

"He knows that Owen guy is missing," he said. "He knows people know he fought with Owen. He left town because he assumed the cops would be after him."

"I know that," Sandy said. "He told me. Yesterday. I wasn't supposed to tell you. He says he's got all this under control, but does he, Jer? This doesn't seem under control to me."

Jerry kept eerily still for a moment. Then he shrugged. It was stiff and exaggerated, like he was once again being terrible in their tenth-grade production of *The Crucible*.

"If he says it's under control, it's under control."

"The police…." Sandy said. "Jer, stop."

Jerry took a few more steps, then halted. Long seconds passed before he faced her again.

"What, Sandra? What about the police?"

"They called me at work. They have the freezer. From the house. They said there was blood in it."

"So he threw some shit in there without wrapping it."

"I told the cops that, but they said it was a lot of blood. They're testing it to see if it's human, and they're gonna try to match it to that Owen guy."

"And it's not, right? So what's the fucking problem? You want me to call Colin and talk to him about his housekeeping?"

"Can you?" Sandy asked.

From that moment until the next time Jerry blinked, Sandy could see something in his eyes. Sad and beaten and… trapped. Then he blinked and his eyes were cold again.

"So what if I can?"

"Tell him he has to deal with this!" she said, yelling because the problem must be volume. Jerry couldn't grasp this incredibly obvious thing because no one had been loud enough about it. "Tell him he has to tell the cops what really happened and what the fuck was in his freezer. Tell him—"

“Shut the fuck up!” Jerry hissed, jutting his head at her like a striking snake. Bank swallows Sandy hadn’t even noticed fled from the trees and shrubs around them. His voice was closer to normal, though still quiet, when he spoke again. “He is not coming back here to straighten things out. Okay? He’s not coming back. And that might be fine.”

They stood there and stared at each other. Neither said anything. Sandy did not, for example, ask why Colin wasn’t coming back. Or why it might be fine if none of them ever saw him again.

Jerry didn’t say that the police were going to find exactly what they expected to find in the freezer. That he knew it for a fact.

The bravest of the swallows returned, rustling the caragana.

“Colin does what he does,” Jerry said. “What can I say?”

Gabe

ELI, BLESS him, had enough sense not to ask Gabe where they were going. He drove, getting them away from the house. Gabe was staring out the window and seeing nothing. He knew, distantly, that he was crying. It wasn’t important. Sandy’s voice-mail message played in his ear and he said, “Call me.”

He thought the tone of his voice said the rest. Call me right now, because this could not be more important.

He shut off the display and bounced the phone in his hand, staring at the lighter black screen within the dark black frame. A murky image of Sandy and Jerry and where they were right now did not magically appear in the liquid crystals. Wrong kind of crystal, he guessed.

Sandy hadn’t said where she was meeting Jerry. Not even a hint. It wouldn’t have been one of the regular spots because they hadn’t wanted company. It wouldn’t have been the house. It would have been somewhere different. Unusual for them.

That could have been a million places. He pictured a map of the town, dozens of little pointers. The casino. The Chinese food dive. He heard Sean yammering at him, something about tracking and beer or coffee and wouldn’t it be cool if they all knew where everyone was so they could meet up when they were in the same area. Pointing at the screen and the little pointers. And….

"Maybe I don't want to see you whenever we're both at the mall," Jerry had said. "Maybe I have shit to do, and it's not like we don't see each other all damned time."

Sean had looked hurt and said he understood, but Gabe had thought he didn't. Sean would never understand someone not wanting to see someone. Not unless they hated that person like poison.

"You can turn it off," Sean had said. "But if you wanna turn it on, you know, I'll have mine on."

Gabe's heart sped up, and he tapped the phone in time with his pulse until the screen lit. He ran his fingertips over the little square pictures, trying to remember which one Sean had been talking about. The one that found your friends' iPhones and told you where they were.

I'll teach you to take the wrong phone.

"Gabe?" Eli's voice was low and calm. Not wanting to pressure him but needing direction.

Gabe rested the tip of one finger against a teardrop on the screen. Not one of his tears, but an arrow shaped like one, pointing to the place where Sean's phone had gone.

"South," he said and raised his finger to point. "That way."

CHAPTER TWELVE

Sandy

THEY WALKED in near silence for a while. Twigs snapped and leaves crunched, but no words disturbed the wildlife. Jerry's shoulders were still hunched and tight. Sandy kept her eyes on them as they moved forward. Normally she would have watched her feet, avoiding rocks or holes or tree roots. Today, though, watching Jerry seemed more important.

He stopped at a point where the trail widened into a small glade, half the size of their living room. Some park developer had taken advantage of the space to set out a bench and a tin sign that listed wildlife to be found in the area. Those signs always made her think of the time she and Jerry and Colin had, on a grade school trip, replaced the display animals in an interpretive centre with chip bags and empty beer bottles. Their argument had been that they'd seen far more of both on the trails than they had animals of any kind. They'd been relegated to the bus after that.

She thought about reminding Jerry of that trip, but the grey and miserable cast to his face said he was probably not in the mood to play Remember When.

Really, she wasn't either.

Jerry sat on the bench and put his hands on his knees. His knuckles were so white, they could have been bones poking through his skin. Like a monster hiding in her garage. Sandy shuddered.

"It could have been an accident," she said and then thought about biting her tongue right off. If it was going to say shit like that, it was not her friend.

Jerry looked up, suddenly alert. "What?"

Sandy tapped the ground with one foot, trying to push her shakiness away.

"He… maybe something happened and it was an accident," she said. "Like he gave Owen a little tap and Owen fell? And hit a car or something with his head?"

"Accidents happen," Jerry said evenly.

"It could have been," Sandy persisted.

"You think so?" Jerry asked, leaning forward as if he couldn't quite find what he was searching for on her face. "Do you think that's likely?"

What the hell was he asking her?

Did he know she knew what Colin could do?

He couldn't know. He couldn't know about Colin and have known for ages and not have said anything. Then again, it wasn't like she was spilling her guts to him about Colin or Gabe.

"There's a rumour," she said slowly. "I know how this sounds… but there's a rumour that Colin is really strong. Like… really strong. Like the Hulk or something. Without the green skin."

Jerry stood there. No expression. No motion.

"I know how dumb that is," Sandy offered. "It's crazy."

"A rumour," Jerry repeated. "Where did you hear this?"

The real answer was in his tone. In how he wasn't saying *Where the fuck did you hear something this stupid*? Not, *What is wrong with you, repeating shit this ridiculous*?

What he'd said was, "How the hell did you find out?"

She wasn't surprised, exactly. She was only surprised by how sick it made her feel to hear him say that. How badly she wanted to walk away.

She set her jaw and said, "Around."

Because she sure as fuck was not going to say she had heard it from Gabe.

"That sucks," Jerry said as he pulled a gun from his coat pocket and aimed it at her.

Gabe

GABE HAD to give them credit for coming up with a place he'd never have expected Jerry to go. Jerry put up with the lake and all of its annoying trees and dirt because there was beer and a firepit. This park, on the other hand, was mostly about exercising amid trees and dirt. Nothing to appeal to Jerry. Except on this day, privacy.

Eli was a few steps down the trail when Gabe called to him to stop. Eli turned, head cocked curiously.

"Yes?"

"Thinking," Gabe said. "I need a sec."

Eli nodded and kept still. It was no less refreshing than it had been the day before, how this guy actually listened to the things Gabe said.

"So, in Sandy's car"—Gabe pointed; sunlight was draped over the vehicle and everything else like a gauzy yellow cloth—"there's a straw wrapper. From Subway. Which means that"—he pointed at a bag in the trash—"is also hers. So they're probably on the trail."

He would have liked to be more specific, but the phone had refused to tell him anything more than that Jerry was on the island.

Eli nodded again. "We've got the right place," he said.

Gabe shook his head, impatient. That wasn't the point. "She left after work, went to Subway, came here, they ate…." He checked his watch. "They're more than halfway through the trail if they've been moving."

Understanding flashed on Eli's face. "It's a loop?"

Gabe nodded and started walking toward the trail's end. He heard Eli behind him, closing the gap.

Gabe crunched down the trail, and his back stiffened as he drew his muscles under tighter control. Walk softly.

A voice in the back of his head, a sneering voice that was oddly like Jerry's, said this might be pointless. Sandy might already be gone. Gabe told the Jerry in his head to fuck off, because that was a useless way to think.

A hand closed on his shoulder, and he didn't startle because it was obviously Eli. Meaning to comfort him or to keep him from rushing into whatever situation they found. Trying to be helpful, either way, and Gabe was grateful for it. Gabe thought that he might have been lying on his back somewhere, kicking and screaming, if his prospective murderer hadn't been around.

Gabe's watch said they'd only been walking for six minutes when he heard Sandy's voice. His watch was a liar. It had been forever. But he felt generous enough to forgive his lying watch, because Sandy was talking—bitching, in fact—and that meant she was alive. Probably not even shot.

"Are you kidding me with this shit?" she asked from around a bend. Gabe froze and held up a hand to stop Eli.

Jerry's voice was next. He sounded exhausted as he said, "I need to know where you heard that, Sandy."

Gabe glanced at Eli, who didn't seem to have any better idea what that meant. Gabe moved forward so slowly that it almost hurt. Patience was not natural to him.

"What are you going to do, Jerry? Kill me? You'd kill me?"

She sounded so sure he wouldn't. That he could never do that. She'd probably have said the same about Jerry killing Sean.

Gabe moved again, and Eli followed, distractingly close. When they reached the bend and Gabe was able to peer around it, he could feel Eli leaning in to see over his shoulder.

Sandy was staring at Jerry with irritated disbelief as Jerry aimed a gun at her.

"I don't want to," Jerry said. Like Eli didn't want to kill Gabe. *I'd rather not.*

"Then don't! And Abby knows, by the way. When I got the subs? I told Abby I was meeting you here."

"Jesus, Sandy. You're making it so I'll have to kill her too."

Sandy's face showed more of that dismissive irritation at first. What a stupid, annoying thing for Jerry to say. As if he was Colin's henchman, running around town covering up for Colin's crimes. Gabe saw the moment when her expression changed. He could see it, the movement of the thought behind her eyes. What if it wasn't ridiculous?

What if that was who Jerry was?

Jerry saw it too. Gabe knew from the way his shoulder twitched and he moved his legs into a better, wider stance. He knew that if there had been any hope left of lying to Sandy, jollying her along, it had vanished. He only had one out now.

The only thing keeping Jerry from doing it was that he didn't want to. That it was, in fact, the last thing he'd ever want to do. And that gave Gabe a little bit of time.

Rushing Jerry would be a mistake. Gabe didn't care if Jerry shot him, but chances were pretty good that he'd be startled enough to shoot at least one time in the direction he was already aiming. And he was too close to Sandy to miss.

The key, then, was to get Jerry to aim the gun somewhere else.

Gabe dropped to one knee and felt for a good throwing rock. Rocks were always the answer. It was the school, round two.

Eli's voice, close to his ear, whispered, "What are you doing?"

"Distraction," he whispered back.

Eli shook his head. “You’ll get shot,” Eli protested.

“Why do you keep worrying about that?”

Eli leaned in so close that Gabe had trouble seeing both his eyes at once. “You have had this field for one day.”

Gabe wanted to say it was closer to two days now, but he didn’t think it would help.

He could see from Eli’s expression, the intensity of the concern, that this wasn’t Eli telling him to keep a lid on his secret. This was Eli reminding him, again, that he didn’t understand this field and that maybe there were things he could do that would turn it off, or maybe it would stop working, or maybe it could only take so many hits. So if he rushed Jerry’s gun, maybe he’d get shot for real.

What Eli wasn’t getting was that somebody was liable to get shot before this was over, and it wasn’t going to be Sandy. The field thing was really beside the point.

Gabe’s hand brushed a rock, and he picked it up, still staring into Eli’s eyes. *What the hell*, he thought.

With his free hand, he grabbed the back of Eli’s head and pulled him the small bit closer that was necessary for kissing him. Then he waited for an objection.

Eli leaned in. That was not an objection.

Gabe didn’t have time to make it a good one, like he wanted, but it was a passable kiss under the circumstances. Eli closed a hand around Gabe’s wrist, holding him in place. It was a tight grip, but Gabe’s field didn’t spark.

They pulled back. They looked at Eli’s hand on Gabe’s arm and then at each other. Gabe pulled his arm away. Eli let go.

And Gabe shrugged, with a smile.

Sandy

PREVIOUSLY, SANDY had rolled her eyes when people on the news, shaking and teary in grey emergency blankets, told reporters, “It all happened so fast!”

She’d been in a few car accidents and a handful of brawls, and they’d happened slowly for her. She’d had what seemed like hours to think, “Oh, shit” or “I should duck.” Maybe she hadn’t had enough time to act, but she’d had plenty of time to notice what was going on. She had therefore assumed that the "it happened so fast" people were stunned in general. They would have said the same thing if asked to describe buying groceries at the Safeway.

But this thing that happened in front of her… it happened so fast. Something had shaken the brush behind Jerry, and birds had flown, and Jerry, twitchy with nerves, had spun toward the bushes.

Gabe, out of nowhere, had leapt at Jerry. Jerry had spun again and fired. Light had flashed, bright enough to hurt her eyes, and a string section had let out staccato screams. Jerry had fired and fired and fired. And yelped.

Now Jerry was sitting on the ground, one leg stuck out in front of him, holding his bleeding left arm and rocking himself.

Gabe was standing before him with Jerry's gun in his hand.

"Jesus," Sandy said with feeling, "fucking Christ."

"Just me," Gabe said. Like his brother had said the day before. Fucking Reeces.

Eli followed Gabe into the clearing, looking as if he couldn't decide between puking in terror and slapping Gabe upside the head. Sandy knew the feeling.

"You've been holding out on us, Younger," Jerry said. His voice shook as if he were cold.

Gabe regarded him, face blank the way Colin's got when Colin was pissed off beyond measure. Sandy couldn't remember having seen that expression on Gabe before.

"We found Sean," Gabe said. "At the house."

Jerry said nothing.

Sandy turned to Gabe. "Gabe? What the fuck? Is he okay?"

"No," Gabe said, still watching Jerry. "I'm sorry. Jerry killed him."

He said it calmly, as if the words meant nothing to him, but Sandy could see now that Gabe's eyes were red and his face was swollen around them. That made it real.

She stumbled into the brush and threw up.

Gabe

JERRY DIDN'T try to deny it. He didn't even seem to care. A decade, almost, of Sean being one of his best friends, and now Jerry was looking Gabe in the eye without sadness or fear. *I shot him. I killed him. What of it?*

Sandy lunged at Jerry, bawling. Eli stopped her. Gabe would have liked to see her hit Jerry. He would have liked to see her take a tree limb to him, and rocks, and hit and kick until there was nothing left. But Eli was probably right. A controlled environment was what they needed now.

"When did you get your magic trick?" Jerry asked.

Gabe said nothing.

"I bet it was you that told her about Colin," Jerry said. "That's why she wouldn't tell me where she heard it. How long have you known?"

"How long have you been killing people?" Gabe asked softly.

Jerry snorted. "You're a baby, Gabe. That's not your fault. You'll grow up pretty fast now."

Gabe stared at Jerry as if he might turn back into someone Gabe would be willing to share a couch, or a car, with. No luck.

"What's with the look, Younger?" Jerry asked. "You know what your brother does, and you're looking at me like you don't get why I'm standing here with a gun? You're smart for a baby. Do the math."

"The math?" Gabe asked softly, wanting to yell but somehow not up to the task. He couldn't picture a row of numbers that would have "Kill Sean" at the bottom. Nothing added up to that.

"You think it was my idea, dumbass?" Jerry said, his tone indicating that this was a clarification and that he was disappointed in Gabe for needing it. "You think any of this has been my idea?"

"Don't you talk to him!" Sandy yelled. Eli, still holding her back, turned away from her face. He seemed desperately uncomfortable.

"Enough," Jerry said, regarding Sandy for the first time since Gabe had interrupted them. "You want to yell at someone, why don't you yell at the heavens? I'm sure God is up there somewhere."

Gabe was back in the lake for a second. Talking to Colin. Like prayer.

"What Lola wants," Jerry said, turning to Gabe again, "Lola gets. Or Lola cracks your arm and tells everyone you fell off a snowmobile."

It might have been snowmobiling weather right then, the way Gabe felt. Remembering Jerry in a cast that past November. Colin laughing over how there were six-year-olds out there on Ski-Doos doing fine, but Jerry had fallen off and taken the machine right over on top of him. Like the dork he was. And Jerry had glared and scratched with knitting needles, and Sandy had taunted him by holding hot chocolate in front of Jerry's one good hand.

What's it gonna be? Chocolate or scratching? Scratching or chocolate? Oh, they both feel soooo gooood....

Gabe didn't look at Sandy. He couldn't. Not that seeing Jerry was a whole lot better, because Jerry was smiling now, and it wasn't a mean smile. It was that weird quivery smile Jerry did when he was seriously, actually about to cry.

"He killed my dad," Jerry said.

It took Gabe a moment to shift gears, to remember that Jerry's dad had vanished from the family home a few months after Gabe's father had died. Jerry's dad had never been seen again. No one had been sad to see the man go because he had been, if anything, a bigger asshole than Gabe and Colin's own father. Or possibly, in retrospect, less of an asshole. But certainly more of a hitter.

"You really believed," Jerry said, "he left town?"

Jerry stepped toward Gabe, not seeming to give a damn about the gun. Gabe thought he could be holding a bazooka and Jerry would be equally unconcerned. What was the worst Gabe could do? Kill him?

"Your brother came back from some trip with your dad, and he told me he was Superman. Showed me some impressive shit. And then he said, 'Hey, let's give your dad a scare. Teach him a lesson about hitting his kid.'"

"It went too far," Gabe guessed and then wished he'd said nothing, because Jerry laughed, and it was the worst thing Gabe had heard in years.

"It got out of hand? Whoops? Fuck that. Your brother picked up me and my dad, and he flew us to the middle of some forest and ripped little pieces off my dad like he was making a pulled pork sandwich." Jerry's eyes went glassy. "I was begging him to stop. After everything my dad did? I was begging Colin to fucking stop. Because *nobody* deserved that, Gabe."

Gabe couldn't stop shaking his head. He didn't know what he was negating. That it had happened at all or happened that way. That any of this was happening now.

Jerry laughed again. "You know what Mr. Sunshine Out the Ass did next? I mean, after my dad bled out? He said I owed him. Huge. Because he'd solved all my problems. It was like...." Jerry looked at the sky, and Gabe wondered if he was looking to Colin for guidance. The thought made Gabe's throat tighten until he couldn't swallow. "It was like when the mob visits you and offers protection. He's standing there with his hands full of my dad's muscle and skin, and he says I've got to keep his secret and help him out because I owe him. And maybe you're a little slow on the uptake, Gabe, but I am not. I got it."

"Colin wouldn't—" Gabe said, and couldn't make himself finish. What wouldn't Colin do? Burn their house down? Kill someone in a parking lot? Keep the body in their own basement, a few feet from where Gabe had found his mom? Where did he think the line really was?

"He caught me with a course catalogue for McMaster," Jerry said. "That's how I got stuck cleaning up his mess at the casino. You get to go to university because you're the fucking golden child, but here's what happens when I try to get out of town. He didn't have to stick a corpse in his freezer and tell me it was my problem to deal with. He could have flown that body where it would never be found. But then," Jerry added, leaning forward to make sure he had Gabe's attention, "I wouldn't have learned anything."

"You killed Sean," Gabe whispered through his narrow throat. And that was what finally made Jerry start to cry. Not loud, a mist of tears and a hitch in his voice taking up the space where the venom had been.

"He made me do it, Gabe. It was me or Sean. It's been me or them every time."

From behind him, Eli's voice came. "And when it's you or them who dies," he said, "it will always be the other person. Won't it?"

It wasn't as if Gabe had forgotten that Eli was there, but he hadn't expected Eli to speak, and so he jumped. Jerry didn't. Gabe didn't think Jerry was any less surprised. He figured Jerry didn't care enough about what happened next to be startled by anything.

"You," Jerry said to Eli. "You're the assassin, aren't you? You take out the guys with the powers. I've heard about you."

Eli eyed Jerry as if he would have made a far better target for assassination. Gabe wondered what Eli might have done if he hadn't had his hands full keeping Sandy back.

"What the fuck did you say?" Sandy asked. She wrestled herself away from Eli and turned to face him. "What the fuck? Is that true?"

"It's true," Jerry said. "He's here to kill Superboy. Gabe, why don't you do us all a favour and let him?"

There was a second, no more, when Gabe saw temper flash in Eli's eyes. It went, and Eli looked Jerry up and down like Jerry was any of the other billion things in the world that didn't confront him.

"Being mean to Gabe," he said, "won't change anything for you."

It wasn't likely there was a damned thing Jerry could say to that, but they didn't have a chance to find out. There was a blur and a swoosh and a rush of air. And then nothing. Jerry's absence. He was gone, the way he'd described Sean being gone, except that he'd been lying about Sean.

"Jesus," Sandy muttered. She was swiping at her tears with the heels of her hands. "Aw, Jesus."

Gabe wasn't sure she was cursing.

"You like holding that gun?" Eli inquired. Gabe glanced at it, then shook his head and passed it to Eli. Eli clicked the safety on and tucked it into the back of his pants.

"Colin?" Sandy stared at the sky, then shouted at it. "Colin, you fuck! Get back here, you fucking fuck!"

It wasn't an enticing invitation. Gabe wasn't surprised when Colin failed to appear.

"We should go," he said. He didn't know where, but he was tired of standing in this place. He couldn't picture himself ever setting foot on this trail again.

"Yeah," Sandy said, her voice low and hoarse. "Okay."

They trudged out of the woods, taking nearly as long in their careless slog out as Gabe and Eli had taken with light, cautious steps on the way in. Gabe thought he should put a hand on Sandy's back or something, offer comfort, but he couldn't seem to manage it. She didn't seem as if she wanted that, anyhow. Her shoulders were drawn in, and her back was hunched. It was as if she was trying to disappear.

She made herself even smaller somehow when they emerged from the trail to find Jerry in the parking lot, sitting on the hood of his car.

Sandy

IT WAS ridiculous. Jerry knew they were gunning for him… so to speak. He had his car keys, as far as she knew. He should have been gone instead of sitting there staring at them with irritable impatience, as if they'd gone into Shopper's saying they'd only be a few minutes and left him in the car for half an hour. He was still holding his arm, keeping pressure on it. Blood had dripped to the gravel at his feet.

Gabe seemed thrown by this development. He went through the motions, stepping in front of Sandy as Eli pulled out Jerry's gun and aimed it at Jerry, but there was no urgency to it. Jerry had changed the rules, so how could they know what to do?

"You should give me the gun," Jerry said amiably. Eli gave his head a little shake, as if a fly had landed on his face.

"Do you think you're using mind control?" he asked Jerry. Jerry snorted.

"I'm giving you good advice," he said. "You don't want to be caught with that gun. Dump the bullets and give it to me."

"Like you don't have more ammo," Gabe said.

Jerry rolled his eyes. "What would I do with it, kid? Shoot you some more? Tell your buddy he should give me the gun before—"

Jerry stopped because he had lost his audience. Sandy, Gabe, and Eli were all staring toward the park's entrance road. Sirens were coming from that direction.

"—before the cops get here," Jerry finished. "I called them to confess. If they ask, you should tell them I met all of you here so I could confess to you first. Now please give me the motherfucking gun."

"Confess?" Sandy said and was disoriented by the sound of Gabe saying the same word at the same time.

"Freakin' *gun*," Jerry said, teeth clenched. He was pale, all freckles and orange stubble dotting paper-white skin. Sandy realized he must be hurting. For a second, before she remembered, she even cared.

Eli glanced at Gabe. Gabe didn't say anything. Eli raised his brows as if using them to shrug and took the remaining bullets from the gun before crossing the lot and handing the gun to Jerry. Jerry took it with the hand of his injured arm. Eli nodded once and crossed back to stand beside Gabe. Sandy moved to stand on Gabe's other side.

"Colin told me to apologize to you," Jerry told Sandy. "So I guess I'm sorry."

"I guess go fuck yourself," Sandy said. Her throat burned, and talking made it a thousand times worse. "I guess that's for both of you."

It was a second or a year later that the cops showed up, and Jerry tried to stand to meet them. That lasted about a heartbeat before he slumped back against his car.

It was Palmer and the redhead, Officer Strembosky. Was it luck of the draw, calling 911 and getting those two, or had they been waiting to pounce on anything to do with Colin and his crew? Driving around in circles hoping someone would break?

"Jerome McClelland," Palmer said. "Drop the gun, please."

Jerry did so, then said, "I want to confess."

"So I hear," Palmer said. "We're going to take a moment and read you your rights if you don't mind. Unless you'd prefer we got you an ambulance and dealt with this later?"

"Get on with it," Jerry said.

Strembosky read Jerry his rights. Sandy almost smiled at the what-the-hell expression on Gabe's face as he listened. They were so used to hearing the American version on TV that this version sounded strange. She'd been surprised by it herself the night she'd fucked up Fitzie's truck. It was almost poetic in spots. "You need not say anything. You have nothing to hope from any promise or favour and nothing to fear from any threat."

But Jerry had plenty to fear.

"Okay," Jerry said once it was done. "I'm confessing to arson of the Reece home. Burned that fucker to the ground and salted the earth. A little. I swiped a salt shaker from the Sev."

No one said anything. Jerry went on.

"I'm also confessing to the murders of Owen Bernier, Tracy Howell, and—" He stopped, and for the first time, the cocky look on his face slipped. "—Sean Boyko."

Palmer watched Jerry's face as his partner took notes. He seemed to want to ask Jerry something, but he kept whatever it was to himself. Over a few deep breaths, Jerry regained control of himself.

"That gun on the ground is the one I used for Bernier. There's another gun in the back of my jeans that I used for Boyko and Howell."

Sandy told herself not to stare at Gabe. She didn't want the cops to see her staring at Gabe. But she really, really wanted to know how Gabe was taking this because she was pretty sure Jerry was talking shit.

Jerry hadn't shot Owen. Sean, yes. He'd shot Sean, and he could have burned the house too. She could see him doing it for Colin, to hide evidence of God knew what. Getting the guitar and violin on

Colin's orders. Torch the place but pull those things out first. And hide them for some impossible day when Gabe can have them back.

Tracy Howell, though. That was different. Hadn't the boogeyman shot her?

And, although she was far less certain of this point, she also didn't think Jerry had been carrying a second gun.

"Well," Palmer said. "That's pretty straightforward."

The man was tough to read, but Sandy didn't think he was convinced, either.

"And the body of Owen Bernier?" Palmer added.

"We can talk about that later," Jerry said. He sounded the way he did when he'd come home at the end of a long day. "I'd like to go to the hospital now."

Palmer nodded. "One last thing. Did you want to tell me who shot you?"

Jerry gave him a tight, nasty smile. "Shot myself," he said. "It was an accident."

At that, Sandy bit down hard on her tongue. Right next to the last bite she'd left in it. She wanted to giggle madly, probably because this whole thing was driving her crazy. But it was true. Jerry kind of had shot himself, hadn't he? By accident.

Strembosky took Jerry's second gun and helped him to the car as Palmer picked up the gun on the ground. Before standing, he turned to Sandy.

"Anything you want to say?" he asked her. "Any of you? Before we take your friend to the hospital?"

"Jerry said it all," Gabe said. Sandy jumped a little when he spoke.

Palmer straightened, put a hand to the small of his back, and stretched. "I guess he did," he said finally. "I would prefer that none of you leave town until we have this squared away. That includes you, Mr. Samm."

"Of course," Eli said, not seeming surprised that the cops knew his name.

Palmer nodded once more and went to the car. He watched them as he walked, and as he got into the car, and as he backed up to turn around. It wasn't until he was driving in the other direction that he took his eyes from them. Sandy was willing to bet that even then the guy was watching them from the rear-view mirror.

"Gabe?" she asked helplessly once the car was out of sight.

"I do not know," Gabe said.

CHAPTER THIRTEEN

Gabe

IT HAD been a quiet drive back to Sandy's house since everyone had taken a different car. Eli in his, Sandy in hers, and Gabe in Jerry's. Jerry had left his keys on the ground next to it. Gabe was the last to arrive and found Eli standing in the hall when he got there. Sandy was in the living room, already ensconced in her favourite chair. The gin bottle was down about a cup, but it might have been like that to start with.

"Close the door, Gabriel," she said. Gabe did and locked it. Put on the chain. It wasn't like anyone else was going to be coming home. He went to stand next to Eli in the hall.

"Am I in shit?" Gabe asked.

"Are you in shit," Sandy repeated. "I don't know, Gabe. I hear your new friend is an assassin."

Gabe glanced at Eli. "Did you want to take this one?"

"It's true," Eli said. "Kind of. But I don't intend to kill Gabe."

"I'd be dead already," Gabe pointed out and then wanted to find and slap whatever part of his brain had thought that would help.

"You'd be dead already," Sandy repeated. "So he's a good assassin."

She took another swig straight from the bottle. Drinking gin straight was something Gabe would only have considered if he were out of floor cleaner. Sandy liked the shit, though. And she was clearly aiming to get as drunk as she had ever been.

"I'm doing this to fix something," Eli said.

"A… fixer?" Sandy waved the bottle as if it were a flashlight for finding words in the dark.

"No!" Eli said, startling both Gabe and Sandy. Sandy blinked and leaned back in her chair. Eli went to the living room and sat on the coffee table in front of Sandy.

"You heard what Jerry said. Pulled. Pork. Sandwich. I wish that was the worst thing I'd heard of one of them doing. They do worse things. They all do."

Gabe wished he could disappear. The fact that he hadn't was driven home by Sandy staring at him. "What?" he demanded.

Sandy glared at Eli. "They all do," she said.

Eli clasped his hands and bowed his head. One more person praying to a god that wasn't a god.

"Gabe seems to be different." He raised his head and looked at Gabe. "You don't behave the way the others do. But who knows what's in your heart?"

"Me," Gabe said. "I think I know."

Eli turned to Sandy again. "I'm sorry. I really am. I do this because I know my father did something wrong, and I have to make it right."

Sandy frowned and drank again. "Bullshit," she said.

Eli shook his head. "It's not."

"Maybe you do it because you like it," she said. "You've got a mean streak. No different from a Reece. What's your special talent, Killer?"

"Mostly that," Eli said. "Mostly killing. It's not as fun for me as you seem to think."

Sandy took another drink. "Gabe's different," she said.

"He'd damned well better be," Eli said, not facing either of them.

Sandy nodded. "You'd damned well better not hurt him."

Eli continued to stare into space. "As long as he doesn't make me have to," he said. It wasn't a threat. Threats didn't come out sounding so defeated.

"Jerry never killed that Tracy Howell," Sandy said suddenly.

Gabe fought back a hysterical laugh as he realized that Sandy was changing the subject. Talking about Jerry confessing to a murder he hadn't committed was less awkward than the previous topic. That was where they were at.

"No," Eli said. "He's covering for Jack and Colin. I don't know how long Jack and Colin have been working together or what they're up to, but obviously they're on the same team."

"And that's the bad guys," Sandy said. "You say."

"Yes," Eli said.

"I bet it was never even the cop that shot at you," Sandy said.

Eli blinked and tucked his head back like an alarmed turtle.

"At the Reece house?" he asked. They'd told Sandy about that in the parking lot before they'd driven back to her house. It had been part of telling her about Sean.

"Think about it," Sandy instructed, pointing at Eli with the bottom of the gin bottle. "Did she say she was a cop before she shot at you? Did she tell you to fucking freeze? That cop never shot at you. Fucking Colin. He shot at you to get you away from the fucking house."

"Maybe," Gabe said. He went to the fridge for a beer. He didn't want to let Sandy drink alone, and Eli didn't seem inclined to join the party. Gabe didn't intend to get drunk, either. Not yet. He was doing his best to seem as if he was keeping up—without even coming close. It helped that Sandy considered him a lightweight.

They drank, or pretended to drink, in silence for a while. The living room grew darker.

"Jerry confessed to murder for Colin," Sandy said. "He killed people for Colin."

She left out the part that made Gabe sickest, where Jerry did it all—or so he said—because he was scared to death of Colin. Because prison was better. Because prison would be like a vacation.

Eli said simply, "Yes."

Sandy nodded thoughtfully and raised her bottle to see what was left.

"Fuck," she said. Gabe couldn't tell whether she was commenting on Jerry or Colin or her encroaching lack of gin. Maybe all of it.

"I'm gonna go for a walk," Gabe said. Eli and Sandy both moved to stand. He held a hand up to them. "Alone. Please."

"Don't kill anybody," Sandy advised.

Gabe shut his eyes and told himself not to take it personally. She was drunk and angry. And drunk. "I'll do my best," Gabe said. He nodded at Eli and left, careful to lock the door behind him.

He did take a walk, several blocks up and past the school he and Eli had thrown rocks at the night before. Had it really been only the night before? Heat lightning turned the sky into the ceiling of a dance club, and Gabe saw a greenish tint to the north. They were about to get what Sandy's mom called "some weather."

"No shit, sky," he said.

He didn't know how much time he'd have before they decided to come searching for him. Since clearly he'd be hit by a bus and killed if he spent more than five minutes on his own. At the age of eighteen. While bulletproof.

He pulled Jerry's cell from his pocket and wondered if the cops had put a trace on it. Probably not. Didn't that kind of thing take time? No doubt the cops would want to see the phone, but Gabe didn't see any benefit in letting them know he had it.

He found the Berlin number, the one that had called Eli with the tip about North Battleford, and called it. He could hear distance, an ocean and a continent of distance, on the line as it rang. Once. Twice. Gabe's heart was pounding so hard that he wondered if it could bruise his lungs.

A click and then nothing. That same buzzy near silence and… maybe… breathing?

"Colin?" Gabe said.

There was no response. Gabe gripped the phone tighter. "We should try our last conversation again," he said. "You can tell the truth this time. I'm in the park by Sandy's house."

Gabe hung up, dropped the phone into his pocket, and walked to a ball diamond at the edge of the park. He leaned against the backstop like he was hanging out, like it wasn't a thing. There wasn't anyone in the park, which was good. Gabe didn't plan to have his talk with Colin there anyway. He planned to suggest they relocate before they got into things. They could go to the country, or another country, or the bottom of the ocean. So no one could hear what they had to say. But it was still better if no one was around to see Colin at all.

He glanced up at the sound of someone approaching. It wasn't Colin. Gabe folded his arms and waited. The heat lightning flashed again. Once the skeletal man was a few feet away, Gabe said, "Hello, Jack."

"Gabriel Reece," Jack said. He didn't look as bad under the streetlights as he had in Tracy Howell's home.

"What brings you by?" Gabe inquired pleasantly. Jack did something with his face that might have been a sneer.

"Bring me Eli Samm," Jack said.

Was he serious?

"I don't work for you, buddy. Try saying please."

"Please," Jack said, hissing the *s* and drawing it out, "bring me the man who intends to kill us both."

"Only one of you has shot me," Gabe pointed out. "And it's not him."

"You're an idiot, Gabriel. And you've been sharing our secrets."

Gabe felt the same fear he had every other time he'd seen Jack, all his life. Instinctive, covering not only this person but everything associated with him. Things Gabe couldn't even remember.

But there was something else in Gabe now, warm in his chest and growing like the buzz from a few rounds of beer. It said, "Really, Gabe. What could this guy do to you?"

What could anyone possibly do?

"Leave me alone, Darth Vader," Gabe told him. "You were scary when I was a kid, but you're Hayden Christensen now."

"You think I'm nothing because your brother took my gun? I can get another one. I could shoot Sssssandra."

Maybe it was because Gabe had a few drinks in him, or because he'd had enough for one day. Or because being so close to a playground made this guy seem like one more tarmac bully. Whatever it was, Gabe rushed the boogeyman.

Jack was too surprised, it seemed, to teleport away. Gabe's field didn't go off when he connected with the boney pile of monster, but it did when Jack pushed back against him. The field separated them and hung between them, blue as bright as the Caribbean Ocean, and violins by the dozen. Gabe pushed the field at Jack and watched as it hit him, throwing him against the backstop. The backstop rang, like it was trying to join Gabe's song. Gabe hit the field again, twice, three times, harder each time. Jack was dazed, shaking like a Halloween skeleton hung from a tree. No more boogeyman. This was Gabe's chance. He could do this now and never see the boogeyman again.

Try not to kill anyone, Sandra had said.

But didn't Eli say it wasn't like that? If you were cleaning up his father's mess?

Gabe hit Jack again. The sound was painfully loud. He saw lights going on in the houses around him. A siren blocks away. He'd have cared more if hitting Jack hadn't felt like scratching an itch, putting aloe on a sunburn, finally letting out a laugh that he'd been holding in for almost twenty years.

"Gabriel! Stop!"

He turned to see Colin coming at him from the height of the tallest spruces. Gabe's field pushed out at Colin, hitting him and making him spin in the air. Colin tumbled back toward the playground, his body taking out the wood fort at the top of the little toboggan hill. Gabe moved toward the hill. Was Colin really hurt?

But Colin popped up again before Gabe could take more than ten steps. He was standing on top of the hill with the remains of the fort at his feet.

"Drop it," Colin said, his voice low but somehow carrying all the way to Gabe. "Drop your field. Now."

"What?" Gabe looked over his shoulder at Jack, or where Jack should have been. Gone. Goddamn it. "You let him get away," Gabe said.

Colin was coming toward him, only walking but still faster than any Olympic sprinter after the gold. "Drop your fucking field before I have to kill witnesses. Come on."

Fuck. Right. The private talk. It was what he'd wanted when he made that call.

Gabe shut his eyes and thought of underwater. Breathing underwater the way he had at the lake. Breathing at the bottom of the ocean.

He didn't realize his field had dropped until he felt Colin's arms around him. It felt like a hug, as if things were right between them. Then Colin's legs bent slightly and they were off, straight into the sky.

Sandy

"MAYBE," SANDY said, "he's gonna bust him out."

She couldn't see what Eli thought of that. The guy was getting fuzzier by the minute. Probably because it was getting dark outside. Sort of dark. Dark green.

"What?" Eli said.

"Maybe ol' Superman will bust Jerry out of prison."

Eli shrugged. "I'd bet Colin promised that. Whether he does it is another story."

"Who t'fuck knows," Sandy said. The sky was glowing deep green. Not like the northern lights; more like the dancing heart monitor lines. Like before a storm. "S'gonna rain."

"Is it?"

"Thunderstorm," she said. "Hail."

Gabe shouldn't be out in that. But it didn't matter anymore, did it? Maybe the storm shouldn't be out with Gabe. The temperature dropped enough that she could feel it even from inside the house. Even with the fan on. Eli stepped closer to the window, and she could see his face. Curious and surprised.

Sandy wanted to tell him to draw the curtains and back away from the glass. More than that, she wanted to close her eyes and put her head against the back of the chair.

"I wonder if Gabe knows he could have accidentally shot you today," Eli said. "Or me. Ricochets in that kind of situation are difficult to predict."

Sandy opened one eye as an experiment. She wanted to know if peering at Eli with one eye would help her understand what the fuck he was talking about. It didn't, so she closed the eye again.

"Rickshaw," she said.

"There are a lot of reasons why it's important for Gabe not to use his field," Eli said. "He's going to be tempted, especially as he gains more control over it. He's learning to use it very quickly."

"Rick-o-shaw," Sandy told him.

"The important thing is that he can turn it on and off," Eli said. "He did it today."

"Book 'em, Ricko," Sandy said. Why wasn't Sean laughing? Sean always laughed when she got really drunk. And then she hit him.

"Please, use your influence. I need your help."

She was forgetting something. She drank to forget. Forget what? It's working! But she was forgetting something. Forget what?

Someone put a blanket over her.

"Thanks," she said. Sean was a good guy. Good for hitting. Good guy, though.

"Good night," Eli said.

Gabe

COLIN FLEW fast enough that Gabe barely had time to notice he was in the air before he wasn't again. His field fired up against the air, and he wondered as they landed what they'd looked like from the ground. Maybe one night he'd see himself on *Unexplained: Caught on Camera*. And Eli would get all excited, and Gabe would have to say, "Sorry, man. That's just Colin and me."

They touched down in a field outside of town. Gabe could see the city lights to the east, but it was dark in the field without bright yard lights or the cozy glow of farmhouse windows anywhere nearby. The crop was something straggly and up to mid-shin on Gabe, with little flowers that seemed blue under the greening sky. Too far along for a grain so early in the year. No point asking Colin about it. *Am I a fucking farmer, Gabe? Am I wearing a shirt with snap buttons?*

Sean would have known what the crop was.

Colin released Gabe and took a step back to give him a good eyeballing. "You okay? It gets cold when I move that fast. But I guess you wouldn't feel it."

"Not feeling things," Gabe said, "seems to be your specialty more than mine."

Colin rubbed his face with his big, heavy-jointed hands. "Oh. It's going to be that kind of conversation." Lightning flashed again, and Colin glanced at the sky with surprise. He seemed to have just noticed that the heat was about to break with violence. "I heard what Jerry said. How much stock do you want to put in that guy's bitching?"

"You were there the whole time?" Gabe said. "But you didn't take Jerry's gun away. You were gonna roll the dice on Sandy getting shot."

"I had things under control."

"Like you had things with Sean under control," Gabe said. He saw Colin's eyes narrow for a second. Less than a second. A flash of honesty before the lies began again.

"I didn't know," Colin said. "Sean caught Jerry checking the freezer, and Jerry decided he had to… he had to deal with that. He told me later. After I saw you at the lake. I didn't lie to you, Gabe. Not about Sean."

"Okay," Gabe said. The power had dropped out of his voice, leaving a breathy sound that was barely a whisper. But Colin heard him anyway. Colin could probably have heard him from space. "I'm gonna put that in the parking lot."

Colin barked out a laugh. The parking lot had been the saviour of Ms. Patel, seventh-grade social studies, who had used it to avoid time-wasting tangents. *Let's put that in the parking lot for now.*

"But," Gabe said, "speaking of parking lots."

He left it at that. Colin's shoulders twitched, and he ducked his head a little, like he was ashamed. Two days ago, Gabe would have believed that he was.

"I know. I lied. I thought it was better for you. Believe me, I didn't mean to kill the guy. You don't know what it's like to be like this. Everything is so fucking fragile. What?"

Gabe realized he was smiling, sort of. The corner of his lip was curved. He stopped as soon as he knew he was doing it. He said, "That's meta-commentary on our whole damned lives."

"What the hell does that mean?"

"You're striking the set. Our whole lives were some bullshit you made out of paper and balsa wood, and now the play's over, so you're tearing it down and throwing it in the trash."

Colin made a face. "Don't be fucking artsy about this."

"It was kind of a genius show," Gabe said. "Like how you cast Jerry as a liar so I'd see blood, and he'd say it was a deer, and I'd think, *Oh, I'm onto Jerry*! *It was a sheep*!"

"Sometimes it was a sheep," Colin said. "Meat's expensive. And don't…. I can see you getting crazy ideas. Owen's the first person who ever wound up in our freezer. I'm not some fucking sicko."

Not a sicko. A murderer. A murderer of people who saw the wrong thing. The guy who'd be standing behind you at the moment you realized monsters were real so he could make sure you'd never tell a soul.

"Holy shit," Gabe said. "Holy fucking shit. You used the same trick on me with the boogeyman. You never expected me to believe you when you said he wasn't real. You just wanted me to think *that* was the big lie."

"Oh, really?" Colin put his hands on his hips. Like Superman. Like Superman in the worst of all possible worlds. "Then what's the truth, Gabe? What was my real big lie?"

"You're the guy under everyone's beds. Jack's not the boogeyman. It's you."

The temperature dropped in an instant. Gabe could feel the pressure of the storm inside his head and against his bones. When the wind finally came in, maybe it would tear his skin away until he was Jack's twin. He could picture it, taking the human skin off him and Colin both. Carrying it away until it hit the trees and hung there like a scarecrow.

"Funny you say that," Colin said. "Funny coming from a guy who was going to push Jack through that backstop like he was making mashed potatoes."

"Reeces have a mean streak," Gabe said softly. "Don't we? We have tempers."

"It's how we are," Colin said. "But, Gabe, the deal I made, it can still hold. You get a handle on your powers and go to school like we planned, and I'll keep doing what I have to do. You can have a normal life. You don't like what I do? That's okay. You don't have to do the bad things. I'll be the monster for you."

Gabe nodded. "It makes sense. It makes a lot of sense. You lost your temper and threw that SUV, and you were still amped up, and you saw Owen and lashed out. I get that. I hate it, but I can get my head around it. Especially now."

Colin took a step toward him. "That's it. And that's why you have to be careful who sees you. Because one of the rules is no witnesses. I would have had to do something about Owen no matter what because we can't have shit getting out. I would have had to scare him or get some blackmail going, some leverage…. There are ways. We can't have the government getting on to us. They'll lock us down. And your boyfriend—I can't stress this enough—what would he do if he'd seen you tonight?"

"I don't know," Gabe said. He didn't. He didn't particularly want to find out.

"I brought that guy to town. I don't know who tipped him off, but I got sloppy and here he is."

"You don't know who tipped him off," Gabe repeated.

Colin cocked his head. "Why? Do you?"

"Someone called from that Berlin number," Gabe told him. "The same one I used to call you tonight. The same one Jerry's been calling for the last few days."

Colin pinched the bridge of his nose. "A lot of people have access to that number," he said. "Damn it. I'll find out. This is fucked-up. I know I keep saying I'm on top of it, but seriously, I will deal with this. We've got a rat in the house."

Did they? Or had Colin done what Eli said and set Gabe up? Gabe felt a strange calm, like the heavy air was a weighted blanket tucking him in. He didn't have to know. He didn't have to figure out whether Colin was lying. It didn't matter.

"The thing is," Gabe said, "I can understand you losing your temper, and it's like you said, things must break for you all the time. I mean, Jesus, how long have you been this way?"

"Since a few months before Dad died," Colin said. "I was in the car when he drove into that truck. I don't know whether he meant to kill both of us or whether he knew I'd survive. I don't know why he did it. But I wasn't next to the road. I didn't grab the steering wheel either, no matter what people say."

"And Mom," Gabe said evenly. "You didn't do that either."

Colin kicked the dirt between rows of whatever those little plants were. "Fuck. Gabe… man, she saw me. I was an idiot, and I landed in the yard. She saw me fly. I wasn't going to do anything about it because who was she going to tell, right? She hadn't said ten words that year. But the next day… I don't know. I guess she couldn't live with it. I'm sorry. I know that one's on me."

"Why couldn't she live with it?" Gabe asked.

Colin's eyes narrowed again, anger and suspicion bleeding through the veneer of regret before he got himself back under control. "I don't know," Colin said. "She must have known more than we thought."

A raindrop landed on Gabe's face, fat and warm and silky soft. He left it there to fall.

"I get you doing things in anger," Gabe said. "They're fucking horrible things, and I think you need to get the great-power speech from Spider-Man tattooed on the insides of your eyelids—"

"Ha fucking ha."

"—but… you say you're Bamm-Bamm with an anger management problem? I'm willing to buy it. You're very strong, and our dad raised us to be fucked-up. I could make some kind of peace with it."

Now Colin was letting his suspicion show. "Thanks, I guess?" he said. "Am I supposed to thank you?"

"What's getting me," Gabe went on, "is Sean."

Colin's shoulders dropped, and his face took on a cast of dismay. The rain was still soft and uneven, like something tossed their way by a lazy sprinkler.

"Gabe… I know. I'm so fucking sorry that happened. Jerry thought he had no choice, and I didn't get there in time to stop him."

"I know," Gabe said. "Jerry had a gun, and he shot Sean."

"What are you—"

"Except he didn't. He didn't have that gun."

"Obviously he did, Gabe."

"No. You gave it to him. You gave it to him when you pulled him up from the trail and moved him to the parking lot. And he told the cops that it was the same gun that killed Tracy. But that was Jack's gun. Jack told me you took his gun after Jack killed Tracy. So maybe you gave that gun to Jerry before Se—before Sean was shot. But I don't think so."

"What fucking difference does it make?" Colin asked. But his face said that he understood.

"Jerry didn't shoot Sean. You did. And you lied about it, and you made Jerry take the blame, and all of that is disgusting, but what really sticks with me is that you didn't snap his neck or punch him in the face or whatever. You showed up with a gun that couldn't be traced to you, and you killed him like another normal human person would kill someone. So you could blame it on Jerry later."

"Jesus," Colin said. "I didn't come out here for an episode of *Law and Order*."

It was a nice attempt to shame Gabe, nerdy over-explaining Gabe, running off at the mouth again. Too bad Gabe didn't care. His field brightened as wind started to drive the rain. It let him see Colin's face as clearly as if they'd been facing each other on a sunny day. The pinched skin at the corners of Colin's eyes.

"And you knew Jerry would take the blame because you killed his dad right in front of him in the worst way you could think of. So he'd be scared shitless of you. And then you got his hands dirty over and over for years so that he could never tell anyone what you were making him do. And then, finally, when you were done using him because you were done with this piece-of-shit town, you made him take that gun and take the blame for you. I don't remember seeing Bamm-Bamm planning things out ten steps ahead and stringing people along for a decade."

"What the fuck is your—"

"Does any of that sound like a guy who snapped?"

Colin froze. He might have been carved from a mountain. All the human sloppiness, the little slumps and shifts, disappeared. He said, "You should shut up now, Gabriel."

Cold and steady, without pity or love or fear. Gabe had heard that voice a few times when he'd done something dangerous and dumb. He'd thought it was an act at the time. He'd thought *that* was the act.

"I'm an adult," Gabe said. "I don't take orders from you."

Colin cricked his neck, and Gabe had a moment to think that it was weird, that Superman shouldn't have a crick in his neck, before Colin said, "Let's see."

He swung on Gabe. Gabe's field threw the force of the punch back at Colin, along with the rain caught between them. Colin staggered and steadied, then bent forward and ran at Gabe. Dirt flew up behind him, furrows forming in the earth. Gabe threw himself to the side, down into the plants, and Colin went past him. Not so fast for Superman, but he'd been knocked off his stride, and the soft dirt had held him back when he ran. Or maybe he'd been holding back, because now he was standing there, squinting into the hard rain and waiting for Gabe to get up.

Gabe scrambled to his feet, getting tangled in the plants as he went. His field didn't protect him from the crops, it seemed. It crossed his mind that it might be nice if his field protected the plants from them. It was probably a cover crop, but still.

And then Colin came at him again.

There was no dodging this time. Colin didn't bother to raise his fists. He ran at Gabe with his head lowered like a charging bull. The field stopped him about a foot from Gabe's chest and lit the sky brighter than the lightning. Violins screamed, but the sound was caught up and swirled into the wind and thunder as if it were part of the storm. The impact knocked them both this time, Gabe a few steps and Colin a hundred metres or more, his body hitting the ground and dragging it up with him for the last few feet.

Colin was on his feet again in a heartbeat, regarding Gabe with interest.

"You felt that one," he said. His voice carried like it had come through a megaphone.

Was his field weakening? Or was Colin more than it could take? Lightning struck again, a flash photograph of his brother standing with rain-slicked hair and shredded clothes, caked in dirt from his knees down. And....

GABE IS nine years old, lying on a table in the basement. He's awake, barely, but he doesn't feel like moving yet. It's too much work even to open his eyes.

He can hear his father and the boogeyman talking. They don't know he's awake. They're trying to be quiet, not to wake him, and the whispering makes the boogeyman's hiss longer, more snakelike.

"...I understand. You wanted an heir and a sssspare. But Colin has expresssssed well."

"It's early days," his father says. "I'll hold on to the spare for now."

"You know having two is againsssst the rulesss. I'll get rid of him for you. I can drop him in the middle of the lake, and he'll drown trying to sssswim to ssshore."

"Give it a year," his father said. "To see how Colin goes. Then I'll get rid of this one myself."

Gabe can't know that, can't live with knowing that, so his brain packs the memory away in some dank, potato-smelling storage room he never goes into, and he doesn't think of it again for eleven years.

"ARE YOU going to kill me?" Gabe asked. Colin said nothing. Then he shot into the sky, and Gabe thought he might have left until he heard a sharp buzzing and realized it was Colin, coming back down, directly at him. Full force. To see whether Gabe's shield would hold.

If it didn't, Colin would go through him like a power drill through pine and brush off the dust as he walked away.

For all Sandy loved him and maybe other people loved him a little… this was Colin. This was the person who had been there Gabe's whole life between Gabe and his father. Between him and everyone. Saying Gabe was his first priority, that he was going to make Gabe's life okay or die trying. Reading to him and bringing home pizza and buying him a guitar.

If Colin wanted to kill him, who was Gabe to argue?

Gabe threw his head back and opened his arms to welcome his brother home.

There was a moment after Colin had almost reached him when nothing moved. Gabe's shield was silent. The blue light went out. He still could make out Colin's face, inches away.

What happened when Superman hit something he couldn't move? Before the first atomic bomb test, scientists had stood in the desert wondering what they'd done. Thinking it might be the end of the world.

The two of them went off like a bomb.

It would have seemed like thunder and lightning from the town. The crash that shook the ground, the daylit sky. Gabe was lying in the dirt at one end of the field, seeing the crops torn out and the earth turned around him. Colin was at the other end, not yet standing. Hail began to fall, and Gabe's shield sputtered back, covering him like a wetsuit. The deflected ice looked like a halo, hailstones colliding and shattering around him, the broken pieces reflecting his blue light.

As one, he and Colin got to their feet. They crossed the ruined field in silence. Met in the middle and stopped, almost close enough to reach out and touch.

"Still love me?" Colin asked.

It hit like nothing before, straight to the gut, and Gabe coughed out a sob.

"Still love me?" Colin asked again. There was no point lying.

"Yes."

"I told Jack to leave you alone. You and Sandy. He will if you leave him alone. He's scared of me. He's probably scared of you now too."

"Okay," Gabe said. It was as much as he could push from his lungs.

"I'm not trying to kill you, you stupid shit," Colin said. "I had to know you didn't need me anymore."

He vanished into the sky.

Sandy

IT WAS God only knew what hour, and Sandy was drunk. Still drunk, the worst kind. The kind where you were finished drinking and wanted to get up and go to the bathroom, get a glass of water on the way back, but you were drunk, and you were staying where you were until you weren't drunk anymore.

She heard the front door open and thought it might be Colin coming to finish them off. It wasn't, though. Colin didn't want that. He could have killed them a million times over. His message, in the form of a confessing Jerry, was clear. Let it stand like this. Let this be the story we all tell and let the whole thing go away. And you may not, God willing, ever see Colin Reece again.

It was Gabe. She heard Eli crossing the floor to meet Gabe at the door. Asking if Gabe was okay. What a dumb question. Either Gabe was completely okay or he was rubble and ash, depending on how you meant it.

But Gabe said he was. More or less. And Colin was gone.

Gabe sounded like he'd been crying.

He asked if Sandy was asleep, and Eli said yes. Sandy didn't have the coordination or the tenacity to argue. Easier to lie there, eyes closed, and let it all go by.

Gabe talked about a fight in a field, first with words and then a real fight.

He said he didn't think they'd see Colin again, or not often. That Colin had warned Jack away.

He said, "You were right. When you said I was being stupid. They did so much shit right in front of me. I wanted to believe things were normal."

"Go to school," Eli said. "Be normal."

"But I'm not."

She heard them sit on the couch, together.

"Leave him alone," Eli said.

"*You* won't," Gabe said.

"I can't."

"I can't go to school while he does whatever he does. And Jerry goes to prison for it."

"Gabe…."

"It was cold blood. The thing with Sean. That was in cold blood."

"I know."

"I'm not sure he has any other kind."

They were quiet again. Sandy drifted. Gabe said he wanted to join Eli's group, and Eli laughed softly. He sounded so sad.

"There's no group," he said. "I wanted them to think that killing me wouldn't solve their problem. I don't know if they ever believed it. They might know I'm alone."

Gabe said, "You aren't now."

And Eli said, "Good night, Gabe."

Chapter Fourteen

Gabe

Gabe and Colin sit on the roof of the house, above Gabe's bedroom. Colin is drinking rye, straight from the bottle. Gabe is using both hands to keep from sliding to the ground.

Their father has been dead a week. Their mom has crossed her own border, from quiet to silent. Now the funeral horde has taken over their home for the reception, chattering and dropping off frozen food. Gabe can't remember most of them saying a word to him before today.

"Do you know how many people have told me I'm the man of the house now?" Colin asks. "Are they playing bingo or something? Are they checking this shit off a list?"

"Why are you so sad?" Gabe asks. He's been wanting to ask for days, but they've never been alone.

Colin takes another pull. "He was our dad."

"He was mean," Gabe points out. "He was an asshole. I'm glad he's gone."

Colin breathes deep, like he's getting ready to sing. He hasn't, Gabe realizes, in years. Not since he used to sing Gabe to sleep.

"Mom's not good for anything," he says.

"She's not bad," Gabe answers. He doesn't mean she's okay or that she's good for anything. Just, she's never raised a hand or even yelled.

"We can just live," he adds, and Colin nods. He's gazing at the meagre city lights spreading to the river and up the other side.

"I'm the man of the house," Colin says.

"Douche of the house?" Gabe offers. "Asshat of the house?"

Colin smiles for the first time in days. "Somebody's gonna get grounded," he says.

An inch at a time, Gabe creeps down the slant of the roof until he's next to his brother. Colin offers him the bottle of rye. Gabe shakes his head.

"Your loss." Colin shrugs. He takes another pull, then rests the bottle between his legs. He's within elbow reach, so Gabe gives him a friendly shove.

"Hey," he says. "Colin? I'm sorry about Dad."

"You aren't. You're having a party."

"I know," Gabe says. "But I'm sorry for you."

Colin considers that in silence. Like the last word on some decision, he chucks the bottle into the tree next door. He's left a few drops for some lucky squirrel. Then he puts one warm hand on Gabe's shoulder.

"Fair enough," he says.

Sandy

THERE WERE times when Gabe's thoughts were so obvious that Sandy could almost imagine she was him. She could feel herself standing at the kitchen entryway, looking at the table where she and Eli sat and thinking that Sandy and Jerry had been there two days earlier. It was like one of those circle-the-differences puzzles.

Eli wasn't the only visible difference in the room. For one thing, Gabe was wearing her clothes instead of Jerry's. Well, not her jeans—those seemed to be his own. But one of her T-shirts, army green and so worn she considered throwing it away every time she washed it.

There was no forgotten toast in the toaster. Jerry was the one who always left toast there. And Sean's lunch bag was on top of the fridge instead of at work with him.

Also, though she wouldn't have known where or how to circle it, there was the main difference that everything was completely, desperately fucked.

"This means the washroom is free," Eli said, pushing his chair back from the table. Gabe ducked his head sheepishly. He'd taken his sweet time in the shower. Sandy wasn't sure there'd be hot water left, but she didn't say anything. If Eli was going to be stuck taking a cold shower, he'd find out soon enough.

Eli left with a nod to Gabe. Gabe took Eli's chair and picked up his abandoned coffee cup. He turned the blue-and-white ceramic around in his hands, staring as if it had been left to him in a will and he couldn't figure out why.

"He didn't want breakfast," Sandy said. She felt she had to explain why her guest had not had food in front of him, though Gabe would surely have known that she had offered. "Do you want breakfast? I'll make whatever."

Gabe raised his eyes to hers. He seemed amused. "Really?"

She nodded. "Heart-shaped pancakes? Scrambled eggs with hot dogs cut up in them, you freak?"

Gabe smiled. "Fuck off. They're good."

"Freak," Sandy repeated.

Gabe stopped smiling and set Eli's mug down. "And then some."

Sandy wanted to duck out of the room and shoot herself then, but Gabe waved a hand at her.

"So I'm a freak. What's bothering me…. Sandy, we ignored everything. Were we so fucking desperate to think Colin was the best guy in the world? Or are we the stupidest people on earth?"

Sandy could have said that of course they weren't. The girl at the Circle K who hadn't known what to charge Sean for ten five-cent candies and had stared blankly at Sean when Sean had said, "There are ten candies and they are five cents each, and five times ten is…?" She was the stupidest person on earth. They had all agreed on that.

She got what Gabe meant, though.

"You can't believe stuff that's… unbelievable," she said, trying to think through her headache. "What's that Sherlock thing? If it's impossible it's gotta be something else?"

"They were hiding some of this shit from us since we were all kids, and we had no fucking idea."

Sandy went to refill her coffee. She proceeded to the fridge and found a can of pop to bring to Gabe.

"I didn't think Jerry McClelland would pull a gun on me."

Gabe shook his head. "I never thought he could turn on you. Especially you. Until I found Sean."

"I think he really would have shot me," Sandy said. She sat down at the table and pressed a napkin to her eyes. Not that she was crying. She was hungover, and her eyes were sore.

Gabe reached across the table and put a hand on her arm. "Remember when your cousin's idiot dog got hit by that car, and your uncle went to help it and it bit him? Because it was so fucking scared?"

Sandy took her arm back so she could use two hands to steady her coffee. "I thought he was my friend. Not Jasper. Jerry."

Gabe sighed. He was toying with the tab on his pop can. If he kept that up, he'd break it, and he'd have to use a knife on the can. But Sandy knew from experience that he wouldn't appreciate the warning.

"Maybe he was. As much as he could be. You know?"

"No," Sandy said. "I don't."

It could have been that the hangover had squeezed her heart until it was three sizes too small, but she wasn't feeling generous enough to cut Jerry any slack. Maybe someday when she'd really thought about Colin and Jerry's dad and living under that for so many years.

But not today.

Gabe opened his pop and touched the condensation on the side of the can. Sandy realized that might not feel cold to him. She had no idea what things felt like to him now.

"I really thought he was the best guy in the world," Gabe said.

So they were talking about Colin some more. They weren't done.

"Me too," Sandy admitted. No sense pretending otherwise with her and Colin's informally adopted kid sitting right in front of her. Sure, they'd been six when Gabe was born, but the adoption had proceeded anyway. She and Colin had been in it together, deep in that scary, amazing, overwhelming responsibility, for nearly all their lives. And he had never, until two days ago, really dropped the ball.

"He is doing very bad shit," Gabe said. "I don't think I can go back to looking away…."

The weight of the previous day was behind those words. Gabe's new understanding of how bad Colin and Jerry's behaviour could be. Gabe was saying, even so, even with what they knew now—Colin was doing very bad things.

Sandy put her coffee down. Two hands weren't enough to keep it steady anymore. "Was he anything like we thought, Gabe?"

Gabe stared at the table. Same table that had been there for the last year and a half, since Sean and Gabe had dragged it home from an alley somewhere. Gabe had called it vintage. Sean had called it a find. Sandy had made them wash it with bleach.

"Either we got him wrong," Gabe said slowly, "or we got, like, a quarter of him."

"The part of him he wanted us to see," Sandy said.

Gabe nodded. "And maybe you and I get a pass," he said. "Because he loves us."

"He loves you the most," Sandy said. "I still think that's true."

"Maybe," Gabe said.

"Maybe your guitar and your violin are in my attic," Sandy told him. Gabe looked up, and Sandy saw tears. Not spilling, just sitting there making his eyes shine.

"What?"

"He pulled them out before he burned the house down. Or before he had Jerry burn the house down. And one of them hid them in our attic. If you eat something for breakfast, I'll let you have them back."

Gabe's mouth twitched a little at Sandy being Good Old Sandy. Pulling out the casual bribery she used on everyone. Then his mouth curved down again. He said, "I really needed him to love me."

"I know," Sandy said. Gabe had tagged along as soon as he'd been able to crawl. He'd been shattered when Colin had been angry with him. Or even short-tempered. Other kids had joked about it, especially Colin's friends. But Sandy had always understood that Gabe was smart and he got the stakes. Knowing his father couldn't be trusted and his mother barely existed, knowing that Colin was what he had, he'd played the game the only way he could.

"Why do you only get what you want," Gabe said, "after it doesn't matter anymore?"

There were so many things Gabe could have meant by that.

Sandy touched his hand. "Is that what happens?" she asked.

"He could hate me," Gabe said, "and I would be okay with it. As long as I could sleep at night knowing we've got the same blood."

She grabbed Gabe's hand, so quickly that it startled him. His field made a noise that was not so much music as it was the squeak of a frightened mouse.

"Gabe," she said. Gabe was glaring at his hand, presumably because it had embarrassed him.

"Gabe," she repeated.

Gabe raised his head. "Present," he said.

Sandy picked up the knife she'd dropped there the night before, after testing Gabe's field. "Let me through."

Gabe's eyes widened. "I can't—"

"Eli says you can," Sandy told him. She held the knife to Gabe's palm. "Lemme in."

Gabe took a deep breath and dropped his shoulders. The knife made a high scraping sound as she pushed it down, but it pierced the skin. Sandy drew it down a little, set the knife on the table between them, then turned Gabe's hand over and squeezed until a few red drops fell.

"You think this shit right here can run your life for you? You think it gets to tell you what to do?"

Before Gabe could answer, Sandy stood and slammed her right fist into the blood on the table as hard as she could. Gabe scrambled backward, knocking over his chair and falling to the linoleum floor as the table's support broke. The tabletop flipped and flew into the wall. Dishes and menus and unpaid bills scattered everywhere. In the silence that followed, Sandy grabbed a dishcloth from the sink and rubbed the blood off her aching hand, then tossed the cloth back into the sink. She'd probably bruised her fist, but damned if it wasn't the best thing she'd felt in days.

She caught Gabe's eye and said, "It's not so tough."

She offered her left hand to Gabe. He took it, and she pulled him to his feet. They stared at each other. Sandy could see Eli from the corner of her eye. He was in the entryway, unmoving, a damp towel around his shoulders.

Gabe blinked away his tears. His shoulders squared. His voice was clear and strong as he said, "You broke the fucking table."

Sandy shrugged, still holding Gabe's hand. "I never liked it anyway."

And Gabe smiled.

Keep Reading for an Excerpt from
The Dominion
By Gayleen Froese.

Available Digitally on YONDER
And Coming Soon in Digital and Print.

Foreword

I HOPE YOU'RE not waiting for *Seven Leagues Over the Dominion* to come out. If you are, you'll be waiting a long time, and you can blame my editor. Or maybe you can blame me, for bringing an uninvited guest to lunch.

I was meeting my editor for a nice business lunch three months after my trip to the Dominion. We were both enthusiastic about a Seven Leagues book covering the most magical place on Earth. At a certain point, if you're writing adventure travel guides, there's no excuse not to go there. The local crime lord will rip your heart from your chest, werewolves can legally eat you, and they had to rebuild City Hall because a dragon burned it down. It's incredibly dangerous, more so than any war-torn republic or 8,000-metre mountaintop. No tourist should ever go there. That's why it was unmissable for me.

She was looking forward to hearing about my trip and to helping me decide what parts I should write about. The Seven Leagues books are pretty strictly structured, with sections about travel to and from the destination, travel within the destination, where to stay, what to eat, how to avoid trouble with the law… all the information you'll need to go places you shouldn't. I know the formula because I created the formula. I'd even written some of the book before our meeting, knowing what would need to be there.

Still, there's room to focus on what's special about a destination, such as the Dominion's lively college scene, or its hallucinogenic wastelands. That's the sort of thing we discuss when we get together.

That day I thought it would be a good idea to bring my photographer along. Karsten Roth was new to the Seven Leagues series, and he was a hell of a catch since his photos had been on the covers of everything from *National Geographic* to *The Cryptid*. I guarantee you've seen his work. You probably don't recognize his name, and you certainly wouldn't recognize his face because he likes it that way. My editor was a fan, and even she couldn't have picked him out of a police line.

She was thrilled to meet him. I told her that would wear off fast, and Karsten hit my arm with his camera bag.

He was polite and dour and funny. He brought her flowers and said he was in awe that she could put up with me. She was charmed.

She insisted we both tell her everything, every detail about our trip, and we stayed so long that we ate dinner at that table too. Over dessert, she declared that *Seven Leagues Over the Dominion* could wait.

I was shocked to say the least. She'd spent hours enraptured by our story. Why wouldn't she want the book?

It turned out she wanted a different book. She wanted a travel memoir, not an adventure guide, about me and Karsten and what happened to us in the Dominion. She wanted both of us to tell the story, not just me. I didn't write that kind of book, and Karsten didn't write at all, not professionally, but that didn't matter. She'd hire a memory extractor, one of the best. All memoirs were created that way these days, she said.

Karsten was horrified at first. Everyone gets their minds read all the time—by customs agents and cops and bored telepaths standing next to us on the subway—but memory extraction is more intensive than any of that, and Karsten is a private guy. He refused, first in his proper Oxford English and then in his more colourful German. Miri, my editor, patted his arm and said it was fine. He didn't have to do it. She'd rather have his perspective and his version of events, but the book could be done without it. Being the evil genius she is, Miri had no doubt guessed what his reaction would be. There was no way he was going to let me tell the story of our trip without his input. He said I was a scoundrel and a fantasist and some word that was long, German, and probably slang, since I didn't recognize it. My version of anything required a second opinion.

Also, though he didn't say it to Miri, there were things that had happened between us that even his sophisticated European sensibility might not want spelled out for everyone to read. If he wasn't part of the book's creation, he'd have no say in what did or didn't wind up on the page. The truth is, I wouldn't have embarrassed him. But he didn't need to know that right then.

As for me, I had mixed feelings. I'd gone to the Dominion planning to write a certain kind of book. I wasn't sure I wanted to change things up.

But the evil genius reminded me that I'd grown up on memoirs of travel and adventure. She said I'd had the real thing in the Dominion—mysterious deaths, a cunning villain, a monster the size of a city block… even my own near demise. It would be a shame to squeeze a story that big around the edges of a travel guide. Besides, we could still do the travel guide, and then I'd have the chance to get two slots on the bestseller lists.

In case that wasn't enough, she waited until Karsten had wandered off to the washroom, then leaned forward and said, "You can find out what he really thought of you right from when you met."

I told her Karsten didn't exactly leave people in the dark regarding his opinion of them. But you'll notice I did the book anyway.

-Innis Stuart, writing from Dawson City, Yukon Territory, Canada

Introduction: A History of Memory

AROUND THE mid-1960s, when most North Americans had become comfortable with magic, some people got the idea that it was ridiculous to have limitations. Old-fashioned, even. If you'd ever been carrying groceries and wished you had a third arm, you didn't have to just wish for it anymore. You could hire someone to make it happen. Why drag a scuba tank around to explore the ocean? Why study for exams when you could pay to never forget anything you'd seen, heard, or done? It was an exciting time in which it seemed as if we'd all be able to be anything we wanted, provided we had the money. Why not?

Today, we know why not. There were the spells that went wrong and the shady operators who would give you a third arm and then leave town before you discovered you'd be growing an arm a week from then on. More importantly, though, there were things we found we could not change.

Take memory for example. We should have known we wouldn't be happy remembering everything. We should have known because there were people in the world before magic who could. They hadn't purchased a spell or potion. They'd simply been born with hoarding brains. You could ask these people what they had eaten for breakfast on a specific day thirty years earlier and they would tell you without hesitation. It's tough to verify an ordinary breakfast that's thirty years gone, so the subjects—as these people were known—would be asked about the weather on a certain day or the newspaper headlines. They were never wrong.

They were also unhappy. They felt rootless and detached. Without momentum. They were haunted by a million small things.

Eventually, the people in the '60s and '70s who bought perfect memories came to feel the same way. It seems there are things we are not built, in psychology or temperament, to be.

These days if you want to remember everything about a part of your life, you pay for a memory extraction instead. The best extractors in the business will find everything you remember and everything you'd forgotten about for a week or a month or, if you can afford it, a year. No one I know of offers more than a year. It's too much effort, too much magic, and too much information.

The police were the first to use this service. It was unheard of at first, so it was legal everywhere. Then it was challenged in court after court and became illegal in most places. Then it was necessary in solving a few downright devilish cases, and people started thinking it wasn't such a bad idea. Now you'll find it used in most places that allow any magic at all.

If something is used for one thing, people will find a way to use it for a hundred. If you're well-off and living in a place where magic is used casually, you may even have bought an extraction yourself. Maybe you wanted to present your child with the story of her birth or preserve your wedding day. Everyone has photos and video of these events, but a good memory extractor creates something more personal. It's your perspective—your memory, your thoughts, in your voice—translated to text. The first extractions read like witness statements, and it was said they'd never replace writing for thoughtful evocation and grace of prose. But the process has developed over the past few decades, and now memory extracts are indistinguishable from the sort of literary works and memoirs that were written two hundred years ago.

Except, of course, that they are accurate. They are coloured by what the subject saw and noticed and by the subject's way of thinking about these things. They reflect misunderstanding and obliviousness. But they reflect these things honestly and without prejudice.

I would be lying if I said I didn't feel a romantic pull toward the image of a lone man at his journal or keyboard, trying to capture his memories of travel and adventure before they flew away. Those are the books I read as a boy living on Canada's boundless prairie. I would read on the porch at my grandmother's farm, then set the book down, look at the horizon, and itch to go there. I had the idea I would write about what I found.

And I do. I write my Seven Leagues books alone at a keyboard, wrestling with memory and sometimes getting it wrong. Sometimes getting it wrong on purpose because, let's face it, adventure travel should be an adventure, in life and on the page.

This book, though, has all the adventure it needs without any help from my imagination. It's about the Dominion and Karsten and me and what happened to us and why and how we're still alive. I didn't want it to be a mistake or a lie.

What you are about to read, ladies and gentlemen of the jury, is the whole truth and nothing but the truth. So help me.

—Innis Stuart

Excerpt from Seven Leagues Over the Dominion

"THE DOMINION is a hell of an idea, and if I ever want to live in an idea, maybe I'll move there."

-Connor Avery, President, One Tir

FAE LEADER Connor Avery was using his famous backhand when he called the Dominion a hell of an idea. The city is said by some to be a hell on earth, full of spectres and monsters of every description. Certainly the Dominion's notorious Scree Quarter is a place to, as Keats wrote, "haunt thy days and chill thy dreaming nights," but there's a lot more to the Dominion—as the thousands of tourists who visit each year will attest.

Formed in 1965, the Dominion was a response to the growing trend of magic regulation around the world. It had been nearly twenty years since the varied forms of magic had sprung from nowhere to become as common as science, and it had taken almost that long for most governments to come up with coherent responses to the new world disorder. When they finally did so, the pendulum, in the opinions of many, overswung. Today, magic is banned in a number of nations and in at least a few regions of nearly every country on Earth. Places where it is allowed impose strict regulations on its use. Where does this leave creatures who are inherently fantastic? Often they're forced to reside in regions or neighbourhoods set aside for them. As you might expect, these usually aren't the most desirable parts of town.

The Dominion was conceived as a response to all of this. A block of Canadian and American land along the Pacific Northwest, including the cross-border Dominion City, was offered as a free space where all comers would, in theory, be welcomed, and those whose personal habits were unwelcome elsewhere could finally be themselves.

Despite what Mr. Avery may have to say about the place, there's no question that the idea of the Dominion was timely and compelling in the increasingly restrictive climate of the early '60s. It seemed sincerely intended as a sop to those who felt alienated and unwanted elsewhere, though critics have since claimed that it was intended to draw undesirables from across North America to one place where, as trillynoid activist Raymond Knot has said, "we can have at each other and leave the normal folks alone."

Whatever it was intended to be, the Dominion stands today as an experiment with mixed results. Werewolves and vampires run wild while less bloodthirsty locals defend themselves by any means necessary—all with the blessing of the Dominion's libertine legal system, in which self-defence is sacrosanct. The murder rate is so high that local newspapers report each night's events as a kind of box score. Death by accident is commonplace, and nearly one hundred tourists each year do not return home. If it can't be said for certain that they've all met with a dark fate, it's only because about half of their bodies are never found.

Yet it has its charms, drawing the curious who want to have mystical experiences not easily available outside the city's domed force field. The Dominion's many body modification shops and psychic transformation facilities attract those who wish to become curiosities in their own right. It can't be denied that a trip to the Dominion can change you, whether you want it to or not. Dollar for dollar, no vacation will give you more unique moments to remember or more incredible stories to dine out on.

Though the territory belongs, jointly, to the United States and Canada, the Dominion really is a country unto itself. When you enter, you give up any expectation of personal security aside from what you can provide for yourself. You give up the law as you've come to understand it, including the laws of physics as Einstein described them—except, perhaps, in the sense that his theory of relativity can be described as "what goes around comes around."

Welcome to the Dominion. It's a hell of an idea.

GAYLEEN FROESE is an LGBTQ writer of detective fiction living in Edmonton, Canada. Her novels include The Girl Whose Luck Ran Out, Touch, and Grayling Cross. Her chapter book for adults, What the Cat Dragged In, was short-listed in the International 3-Day Novel Contest and is published by The Asp, an authors' collective based in western Canada.

Gayleen has appeared on Canadian Learning Television's A Total Write-Off, won the second season of the Three Day Novel Contest on BookTelevision, and as a singer-songwriter, showcased at festivals across Canada. She has worked as a radio writer and talk-show host, an advertising creative director, and a communications officer.

A past resident of Saskatoon, Toronto, and northern Saskatchewan, Gayleen now lives in Edmonton with novelist Laird Ryan States in a home that includes dogs, geckos, snakes, monitor lizards, and Marlowe the tegu. When not writing, she can be found kayaking, photographing unsuspecting wildlife, and playing cooperative board games, viciously competitive card games, and tabletop RPGs.

Gayleen can be found on:
Facebook @GayleenFroeseWriting
www.gayleenfroese.com

Follow me on BookBub

Can a disillusioned former cop track down a missing girl before it's too late?

Seven years ago, criminologist Ben Ames thought he'd change a big city police force from the inside. He failed. Now he's a private detective trailing insurance frauds and cheating spouses through the foothills of the Rocky Mountains. Like police work, the job would be easier if he didn't have a conscience.

When university student Kimberly Moy goes missing, her sister begs Ben to take the case. But before Ben can follow up on any leads—What does the Fibonacci series have to do with Kim's disappearance? What do her disaffected friends know? And where is her car?—chance and bad timing drop his unexpected ex, Jesse, into the mix.

Ben doesn't have time to train Jesse into the junior PI he seems determined to become. Amateur sleuths are always trouble. Unfortunately, this is turning out to be the kind of case that requires backup, and his intuition is telling him Kim's story may not have a happy ending….

GAYLEEN FROESE

THE MAN WHO LOST HIS PEN

Everybody freeze.

Calgary PI Ben Ames expects a relaxing evening off as he supports his boyfriend, Jesse, one of the star performers at a charity concert. But it turns out relaxing isn't on the program.

When last-minute guest Matt Garrett shows up, it creates a frenzy backstage. An A-list movie star with an ego to match, Garrett has bad blood with many of the performers—Jesse included. So when Garrett turns up dead, Ben begins to dig for the truth, both to protect Jesse and to satisfy his own instinctive curiosity.

So much for his night off.

When the police arrive, emotions backstage heat up, but no one can step out to cool off, because the Western Canadian winter is so cold that hypothermia waits outside. With such a high-profile crime, the lead detective seems poised to make a quick arrest… and Jesse's a prime suspect. Ben has his work cut out for him to solve the murder under the police and paparazzi's noses before Jesse's reputation becomes collateral damage.

For more
great fiction
from

f